# SHARPSHOOTER

This Large Print Book carries the
Seal of Approval of N.A.V.H.

A BYRNES FAMILY RANCH NOVEL

# SHARPSHOOTER

## DUSTY RICHARDS

**THORNDIKE PRESS**
A part of Gale, a Cengage Company

Farmington Hills, Mich • San Francisco • New York • Waterville, Maine
Meriden, Conn • Mason, Ohio • Chicago

Copyright © 2018 by Dusty Richards.
Thorndike Press, a part of Gale, a Cengage Company.

**ALL RIGHTS RESERVED**
Thorndike Press® Large Print Western.
The text of this Large Print edition is unabridged.
Other aspects of the book may vary from the original edition.
Set in 16 pt. Plantin.

**LIBRARY OF CONGRESS CIP DATA ON FILE.
CATALOGUING IN PUBLICATION FOR THIS BOOK
IS AVAILABLE FROM THE LIBRARY OF CONGRESS**

ISBN-13: 978-1-4328-5543-7 (hardcover)

Published in 2018 by arrangement with Pinnacle Books, an imprint of Kensington Publishing Corp.

Printed in Mexico
1 2 3 4 5 6 7 22 21 20 19 18

To my readers,

I certainly enjoy your e-mails. I hope by the time this book is published you have found my new site at dustyrichards.com. That is going to be the place to check on my new books coming out.

The West rides on. I am doing what I have loved all my life to do: read and write westerns. I have met so many western fiction writers — the list is a mile long — and many are not here any longer. Jory Sherman handed me a membership for Western Writers in February 1985 at Branson, Missouri. I went to my first WWA convention in San Antonio in July of that year.

That was my lucky day, when I also met book editor Frank Reuter, and he made a salable writer out of me. Through time I met and was helped by many greats. I am very proud of my Spur Awards, my Wrangler Award from the Cowboy Hall, my Will Roger Medallion Award, and others.

But most of all, many thanks to my readers.

Keep up the good work. It helps me sell more.

Till the next novel, keep that horse's head up so he don't buck you off.

DUSTY RICHARDS
A lifetime member of
Western Writers of America

# CHAPTER 1

On one of those Sunday afternoons when they were caught up on the ranch, work-wise, Chet Byrnes was seated in his spacious living room in the new morris chair that his wife, Lisa, had recently bought for him. The slender woman in her early twenties who had taken on the job of being Chet's wife only months before, was in the kitchen busy making coffee and slicing her sweet raisin bread for the gathered company of some of his top men. They were in the living room, discussing ranch matters and other things that came up.

The lanky Cole Emerson was slumped on the leather sofa with his dusty boots stretched way out, and Jesus Martinez was seated on the other end of the sofa.

"I know we have heard lots of rumors about some real remains of the first pure Spanish horses, but do you reckon there are any left?" Jesus asked.

Cole shook his head to dismiss the idea. "If there had been, they'd've been found and reported."

"Hell, Cole, they haven't looked in every back canyon for them."

"Then where are they hiding?"

"Maybe on the North Rim of the Grand Canyon."

Cole drew up his lanky legs when Lisa, a tray of coffee cups in her hands, came into the room. He said, "Smells great to me, Lisa. Yes, Jesus, if there is one place undiscovered it has to be that land north of the great hole."

"How did that land get cut off from Utah, anyway?" Jesus asked.

"Well," Chet began, "the story goes that Washington, DC, was angry with the Mormons in Utah over their bitching and fussing and ran the survey straight west instead of making the Grand Canyon the border between the two territories."

"That's why people have to go out of state through Nevada to come to Preskitt to their county seat." Jesus took his coffee cup off Lisa's tray and thanked her.

"It wasn't drawn to be easy."

"It really is the lost land for the Arizona Territory."

"I overheard someone say, while I was out

8

in the kitchen, there might be real wild horses up there?" Lisa asked.

Chet shook his head. "Lisa, no one knows much about what is up there."

"I say, since we have the cattle all worked and the hay up, that we go up there and explore it," Cole said.

Lisa set the tray down. "I'd like to tag along. I've never been up there."

"Jesus, would your wife let you go along?" Chet asked.

"If I went with you, she would."

Everyone laughed.

"So would mine." Cole chuckled

"Several years ago, Lisa, Jesus, along with Cole and me, nearly froze to death coming off of there with some criminals we were bringing back from Utah."

"That was midwinter then," Cole said. "We are just going exploring in the summertime. We are not staying up there that long."

"Who else do we need to go with us?" Jesus asked.

"Me?" Lisa pointed at herself.

"You sure can tag along. But it is not a peaches-and-cream place to explore," Chet said. "There are no hotels or cafés."

"That doesn't matter. I'd just love to see it."

Chet agreed. Lisa had come a long way since he laid his orders out to the snobby girl who'd been living with outlaws. After they had captured the gang of marauders who'd attacked one of his stage stations on the Marcy Road, this tough-acting girl told him she had no means or way to get out of that desolate Four Corners country now that her ex-boyfriend was Chet's prisoner and faced several years in prison. Chet let her know right off she was not his responsibility, but if she would work hard with the cook and do her part in camp, he'd find her a packhorse to ride back with them. She had bowed her head and thanked him.

From that time on, that girl carried her share of the load. On the second day, without saying a word to Chet, Jesus found her a saddle to ride. Back at the ranch she worked even harder and married one of Chet's foremen. Then she took over the job of running the big house when his wife's majordomo, Monica, suddenly died from a heart attack. Lisa taught the Mexican ranch children English so they could attend the Cherry School. Then her husband was killed in range war shoot-out over east at the Wagon Wheel Ranch, and terminal cancer swept Chet's wife, Elizabeth, away as well. Lost in their own personal sorrow the two soon found each other to lean on, and he married her. Ten years or more his junior, he never noticed the difference except when their ages were mentioned.

"Can we get Hampt to go along?" Cole asked.

"May might not let him go with you all," Lisa said.

Jesus shook his head. "She would if Chet asked for him. She'd do anything for him."

Lisa quickly agreed. May was Chet's widowed sister-in-law who'd later married Hampt, one of his original ranch hands, and the two were raising a second family. She nearly didn't come along when he packed them up to go from Texas to Arizona. His second wife, Elizabeth, once said his sister-in-law probably expected Chet to marry her out there — but she settled for Hampt and they were very happy.

"I am sure Hampt would love to join us and he's a good backup. He saved many lives arming the black cowboys in the lost herd deal in Texas. Plus, he's the greatest expert at growing alfalfa in the Territory."

"Will you ask her, then? Thanks for the coffee, Lisa. I better get home and ask my wife if I can go, too."

"Cole, as well as you two get along you're going north with us," Lisa said, gathering

11

up the empty cups.

"When are we leaving?" she asked Chet.

"Oh, three days or four. I want Tom and Millie to stay up here while we are gone."

She agreed and headed for the kitchen with her tray full of empty cups.

He stopped her by clearing his throat. With a head toss toward the stairs and a smile, he waited for her answer.

"As soon as I get these dishes on the sink I am coming up there. I thought you'd never think of doing that."

They both laughed.

Being married to her had brought lots of things back to his life. Their sessions at making love were just a portion as sweet as the other intimate things they shared, like swimming naked in the Verde River when they were alone together, checking on things, taking showers with each other under the sheepherder fixture out back before bedtime. They had settled into a good life together with few restrictions on things that they enjoyed.

Climbing the stairs, he smiled. What would they find on the north side of that big gorge? No matter. It would be mostly new country and he looked forward to going up there. Maybe his back would complain some, sleeping on the ground, but Lisa could get those kinks out with her powerful hands. Not much his missus couldn't do — though she wanted children or said she did. They were trying.

Those would come along, he felt certain. Raised by her father, he'd spoiled her when her mother died young, and Chet learned that when she was still a teen, she'd left home with an outlaw who'd promised to marry her. In their flight to escape Chet and his persistent posse, she discovered she was simply the outlaw's whore, but it was too late, too dangerous for her to leave him and strike out alone in the vast, tough land she did not know a thing about. And she had no money.

The next day Chet and Lisa drove down to the Verde Ranch to talk to Tom and Millie. The women were left at the house while the two men walked about the ranch pens to talk.

"We're going looking at the North Rim country in a few days."

Tom nodded. "Any particular purpose?"

"Jesus wants to find some pure Spanish horses."

They laughed.

"No, we'll just look. We're caught up with things and want to see some new country."

"Say, I have a top hand for you to take along. His name's Salty Meeker and he's a real sharp guy."

"Where's he out of?" Chet asked.

"Texas, but he is a guy who sees things and fixes them right there."

"I have to clear him with the guys, but sure, send him up. You and Millie willing to watch things from our place?"

"Aw hell, Chet, you know me. I'll do anything you need done. It ain't no big trick."

"Lisa will feel better with you and Millie looking over things up there."

"I understand. What will you find up there, do you think?"

"Oh, who knows? I think it is just a boy's-night-out deal. Lisa is a tomboy and of course wants to tag along."

"More than that. She makes a good woman for you."

"I agree. When I first found her in Colorado, I never expected her to amount to a hill of beans."

Tom shook his head. "She's taught school to those Mexican children until they knew enough English to attend that Cherry School. She took over that house when Monica died like she'd done it all her life. I hated when her husband got shot over there in that range war. He'd made a great foreman to replace the old man who'd retired."

"He was a real dedicated person. We all hated it when he was killed. But Lisa is a great wife, too."

"Oh, Millie and I both agree. She was the right one for you, and you needed a wife."

"Be sure to send this Salty up. I have to go see May and Hampt when I get back. We want him to go along, too."

Tom agreed. "I wish the railroad would get done up there. I need some new Hereford bulls to use in our purebred herd, and they'd need to be shipped out here, not driven from Kansas."

"You better get them hauled out here in a wagon. That track, at the rate it is coming, will be several years getting to Flagstaff."

"What is stalling them so much?"

"Money. They run out and don't have the business on the rest of their tracks to build it fast enough. I think freight is not coming on it like they first thought it would. The country they are coming through has not been developed. You and I know cattle ranching without the Navajo sales would be tough on us. Other ranchers on this dry land couldn't exist for long out here with no markets."

"I know you are right. But it won't get

any better until they get tracks, pens, and cars to haul the cattle out of here."

"Tom, you and I have talked about markets since we took the Quarter Circle Z away from those bandits who had it. JD and the brothers down south are making cattle sales down there but it isn't that good and the Tucson Ring still has hold on lots of things, like the army and Indian sales. In time those rails at Flagstaff will make us rich but they are a long way off still. While I am gone I want you to handle all business like it was your own."

"Been a long time since you fed those starving Indians down on the Verde and had to get General Crook to straighten the agency out."

Chet laughed. "We've sure had some times."

"Cole shot his Apache prisoner you gave him, on that first cattle drive you made, and he feared you'd fire him over it."

"That was our first and last Apache war until we had to stop those wild ones over at Rustler's Ranch."

"How are Toby and Talley making it?"

"He's fenced more of those homesteads that Bo's bought for us. He'll have several hundred calves to wean this year from the cattle we got him. He expects to be at five hundred mother cows in two years and he'll have the feed to do it."

"Talley was one of those strays you brought back, too?"

Chet nodded. "And when Toby married her I thought she'd never straighten out of her sullen self. But she lent him a hand and their operation is going great."

"It started with Cole's woman. You sent her up here to help in Jenn's restaurant. Valerie didn't like that dove business after she got down there."

"Right. We brought the hardware-mercantile man Ben Ivor and his wife, Kathrin, back with us from Utah."

"And you rescued JD's wife-to-be, Bonnie, then down in Mexico."

Chet agreed. "You know, Tanner at the bank married the woman who about ruined JD. And they're looking for number two child. He must be twenty years older than her but he brags on her."

"And your land man Bo's building a family, too."

Chet laughed. "That woman was married to her first husband ten years and never had a child with him."

Tom agreed. "I know. Over the years we all talked about you and that tall Navajo woman."

17

"Blue Bell. Jesus even asked me about her. No, we never had an affair. She is so busy helping her people she didn't need a white man to court her."

"You went to Washington, DC, once to help them?"

Chet shrugged. "I went. Tried, but they gave the Navajo coal to some company to sell to the railroad. I sure lost that fight."

"You've won a lot of battles against outlaws and made Arizona a better place to live."

"We tried."

"Hell no. You led all those battles and we did stop lots of crimes."

"Enough of that. Tom, I am damn proud of that Hereford herd and what you've accomplished."

"We did that right. I never believed we could accomplish that, but now we are a large breeder of purebred cattle and we have good ones."

They stopped at the corral and watched a young wrangler sacking down a wall-eyed bronc tied to a post. The horse was having a fit every time the wrangler waved the sack at him, but he'd get over that.

"My kids are getting along fine over at your sister and Sarge's place. Cody's taking a herd every other month to New Mexico for Sarge, letting him stay home more. That boy is making a real hand. I saw him as the boy stealing my daughter and you saw him as a foreman — taught me a lesson there."

"He was cut out of the same wood as Robert, who runs the timber-hauling business up on the rim."

"I see those reports. He makes real money for this outfit and he isn't much older than my son-in-law."

"You know Robert's Mormon wife fixes coffee for us when we go up there?"

"He takes her to church, too."

"They kind of picked at her for marrying outside the church. But not anymore. He makes a real good living and she has a new house like yours."

"A good-paying job in Arizona is hard to find."

"Things will change when they get the tracks laid, but it won't be tomorrow. We'll have a small ranch party Wednesday night and leave Thursday."

"Millie and I will be up there at lunchtime Wednesday but I'm sending Salty your way in the morning."

They shook hands and Chet went for the rig he'd haul his bride home in. He already had Hampt set to go along, a camp cook borrowed from Tom, and some good hands

— this Salty would be a good addition for the trip if he was half as good as Tom said he was.

The trip back up the canyon to the upper ranch ate up the rest of the day. Lisa told him stories she'd heard that were funny and when they topped out he let the sweaty horses stop and rest.

"Chet, I am kind of excited about this venture. Millie thinks there are some little people that live up there by themselves."

"I doubt we'll find them. People, beginning with the Spanish centuries ago, searched this land out with a fine-tooth comb, even up there."

She hugged him hard. "I don't care. I will be with you, seeing land not many others ever saw."

He kissed her. Damn, she was neat to love. How lucky could one man get? They'd have some fun exploring a new country.

# CHAPTER 2

The ranch crew at the home place knew how to have a party. Roast a big fat steer over a pit of dry hardwood for a long while. There were roasting ears cooked in a similar way. Fried onions, green and red sweet peppers, and lots of cooked hot peppers as well. Two giant kettles of frijoles, flour tortillas, corn tortillas, and several large Dutch ovens full of peach cobbler from the ranch orchards in Oak Creek Canyon.

All the ranch people worked shoulder to shoulder to get it set up and completed. Plenty of musicians and singers were there, their fiddles crying in the setting sun. Townsfolk and ranch people alike all came, and everyone enjoyed the comradery of the party. The Quarter Circle Z had a great reputation as the place to be when they hosted any event, large or small.

Salty had fresh-shod all their horses with a crew of two. He wanted to start out with everything fixed and both wagons' wheels were gone over and two spare wheels loaded. Harnesses were gone through and then even a collar was changed to better fit a draft horse. Chet had to agree this new guy was thorough and he'd added things to the load that they might need, including two spools of rope.

Chet had a good visit with both his sons and promised them they'd elk hunt with him in the fall. Rocky lived with Cole and his wife, Valerie. Adam lived on the Verde with Victor and his wife, Reba, at the big house down there.

Before Chet moved from Texas, a woman he'd had an affair with was murdered by members of the family that he had all the hell with. She used her own blood to name her attacker on the sheet. When he discovered Marla's body, he'd found a note she'd written to her husband earlier that she was quitting him for Chet. He never let anyone see the good-bye note but destroyed it instead.

His first wife, Marge, had paid the bills he left behind him when he first came to Preskitt, thinking he needed help. He finally paid off the debt and told her that he had a woman in Texas and never offered her any part of his life. When some ruthless stage robbers murdered his nephew on his return trip to Texas, Marge came to his aid. The woman in Texas had invalid parents and she couldn't move out with him. Later, when she died of pneumonia, her daughter told Chet he had a son he didn't know about. Chet's first wife had been killed in a horse-jumping accident so Cole and Valerie were raising Rocky.

He met wife number two, a Spanish woman Elizabeth, on the Santa Cruz River below Tucson. After he'd seen her wading in the river, he dried her feet and she always felt he was like Jesus, who washed his disciples' feet at the Last Supper. Elizabeth died of cancer unexpectedly, and now he had married Lisa.

That last night in their own bed at home, Lisa told him how much she loved the things he did for her and the people — how fortunate she was to have him. Then she buried him in her kisses.

The next morning in the predawn with Lisa on the wagon seat beside big Hampt, those two were warning Chet that the sidestepping horse he rode might throw him before he passed under the gate bar. He even believed the big bay horse under him might break in two at any moment — but that time passed. He was still in the saddle to saw at his mouth, getting the bay's attention off bucking, and they short-loped away. The wagon train caught up with him at the north-south road junction before they went off the steep downhill road into the canyon. By then the gelding was settled, and Chet smiled big when the lead wagon and the rest of the riders joined him for their steep descent down to the Verde Valley.

They didn't stop at the ranch and were over on the North Rim of the Verde River Valley by late afternoon, ready to camp out. Next day they'd pass by Robert's house at the sawmill south of Flagstaff. Things went without a hitch. No doubt the efforts of the new man, Salty, who made the preparations for a long haul, were paying off.

After supper, he gave the younger guy, Eldon Grimes the horse wrangler, the name of the roan horse, Butch, as the one he'd ride out from the remuda in the morning. Lisa was in charge of dishes that night and when she completed them, she and Chet went off to the bedrolls he'd laid out for them. Like he guessed, she planned to sleep together with him, which didn't upset him one bit. Nice to have her, and he told her so.

They were up early. As the smoke from

the cooking fire began to rise, Tom's second roundup cook, Tad Newman, was getting breakfast under way. Lisa planned to ride horseback that day with Chet. So he saddled the horses the wrangler brought over. They were high up in the pungent pines that morning.

Cole came by and commented how cool and nice it was up there.

"Except for when we are on the main Kaibab Rim. It won't be this cool over there."

His man laughed. "Still be nice to see some new country."

"I agree. Take us three days past Flagstaff to cross the Colorado at Lee's Ferry and then another day or so to cross House Rock Valley."

"Are those deer up there as big as they say?"

"There are lots of big antlered mule deer up there."

"Hey, I am enjoying every day of this trip."

"So am I."

"Are we camping at the part you kept of the old stagecoach yards in Flagstaff tonight?" Cole asked.

"Yes. I have two of those houses rented to keep them in shape to use if we ever need them again."

"Good idea. They may be worth something when the rails arrive."

"I don't need to sell them. So, if I do, they will have a husky price tag on them."

Cole agreed. "I sure enjoy ranching a lot more than the stagecoach business. But I always knew that."

"You did a helluva job running it. I don't think those people now running it do one serious thing to make either it or the telegraph office operate like a business. I hear horror stories all the time from folks dealing with both the wire and the stage line."

Cole agreed. "They like steam engines and whistles better than working at that."

"They do. That operation made money for us. It is costing them but I don't care."

"They're not stage line people."

"Amen." They crossed the proposed graded train track bed going east to west, which had been scrapped up to appear like the ties and steel were only days away.

Chet stood in the stirrups. The builders wanted to sell more of the sections they owned on opposite sides of the train route, sections that were of high value. The government gave them a mile-wide and -long strip on one side, then the other side, land adjacent to the tracks, to sell. So, this grading was to show any potential buyer where they would be if they bought a section. It was smart for real estate sales and this was where folks wanted land adjoining the tracks. His own land on the tracks was west of town, where he felt he could build a loading area and stockyards if it showed a profit was out there.

Chet made his shy horse cross the railbed, moving on to his own land. The day was about over and they'd made good time, but everyone, including Chet, was tired. Both wagons and remuda followed him up the hill to the land he kept out of the sale of the company.

To close the day, some late-afternoon monsoon showers hurried the tent-raising as thunder rolled off the mountains rising above them. In record time, they had the tent up and saddles with bedrolls went inside to stay dry so they could be used later.

Once unsaddled, horses were gathered up and put in a rope corral until the shower went on its way. Men worked in raincoats and soon the camp was set up. By then the sun peered out. Chet smiled and shook his head as the curtain called rain moved away.

Lisa found him. "Supper is cooking and things look good. You need anything?"

"No. Glad things are happening. You all right?"

"I am fine. I'll go help them get the meal out."

He kissed her forehead. "Go. I know you can hustle them along."

She ran off.

"Sir?"

"Yes."

"Where did you ever find a woman that sharp about things?" The question was from Salty. Chet hadn't had much chance to talk to him during the trip.

"Lucky, aren't I?" he asked.

"Luckier than most men I know. She gets more done than two people could."

"Salty, she was standing in a patch of sagebrush in Colorado. Said she was broke and had no transportation out of there. I offered her meals and a ride on a packhorse I had left if she'd make herself handy helping my crew make camp and meals on the way back to Arizona."

"She's been handy ever since, I guess?"

"Well, I am not leaving her behind."

"She's cute and smart."

Chet nodded. "Tom told me that you were pretty sharp, and I believe him now we've come this far."

"Thank you, sir. I appreciate being invited."

"Well, let me know when we begin to fail."

"You won't fail. Thanks again for inviting me."

Chet gave him a wave and went on to eat supper. They were a week away from what they called the North Rim. But they'd soon be on the road again and headed for their goal.

Chet found Lisa seated on a bench, scooted in, and began eating the plate of food she'd filled for him "You have a new fan."

"Who?"

"Salty Meeker. He says you do two folks' jobs."

"He is unreal himself."

"He's a good man. It was a compliment."

She nodded. "You satisfied with the progress we are making?"

"It's going fine, for my part. Take three to four days to get to the ferry from here."

She agreed. "Just so we are doing what we should be doing. You want more peach cobbler, I'll go get it."

"My legs are not broken."

"I just want to save you for when we really need you."

He laughed. "I'll take it, then."

She tweaked her nose at him, then took his tin plate and left to get more.

He shook his head after her cute exit for

the Dutch ovens.

They turned in early that evening. As planned, they headed for the Little Colorado Crossing in the morning. Chet knew it was a gathering place for horse thieves and riffraff. By midday they were able to view the distant deep cut of the Grand Canyon on the left-hand side of the road. By dark they reached the trading post. Chet told the men to buy some hay from a Navajo squaw and keep the horse stock under guard that night since the reputation of horse thieves ran high in that area.

Salty and the other wrangler, Eldon Grimes, took over guarding the horses. Chet and Lisa went to eat in the restaurant in the trading post. Chet promised to bring Salty and Eldon back food later, and they agreed. He stopped Lisa outside the doors and told her to go inside, to get them both a plate plus a place to sit. When she had gone inside he knelt down before a Navajo woman seated cross-legged before her silver jewelry.

He asked her the prices of the silver necklaces on the colorful blanket, and he shook his head. "Too high."

"Silver is not mold that grows on rocks," she said.

He agreed, found a turquoise-and-silver one he liked, held it up, and asked her price.

"Too high," she said.

"No. How much?"

"Hundred and twenty dollars."

"Give you eighty."

She shook her head.

"Ninety."

She gave him the same sign.

He whipped out a hundred-dollar bill from his wallet.

She smiled and held out the necklace, then took his money. *"Gracias, amigo."*

*"Mucho,"* he said, and got off his knees.

Inside, he found Lisa, looking worried and seated with two plates piled with barbecue, beans, and biscuits. "Shut your eyes."

"Huh. You better eat. It won't taste good cold."

"Close your eyes."

She did and he made her put her hands down. Then he hung the necklace on her and snapped it in back.

"What have you done — oh my gosh, what is it?"

"Looks damn pretty on you," Cole said.

"He did good," Jesus said.

"Sit down," she said, and Chet slid in beside her. "I don't deserve this."

"I'll decide that. Give me that bottle of hot sauce. These beans need firing up some."

"Chet Byrnes, do you hear me?"

"No. Eat. It looks better on you than it did on her."

Then she broke out laughing. "He won't listen to a thing I say."

"Better eat. It will get cold."

"You tricked me."

"Haven't I got that right? I mean, can't I do that?"

She shook her head. "Guys, there is never a dull moment being his wife. Never."

"Lisa, the two of you make the greatest couple in the whole world," Cole said. "Keep him. We love him and you won't find a better man on this earth."

She dropped her chin and shook her head. "I love it but I may get a crooked neck wearing it."

Everyone laughed.

"Two more days and we should be across the Colorado and headed for Kaibab."

"We made great time today," Cole added.

"Really good time. Jesus, you getting food for the horse wranglers? Who gets the first shift watching the horses? I think we need two men."

"Jesus and I can take first run," Cole said.

"The cook's helper, Eddie, and Billy Bob Kimes can take the second one. See you at daylight, men."

Chet and his bride went to the camp area.

"I hope you aren't mad at me. No one — but no one — ever gave me a pretty hunk of jewelry like that ever before."

"No one ever appreciated anyone as much as I do you."

"No. No one ever did that, either."

"We're going to make it, girl, and have fun doing it."

She agreed.

He wondered if they'd make it to the ferry in two days. The sun squeezed shut for the day. Heck, he still had her to love — oh hell, it was going great.

They woke up in the predawn. The cooking team boiled oats. They had not lost a single horse to thieves but Chet felt that was the results of his guard shifts and penning the horses up overnight. They set out before the sun was full up and were headed to the ferry across the roiling muddy Little Colorado. On the far bank, they crawled north, skirting the Grand Canyon's gorge on the west side of them, and the red cliffs rising on the right-hand side. It was no grassy land and Chet wondered what those small flocks of Navajo sheep and goats that grazed along the road ate.

Several buggies and small wagons were

headed south on the road, with red-faced young freshly married couples out of Utah, who were headed south to settle around St. David or Thatcher, the prime areas for young Mormon couples to settle in the Arizona Territory. He pointed them out to Lisa and she agreed that was who they were.

"What will they do for a living?" she asked.

"Oh, they are clannish enough to find jobs among their own."

"I am glad I am married to you."

"Hey, so am I. I doubt anyone would hire me." He laughed as they rode apart from the train.

"Don't offer to go to work for anyone if you don't want a job," she said. "I know several outfits that could use you. You built a four-hundred-mile-long telegraph line across a vast wasteland in record time."

"You know I have never worked much for the other guy, besides that stage line–telegraph deal, in my life."

"You said your dad ruined his health looking for your siblings."

"Yeah, the Comanche kidnapped them." He always felt guilty about the loss of his two brothers and a sister but there was nothing he could have done at the time. And he was only a teenage boy. If his father couldn't find them, how could he have saved them? Still, the notion stayed that savages kidnapped them, and it was doubtful they were even alive after all this time. Even talking about it upset him.

"Are there Indians on the North Rim?"

"Paiutes. General Crook called them *grasshopper eaters*."

"Oh, that would be awful."

"I agree, but they were driven there, I bet, by superior tribes into a desolate land situation they couldn't escape."

She nodded that she heard and understood.

At the noon break low clouds came in overhead and the rain they shed was more a drip than drops. Still, the two of them wore raincoats and the train pushed on. Chet decided they would still be a day away from the ferry when they camped for the night. He'd either misjudged the distance or they'd not pushed as hard as they usually did. No matter, this trip was supposed to be pleasure, not work.

The next day they crossed the Colorado River via the ferry barge and Chet spoke to Lee's English wife when he paid her.

"You come after them no-account Logans?" she asked, counting the money.

"No. We are sightseeing."

"Hmm. When will that worthless sheriff

down there send some deputies up to round them scallywags up?"

"They doing anything wrong?"

"Only robbing and murdering folks. Folks disappear all the time and are never heard of again. I keep my guns loaded all the time."

"I am not on law business coming here."

"You need to be. You used to be a U.S. Marshal, didn't you?"

"Yes. But today I am a rancher looking at empty land."

"Look all you want but them no-accounts may murder you."

"I will be very careful. Thanks."

When they were back on the road headed west, Lisa asked, "You think the ones she calls Logans are that bad?"

"I think there may be some bands of outlaws up here. There is no law up here I know about. And it has to come out of Preskitt to have any authority."

"That would be impossible."

"I agree but I had nothing to do with drawing boundaries."

"Where will we stop tonight?"

"There is a good spring west of here some ways at the base of those Vermilion Cliffs on the right side of us. This vast sagebrush plateau on the left is House Rock Valley."

"Good. And the mountain range in the west is our goal tomorrow?"

"Yes. That is Kaibab North. We plan to go down it to the North Rim and spit in the canyon from there."

"I always wanted to do that." She chuckled at his words.

The "good spring," like the rest of his estimates, was farther west than he thought. They had to use lamps to set up camp since the sun had long before set.

In the process, two men rode up and asked for some information.

They both wore suits and one man had his bloody arm in a sling. Chet invited them into their camp and learned their names: Arron Carte and Joseph Hammer — Hammer was the wounded one. Both were dressed as businessmen, and they appeared to have been in a scuffle. Carte told their story.

"We were coming down from Salt Lake to start a business in Arizona. Four tough strangers tried to rob us. Well, they robbed us but I managed to shoot one of them before they left. He dropped part of the money but they all got away."

"You know their names?" Chet asked.

"Just what the three called each other. I didn't hear the name of the fourth guy. One

37

was Hutch. Another was Knobby. And Samson. I shot Samson."

"I told him we needed to telegraph the law," the wounded man said. "Is there a telegraph at the ferry?"

"No," Chet said. "It is a three-day ride south of there on the Little Colorado Crossing."

"My arm may rot off by then."

"No," Salty said. "We are going to redress it for you. You guys were packing that much money in cash and you had no guards?"

"Peaceful country, someone told us."

"Mister, this no-man's-land is far from being that." Salty busied himself redressing the man's gunshot wound, sending for alcohol and fresh bandages from the wagon.

The man's wound was soon cleaned and wrapped. He thanked Salty and his helper. Supper was beans, and they learned some more about the two men and the business they planned for Flagstaff.

Chet finally asked if they thought there would be enough business in the start-up there to survive until the train tracks came to town.

"Why, we were told they had the tracks already graded through town. How far away are the end of the tracks?" Carte slapped his forehead. "And those bastards got most of our money."

"A lot closer to Santa Fe than Flagstaff. They made those graded sections to sell the land they own beside it and pay for more tracks clear over in New Mexico, where they end right now. Not counting the tracks to still be laid over in New Mexico, they lack over two hundred miles in Arizona to get to Flagstaff. At the current rate, I'd say it will be four years before you hear a train whistle down there."

Both men looked sick to their stomachs at Chet's words.

"What will we do?" Carte asked his partner.

"With this throbbing arm, I can hardly worry about our situation except I can hope some surgeon, when we find him, won't cut it off to save me from dying."

"I understand your concern. But we have to continue, after all."

Chet had no answer for them.

The next morning the men rode on. Chet told his wife he felt bad they'd lost their start-up money but Flagstaff wasn't ready for business, either.

She agreed.

They made it to the small settlement of Joseph Lake in midafternoon. A new man owned the store, and the lake, Lisa later told him, was hardly more than a cow tank. Rory Lincoln was a tall man with a slightly bent back. He and Chet hit it right off.

"You met that pair got robbed on the road coming down from Utah?" Lincoln asked him.

"Yes, and they thought the rails were at Flagstaff."

"I heard them say something about it and wondered how the train got that far that fast."

"They are not halfway out of crossing the Rio Grande and the western border of New Mexico."

"I bet business isn't much better than up here."

Both man laughed at his joke.

"From their description, do you know who held them up?"

The tall man surveyed the open area to be certain his response was private. "More than likely the Logan bunch. There ain't room for many outlaws up here but they kind of lead the crime we get."

"Mrs. Lee, over at the ferry, thought I'd arrest them or wanted me to do that."

"I'd help you."

Chet shook his head. "You have to have proof. Good witnesses. A lawyer will get them off. Hearsay won't put them in prison."

"I understand, and Preskitt is over a week away from right here."

"Yes, a long way away. Nice to meet you."

"Yes. I'd heard about the big rancher Chet Byrnes and I am proud to meet you."

"We are headed south to look off in the deep trough and then ride over some of the country."

He laughed. "Don't fall in."

"I aim to avoid that."

# CHAPTER 3

The next morning, Cole shot a big buck with a beautiful twelve-point rack. He had the rack packed to mount when he got home. They dressed the deer and headed south. The country on top that they rode through was like Flagstaff, mostly ponderosa pines.

Hampt rode horseback alongside Lisa and Chet and mused about how pretty the country was they were crossing.

"No market up here, either."

"And there won't be one for years, will there?"

"You have the answer right there. You couldn't afford to ranch up here even if they gave the land to you," Chet said to him.

Late that day they reached the last jumping-off place, as Cole called it, and stood on the North Rim to take in the vast canyon of the Colorado. There was so much to see on the clear day that they shared with buzzards drifting across the vast sky, it impressed both Lisa and Chet.

They rested around camp. The next day Cole, Salty, and Hampt were going off to some side canyon they said led down to the river. Lisa and Chet were going to ride off east into House Rock Valley.

In the morning, the two parties went in opposite directions. In a few hours, Lisa smelled woodsmoke and reined up. Chet nodded that he smelled it, too. They rode into a valley that contained a new log cabin, the source of the smoke.

A pretty blond woman with two children on her skirt came to the open doorway.

"Howdy, folks. Welcome to the Bar Double O Ranch. I am Jeanie Meadows. Those bashful kids are Mark and Sally. My husband, Michael, is gone checking on the cattle we have here."

"I'm Chet and she's my wife, Lisa. We have some ranches over in the Verde River country and Preskitt Valley."

"Oh, you own that lovely place in Preskitt Valley?"

"I can tell you've been by our house," Chet said.

The young woman nodded. "I sure admired it, too, ma'am."

"Jeanie, I have only been there a few years.

I am proud you liked my house. It's a big one, and takes three maids to keep it looking nice," Lisa said.

"Oh, I bet so. Come on in. I don't have coffee but we can sip spring water and talk. I don't get much female company or many men, either, to drop by."

"Would you drink coffee if you had it?" Chet asked, undoing the flap on his saddlebags.

"Oh yes. We aren't Mormons. We just ran out — well, a few weeks ago."

"Neither are we, and I have some." He drew the cloth sack out and they headed inside.

"Michael will be jealous he missed it."

"You can have the rest of it. We have more in our supplies."

"Well, thank you."

In their conversation, they learned Jeanie, her husband, and both their brothers had brought a small herd of cows and bulls up there the year before. They'd wintered well and calved out with low losses. They filed for a homestead claim and had it registered in Preskitt at the courthouse. Their brothers came up earlier and the three men and Jeanie raised the well-built cabin.

Chet was impressed with their dedication to building a ranch. The children were bashful but polite. Mark was four and his sister, Sally, was three. They rounded out the family.

After a nice visit, Chet and Lisa set out for their own camp and, riding back, Lisa asked him about how the children would get educated.

"Either teach them themselves or send them to boarding school."

"Oh, Chet, if I had children like those two I would die if I had to send them to boarding school."

"There is no option when you live this far out. Educate them at home or boarding."

"I am so proud that Elizabeth and I enrolled all those ranch children up at the Cherry School House. She was so progressive and she wanted them to grow up and be citizens. I know you miss her and so do I."

He nodded to show her that he cared, but in a decade he'd lost four women who had touched his life, and that had been hard on him. Life was for the living and Lisa was the joy of his life, but it was hard to keep it all canned up inside him.

They got back to camp before the adventurers returned and she started supper. Chet gave her a hand at peeling some potatoes. She felt they'd eaten enough beans at that point, and told him potatoes and flour gravy might be a good change.

Her observation amused him. Cowboys ate beans every day and any holiday they came to, in his book. But he wasn't going to argue — it would be a good change.

When the others rode in he read on their hard-look faces that his men were upset about something and it was serious.

He caught Cole by the sleeve. "What went wrong today?"

Cole stopped and shook his head. "We met this Logan bunch today. The leader told us we had no business up here checking around on things and if we didn't go home he'd see we were eliminated."

"You men put up with that?"

"Chet — I didn't want any one of us shot. He had the canyon trail covered where we came out, surrounded with rifle-armed men."

"Chet, Cole did the right thing," Jesus said. "They had over a dozen hardcases all armed with new-looking Winchesters and there was no doubt they meant business."

"We had a nice day in the canyon and went clear to the muddy Colorado earlier. I never saw a horse print going or coming out but our own," Hampt said. "But they had the high card, Chet. Cole did the right thing."

Chet let out a held breath and nodded. "I didn't want anyone hurt. Did you recognize any of his men as wanted criminals?"

The crew shook their heads.

"What do we do next?" he asked them.

"Oh, they won't ever get the drop on us again," Salty said. "I promise you they won't. Guess we thought we were too tough to be challenged. They made a big mistake today leaving us alive, and if they try again, they won't survive the attempt."

"Thanks, men. We came to have fun. I am sorry this happened."

The camp crew nodded they understood.

"Lisa has made chicken-fried venison steaks with mashed potatoes and gravy, plus sourdough biscuits. Brag on her for me."

Cole threw his arm over Chet's shoulder. "We can damn sure do that."

And they ate like they were celebrating some major event. But Chet knew they needed to do something about Logan and his threat to them. He damn sure didn't own the North Rim country, and his bunch needed to convince them of that fact.

"We need to know more about Logan and his men. Their habits, strengths, and weaknesses."

Cole, enjoying the crisp meat, agreed with a nod. "Lisa, you did real good cooking this."

The men applauded.

She blushed. "It was nothing. Just a change. I don't want to upset the cooking and take that over, is for certain."

"Shucks, Lisa," Hampt said. "We thought you were about to open an eatery up here."

"Aside from you guys and a few black bears I'd be awful thin on customers."

Everyone laughed and agreed.

# Chapter 4

When the sun came up the next morning, Chet was no closer to having an answer about what to do about Logan than he'd been the night before. After a breakfast of hotcakes, homemade syrup, and crisp bacon they drank coffee and discussed the matter.

Cole and Salty offered to try and scout them out. Chet agreed they'd be the best two and said for them to be careful but learn what they could. Hampt had seen some mustang tracks, and while two men stayed in camp to keep an eye on things — the rest planned to go wild-horse hunting.

The party of six left in search of the broomtails.

Midmorning, they had them in Chet's field glasses. The riders were parked on top of a tall sand dune to view the band from a distance.

"Some nice-looking mares." Hampt shared the glasses with Lisa.

49

"Chet, you see any you like?"

"Couple of red roans might make good horses someday."

"They're close to weaning, aren't they?"

He nodded to agree.

"Well, let's shake loose some lariats and capture them. No need to go home empty-handed," his wife said.

Did she rope mustangs? Not too much she did shocked him but he saw right off when she made a loop to catch one, this was not her first trial at it. What a woman he had married.

They divided forces. He followed her, and Hampt went with them. The others, including the horse wrangler Eldon, set in to catch some older colts.

The lead mare made short work of rounding up her band when she discovered them as onlookers. The herd went over the rise between some juniper groves. Lisa and her hands fell into hot pursuit, ropes ready to swing wide and catch some horseflesh.

Pounding after them across some purple sage patches, they were having lots of laughs. One of the camp boys' horses spilled and Billy Bob was tossed into the grass. He quickly rose and shouted, "I'm fine. Don't let them get away."

"We won't," Chet promised him over his

shoulder, grateful the youth was okay.

In the confusion one of the roan colts found itself blocked in by some fallen dead cedars, and Lisa closed in on the panic-stricken critter. He started to dart back past her but she threw the lariat over his ears and then she jerked the slack. Like a large fish on a hook he settled into having a walleyed fit. But she had him on her rope and was keeping her mount looking at him and not giving him any slack.

Chet ripped a denim shell out from behind the cantle, bailed off his horse to cover his head, and hoped, when he was blinded, it would settle him down. He could see they had two more colts caught out in the next sage flat and were having a fight, too, with them.

The jumper was over his head and big Hampt had him caught around the neck, and the three were laughing hard at their wild horse's antics.

"Where did you learn to rope like that?" Chet asked his wife, who was holding the rope they had the colt caught with.

"Chet Byrnes, I never was some charm school graduate. You just never saw me at roundup before."

He guessed he had that coming. Keeping the fighting young horse on his mind he'd sworn that damn colt wasn't a broke livery horse, either. He had to duck a flying hoof or he'd be clubbed with it. "Whoa, pony boy. You are going to be her next horse to break."

A halter was formed and slipped over his head, with Hampt holding him around the neck so he had little chance to get going on a wild charge or jump.

Recoiling her lariat, Lisa, looking, a little triumphant, came to where Hampt held the colt.

"He's going to become a great horse," she said, and the others all agreed.

Chet shook his head — still amazed. He damn sure never expected her to catch the colt but she did. He took the reins of his returned mount from the hand who'd caught him and thanked him. In a short while they were headed home with four soon-to-be-willing-to-be-led colts.

Making camp later, he knew by their absence that Cole and Salty were still out there checking on Logan. He hoped those two were all right. He was pretty well convinced that, before it was over, they'd have to do something serious about Logan and his gang. Those outlaws were no differ-ent than the rest of the lawless elements and in his book they all needed to be stopped or

Arizona would never become a state.

His crew, even without Cole and Salty, set in with saws and axes to build a small pole corral to hold the two colts. By suppertime the pen was built and Lisa's wards were nickering for their momma in this new world. Taking hold of her shoulders from behind, he kneaded them as she observed her "herd."

"I am more than a little amazed at your ability to rope."

She nodded. "I never needed to rope anything before when you were around. It was learn how to rope or be the cook's slave, and I mean *slave*. I learned how to beat those neighbor boys at roping pretty damn quick."

"How old were you then?"

"Twelve or so. I beat those big boys — sixteen and older — at it."

"I can recall riding out at dawn with the rest of the roundup crew and that big Gary Sampson was waving a big knife at me, peeling potatoes and shouting, "You bitch, you won't beat me again at roping.""

"Did you?"

"Yes."

"What you going to do with your herd?"

"I never owned two horses before. Guess I'll have to think on it. How did those boys build that trap that quick?"

"I figure between Cole and Salty gone they knew when those two got back they'd have them hopping to do things. So they didn't need any prodding to build it."

"We do have a good crew, and they wouldn't want to be camp dishwashers left in camp, either, on this trip." She turned around and stood on her toes to kiss Chet.

"You worried about those two men of yours?" she asked him.

He looked off over her head across the vast abyss of the canyon and shook his head. "Not yet. They want a good picture of the enemy. Those two are smart and will want all the information they can get before they come back."

"What if they took them prisoners?"

"A big part of his gang will be dead."

She hugged him and shook her head. "You know them well enough."

"That may be the toughest pair I could have found to do this job."

His detectives rode in after dark. They looked hollow-eyed in the campfire light but Chet could tell they'd learned a lot.

Lisa and some of the help fed them when they settled down at the fireside circle.

"You all been catching wild horses?" Cole tossed his head toward the corral.

"Lisa owns them."

Cole took a sip of the hot coffee they'd served him and nodded. "Salty, tell them about the Logan gang."

"They have about a dozen men. Some have wives. Mates, huh, anyway. They're Mexican women or squaws. They have some dome hide lodges and a few raw cabins. Kind of a sorry camp, and a part of those men we think were gone somewhere. Nothing like we expected to find. I thought they were more military-like when we met them coming out of that canyon. They don't look it to me."

"Salty and I figured they are like most outcasts. They just exist out here so they aren't imprisoned or hung. I say we go on having your vacation that you and Lisa are taking. Be a little more cautious and handle them when we need to."

"Sounds good to me. Get a bath and some sleep."

"Lisa, are you going to need a ranch up here for your horses?" Cole teased.

"You want the job running it?" she asked him.

He held up his hands to protect himself. "No. No."

"Well, let's look at more country tomorrow," Chet said, and they agreed.

■ ■ ■ ■

West of there the following day, they were out on a point and Cole directed their attention to a cave opening under the face of the sheer cliff, maybe thirty feet below the rim. Nothing would do but tying some lariats together and lowering someone small like Salty down there and have him explore it.

They tied the end of the rope to a good-size juniper tree and two men let hatless Salty off the edge using Chet and Hampt as the main force on the rope to allow him to drop down. Salty managed to get off the rope and into the cave. In minutes he shouted, "Send Cole down. I found something. Make another rope to pull things up."

"What did he find?" Chet couldn't imagine finding anything but bat shit in that cave.

He shook his head, and Cole shed his hat to give to Lisa. Cole smiled and got on the rope with his gloves. "Hell only knows."

He soon disappeared into the cave entrance, waving his thanks. In a short while Cole and Salty shouted they had something to pull up.

Chet frowned. The fish on the line they hauled up were breastplates of Spanish armor. He looked at them in disbelief.

"What is it?" Eddie asked.

"Something a Spanish soldier left in that cave," Chet said.

"Is there any more treasure?" Hampt shouted.

Cole stuck his head out. "There is a damn museum of those things. Even some skeletons of the men who died down here."

Chet turned to two of the boys. "We may need to get one of the wagons over here to haul it out. Can we do that?"

"We can get one close. That last wash might be as close as we can get one on top."

Chet agreed. "We better get what we can hauled up."

"Is this stuff worth much?" Billy Bob, the freckled-face cowboy, asked.

Chet nodded. "No telling. But all these years in this dry atmosphere it is in really good shape and probably worth something."

So, the job began with them piling the bounty coming from the cave well back from the edge. Some old flint-sparked muskets, hand pistols, swords, and metal hats, and then Cole shouted up to them, "Be careful. This is the good one."

Chet was standing on the edge and could not make out the contents of the bucket they hauled up the cliff's face. Hampt even strained to pull it up, and it was obvious that it was heavy enough that he had to move back from the edge and use both his hands.

After the pail was set down, Chet knelt and took a handful of the shiny red stones out. "Rubies."

Raw, red, uncut diamondlike stones — why, there must have been thousands of dollars' worth of them.

Chet's wife knelt beside him. Her face was very pale. "Are they real?"

All Chet could do was swallow and nod. "They're the real things. Wait. Cole's shouting again."

"What comes next?" Hampt's voice echoed back.

"Damned if I know what they are," was the reply.

The big man hauled up the next bucket more carefully than the last. It was only half-full and Chet, still on his knees, scooped up some in his palm. "Emeralds. Equally as good."

In all this time Jesus was carefully reading the parchments they'd sent up earlier. "I am not a good translator but three officers must have been trapped in the cave waiting to be rescued by the soldiers that were with them, and no one came back for them in time to save them. One committed suicide by jumping out, the other two died down there."

"When was that?" someone asked.

"Seventeen hundred–something," Jesus said.

Next came crude gold bars, melted, poured, and branded. They were real and damn impressive, Chet decided.

"How much more is down there? We about have a wagon load now," Chet told them.

Cole stuck his head out. "Another wagon load, I bet, if it is worth hauling off."

"What else?"

"Gold nuggets they never got melted, and we need some sacks for them."

"Well, we need to make arrangements for more wagons, and that store isn't close." Chet was laughing. What a deal to have a problem with.

Someone obviously would be able to read the signs that they'd been removing things from that cave. They would need to get all that was worth having out of there. He'd need to buy some more wagons and conceal all they'd gotten to get it back to Preskitt. Nothing ever came easy.

"There is a fortune here, isn't there?" Lisa asked him under her breath.

"Yes, but we'd need more wagons to ever get it all back home."

"Where are they at?"

"Maybe Joseph Lake. Maybe Utah. We need to send for them."

She nodded.

"When we get all the valuable things up on top we will move this to our camp."

She agreed.

No time for lunch. It was midafternoon when they ate, and all hands were up on top. Two of the men went back to camp to get the empty wagons as close as possible to the site. Chet and Cole appraised the deep cut wash as a barrier and decided it had too much depth to fill in with no more than the hand tools they had to move the dirt. They decided to build a walkway made out of poles to go across it.

That meant the crew must spend another day there, considering the effort needed to build that bridge. No one complained. They set in to find trees nearby to cut down to build their crossing with, and the men who'd gone for wagons had been instructed to bring back saws and axes.

Hands rested, waiting until they got back. Then trees were cut, limbed, and skidded by dark. They rode their horses back to camp in the dark, accompanied by some howling wolves stalking the ridges who no doubt wondered what the hell they were up to riding around under the stars in their territory.

# CHAPTER 5

The bridge over the newly christened Dry Fork took shape by noon. Chet told the ones there that if they fell off it packing stuff across this bridge about twelve feet above the base they'd have to stay there permanently. Earlier he'd sent Cole and Billy Bob on a mission to buy at least one more wagon. If there was not one at Joseph Lake, he'd told them to go on to find one or two at Kanab, up the road.

When everything was piled into the two rigs, they drove them back to their original camp in the fading sundown. They ate what they found and fell exhausted in their bedrolls. The next day passed and Chet decided his men had gone to Kanab, Utah, to find another wagon.

He was busy writing in his diary when Lisa came back from feeding her horses herd grass she and some hands cut for them.

"Chet, the wagons are coming. I can hear them."

He finished his last paragraph about finding the Spanish treasure and closed the inkwell. "I hear them, my dear, and a finer sound never came to me like their arrival is."

After Cole tied off the reins in the brake lever, he nodded to Chet. "Yes, we had to go to Kanab to get these rigs. But these horses are sound and the rigs are, too. They just cost a lot of money, which I had no time to dicker over." Everyone laughed and clapped.

"Everyone rest. We load up tomorrow and leave for Preskitt when we get that done."

The boss's decision was well accepted by the hands.

In the late afternoon, the Meadows family rode up on horseback. Lisa ran to meet them.

"So glad you came to see us, Jeanie. Get down and meet my crew," Lisa said, taking Jeanie's young daughter off the horse.

Jeanie's handsome husband, a man in his late twenties, handed Chet the boy to hold and smiled as he dismounted. "She talked about you and said you all might still be here, and we decided to ride over. Hope we aren't interrupting anything."

"No, we are resting. We found some Span-ish treasures and are heading home tomor-row."

"A lot of it?"

"Yes, to be honest, a lot of it. We had to pack it out to where we could get it in our wagon and now have it loaded."

"How did you find it?"

"It was in a cave about thirty foot off the top of where we were looking at the canyon. By the notes we found, and Jesus translated, the three men were left in the cave and were waiting for their soldiers to come back and rescue them. One committed suicide and the other two died in the cave."

"When were they here?"

"Seventeen-forty."

"And it was still there?"

Chet nodded and showed him the metal armor and hats they wore. Then the guns, swords, and books.

"Any gold?"

"Some."

Michael said, "They didn't get it from close around here. I have been panning in all the dry creeks."

"Ever find any rubies?"

"Were there some of them there, too?"

Chet showed him some samples of the ones they'd found, taking a few from his pocket. He held them up to the sun.

"I never found any of these, either."

"I don't know where they came from but they're gem quality."

"Where is this place you found them, if I may ask?"

"None of us plan to go back, do we?" he asked his men.

They all shook their heads. "It is about ten miles west over there, but we cleaned out the cave in the face of the bluff. You find the bridge we built to cross a deep dry wash then you can find the cave, but don't try to go down to it alone. We found these gems and artifacts in that hole, but we have ranches to run and no time to look for more of them."

"I'd love to find the source. And thanks for telling me how to find the area."

"They also found some emeralds when they were here. We never found the source of any of them."

"What made you look in that cave?" Michael asked.

"Ask Cole. We let him and Salty down there on ropes. They found it all."

"Whew, you were real lucky."

"We've been looking all over at things. Jesus came to find some original Spanish horses. They caught my wife four colts she likes."

"Michael," Cole said, swinging the boy around and making him laugh. "We had to see what was down there after we discovered it was a cave."

"I'll be more attentive to things after this — thanks for the tips. Mr. Byrnes is your boss. How did he get to Arizona?"

Cole laughed. "He told us they ran him out of Texas."

Chet nodded. "My family got in a feud. They murdered my brother while we were taking a herd to Kansas."

"I understand feuds. They're bad deals."

"Why are you up here starting a ranch?" Chet asked him.

"I had some money to buy some cattle. I couldn't afford a ranch down south. This is unsettled country and I could homestead the land. Jeanie said she was brave enough to try it. Our brothers helped me get the herd up here. They came back and we built the cabin. In four or five years we will have cattle to sell."

Chet nodded that he heard him. "If you see that it doesn't work, come find me up at Preskitt Valley. We could find work for you. We have lots of couples working for us."

"Wish I'd met you two years ago. I'll stick

with this plan, but thanks, and I may need to find you, Mr. Byrnes — someday."

The couple left to get home by dark. Lisa was on a high. She'd played with their daughter, Sally. Chet knew she wanted a girl of her own to show her how to live her life better than she'd handled her own early on.

They set out for Joseph Lake in the morning and made it by evening. Chet and Rory Lincoln, the storekeeper, talked about his business and the Logan bunch and their threats. Lincoln said he was glad they had no more problems than the one threat. He apologized, too, for not finding Cole the extra wagons and teams they needed, but he did send them to a man in Kanab who had them.

Lincoln never asked what they were totting out and Chet wasn't going to broadcast any information about it. They camped for the night and started for the ferry in the morning.

A day and a half later, Mrs. Lee talked to them about ferrying two more wagons besides the two original ones. Chet merely told her they needed them and let it go. The entire cave treasure was well concealed in each wagon. Lisa's colts, by this time, were broke to lead in a line, and they were another topic of the questions streaming from Mrs. Lee's English-accented mouth.

"Those are her horses. She picked them out. Better ask her." Chet put Mrs. Lee off with that and paid her the fees.

"You coming back up here to settle?" she asked.

"I don't think so. We have a lot of good range land down there for now. Thanks."

"I'll be here if you need to cross back over. Thanks, sir."

When he joined Lisa at the head of the line, she said, "I think Mrs. Lee likes you."

"Sorry. I am taken."

They both laughed. It was a good two days ahead of them to the Little Colorado Crossing.

Riding along he told her, "Make a list of each man here. I'll pay them half whatever this stuff brings when we get it settled."

"Eight shares, then get fifty percent of the final settlement?"

"Fine."

That evening at supper he announced he would split the treasure's final sales in half and each of the eight party members would get their share of that half.

They applauded and thanked him.

Jesus shook his head. "I get that and I will

have to whitewash all my buildings at home."

"At least it won't come out of your pocket," Hampt teased.

"It isn't the money for the paint I worry about. It is me having to paint it all."

They laughed some more.

They had no trouble at the Little Colorado. But Chet noticed they had many suspicious eyes and back-of-hands comments on how they went up there with two wagons and now had four.

He bet the onlookers really worried about what he'd found up there that was worth dragging home. They would never know until the word got out that they'd found Spanish gold and gemstones, and that they'd slipped a fortune past them in those farm wagons.

"What is so funny?" Lisa asked, riding in close to Chet.

"There were several greedy eyes back up there wondering what we found. Why four wagons to go home with?"

"Yes. It is funny. Where will you store it?"

"The gold bars and the nuggets in the bank. The same with the gems. I want them appraised. Tanner at the bank can keep them for us. I know a man in Tucson who collects Spanish antiques. I'll invite him up to look at those."

Five days later they met Tom and Millie at the Preskitt Valley ranch. Chet made Millie put out her hand when she frowned at the four rigs. He dropped four uncut rubies into her palm.

Her blue eyes flew open. "Oh my goodness, are they real?"

"Yes. Very real. Those are yours for guarding the house."

Tom laughed and shook his head at his wife's reaction. "I'd say you got top wages."

"But — but they are real — not glass?"

"The very real thing."

Jesus and Cole were taking the loot to the bank with the rest of the men except for Hampt, who they shook hands with since he planned to ride home to join May and his children.

That all settled, Chet took the rest of them back into the house and explained what they found and the one incident with Logan. When he completed the story, Tom shook his head. "It was all in a cave in the face of a towering cliff over the Grand Canyon?"

"Yes. They left a diary. Jesus translated it. Two died in the cave when no one came back for them. The other committed suicide."

"Wonder why they didn't come back for them and the gold?"

"I figure an Indian bunch wiped them out — somewhere up there. So they never got back to get the live ones or the treasure out of there."

"Helluva a deal, and it happened in the seventeen hundreds?"

"Yes. A long time ago. I never went over the cliff. Your man Salty and Cole went down on ropes and loaded the things and we pulled them up. It made a great hideout but also a death trap for the ones left there when they did not come back for them."

"Where did they get the rubies?" Millie asked.

"Somewhere up there I imagine there is maybe a caved-in mine. A prospector may someday trail the mine up. But we never saw any gems laying around any source on the ground. We didn't do much gold panning. There simply was not that much looking-around time and, let me tell you, I don't think you could walk all over that entire portion of Arizona in a lifetime. It is a dry land with few rivers or streams.

"They tell me the emeralds we brought back came from a different vein than the rubies. The Spaniards found gold, rubies, and emeralds up there. We found skeletons, metal uniforms, old, old guns, books, and letters. There's some bands of outlaws, at least one, anyway, who run roughshod over the citizens up there. They need to be removed but that is a job for the territorial law to handle, not the ranch folks."

"Were there any pure Spanish horses?" someone asked.

"Not that I observed. Those colts are my wife's and she will decide their fate. I made a deal with the men that went along with me. I will share half the treasure profits with them."

The gathered folks clapped and approved the deal. He also told them he had no plans to run a ranch on the north side of the Grand Canyon. They applauded again. He hugged his wife by the shoulders. "Thanks. This ranch looks wonderful and a better site to be at than the whole north part of Arizona above the Grand Canyon."

He waved good-bye to Tom and Millie. Cole's wife, Valerie, was there, in a buckboard, by then. Standing before the spring seat she shouted, "Chet Byrnes, thank you again for bringing him back to me. You've saved my life several times."

He agreed and waved at her.

He and Lisa went into the house.

"They have baths for us drawn upstairs. I

will bring our meal up, all right?"

"Sounds wonderful."

"I am not rushing you, am I?"

He shook his head. "I am really bushed. Be good to sit down finally. Thanks, honey."

Bathed and full, they went to bed early.

# CHAPTER 6

The alarm bell in the ranch center was ringing. Chet sat straight up in bed. It was still night dark outside. Something bad had happened. He went to the open window to shout at the bell ringer. "What's wrong?"

"Mr. Byrnes, they've stolen several horses over at our ranch tonight. Hampt has his arm broken. He tried to stop them. Louis told me to come get you and more men."

"I am coming down. Vance, send word to Jesus and Cole for them to come at once.

"Messenger?" Chet asked the man.

"My name is Hal, sir."

"Didn't recognize you in the dark. Hal, come to the back door. My wife and I'll be down there after we dress. I want to hear the whole story."

"Yes, sir."

Busy dressing in the lighted bedroom by the bedside lamp, Lisa shook her head. "You

74

aren't home ten minutes and all hell breaks loose."

"Glad I am here."

"Oh, I am not complaining. Where would they go with stolen horses?"

"I'd say south. Not much market anywhere else."

She nodded that she heard him and finished buttoning up her dress. "Just be careful, all right?"

"I intend to be that." He kissed her quickly and dropped his rump on the bed to pull on his boots. "Sorry, this will be too tough for you to go along."

"I understand and I really appreciated the trip north. What shall I do about all this treasure business?"

"If it sounds like a good offer, accept it."

"No. I have no idea about the value. It can wait until you return."

"Fine. Tanner at the bank knows the gold's value. Have him sell it."

"I will do that, then."

He hugged her, thanked her, and they went downstairs. Hal rose when he saw Chet's wife. "These girls let me in."

"Fine. Sit down. And tell me the story from the start."

"I was asleep in the bunkhouse when the dogs went to raising hell. Earlier we had a big welcome home for Hampt getting back from your trip. I jumped out of bed, put on my boots, and grabbed my gun before going out the door. But the horses they drove had already gone by the bunkhouse door."

"What happened next?"

"One of the rustlers whirled his horse around to come back to help a rustler that Hampt had ahold of. I guess he ran out of the house, caught this last one, and jerked him off his horse. The outlaw who rode back crashed his horse into Hampt. That sent him and the one he had hold of down on the ground and broke Hampt's arm in the wreck.

"The rider shot at Hampt but the horse he rode was all upset so he missed — the rustler that Hampt had hold of jumped on the other one's horse behind him and they skedaddled. I shot at them, but in the dark, you can't hit anything except by luck."

"How many horses did they get?"

"Last count I heard was two dozen. May sent me to get you. Walt Stroud and two others were going after them when they found horses to ride. I caught this old horse and rode fast as I could over here."

"How is Hampt?"

"Hell — sorry, ladies — he was ready to go after them, broken arm and all."

Chet knew Hampt would be upset. He hoped May could hold him until they got the arm set, anyway.

"These were the horses that Hampt's stepson broke for him?"

"Oh yes, sir. They were the best horses to steal."

Lisa brought them both a cup of hot coffee.

Boy, he knew how mad Hampt must be. He'd bragged on the new addition to his remuda up on the North Rim, and to have rustlers take them was not an easy thing to swallow, especially for a man like Hampt.

The house girls and Lisa fixed them breakfast. Vance came to the house and reported how he'd sent for both Jesus and Cole. His men were loading the packhorses with supplies.

His ranch foreman asked if they needed a horse wrangler to keep up with them.

Chet nodded.

Chet thanked the girl who delivered his plate heaped with scrambled eggs, bacon, hash browns, and biscuits in gravy.

"Wow, you girls are fattening me."

"Eat up," Lisa said. "There will not be any kitchens where you'll be camping."

"Yes, ma'am. Vance, to come back to your question. Yes, a good man like Vic wouldn't hurt to have along, and another man to manage the horses."

"Vic will be proud to serve."

"Yes. He'd be good."

"Pick that boy who went north with us. He's up here," Lisa said. "His name was Eldon Grimes."

Chet nodded and told Vance to stay there and eat — it would take a while for Cole and Jesus to get there.

Vance did as he was told.

"It is a shame that Salty isn't up here," Lisa said.

"By the time he got up here we'd be long gone."

She agreed.

"I can send a word to him," Vance said. "He'd be up here in four hours and grab a fresh horse here. He'd catch you pretty quick on the trail."

"There won't be anyone to look after things if we all go. Send word for him to help you while we are gone. We are taking some of your men as it is."

Cole arrived in a buckboard with Valerie and Chet's son Rocky, who came on the run to the house.

"Is Hampt all right?" Val shouted at him.

Chet went over and hugged Cole's wife, Valerie, and tousled his son's hair. "We think so. How are you two?"

"Fine. How bad off is Hampt?" she asked.

"I figure by now he's on his way to Preskitt to have the bone set. And mad as hell about the whole thing."

"You have many details?"

"Hampt got hold of one of them and jerked him off his horse. Another rustler came back and that guy ran over them with his horse. In the wreck, they say Hampt broke his arm and the second one got on and rode off with that other rustler."

"Boy, if Hampt had got hold of one of them he'd have pumped the information about who they were out of that outlaw."

Chet agreed. "Have some breakfast. Rocky, are you all right?"

"I'm fine. I like Hampt. I hope he gets all right."

"So do I. You need to see Lisa's new horses we brought home with us."

"I will be sure to look at them."

"How long before Jesus gets here?" Cole asked.

"Maybe an hour. Vance is sending Vic and the horse wrangler Billy Bob, who went to the North Rim."

"That's good. Any idea who the rustlers are?"

"No. But they must be well organized to

slip in and take only the good horses."

Cole nodded. "Didn't horse rustlers take some valuable horses from this ranch before you married Marge?"

"My first wife. Yes. They went through Bloody Basin and some damn rough country."

"They ambushed the ranch's foreman and his man?"

Chet nodded. "I made Raphael stay with their bodies and rode on after them. Our deal was for Raphael to come after me when they got there."

Cole nodded. "That old man never forgot the sheriff's deputy. When he got there he wouldn't let him go on and help you."

"He always told me that."

Jesus arrived by buckboard about the time daylight lightened the eastern sky. He handed over a bedroll and war bag with a rifle. "How is Hampt?"

"I imagine he's had his arm set by now," Chet said.

Shaking his head, his aide said, "I hope he's all right. The boy said they stole those good horses that May's son broke for him."

"I'd say they had a spy over there, or someone knew those horses were broke and ready for when they got there. It was well planned."

"They going to Bloody Basin this time?"

Chet smiled. "Most rustlers use that route. Is your wife all right?"

"She's fine."

"Thanks for answering my call. Cole's here and two ranch men are going along — Vic and the horse wrangler Billy Bob, who we used on the North Rim."

"Good. I will be ready shortly. I want to check on the supplies they have loaded."

"Fine. We are also taking along a few extra horses."

"Good."

Jesus shook his head in disbelief. "It is a wonder Hampt is alive."

"I thought the same thing." They both laughed.

"How many head taken?"

"No one had a count of how many got away. He originally bought twenty head. We'd hoped to start out with some real good horses for him to have for roundup next spring."

"These supplies will work," Jesus said, telling the hands standing by to replace the diamond hitches over the panniers.

"I think the others are here. Mount up!"

Chet took the reins to the stout roan mountain horse they called Gilacarty and swung into the saddle. His boot soles set in the stirrups, he smiled at Lisa. "I'll be back."

"You better or I'll haunt you to hell."

"I believe you'd do that."

She moved in and slapped his leg. "Wear chaps in the brush. It will save you needles in your legs."

"I promise. I get down there, I'll wear them. Love you."

She shook her head, her lashes wet. Parting was hard on him, too.

The horse the vaquero Vic chose bucked some going under the gate bar. The others shouted him on but the gelding quickly broke into a lope and he led the procession to where the highway turned southeast.

"How far will we get today?" Cole asked Chet.

"We should make the turnoff to Bloody Basin by sundown."

"They have a half-day's start on us?"

Chet nodded. "Unless they pour it on hard today."

Cole agreed. "Oh, thanks for inviting me."

Chet found that funny and laughed.

Before sundown they located water off the Black Canyon Road at the Bloody Basin cutoff. There was no doubt in Chet's mind the rustlers had gone into the wilderness with the stolen horses. It was a long ways to any civilization, crossing this way, and there were not many folks to say they'd rode by. He wondered what their plans were to sell the horses and where?

They made camp and the stopover was well organized. Where would they land? He sat cross-legged on an Indian rug and flipped pebbles out in the short dry grass while they set up camp. There had to be an answer to his question. Maybe he'd ask a raven how far ahead they were.

That amused him — talking to birds. Wouldn't work. But then the next day he needed that information to continue after them. *Lisa, I am thinking of you . . .*

# CHAPTER 7

They were up before sunup so that when the pink lighted the eastern sky the fires for breakfast were flaming. They began loading the packhorses and saddling the riding ones. Bedrolls were tied on behind cantles and the men came into camp to sip too-hot coffee and fill their plates with cooked food out of iron kettles.

Everything packed, they set out. No doubt the fresh-shod ranch horses were going ahead of them. Chet rode up on some rises to see if there was any dust boiling up. Nothing. They reached a long-abandoned ranch to water the herd and could see that the rustlers had been there earlier in this densely crowded juniper brush–clad rolling country.

Many buck mule deer stiff-legged bounded away at their appearance. Their antlers in the velvet they soon disappeared in the vegetation. It would have been a great place to hunt deer, Chet decided when a near-blue-coated male snorted at him and left the area in a bounding run.

At noon they took a short break and ate some leftover breakfast. Chet told them they'd find some water midafternoon and might consider camping there since the next water he knew about was the Verde River and it was a day's drive past that place.

They agreed.

"How far away are we from where they were hung?" Cole asked. He referred to the place where Chet had lynched the last two of the killers of the two ranch foremen.

"I'd say we're four to five hours from the Verde now. That lynching was at Rye and it is way the hell over there," Chet replied, pointing in the direction it all happened.

"Will they go there?"

"Best horse market is Tombstone."

"You think they'll go there?"

"I have no idea, but there's money there and horses come high priced."

"Who hung them killers, Mr. Byrnes?" Billy Bob asked.

"A man who followed the bloody trail close behind them."

"You did?"

"Those men had murdered both the Preskitt Valley ranch foreman and his number one man. They raped two women as well. I trailed the killers down here and then way over there to Rye and decided the world didn't need them any longer. Today I would drag them back to be hung — law is better than that — but then I didn't."

Billy Bob nodded that he understood.

Chet began to unsaddle his horse.

"Sir, let me do that. That is my job."

"Not today. But thanks."

"Yes, sir."

Jesus and Cole soon were at his side.

Cole began with authority in his voice, "We have four hours of sunlight left. Let's take fresh horses and ride like hell and maybe catch this bunch."

"The three of us," Jesus said. "Two of us already think we are really close to them from the signs of things."

"The rest of our crew and the packhorses can come on in the morning if we don't catch them," Cole said.

Chet nodded. "I'm game."

"Guys, saddle us the toughest fresh horses we have. The boss man, Jesus, and I are making a hard rush this afternoon to catch these thieves and if we don't, so what. You all come in the morning and bring the pack-horses."

The crew rushed to get them mounted.

Jesus got them some jerky and in no time the three of them were ready to race off after the rustlers. Chet had put on his chaps to save his legs, since he knew rushing like this would get them in some fixes in the brush or even a pancake cactus bed.

Mounted, they saluted the men, left, and charged away. Cole took the lead and they wasted no time going from hill to the next hill on the faded wagon track through the dry washes and up the other side. Hooves drumming, saddle leather creaking, the determined threesome crossed lots of country.

Coming off a long grade, Chet stopped them and dug out his field glasses after he saw what he thought looked like the flash of a dark bay horse farther down the mountain. Glasses to his eyes, he adjusted them and he saw another horse through the openings.

He handed the glasses to Cole. "They are half a mile downhill from here."

"Reckon they've heard us?" Jesus asked.

Chet shook his head and fought his heated horse to be still. "Not herding their own horses."

"Yes, it's them. Range horses don't shine like those horses do."

Jesus took the glasses next. "How do we

sneak up on them, then?"

"Keep moving. We have some time till sundown. I think they plan to stop at the Verde."

"Good."

They trotted their mounts from there on. All they could hope for was that the rustlers didn't see them coming. But either way they'd soon be in range of them. Chet began to grow more confident they were about to recover the stolen horses. He saw the rustlers again on the wide sandy beach, watering men and horses.

He slipped his Winchester out of the scabbard. The three of them were nearly under the ancient gnarled cottonwoods that lined the river. He motioned for his own armed men to spread out.

At that point, the rustlers had only sidearms. Their rifles were in the saddle scabbards.

One of them shouted, "Look!"

Chet took aim, and the man never reached but six inches for his Colt when the rifle slug sent him sprawling on his back. The report spooked all the horses and they stampeded into the rustlers trying to get their guns out. Their resistance lasted only minutes and a few shots from his men. The rustlers were either shot or trying to get up after one of the scared horses collided with him.

Off their horses and taking charge, Jesus and Cole were busy disarming the rustlers and making them get facedown in the sand. None of them offered any resistance, but they cussed a lot.

Two of the wounded ones moaned real loud. The last man standing wore a black business suit and he told Jesus no way was he lying down in that mud. Cole busted him over the head with his pistol and he, too, lay on the sand.

Satisfied the fight was over Jesus went to his horse for some rope to tie them up with.

Chet, gun in his fist, stepped down off his horse and waded over to Cole. "Who is the preacher you knocked out?"

Cole smiled and shook his head. "Damned if I know. Jesus, who is he?"

The rustler on the ground said, "Dean Louray."

Chet shook his head. He'd never heard of him. "You all are under arrest for horse stealing, attempted murder, and I'll find me some more charges up in Preskitt to keep you in jail for a long time."

The two wounded men were carried to the shade. One was going to die from a bullet in the chest. The other was shot in the arm but a tourniquet had stopped the bleeding. The rest had their hands tied behind their backs. They'd been disarmed and searched. The rustlers, save for Louray, had little money on them. He had over five hundred dollars on him.

Chet had Jesus make a list in his herd book of the names they gave him. Horses were rounded up and a few hobbled to keep them close and grazing as the sun set. But before it went down two of the lesser prisoners stacked up driftwood for the night's campfire. Jesus had found some frijoles on one of their packhorses, boiled some, and served them as supper.

The worst wounded one died and they rolled him in a blanket to bury at dawn. The guard shift was chosen and each man had a few hours, by Big Dipper time, to oversee them.

Cowboys didn't invent keeping time on the Big Dipper, but Chet knew anyone who ever drove cattle herds to Kansas could use it.

The rest of Chet's crew must have gotten up early and pushed hard to join them. They were smiling when they rode up the Verde bottoms with the pack train and nodded in approval at the tied-up outlaws.

"You get them all?" Billy Bob asked, reining up his horse.

"Every damn one we could find," Cole teased him. "Get some coffee out. These cheap bastards didn't have any."

At that, they all laughed.

# CHAPTER 8

Five days later Chet had driven into Preskitt to talk to Tanner at the bank. He left Lisa off at the dress store and parked his rig out in front of the bank. His men, on their arrival back, had the rustlers put in jail. Cole and Jesus handled the booking and the sheriff never sent word to Chet he was pleased or unpleased about their efforts.

When Chet walked in the lobby of the bank that morning, two ranchers leaving shook his hand and thanked him for a job well done. Standing at Tanner's desk he saw the *Miner* newspaper headline read: AREA RANCHER ROUNDS UP THE HORSE RUSTLERS. He bet the editor had asked why couldn't the Yavapai County sheriff have done the same?

"Morning, Tanner. How is banking going?"

"Good enough. The gem buyer wants to examine them. He will pay freight one way and look at them. He doesn't want them, then you pay the return freight."

"How much will it cost?"

"Oh, five hundred by Wells Fargo."

"Tell him if he takes them the bidding starts at over a hundred thousand dollars."

Tanner chuckled. "I doubt he'd pay that for them but I will do as you say. He wants the emeralds and he says he will pay you fifty thousand if they are that good."

Chet shook his head. "If he wants them and the rubies, the bidding on both of them starts at two hundred fifty thousand."

Tanner kind of winced. "I'll wire him but I doubt he will pay that."

"Then he won't buy them. Have you sold the gold?"

"The gold bars gave you two hundred twenty thousand dollars. The loose gold is being smelted and may amount to more than that."

"My cowboys may quit me after I pay them their fifty percent."

Tanner looked in shock at him. "How many hands were with you?"

"Eight men will share in half of the total."

"You get your prices they could earn fifty to sixty thousand dollars apiece." Tanner shook his head.

"They could have gotten killed by some

bad men while up there, and possibly ended up being eaten by buzzards."

"I understand. It is a helluva lot of money. I understand, by gossip, three of those rustlers that your men brought in have bounties on their heads."

"Good. I'll split that with the men if it ever gets paid."

"That's Wells Fargo rewards. You will be paid that money."

"Anything else comes up, holler."

"Any more offers on the other things you found?"

"Some rich guy is coming from Mexico. He wants to buy that armor, the swords, and the books."

"What are they worth?"

"Lots. Your wife and babies doing good?"

"Oh. Wonderful." Tanner stood a little straighter and beamed at being asked. A man who waits till he's forty-some years old to get married to a much younger woman and has two kids in two years out of his bride should stand tall — but Chet still didn't trust her.

"I better go get mine. She may be tired of trying on outfits." He left the bank whistling and drove around to the dress store. Lisa waved to him and quickly came outside.

"Any details on the value?"

"Tanner says a half a million in gold when the free gold gets smelted."

"My heavens. What are the gems worth?"

"Maybe a quarter million or more."

"You need to take more vacations."

"Like that, I do."

They drove home, laughing all the way. She was a great companion and he enjoyed her company.

"Could I give my colts to your sons? I am not a horse breaker."

"They'd both probably love them."

"Good. I will do that." When he set her down coming off the buckboard, she kissed him. "Thanks."

Things held good the next few weeks, the precious stone buyer bid him three hundred fifty thousand for both lots. He told Tanner to take it. Smelting was not completed on the raw gold, so that waited on them.

Word was out a fortune was coming to some of his ranch hands and those on the list met in the big house living room.

"Don't spend a dime of your money until you know what you want to do besides take siestas," Chet told them.

"You will have more friends and relatives who want to borrow money and, in truth, they will never pay you back. Personally, I don't care, but that sum of money is not endless. You can blow it all on wild women and alcohol in a year or you can park it in a bank and only use it when out of work or to buy a place of your own.

"Remember, folks can skin you out of your money and you'd not get any land. Hire a lawyer, a banker to do the job for you."

The men shook his hand and left, except for Jesus and Cole.

"Think they will listen to me?" he asked them straight out.

"Not good enough. They have no education and no idea what it is like to have that much money," Cole said.

Jesus agreed. "When I was a boy in Mexico, I saw a man who prospected in the mountains. If he found some gold he hurried to town and spent it immediately on *putas,* wine, and fancy clothes. Soon he was broke, hungover, and those whores wanted no part of him. I asked him why he never learned his lesson and kept some back. He said, 'Jesus, you do not understand. The only reason I go prospecting is so I can afford to live with them for a short while like a wild man. I love to do that, and for them to snub their noses at me sends me back to find more.' "

The three men laughed loud enough that

Lisa came into the living room and asked what was so funny.

"I will tell you later. I warned the men how they must manage the money they will receive."

"I can tell you right now they will all — maybe a few won't — but most will blow it, and fast."

"That rich rancher's son who hauled me to Colorado. His father sent him five hundred dollars so he would have money to escape on. He blew that in four hours gambling in a saloon. Most men are stupid — you three are excused — but my brother sold a racehorse when I was twelve. He was older than me by several years. He got a thousand dollars for him and came home that night dead broke after promising to pay our grocery bill. That is what most men do with money — blow it away as quick as they can."

"I hope not." Chet shook his head.

"They can't help themselves. It must be in their bloodstream. The girls are counting supper plates. Are either of you staying for supper?"

Cole shook his head. "I can't. I promised my wife I'd be back by then."

Jesus said, "I'm like Cole. I better eat there. Tell them thanks for us."

"They're very good girls. Work hard and always feed anyone loose around the place who needs food."

Chet walked them to the back door. "Take tomorrow off. We're caught up. That prosecuting attorney never asked for any evidence on the horse stealing?"

"We brought in six of them. Four were wanted elsewhere," Cole said. "He must be shipping them to Texas and Colorado, where the crime is murder. Then he saves the court costs on four. Bet he's scratching to find a place to ship the last two out of this county and slam them in someone else's jail so he'll save himself the work and court costs."

Chet shook his head and put his hands on his hips. "If they get free from those charges they can go free and steal more horses. Does anyone on the *Miner* know about his scheme?"

"Damned if I know," Cole said. "Let's go talk to Bo tomorrow and let him put the bug in some folks' ears."

"Right. I'll have the horses hitched for when you get here tomorrow. Jesus, we can handle it if you have work you need done."

He shook his head. "We rode our asses off to capture them, and letting them loose will not curb the rustling. Pick me up at my house."

"Amen. See you two then." He showed them to the back door and, when they were mounted, waved good-bye.

Lisa said, "I heard most of that and could not believe my ears."

"Lots of folks need to learn that."

In the morning, they took the buckboard to town and parked in front of Bo's office. He met them at the door, smiling big. "What brings the three soldiers to my door?"

"Find a chair. We have a problem you need to solve."

"What is that? Take a seat."

"Those horse thieves we arrested."

"Yes, what about them?"

"The county prosecutor isn't going to try them if he can help it. Instead he is having the other law agencies that want them take them off his hands. But when they get wherever they came from and are found not guilty they get off scot-free."

"He's lazy. But I can get that changed."

"Good. That was all we needed."

"Man, you three are easy to please. Now, tell me who all gets money out of the North Rim business?"

"I get half."

"Good. Who gets the rest?"

"Cole and Jesus plus six other guys who went up there with us."

"Sit back down. Do I have some land deals for you two? I already have his business."

Chet winked at them.

Bo said, "Talk is they will get fifty thousand each?"

"More than that."

"More than that? How much are rusty old suits of armor worth, anyway?"

"There was a water pail full of uncut rubies. Another half pail of raw emeralds, plus forty bars of gold, and that much more gold dust."

Bo shook his head as if impressed by the amount. "Damn, you guys really did find the Spanish gold."

"Yes, they did."

"What will those others do with their share?"

"Lisa says most will go get drunk and spend their money on some loose-morals women."

Bo laughed. "Man, oh man, I had less money than that and stayed drunk all the time. Whew, am I glad that is over for me."

"It better be. But I will have no control after I pay them."

"Any of them want ranches?"

"You can come out and talk to them."

"I could find them some great small ranches."

"When do you want to come out?" Chet asked him.

"I'll send word. I am going to the courthouse and straighten out this rustler deal for you. I'll have an answer by morning. Those judges we have are all federal and they won't let him do that."

"We're going to have lunch at the Palace Bar. I'm buying. You want to join us?"

"No, I told my wife, I'd pick up some things for her at noontime."

"Tell her we said howdy."

They drove downtown after leaving Bo's office.

"Bo has bought you lots of land, hasn't he?" Cole asked.

"It all turned out pretty good. The folks on them had all gotten deeds but there was no way to make a living out there. He bought them cheap enough. They are going to all be fenced this winter and we will cut more hay off them next year. Toby and his wife and his Mexican help can put up more hay than anyone I know. But he's up to nearly a dozen mowing machines, rakes, beaver boards, and twice that many teams of horses. They break mustangs in the winter and use them for teams. He has hay stacked all over that country on the rim and he sells lots of it off the homesteads that Bo bought cheap."

"We brought that wife of his, Talley, back, too," Cole said, shaking his head. "And your wife Elizabeth said she'd grow up. I doubted it. I know she works harder than he does now. They are a pair I couldn't believe ever would make it running a ranch."

"They damn sure do it. I appreciate all my help, guys. But those two are damn sure neat at getting after it."

"If Bo gets this straightened, what do we need to do up here?" Cole asked.

"I should go see Toby and Talley. Then go over east and see the Wagon Wheel."

"I can go with you starting next week."

"Jesus?"

"I'll be ready then, too."

"I don't know Lisa's plans but she may ride along."

Cole agreed, so did Jesus, and the matter was settled over lunch in the Palace Bar.

On Thursday Bo came out to the ranch and he met with Cole and Valerie, Jesus and Anita, plus Hampt and May in Lisa's living room

"You folks getting this money, I want to

tell you I have several ranches for sale if you are interested."

"Bo, May and I have a new family. These two babies will need a place somewhere. We helped her sons get into what they wanted to do. And we will do the same for them."

"Sure, I understand."

"I don't need another ranch right now. One is enough," Jesus said. His wife agreed with a nod.

Cole said, "I am plenty pleased to be back in the foreman business here. Val and I will bank our money, too."

"Thanks. All of you know who I am and what I do. Anytime I can help, call on me."

"We can go to the Verde Ranch tomorrow, if you can come, Bo," Chet said.

"Thanks. I'll be here in the morning. Lisa, you may be wrong about half of them," Bo teased her.

"You haven't heard from them all." She laughed and spoke to Chet's son Rocky. "Did your dad tell you I wanted to give you two colts that we brought down from the North Rim?"

"Yes, he did. Thank you. I hope they make good horses."

"They will. They're real mustangs."

Rocky smiled at his stepmother. "Hear that?"

Valerie nodded and then shook her head at him. "I still say they will kick you."

Both women laughed.

# CHAPTER 9

Bo gave him the report the next morning when he arrived at the ranch.

Dear Chet,
   Two of the rustlers have already been removed from Prescott by officials from other law agencies. But officials will prosecute the remaining four. You were right. They wanted to save court costs and had not considered another court might find them not guilty and they would get off scot-free.

Chet went on to the house while Bo stopped to talk to Chet's foreman Vance.
   "What does it say?" Lisa asked, pouring him coffee while he read the note.
   "The four left will stand trial. Bo said the prosecutor admitted the original plan was to save the county court expenses."
   Lisa shook her head. "You have to watch

everything, don't you?"

"Yes. I don't think the prosecutor wanted them loose. He figured how they'd save the cost of more trials and the rustlers would still be behind bars elsewhere."

"What are you going to do next?"

"Take Bo to the Verde Ranch today. He wants to talk to those others who are receiving money."

"He wanted you to know the trials were being take care of?"

"Bo and I are close. He's considerate."

"You hired some tough guys to guard him night and day to make him quit drinking, they told me."

"I had to. He'd sell something and go get drunk for a week. You couldn't count on him but he was good at selling and buying land. He was married but the gal died. That's why he drank."

"I knew Shelly was his second wife."

"She was a widow with money who moved here after she lost her husband. By then he was respectable enough to marry."

"And she never was pregnant with husband number one, was she?"

"No, but she's had two since marrying Bo."

"Maybe that will happen to me."

"Quit worrying. We do all we can."

She put down some dishes and hugged him. "I know, but that doesn't make it easier."

"Hey, get dressed and come along with me. You love to visit with Millie."

"Thanks, I will do that. Who else is going?"

"Cole and Jesus."

"I'll be ready." She rushed off to change.

One of her house girls brought the coffeepot over. Her name was Oleta. "Señor, you want more coffee?"

"No. Thanks anyway."

"May I ask a question, señor?"

"Certainly. What is it?"

"Is there an hombre named Salty down there where you go today?"

"Yes."

"Would you see if his foot is broken?"

"Sure. But I am sure he is sound or I would have heard about it."

She looked around like she wanted no one to hear. "He promised he'd come back and see me."

Chet nodded. "You want me to remind him?"

"Oh no. If he don't want to, I sure don't want to see him, either."

"Can I say, 'Oleta sends her blessings'?"

"Only if he still wears my cross. It has

some black stones and a cross on it. If he wears it, he still remembers me."

"I will check."

She crossed herself. *"Gracias, patrón."*

"No. I am Chet, not *patrón.*"

"Excuse me. You know that Julie and I are very proud to work here. Your wife is so generous to both of us — more like a mother than a boss. We grew up here on this ranch and this has been a fine place to live, but when she became head of the house she brought us both inside because we helped her with schooling the children. Now we run it for her and we appreciate you and her confidence in us."

Julie joined her, nodding her head. "Chet, we will get your name right. We really appreciate all you do for the people of this ranch."

"It is a wonderful ranch because of the people who work here and how they all pitch in."

Bo soon joined them for breakfast.

Lisa rode horseback with the four men to Tom's house at the base of the mountain. They teased her about things and she laughed most of the way down the steep grade to the base.

Chet told them about his sister, who ran

the household back then at the start, and how May's two boys growing up caught fish out of the Verde River for Sis to cook, and when they took her the huge carp she threw it out. "Why, those two about disowned her over doing that."

"I heard you fed the Indians down here, too?" Lisa asked.

"They had a sorry Indian agent when we first came to the area. I fed the Indians and he got mad and threatened me. I went and saw General Crook at the fort up here and he got that straight. Why, those people and their children had no food. Some big officials came down from Washington, DC, after General Crook spoke to them, and when they saw the mess, they removed that agent."

"Yesterday I was glad to see Hampt's arm was nearly healed," Jesus said.

"Yes. He's fine. Hated he didn't get in with the chase we had getting those rustlers rounded up."

Cole agreed. "I'd pick him anytime to be on my team. That big guy is tough when you make him mad."

"Bo, you've missed out on lots of great adventures the three of us have had together," Chet said.

Like he'd never catch up with them, Bo

shook his head. "Now, I would not have gone off on that rope to get inside that cave, dangling thousands of feet over rock piles below, but I'd damn sure liked to have been on the receiving end of the final count. Maybe had me some of that armor."

"It was one helluva find."

"I'd say so. I think we told you we never found anything else up there."

"No sign of the mine that gave them the rubies?" Bo looked at the men for an answer.

They all shook their heads.

Cole spoke up. "We never saw even a speck of those rubies anywhere we went. Not any color in the creeks. That place holds its secrets tight."

"How did those Spaniards find them?"

"Hell, Bo, you couldn't see all the country that is inside the boundaries of that strip in over a lifetime. There were no maps to show where they got it in those books, either."

"Isolated and dry," Cole added.

Salty greeted them when they arrived down there. Chet recalled the girl's words: "If he still wears my cross." The stones were black, and he could see that Salty wore something around his neck, inside of his shirt. "Oh yes, Oleta said to say hi to you."

Salty grinned big. "Tell her I am coming

in a few days. Tom has had lots of work for me down here."

"Maybe Lisa should send her down here?"

"No, then I would get nothing done."

The crew laughed.

The meeting with Bo and the five recipients was held in Tom's living room. Bo introduced himself and explained they were going to soon have lots of money, and the danger of losing it loomed over them.

"Don't make loans to friends. You will never get it back. We know now it will be over fifty thousand for each of your shares.

"Wow."

"Land swindlers are all over. Only buy land with a clear title. Do it with an honest broker or a banker you trust handling the paperwork. Don't drink it up. Don't spend it on wild women. I'd like to talk to any of you interested about buying a place of your own."

"I don't want a ranch of my own yet," the cook Tad Newman said. "If I can stay here and work the roundup cooking I will be fine. Tom said Mr. Tanner at the bank would treat me fair and maybe someday I will go back to Sonora and ranch there."

"Good thinking," Chet said. "You can have that place as long as you like."

Eddie Maine, the cook's helper, raised his

hand next. "My grandmother lives near Nogales. She needs a windmill to pump a storage tank full so she does not have to pull up buckets. Nana raised me, so could one of you help me get that done?"

Chet told him yes. "Eddie, we can find some honest folks to do that down there and have her running water in her house, even."

Eddie smiled. "I'd sure appreciate that."

"Billy Bob, what about you?" Chet asked.

"I been thinking my mom and dad ain't got a tombstone back in Decatur, Texas. Would you all help me get one up?"

Tom spoke up. "Yes, we can help you and get that done. Nice thought on your part. Salty, what have you thought about?"

"You know. I bet Chet knows, too. I'd like permission to build a house on either place if some gal says yes, for us to live in it together. You can have it when I leave. I hope that isn't soon."

Chet smiled. "I bet she'd want to live up at Preskitt Valley."

"Probably. Don't tell her — I want to shock her so she can't say no. But would that work?"

"Salty, Tom and I would approve it at either ranch."

Salty smiled big. "On top?"

"Either place. Let us know."

"I'll sure do that."

They rode back from the Verde to the Valley ranch. Bo thanked them and rode on to town.

In the kitchen, Lisa spoke to Oleta. "He's wearing it and said when he got caught up on his work to tell you he would come to see you."

The girl blushed. "We should have taught him how to write, like we did the children."

"He can't write?" Lisa asked her.

"I don't think so."

They both looked at Chet.

"Something else you must teach him, then."

Oleta said, "I can do that."

"Good. He is in your hands. He can break horses up here if you like."

"If you promise not to tell him I told you about his not writing."

"I won't say a word."

"I am so grateful."

Soon after that, Salty moved to the upper ranch with the ranch's unbroken two-year-old colts. The foreman, Vance, gave him two large teenage boys who were tickled to death, to help him. They came off weeding and watering the large patch of frijoles they raised that fed every ranch member. Chet figured they may have been even happier than Oleta was over the move.

He knew that those boys would work harder at their new jobs.

Late in the week he and Lisa went into Preskitt to check on things — get the mail — and for Lisa to get some dress material for what she called *pending.* The weather was still nice but the days had gotten shorter and fall was coming. The couple Betty and Leroy Sipes up at Oak Creek Canyon with the orchard, berries, and summer garden had brought by several bushels of apples for the last time that year and said they had them all picked.

Chet went by the mercantile and talked to his friend Ben Ivor.

Ben rose from behind the desk. They shook hands and then he shook his head before he said, "I have three of your mowers for next year in Fort Worth. Three are in El Paso, and six they shipped to Iowa."

"Well, we have all winter to round them up." Chet took a chair while he was laughing.

Ben shook his head. "They must not have maps. Where do they think Preskitt is next to?"

"I have no idea. But I may need to up the number by another half dozen."

"How much hay do you have to cut?"

"When Bo bought all these homesteads, they were cleared of sagebrush and grew tall grasses when people quit farming them. My men fenced them to keep the range cows out and now I have hay farms all over the north county."

"How many have you got?"

"Those farms? I think maybe thirty of them."

"A hundred sixty times thirty is forty-eight hundred acres."

Chet agreed. "We have lots of hay to mow. Shane and his bunch cut lots of hay over at Hackberry. The Verde Ranch must have a few hundred acres. Toby had all those old homesteads and his own fenced land became hay fields. Spencer has maybe three sections. Sarge gets his hay now from Toby. They have to haul hay up to the sawmill for the timber-hauling horses and mules. And Hampt makes lots of good hay — most of his is in alfalfa."

"Makes me the biggest mower salesman in the West."

After a good cordial laugh they shook hands and Ben said he'd check on their delivery being there before spring.

"I'll tell Kathrin I said hi to you from her. She never got over you bringing her down here from Utah. She claims you saved her life. And she sure made a great wife for me."

"It all ended good."

Late in the afternoon, he picked up Lisa and her purchases, and with those loaded in the buckboard, he set the team in a trot for home. It had clouded up some during the afternoon. As they were coming through some woods three armed riders busted out of the thin pine cover.

Shocked by the pop of a pistol, Chet handed Lisa the reins and reached for the Winchester rifle in the scabbard on the buckboard's dashboard. "They're shooting at us. Get us the hell out of here."

He levered in a cartridge and knew with the rough ride of the buckboard he'd be lucky to hit any of the three. He struggled to hook his right arm over the seat back, to steady the long gun. The rough ride made his taking aim through the sights a real chore. But he shot anyway. If nothing else, maybe he'd stop them if he hit one.

"What do they want?" she shouted at him, and whipped the horses with the lines to make them go faster.

"I have no idea. Maybe they want us dead." He squeezed off another shot. They were worthless attempts. He made two quick shots without much sign of success.

"Make them go faster, Lisa. Head for the Black Canyon Stage office, the next dip in the road. They may help defend us."

"I've got it."

Over the swaying buckboard bench seat, he fired the rifle again and again back at their attackers, but it was only in defense. Hitting anyone or anything would have been by sheer luck.

She shouted at him, "The stage people are coming out, Chet, and they're armed."

"Keep going. Get to the stage building. Those outlaws have reined up but we need more cover and distance from them."

"Mr. Byrnes, what did they want with you two?" wide-eyed Ed Samson, the stage line manager, asked after they finally pulled up. He helped Lisa down from her seat.

Still upset by the attack, Chet couldn't see any sign of them. "Damned if I know."

"Where are your guards at?"

He shook his head and jumped down to hug his upset wife. "We didn't need them until a while back."

"Did anyone recognize who they were?" Lisa asked.

No one had recognized any of their pursuers.

"My men are going to saddle horses and see you two get home," Samson said. "You are too good a customer of our stage line to let you go home unprotected."

"Only up to Jesus Martinez's ranch. He will get us home. Thanks."

"You ever see them bandits before?"

"No, and I didn't see them well enough to recognize them, bouncing around and shooting at them the way I was." He kissed his wife's forehead. "Thank God you're all right."

"I'm fine. I'm mad they chased us here, but grateful these men were here. Thanks."

Samson shook his head. "They must have been desperate for money. They damn sure picked on the wrong guy, getting after you."

Chet agreed. "I'll find out who they were one day and make them wish they never tried that trick on us."

"Here come my men on horseback. Joey, he just needs guards to Jesus's place."

"Whatever. Mr. Byrnes, you didn't know them?"

"No. They were wearing masks and they were too far back, when she went to driving those horses, to see them clear enough, except they sure did want us."

"Thanks," Lisa said after Chet put her back on the seat and climbed in himself. "You ever need a favor, come get me," Chet added to Samson.

"You all be more careful," Samson said. "We need your business."

Chet laughed and agreed, clucked to his team, and they were off.

When they got to Jesus's place, he came out on the porch to greet them.

Chet thanked the stage company workers, offered them money that they declined, and they headed back. Jesus's wife, Anita, holding the baby in her arms, came out to talk to Lisa.

"Why were those men riding with you?" Jesus asked.

"Some outlaws got after us after we left town and chased us to the stagecoach office."

"Huh?"

"I am not kidding. Three masked men busted out of the woods, shooting at us. She drove and I emptied the Winchester at them. Samson and those two men rushed out and ran them off."

"You shoot any of them?"

"Going down that rough road at least forty miles an hour. Not likely."

"No idea who they were?"

"They were masked and too far back."

"I'll get my gun and ride home with you. What did you promise us?"

"I'd never go alone again."

"Good. Promise us again."

"I do."

"Jesus, we just ran into town and were on our way home," Lisa said in Chet's defense.

"Lisa, you two need protection. There are too many outlaws still running all over."

"Yes, sir."

When they arrived back at the house, Jesus with them, they drew a crowd in the ranch yard. Someone rang the big school bell before Chet could stop them, and in no time, they had everyone there, including Cole and Salty.

Jesus took charge, standing in the buckboard bed. "This afternoon three gunmen shot at and chased the boss man and Lisa into the Black Canyon Stage yard. He didn't recognize any of them but in the morning, some of us are going that direction and find out who they were.

"Now, everyone who works here knows how important for our jobs the lives of these two are to all of us. So, if we don't find them tomorrow, you all be listening for talk. Someone will brag they did that when whiskey loosens their tongues, and I want their names or descriptions. I don't want any of you to try and take them. We are the pistoleros on this ranch, but we sure may need your help to find them. Thanks that we are all safe tonight."

He began to clap and so did the family.

Cole was standing next to Chet by then. "Any idea who they were?"

Chet shook his head. "Lisa was driving the buckboard so hard I never got a good shot off at them."

Cole laughed and hugged her. "Good for you, girl. No idea why they wanted you two?"

"No. I can tell you right now I have never, even under Indian raids, been as shocked as when those three guys wearing masks came busting out of the pines firing their pistols at us."

"They are fine," Cole said to his wife as she and Rocky joined them.

"Good. We heard Jesus's speech. He's becoming a leader, isn't he?"

"No doubt," Chet said. "Rocky, how are you?"

"A little sore."

"What happened?"

"That North Rim colt kicked me."

Lisa hugged him. "I am sorry."

"No, ma'am. He's my horse now and I'll break him of doing that."

Lisa was amused. "Yes, Chet Byrnes Number Two. I bet you will break him."

"Sounds just like him already, don't he?"

Cole teased.

Chet shared a private nod with his son. "You'll show her and the horse."

"Naw, he's just got things to learn. Besides, she might get more horses and give them to me. I'm not saying anything about her."

They all laughed and headed for the back porch stairs in the bleeding sunset.

Chet shook Jesus's hand and thanked him for the job he did. A boy brought up a saddled horse for him to ride home. Things were settling down in the evening when Chet climbed the steps and looked across the yard as the ranch people headed home.

Oh, they'd find those cap busters. Might take some time but they'd wish they never tried that robbery or whatever it was those devils wanted.

# CHAPTER 10

The women were busy in the kitchen, examining the material Lisa bought for Oleta's wedding dress. While in the living room Chet, Cole, Salty, Vic, and Vance were laying down plans to try to find the masked thugs.

"Daylight, two of us will do some tracking back there," Salty said. "Vic and I bet we can find their tracks."

"Lots of luck. Be careful. I lost Lisa's husband, Miguel, in a deal like this. They aren't worth anyone getting killed over."

"We will, boss man. I can't figure why they'd make a breakout like that at you."

"When the masked outfit started shooting, I handed her the reins and jerked out the Winchester. I was rocking around on that seat and finally figured I'd shoot some and maybe scare them off. We topped the ridge and she had that team running dead out. They weren't quitting until we came in sight of the Black Canyon Stage office and by then they probably had emptied their six-guns. It wasn't the bullets from my rifle slowed them up, but the Black Canyon Stage boys were shooting at them, too."

"You notice the color of their horses?" Salty asked.

"Two were bays but one of them had a gray or light roan horse. May have been dirty white."

"That's good. He would be easy to find even at a distance. We might catch a sight of him we'd miss ordinarily." Salty was nodding his head, going over the discovery.

The girls served them some supper. The visitors left for the evening and Oleta said, "I am glad you moved him up here. The dress material your wife bought today is very nice. Maybe more than all I deserve, but no one ever before did so many things simply for me."

"When I saw him wearing those black rocks, I figured he was still serious about you."

She bobbed her head and laughed. "I told him I said if he was wearing it for you to tell him. He kind of got all over me. Like, why wouldn't he wear it?"

"He's serious or he'd never have worn it."

"Oh yes. *Gracias,* my — amigo, huh?"

124

"Yes, no *patrón*. You two are both hard workers and you will do well together."

She lowered her voice. "I can't believe he is that rich?"

"He is."

She left the kitchen, cranking her head around like she'd gone off the deep end.

Later in their bedroom he told Lisa about Oleta's conversation with him.

Amused about it, she agreed, and told him they'd make a good couple, and then she asked where she and Chet would go next.

"I guess we better go see the kids up on Crook's Road. Toby and Talley work so damn hard I don't want them to think we don't appreciate or see it."

"He's grown up a lot, too."

Chet agreed. She rolled over and kissed him. "We get into another fix like that, don't worry about me. I can drive horses, can't I?"

He shifted a little to kiss her back. "You damn sure can."

She gave a great sigh. "Aside from those three trying to bust it up, I want you to know I feel as fortunate having you as Oleta does having Salty."

"Good. I don't ever want that to end."

"Good. I have a black rock necklace —"

He tickled her until she said, "You don't

125

have to wear it."

Chet and Lisa's plan was set for the next morning when Salty and Vic would ride out to investigate the road bandits' deal. Cole and Jesus would ride with Chet and Lisa the next day to the Rustler's Ranch. Jesus was to set up the pack train so they could go on from there to see about the new easternmost Wagon Wheel Ranch, run by Spencer Horne and his wife, Lucinda, along with Fred and his wife, Josey.

It was a nice day when they crossed the Verde River and struck easy on the road that General Crook built to make a way for troops to get from Preskitt over to Fort Apache, far around in the White Mountains of eastern Arizona. The mountain road clung to the Mogollon Rim's towering heights, which made this route a picturesque one, but it was not a graded, smooth highway, having some real steep stretches. Easier used by horseback rather than in a wagon but still, not a simple path.

They reached the Rustler's Ranch, where horse thieves had fought Chet and his posse to their own deaths rather than serve long terms in prison. Bo had secured the deed and Chet had bought the ranch at the same time he was busy building a stage line and then a telegraph line that stretched across four hundred miles from east to west on the Marcy Road.

The ranch had vast meadows. The meadows were all brush, and any ranch this far north needed a hay supply. This brush couldn't be simply mowed. It had to be chopped away, and no cowboy likes to get off his horse to swing an ax or machete at brush.

So, securing a foreman to run it, Chet had less options than he'd had for any other place he'd ever purchased. Toby had helped him, and Chet knew he had a hard work personality. He was still a young man with no past experience as a supervisor of men. But his tenacity to get a job done made Chet try him.

His wife, Talley, was one of those young women who had run off with a band of outlaws who raided the stage stopovers. She'd quickly discovered a woman like her was only being used by those men and that none of them would ever marry her. Chet had found her the laziest one of the women there. She had a snobby way about her, and she wasn't half as pretty as she thought she was. Then she woke one morning and must have discovered she had no boyfriend and she'd faced being a common housemaid for the rest of her life. Chet saw she'd set to convincing Toby he needed her, since he looked like he had the best chance at becoming a ranch foreman.

Chet knew how everyone at the Preskitt Valley headquarters, including himself, thought that Talley would never stay out there on the Rustler's Ranch past six weeks with a husband she'd earlier snubbed. But like the woman who'd jumped into the sailor's arms when the captain rushed by her to save a prettier woman, Talley jumped into Toby's hug. Chet and Lisa laughed over that story.

With a brush-cutting team of eight teen-age Mexican boys and her husband to feed, she proved them all wrong about how the isolation of this far-back place would bring her in a hurry to separate from her husband. Instead she became his closest sidekick and even became his pusher at times to get things going despite Apache war party's raids and the rigors and the size of the job.

Soon Toby talked Chet into doubling the number of brush cutters to do the job, and for her to feed. They cleared all the once-open meadows on that place and fenced the ranch in record time. After Talley, Chet surmised, discovered how he owned all those homesteads Bo had bought, she came down to the ranch and asked for barbwire and permission to fence those plots and use them for hay making.

Chet couldn't tell them no. Not that determined married couple who swam the flooding Verde River to come to a main ranch party to tell everyone they had most of them fenced and would hay them that year, too.

The plan to stock that ranch with beef cows was moved up to three hundred head, and in the next two years with the hay supply to feed them, he'd be at six hundred mother cows or more. Even while she was pregnant Talley worked hard every day.

Lisa had commented that some women had children and gave up all the side work. Not Talley — she grew more involved.

Talley was excited to see them and sent word to Toby, who was working on a windmill setup to come in. The boss was there.

Talley gave the baby to Lisa to hold and told one of the younger hands to show the boss all the new corrals they'd built since the last time he was there while she'd make supper. Jesus and Cole took off to look at the meadows and water development.

Chet had to admit the corral additions were really inventive. They also were as strong as an army fort stockade.

"I guess you helped build them?" he asked his teenage guide.

"No, señor. I help the señora do the cooking. I work in her garden. I rock the baby when she is busy. She promised me when Ruben goes to work on the hay crew I can milk the cow."

"Well, that will be lots of work."

"Not so much. Someday I will be a cowboy, huh?"

"I hope you make it."

"Oh, I will."

Toby arrived on a sweaty horse and slid to a stop. "Oh, Chet, I didn't know you were coming. I was working on a windmill when I got word."

"You get it fixed?"

"Oh yeah. Jud will finish it and there is still water in the tanks for the cows that come by."

"How many mills have you got?"

"Twelve, counting the new one I got last week, but I need that many more. I am putting them in every well I have on the homesteads, then I pipe it outside to a tank to water the cows outside of the boundary fence, so I have my hay and those cows outside have water."

"Robert told me last trip your boys were getting him enough hay up there."

"That is a long haul for me. Is there any way Victor could supply part of that?"

"How far is it?"

"It takes my men six days to go up there, unload, and come back."

Chet considered the distance. Victor's men could make a round trip in three days yet they were letting Toby handle it. "I will see what I can do. You providing Spencer?"

"Oh yes. He had no hay land fenced yet. In some cases, those far east homesteads are only a three days' round trip hay haul over to Spencer. I have some homesteads right beside Sarge and use them. He said he wouldn't miss that hay equipment he gave me. But I sure needed it."

"I bet you did."

"Met Spencer over at his fenced place south of the road two weeks ago. That was the only fenced ground he has. We can put hay up there next year if he can get the brush and cactus cut off that land. Says there are some Navajo boys would do it."

"This is where that past owner tried to grow corn that time?"

"Yes. The perimeter fence is pretty good."

"I appreciate all you do but can your men really get over there, mow it, and all?"

"Yes, we can handle it. I don't believe his Navajos will get much hay land cleaned.

You'd just have to buy the hay equipment for him and hire him more help. My boys can do it easier."

They rode up to where the water came out of a pipe from a windmill on a rise a good distance away from the tanks. Well designed, it flowed by gravity into a series of homemade rock-and-mortar tanks to hold it. Chet nodded in approval.

"Where was the closest water before you built this?"

"Over a mile and a half south of here. The cows never came up here to graze before we fixed this. I was riding with the ranch foreman in west Texas on the HFT Ranch. I didn't know much back then so I said, 'Lots of good grass here.' He said, 'Yeah, there ain't no water in three miles is why.' "

Chet laughed. "That's how you learned about water and cows?"

Toby rubbed his three-day-old whiskered cheek with his palm. "Embarrassed me. But I damn sure never forgot it."

"I noticed those New Mexico cows we brought in last year are doing good on your water."

"I heard that lie, too, about damned old Arizona grass ain't worth nothing to a cow out here."

"Unless she's got water, I agree."

"We haven't upset you in any way, have we?" Toby asked. "I know the place could look sharper."

"How? You and Talley are working your backsides off."

"Yeah, you aren't mad at us about anything we didn't get done?"

"Let me put it straight — hell, no."

Toby smiled. "Good. Not seeing anyone, you wonder if you pissed in their soup bowl is why they ain't coming by."

Chet laughed. "Guess all those folks who said Talley won't stay out here and you won't make it have learned better."

"I can see why. She come from some folks I'd say had more than most. And she resented that folks were getting along better than she was — but, Chet, I told her nicelike as I could, she and me had to really prove who we were and what we could really get done.

"We were about to be married. I could tell she didn't hold no big ambition for me. I said we'd have to prove to folks who think we won't make it they're wrong. They were all wrong, and they didn't know what we could do as a team. Now, she had more education than me. I told her if I wasn't running a great ranch in five years I'd divorce her and let her find a better provider. But she had to lend me her education."

"That's what changed her?"

"Part. We had a real big honeymoon over at Oak Creek. I think it changed things, too, because she began to want to sit close to me, be a part of me, and she began to say, 'How did you see that?' And we began challenging each other after that."

Chet, riding beside him, was nodding his head. "I knew something had swept you two away."

"Whew." Riding along, he stripped off his dusty, stained hat and waved it. "It's worked, then, hasn't it?"

"Yes, you have shown them. Don't stop."

"I won't. I promise. Nor will she."

That evening, sleeping in their tent, he and Lisa talked.

"Their honeymoon in Oak Creek was heavenly," Lisa said. "And I bet she realized that a good man would treat you good as compared to probably what she'd had before. But she read his cards and must have decided to help him reach their goals."

"It has worked."

"Oh yes. You know, she worked for me at the house. She is not now the same one who did that. Somehow I'd like to dress her up and make her be prouder of herself."

"Maybe we can dress both of them up?"

"Let's do it."

They shook hands and sealed it with a kiss.

# CHAPTER 11

Each day, Chet and Toby rode out and looked at, lots of his different homestead farms and windmill setups. Two rock-and-mortar dams on small creeks, both with a spillway, showed his men's masonry talents. Chet marveled at his accomplishments and at the neat haystacks on those separate places. There was plenty of feed stacked high on those places, which were well fenced so even if range animals penetrated the very well-constructed boundary fences they could not get to the hay.

"No rustlers up here?" Chet asked.

"We have not seen any cases of it. Spring roundup we worked two hundred thirty-eight calves. I guess I lost seven calves at birth or that many had aborted for some reason."

"That's a good calving percentage."

"We've had a good year and I expect close to that many to be weaned. I am going to wean them on a few of the places close to the house."

"Your bulls I've been seeing look good. Next fall we can sell a hundred head of big steers and make eight thousand dollars."

Toby made a sour face. "Wow, we will be a long time at that rate to being profitable."

"We get to five hundred mother cows and the calves get to be two years old, we can sell four hundred head of heifers and steers, retain a hundred head of heifers for replacement, cull fifty-sixty cows each year. That would make us at eighty bucks a head or gross of sixty-some thousand."

"I'll go easier on you about expenses until then."

"No. Your hay sales this winter will pay your labor bill. I am replacing some worn-out mowers this coming year but all in all we are going to be in good shape."

"I need this experience of running a ranch, but Jesus told me those guys went to the North Rim with you made seventy thousand on that Spanish gold?"

"It was a once-in-a-lifetime find. Nice if you drew some of it."

Toby shook his head. "I just couldn't imagine that much money."

"I hope they know that and manage it well."

"Then, in four years you will begin to realize a profit on this place?"

"Oh, we will have the startup covered and be ready to make some money."

"That's great. I'd like to have some of those artesian wells drilled that push water out enough to irrigate with."

"If we can find some land that's worth the money to buy and level in an area where there are other wells, we can try to drill some."

"I will be looking for it."

"Good. We're going on to Spencer's next. Send my accountant a list on this hay you haul to everyone. I will be sure you get credit for it. I'll tell Spencer you will cut his hay next year if he can get it cleared, and that way he doesn't need a hay crew."

"Thanks. Talley can send you all those hay receipts we delivered and then do it monthly. We have hauled a lot to Robert, Sarge, and Spencer, and I have lots spoken for from other ranchers."

"Good. I want you to take a week or so off this winter. Take her to Tucson, see some shows, wine and dine her. You can hire a babysitter to take along and take a stage down there."

"I don't know —"

"Lisa and I are sponsoring it. Call it a

bonus for doing such a swell job."

"Well. Thanks. Best part of this job is knowing you've done something."

"You two most certainly have."

At supper that evening, Toby told his wife about their vacation coming, and she held her hands over her mouth and cried.

Lisa went on, "And you will need a wardrobe, so plan on coming to my house a month before and find the clothes you two will need to wear."

Chet and his bunch packed up and headed for the Wagon Wheel Ranch the next morning. Leaving, riding north for the Marcy Road, they came out on top in the wide-open grass country and hit the main road eastward. The second day they crossed the staked-out survey for the railroad tracks north of the main road and then rode on onto the neat ranch setup.

"This place is beautiful," Lisa said, looking over the expanse of the headquarters. "It was to be a hunting lodge?"

"Some rich guy out of Saint Louis had it built as hunting lodge/ranch. He got mad, never slept here, and dumped it. Spencer found it and we bought it for ten cents on the dollar or less. The main ranch land lies south of here, but that place had no headquarters on it."

He noted her biting her lip and he rode in close to her. "Yes, it was here where Miguel died. I am so sorry I forgot. Will you be all right?"

"Yes." She swallowed. "I will be fine. I bet he liked it, too."

"We all did."

Spencer's wife, Lucinda, came out on the porch, her two children hugging her skirt.

"Good day. I think you have met my wife, Lisa? That is Jesus, and you know Cole."

"Welcome to the Wagon Wheel Ranch. My husband and Fred are off in a cow camp. I will send a boy for him to come home, now that you are here."

"We just dropped by to see how you two were getting along. Not to be any bother or interrupt any business."

"You are no trouble. Spencer, Fred, and his men are trying to stop some rustling activities. They've spent lots of time this summer trying to close the loop on them. All they were able to prove was a butcher shop bought three head with our brand on them. They paid for the cattle but Spencer suspects they weren't the same rustlers that moved several bunches out of state."

"They take some to New Mexico?"

"He has some letters that he will show

you that say they did that. Come in, and my cooks will fix you supper. Those three fine boys will unload your packhorses and put up your mounts. Hitch them. All of you, wash up and come into my casa. I am so glad you all came."

Everyone thanked her.

The woman took Lisa's arm and led her inside. "I am so glad you came to our ranch. You know I was the wife of a vaquero who was killed at roundup down on the border of the Diablo Ranch. After that I still lived on that large ranch Diablo, with my small children. Bonnie and JD operate this ranch for the Byrnes family. When I met my husband, Spencer, he asked me to marry him. I had the little children. He didn't care so I married him. I know this ranch has some sad memories for you but its beauty has hugged me ever since Spencer brought me up here. Since this rustling started, Fred's wife, Josey, and I must keep our own company. Spencer and Fred stay gone all the time."

"How are you feeling, Josey?" Lisa asked the quiet pregnant girl.

"Big, and I still have two months to go."

Lisa shook her head and hugged her. "Girl, I'd love a lot to be where you are at today."

Josey blushed. "I am grateful to be here and married to Fred. But I do get lonely and feel sorry for myself with no one around, just Lucinda. How have you been doing?"

"I am doing fine. You two have such a lovely house here, but I understand how you feel. With so few close neighbors. I was lonely, too, when I first came to the Preskitt ranch and lived in a casa. But I was glad to be there. My husband now had brought me back there from Colorado after I agreed to work as a camp helper. At the ranch, I worked in the large house as a maid. When the woman Monica, who ran the house, died of a heart attack, Chet's wife asked me to try and do her job. Miguel took me horse riding — I thought he was a very smart man and we had a courtship, but I liked my job running the house. Elizabeth told me I could marry him and keep my job. He was killed up here and it broke my heart. Then Chet's wife, Elizabeth, died suddenly from cancer.

"Chet and I leaned on each other. We had no immediate family. So we married. And we have had such a great life. I knew we were coming here. I had some dread but my life goes on and needs to. Thanks for your comfort and concern. I will be fine."

"Lucinda and I try to cheer each other up. She has become a dear friend."

Lucinda crossed herself. "I agree with her. This ranch is far out. When my first husband was killed, if the Diablo Ranch had not been so kind to me, I would be living in the Tucson barrio as a woman of the night. They told me to stay there as long as I wanted and paid me my husband's wages. I thank all of you and God every night."

"And I'd be in the alleys of Preskitt trying to make a living, too," Josey said.

Lisa nodded. "Yes, we all owe them."

Their conversation ended, Chet seated her at the table and then took a place beside her. The food came piled on their plates and the fresh coffee aroma filled the air. The kitchen girls swirling around to feed them were all dressed very well and looked very professional under Lucinda's command.

Horses were coming in. Lucinda went to the front door. "My husband is here."

Chet rose and went to meet him.

"Boy, boss man, good to see you. I was over at the cow camp trying to put an end to the rustlers."

"Lucinda said they were pestering you."

"Go back to eating. I can pull up a chair."

"Fine. You know my men Cole and Jesus."

Spencer nodded. "You fellows come

straight up here?"

"No. We stopped down at the Rustler's Ranch and spent a few days with Toby and Talley. You leave Fred down there?"

"Yes. This rustling deal has us both concerned. One of us stays down there in the bunkhouse at all times. He is a great worker and we get lots done but these rustlers have about beat both of us in the ground trying to catch and stop them."

"Maybe the three of us can lend you a hand in finding the source of this rustling."

"I hope so."

"Toby has delivered you enough hay?"

"Man, he is a hay-mowing-and-moving guy. I offered him some hands at roundup to pay him back but he thanked me and said he had enough. He's delivered plenty of hay to us for next winter. I am surprised how much he has stored on those homesteads. Of course, unfenced, the range cattle had grazed them down before so there was nothing growing on them. But he has a bunch of them fenced and using the dug well there and windmills to water the range stock. Last we talked he had several ranchers contracting hay for this winter from him."

"Those two are workers, both of them. Lucinda told us some about the rustler deal. How does that stand?"

"According to some letters written to me, they have been slipping out of Arizona with bunches of my cattle. My men are careful and I thought we'd see more tracks of that activity but we haven't seen a thing that looks like they moved a dozen or more critters off the ranch."

"Hey, we have time to check this out. Who sent the letters?" Cole asked.

"I'll get them."

"Stay there. I know where they are," Lucinda said, and went for them.

Cole began to read aloud the first one. " 'Dear Spencer Horne. My name is Ira Brown. I ranch in western New Mexico and rustlers have been driving cattle bearing your brand by my place. In June, I'd bet they drove fifty head over here past my place. July, maybe more. I am seventy years old and I don't want to tangle with them. But I hate rustlers or thieves of any kind — but please don't involve me.

" 'These thieves have many relatives over here who might seek revenge on me if they knew I told you so. Ira Brown.' "

"I sent one of my men over there but the old man was worried they might make a connection between him and us. So he came back empty-handed," Spencer said.

"I understand territorial lines are almost

like national borders. But we need to talk to the law over there, not mention Brown, and find out the truth," Chet said.

Spencer agreed.

"A lady wrote this one," Cole said. " 'Dear Mr. Burns, My name is Nita Rochester and I live close to the Arizona–New Mexico border. Some New Mexico cattle rustlers have been driving your branded cattle across the line and selling them over here. For a small fee, I can give you their names and who they sold them to. But I am a widow and I could be killed for giving out this information. So please keep my name out of this.' "

"I had not contacted her yet. She lives closer to Gallup."

"Well, you have three of us to help you. Let's get to the bottom of it."

"I may even help them," Lisa said, and they laughed.

The next morning at breakfast it was agreed the men would ride out and check on things across the road, where the bulk of the ranch's cattle were, and where Fred was staying. Then they'd form a plan with the five of them to check on New Mexico locations and possible thefts. Lisa stayed with Lucinda, Josey, and the kids.

When the fresh ranch horses were saddled and the men's legs were thrown across the seats of the saddle, Cole found he had drawn the head-bogging one, and he went off bucking down the short grass-clad open bowl out in front of the house. Chet and Jesus plus Spencer's men made a great cheering audience. The horse that Cole was on must have had springs on his legs because Chet decided Cole was getting high enough for him to maybe see the San Francisco Peaks a hundred miles west of there.

They finally all rode south out of the great bowl that held the corrals and buildings that made up the home place. Chet always enjoyed himself when the other feller's horse bucked that powerfully. Cole rode in beside him and Chet asked him, "You call that pony Wings?"

"No, worse than that. Boy, he got sky-bound on me. Spencer, you need to promise me a pony to ride for tomorrow."

"I have to apologize, too," Spencer said.

Cole was shaking his head. "He was like that wild Apache that Chet gave me as a prisoner that time. I shot him and was thinking the same of this horse, too."

Chet laughed and then to explain it to Spencer, said, "That was out on our first drive to feed the Navajos over at Gallup and we'd never have made it out here without that contract all these years."

Cole agreed. "But you have fulfilled that contract with sound animals. That stuff they feed the Apaches down at San Carlos was horrible. It is no wonder that they're mad and running around — Old Man Clanton and that Tucson Ring deliver some damn sorry stock for them to eat."

Chet agreed "Oh, we've had some real breaks, but all in all it wasn't because we didn't try hard, too."

"Yes, we did, and I love working here even with your bucking horse. When I quit the stage line, Valerie asked me if I was ready to take off on my own. My share of the telegraph-stage deal would have set us up. It is in the bank untouched but I told her no, that I was having too much fun working for Chet and his outfit. Plus, we may find another Spanish cave."

They had to tell Spencer about the cave in the Grand Canyon cliff wall.

"I never knew Arizona had rubies," Spencer said.

"Yeah, if we could have found the source we'd have it made."

Jesus spurred his horse up beside them. "They have them in Mexico, even. But I

148

never saw that many. Spencer, they hauled up a big bucket of them. I thought at first it was only red broken glass. But the half bucket of emerald stones made me the most excited, and then gold nuggets, many bigger than my fingernail."

Chet said, "And they'd done some gold melting, too. I had to buy two teams and horses to haul it all out."

"Who went over the edge to look in the cave?"

"Cole and a new guy named Salty. He's half monkey anyway. I stayed up on top," Jesus said.

"Spencer, Jesus translated their writing. They had all this stuff in a safe cave twenty feet or more below the lip of the North Rim and three men waited there to be pulled up and load all those treasures on pack mules and go back to Mexico and live like kings."

"One in desperation fell to his death by jumping out. The other two waited and died. We don't know what happened to the rest who never came back or where they found the rubies."

"Indians probably killed them and they never knew they had treasure in a cave like that," Spencer said.

"Chet saved a few things. An old Mexican man who lives on the ranch is cleaning it for him. One great find is a real old flintlock rifle. He may need to make a stock for it. It is amazing that that cave was so dry."

"There were a few rubies showed up in the Bill Williams area west of Preskitt," Spencer said. "A prospector showed me a handful he found in that region."

"Not a bucketful," Cole said. "And some were bigger than my thumbnail."

Fred joined them at the bunkhouse and they went out and spent the day looking at tracks. Eating a sandwich lunch, Chet talked to a few of Spencer's hands who were also trying to see where anyone drove off stock. But not much sign of any kind of a cattle drive made in the area showed in the great rolling grass prairie. From the bunkhouse Chet was surveying all the grass. He considered his bargain ranch a real place to run beef cattle on.

Chet saw the rustler business had Fred about as worn down as Spencer was. Both men, no matter how tough they were, needed a break.

Midafternoon Chet and his men, along with Spencer, went back to headquarters. Fred stayed with the cowboys.

"What next?" Spencer asked.

"Break up to going in twos and ride over into New Mexico in working clothes. Talk

150

to those people who wrote the letters, pay them a little money, and see what else we can learn. Where there are some sparks there can be fire."

"Sounds like a winner. I owe Cole a better horse tomorrow. I'll ride with him," Spencer said.

"Fine. We need to take some gear along and stay a few days. Someone will know something about this rustling deal over there, I bet, if there is anything going on."

Jesus jogged his horse up closer to the two of them. "And don't you find me one of those winged horses tomorrow, either."

Spencer laughed. "I swear on a stack of Bibles that horse never bucked that hard in all his life."

"Just remember that."

Later that night in bed Lisa asked him, "How long will you be gone?"

"I hope only a few days. But say five. You be all right here?"

She snuggled against him. "I will miss you. Yes, I will be fine. Lucinda is an intelligent enough person and her children are smart. Josey can use the company — she's in a hard place mentally. I understand that rustlers need to be run down and stopped, but know I treasure every day I am at your side and I worry when I am not there. You see what marrying you has done to me?"

He rolled over to face her in the bed. "Yes. You've lost some of your personal freedom."

"Exactly," she said. "But I will look forward to your return."

So would he.

"I worry about Josey being pregnant and having any trouble to need a doctor. In another month or sooner I want her at our house. Being her first child she might have problems."

"Once we get past these rustlers, Fred can move her carefully over there."

"Good. Do that."

"I will." He kissed her and held her close.

# CHAPTER 12

They crossed the border into New Mexico and rode on into Gallup. They stabled their horses, found rooms, and went out to eat. Over a great Mexican restaurant meal of beef, flour tortillas, and enchiladas they laughed and planned the day.

Chet and Jesus would look things over around town. Spencer and Cole would ride south and find the letter writers, maybe take three days, and meet back in town on Saturday. By then they should all know something. If they needed help they'd send Chet a telegram at the hotel.

The cantina music was loud, and several people stopped by the table. A young man who once worked for Cole on the stage line, Kenny York, had not heard about any rustling but promised to leave word at the hotel for Chet if he learned anything.

A Mexican woman about thirty by the name of Rita Miranda, who worked at the

Navajo Agency, recognized Chet and spoke to him. When he told her they were secretly looking for rustlers she told him she would also leave word at the hotel if she learned anything. A widow woman in her thirties, she took the opportunity to dance with each of them.

Before she left Chet, she whispered, "Next time you come to Gallup bring some single hombres. I need a man, too."

Laughing with her, he promised to do that.

Going back to their room, Jesus said, "I remember going places with you and meeting these women — all kinds. But I am so glad I have Anita now and the baby. I can go home and be in heaven, huh?"

"Amen."

The next day they went around to several butcher shops. None had seen the Wagon Wheel or the Bar K brand on cattle they'd bought. But Chet figured they wouldn't tell if they had butchered some, because telling might get them involved in a felony.

Chet knew having someone like Jesus speaking fluently in Spanish was an advantage in a town like Gallup. Day one came and passed without any leads. They ate in the same cantina and the man who owned it joined them while they ate the rich, well-prepared food again.

"You learn anything today?" Fred Orr asked.

"Not much. Most say they never saw that Wagon Wheel or Bar K brand around here. But I figure they would have to play dumb so they don't become a suspect."

"I know a man who might know something for a few dollars. He would not lie to you."

Chet nodded. "What does he charge?"

"Oh, say, for twenty dollars he may have some very good pointers."

"Where will I find him?"

"Before breakfast tomorrow in that little park up the street. He will wear a yellow bandanna. His name is Yeffie."

"Yef-fee?"

"That is close enough. Good luck, my amigos. The food was okay?"

"Terrible food," Jesus said in Spanish to tease him.

He left laughing.

Chet didn't fall asleep very fast that evening. Lisa had spoiled him. For certain she wasn't the only one missing someone who wasn't in their bed. Were Spencer and Cole doing any better? He and Jesus would meet Fred Orr's man in the park before breakfast.

Chet easily found the man in the empty park. A few drunken drifters, lying prone on benches, snored away, but he was sitting alone at a table.

Standing above him Chet asked, "You must be Yeffie?"

The middle-aged man nodded.

Chet slid in across from him. "Do you know anything about my rustling problems?"

"Some."

"What will I get for my money?"

"Do you have the Arizona brand for the Wagon Wheel and the Bar K?"

"Yes."

"Well, in June, July, and August around fifty head with one of your two brands on them each month were slaughtered at the All Right Slaughter House."

"Did the brand inspector report them?"

"No. He never saw them. They were hurried in after dark and each time slaughtered at night and the carcasses removed before they made their normal opening time the next day."

"Where are their hides?" Chet asked.

The old man smiled. "I imagine in the

green hide stack. The inspector never looks at them."

Chet knew what he had to do. Get the county law to secure a search warrant, and if the hides were there, those people would have to admit who sold the cattle to them or face a long prison sentences themselves. He peeled out three twenties and handed them to the man. "You know anything else I need to know about my cattle or ranch?"

"I understand a man that works for you on your Wagon Wheel Ranch is wanted for murder in Texas."

"Who did he kill?"

"A Texas sheriff's deputy that he found in bed with his wife."

"My Lord, man." Chet shook his head in disgust. "What is his name?"

"Frank Edwards."

Chet shook his head. "That all?"

"Can I ask what you will do about that?"

Chet looked around to be certain no one could hear him. "Maybe buy him a stage-coach ticket."

Yeffie waved away Chet's offer of giving him some more money. "Give it to that man on the run. That deputy was a no-account sumbitch."

Chet put the money back in his pocket. "Thank you. I'd looked long and hard for those facts you gave me on the rustling. *Gracias.*"

Yeffie made no effort to move. Chet left him and joined Jesus at the edge of the park. They went on to eat breakfast and on the way, Chet began to explain what the man had told him.

"In June, July, and August he says that they slaughtered about fifty head of our cattle at night and each time they did it before the brand inspector got there and the carcasses were hauled away before the inspector came to work."

"How do we prove that?" Jesus asked.

"Our man thinks the hides from our cattle were not hidden but stacked in the green hide pile, waiting for someone to pass through and buy them."

"Sounds like greedy people, huh?" Jesus's smile beamed at the notion.

"Yes. Let's eat breakfast and then go see the county sheriff."

The meal of scrambled eggs, bacon, frijoles, and flour tortillas was done well and the coffee rich and good. When he paid the cashier, Chet asked where the courthouse was located, and the man making change suggested they take a taxi.

Outside, Chet waved down one and the man reined up his single horse.

"Take us to the courthouse."

"There is no county courthouse here yet."

"Is there a sheriff here?"

"No, señor, but we have some deputy sheriffs."

"Go there."

They soon learned that New Mexico had so far not divided parts of that state into counties, but there were lawmen in the office and they listened to him. One of them set out and brought a state brand inspector back to the conversation. The inspector's name was Morris Granada.

He listened to Chet's story about the cattle being slaughtered under the cover of night and the idea that those hides might be in the green stack. The man nodded that they could still be there if they had, indeed, been slaughtered there.

"Señor Byrnes, I know about your work with the Navajos and how you tried to get them the coal sale to this railroad but did not get it in the end. I don't need a search warrant to search their green hide piles. That is covered in my job description."

"Can we go along with you?"

"Sure."

A deputy named August accompanied them. They took a buckboard to the slaughterhouse, which, in the hot near-midday air, reeked from the processing of animals.

A big man sharpening a large knife met them at the door. He asked what they wanted, suspicion in his voice. During the man's conversation with Granada he shifted his dark glares to Chet and Jesus.

Chet didn't know the man and felt he was suspicious of the entire foursome, not only himself and Jesus.

The deputy sheriff, August, then forcefully pushed Granada aside and he entered into an increasingly angry conversation when the big man said he would not let none of them into the plant.

Between the giant flies, other flying bugs, and the sour spilled-guts aroma the voices became more heated than the glaring sun had been outside. Once inside, the deputy ordered the butcher to stand back. When he did not obey, the officer unholstered his gun and forced him back. "Go ahead, Granada. You two can come in, too."

While most of the conversation was in Spanish, Chet felt this man damn sure didn't want anyone to look at his hide pile. Both the deputy and Granada insisted they must see the ones he had on hand. The lawman made him lay down the knife, and they hurried to the back into the warehouse portion, which stunk as bad as the rest of the

160

plant. Granada pointed out the hide piles, which reached almost to the ceiling.

"Each take a pile and restack them. You find your brand, keep the hide separate in a stack over here for reexamination."

"They will bear a Bar K or Wagon Wheel brand on ours." Then Jesus took a deep breath and started on his pile. Chet had another large stack to look at.

"Here's one," Granada said. "Butcher Man?"

He directed his question at the disarmed butcher. "You realize that this hide could put you in prison for ten years?"

The big man didn't answer him.

Jesus spoke up. "I have several here."

"That is enough," Granada said. "I will have some jailhouse prisoners to get the rest out. I think you're right, Mr. Byrnes. There may be a hundred and fifty of them in here."

"Good. We need this situation stopped."

"I am going to arrest several others who are working here and find out who knew about this illegal slaughter and did not report it," the deputy said, slapping cuffs on the plant owner. "Wentworth, get to walking."

"Anything else you need of me or Jesus?" Chet asked them.

"No, but thanks. We'd never have known

this had happened without you telling us." Granada shook Chet's hand and Jesus's, too. August also thanked them and shook their hands.

Outside, Chet waved down a taxi. "Where is the best bathhouse? Me and my friend need a bath and our clothes washed. Badly."

The man wrinkled his nose. "You damn sure do. I know the place you need to do that at."

"Take us there." He and Jesus climbed in the cab and the driver hurried his horse to the Shanghai Bath House.

Chet tipped the driver a dollar above his charge and the pleased man thanked him. Inside the bathhouse office, he knew from the shocked look on the Chinese woman's face that she smelled them before they reached her.

"We both need a bath and our clothes washed."

"Be a dollar apiece," she said like that was her top price.

He paid her. She held her nose with one hand and pointed to the green door that went into the bathhouse.

Both Chet and Jesus laughed all the way down, undressing along the way.

"Most fun we've had in years."

"Jesus, do you realize we may have caught

the rustlers, too?"

"Hell, yes, I do. That is why I am laughing. Cole and Spencer will be back here tonight and they don't know it,"

Chet shook his head. *Lisa, I'll be home shortly.*

# CHAPTER 13

About seven that evening, the dusty pair entered the Mexican café. Chet and Jesus in their fresh clothes toasted them. "Here's to the outlaw rustlers — half of them are in the Crossbar Hotel tonight."

Both men looked in disbelief at them.

"You what?" Spencer asked.

"We have six rustlers in the Gallup, New Mexico, jail. A posse will ride in the morning to arrest five more."

"Who are they?" Cole asked.

"One is a big fat butcher named Wentworth. Him and five more who concealed the slaughter. We think he butchered about one hundred and fifty head of our stock. The outside men, who are at a so-far-undisclosed ranch, they will arrest tomorrow."

Spencer collapsed in a wooden chair, dropped his dirty hat on the floor, and swept his graying hair back. "You mean you two solved this rustler deal today?"

Chet nodded. "They slaughtered about fifty head a month in June, July, and August. They did it at night, then hauled the carcasses away to the plant before it opened. But they made one mistake. They put all our branded hides in the same stack, in the back, with their green hides."

"What next?"

"We broke up a large ring of rustlers."

"I want to know how they got them off the ranch," Spencer said.

"They will be in jail tomorrow night when they bring them in. The deputy can tell you all about it later. I am going home in the morning, to your house."

After their meal, Cole and Spencer went for baths. The four planned to have breakfast together and to head home in the morning. It would take two hard days' ride to do it but it made no difference. Chet wanted to be back with Lisa even if it took three days.

Things went smoothly and the third day they rode into the Wagon Wheel Ranch headquarters. Fred Taylor and Josey, with Chet's wife and Lucinda, were on the front porch, beaming at their return. Spencer's two stepchildren ran to him shouting, "Candy?"

He had pockets full for them and they knew it. Packing one of them in each arm, their dark faces puckered out, sucking on hard candy and beating on him happily.

Lisa looked snug enough, running in for a hug and kiss. That was worth the two-and-a-half-days' ride.

"I really missed you." Then she whispered, "Don't you ever sell Preskitt Valley. I miss it, too."

He laughed. "I know what you mean."

"What's next?"

"They have the rustlers in jail. The chief deputy promised us a letter on what he learned from the rustlers that are now in jail."

"How much did they get away with?"

"A hundred-fifty head over three months is the estimate."

"Lots of money, wasn't it?"

"Yes, but Spencer and Fred were doing all they could to stop it. They were pretty sharp rustlers at sneaking cattle out of here. I think a few at a time on horses with hooves wrapped in blankets and getting them over there and butchered. We decided they never took many at any time, which made it hard to track. But they kept the hides, which hung them."

"Where to next?"

"Visit my sister and slip home."

"Wonderful."

Chet told Spencer that things looked great and he still had lots of steers to ship on the Navajo run in the fall. Things would work out and he and Fred had a great ranch operation going. Then Chet made Spencer step out on the back porch. "I don't recall his name but word is out one of your men is wanted in Texas for shooting a deputy."

"Oh hell."

"Frank Edwards, that's his name."

Spencer made a sour face. "Best damn man on the list."

"I heard the story. He shot some deputy for being in bed with his wife. My informant in Gallup must have liked Edwards, too. He asked that I buy him a stagecoach ticket west."

"What do you say I should do?"

"Pay him a hundred and have him jump on the next stage goes by for California."

"Chet, he is a marvelous worker and I wanted him to be my number three man. He refused my offer but lots of guys don't want to be the boss. Thanks, I'll get that done. Who in the hell told you all this information?"

"An old man named Yeffie, who lives around Gallup. He don't miss much."

"Wish to hell I'd known this guy, huh?"

"You still may need him sometime."

"Oh, I have his name down. I won't forget it."

The next morning, Chet told Spencer, "Tell Lucinda thanks for her hospitality. We better ride if we are to get to Sis's by dark."

"Rustlers aside, it is sure nice to run a ranch and be out riding cross-country. No worries you'll run out of nails or boards. Thanks."

"Now that the rustlers are in jail, I want you and Lucinda to take the kids to Gallup. Take two weeks. You need some time off. I want to pay the tab for all of it. Clothes and all. Don't spare me. This rustler deal had both you and Fred exhausted. Then when you get back I want Fred to carefully bring Josey to Preskitt before she delivers. Lisa is concerned about this baby, being her first and all. He's as tired as you are. Ranching can be fun but next time you get so worn down — write me a letter to come help. If I can't come, I'll send someone. Now, we worked hard getting to this point. It is time to step back and enjoy it. Savvy?"

"Yes, sir. You know I'm serious. And Fred is, too, and in time he'll be a great leader. We will settle down and do all that. Oh,

Frank Edwards caught the westbound stage last night down on the Marcy Road. Damn, he and I both cried. I gave him a hundred and paid for the ticket. Fred felt like I did. A good man like that — no place to go — no wife — just shuffle on ahead of the law."

"No one said this job would be easy."

Chet joined the others and they rode west toward the Windmill Ranch with the meadowlarks singing and chasing bugs on the road all the way.

# CHAPTER 14

Chet's prediction was right. Despite the push they made, the sun was down when they finally reached Sarge and Sis's Windmill Ranch.

"Howdy," Sarge shouted. He was holding up the lantern on the porch steps.

"Just us, Sarge," Chet shouted. "Lisa, Jesus, and Cole."

"It's your big brother," Sarge said over his shoulder to his wife.

"I'm coming. I'm coming. Don't let them ride off."

"Hell, darling, we're too tired to go another mile," Chet shouted, undoing his sweaty latigos on the girth.

"Lisa, where are you?" Sis shouted, coming down the porch stairs.

"Let them horses go," Sarge shouted. "My men are coming. They'll put them up for you."

Cole agreed and he shook Sarge's hand.

"How are you?"

"Been a long time since you've been here. Do you miss the stagecoaches and the singing wire?"

"Hell no, Sarge."

"I just wondered. How are you, Jesus?"

"Good now that we've got here."

"Where did you come from, Chet?"

"Wagon Wheel Ranch."

"That's a pretty long ride."

"Going anywhere to another ranch is a far piece," Chet said, and they headed for the stairs and the lighted door at the head of them. They went on into the house.

"Cody Day and his wife, Sandy, with the baby ran over to the Verde Ranch to see Tom and Millie."

"Who goes to Gallup this month?" Chet asked.

"I do. That's why they took the break. Their turn to watch the ranch."

"Handy to have someone who can make the drive, isn't it?"

"You bet. That boy — well, he's a young man — could run any ranch you have."

"With all the men that you tried to train I figured at the time I sent him to you he could do it."

Sarge laughed. "Tom didn't."

"Tom didn't want to give up his daughter."

"You're right. Those two have made it good, too."

"So have you and Sis. We've been to see Toby and Talley first and they are doing great."

"Boy, he is a worker. We have plenty of hay, and people ask me who owns all these fenced homesteads and haystacks. If they want to buy hay I send them to Toby."

"He's the hay man for us."

"They tell me they have the roadbed in at Flagstaff. Is it that close?"

"I think they want to sell those high-priced sections. That train won't be there for four years, if by then."

Sarge laughed.

Sis came by then with a dish of food and kissed Chet on the cheek. "What is so funny?"

"You know about the roadbed at Flagstaff that we heard about?" Sarge asked her.

"Yes."

"Your brother says the tracks aren't even halfway across New Mexico. Chet says it is so they can sell the high-priced land over there at Flagstaff."

"Dang them. They had me all excited we could get out of here."

Sarge and Chet laughed.

Later in bed, Lisa asked him, "You and her ran the Texas ranch before you came out here?"

"Yes. My dad lost most of his mind trying to get the kidnapped kids back from the Comanche and he stayed out too long. Texas Rangers found him and brought him back home. He never was right after that. I was fifteen. Our mother had been upset over the loss of them from the start. Her mind sank away. Sis and I ran the place. I bet she wasn't twelve then. My brother was no help and he wouldn't take any responsibility but he'd gripe at everything I did. I finally quit listening to him."

"No wonder you can manage all this — you've been doing it forever."

"I have big shoulders."

She snuggled in his arms. "I'm glad I fit into this tight bunch. I couldn't believe that you'd ever marry me. You could have had anyone you wanted. But if I hadn't been so dumb and ran off with that stupid rich boy — I'd never have meet you. You reckon God planned it that way?"

"Call it fate or whatever. I'm pleased. You said that for days with those raiders you had little food or water while trying to escape my posse going up through that Four Corners country."

"Oh, Chet, they were some real bad times and I can't believe I survived that. Those boys — hell, they were men — they didn't care if any of us girls ate or drank water. They spoke about you hanging all of them when you caught them. They really believed that was your plan — to lynch them."

"That country up there is bleak, too."

"Tell me about it. I considered shooting myself to escape it. But I didn't have a gun. My system was messed up inside. If I ate anything I threw it up. He shook me by my arms once when I was bent over retching it all up and demanded to know if I was pregnant."

"Think you were?"

"No. But I had no idea. I was bleeding. Hell, at that moment I thought being hung would be a great escape. After that he double-handed slapped my face until someone told him to stop. Then, weak as I was, I knew they'd leave me out there to die, and despite the pain I got up, caught my weary horse, and rode after them."

"I never knew it was that tough."

"Yeah, a few hours later, he came begging and pleading for me to love him."

"What happened then?"

"I told him go ahead but he wouldn't like

doing that. I was bleeding."

"And?"

"He stalked off mad and then he openly raped an Indian girl named Little Deer. Next morning, she was gone. I never knew if she ran away or they killed her. Your bunch ran us down three nights later."

"She didn't die. We found her the next day and she told us where they were going. We gave her a fresh horse and enough food and money to get her back home."

"Thank God and you. What did you think when you saw me the first time?"

"You were a very rich, dirt-filthy bitch running with those stupid boys for any wild adventure that you could find."

"I thought, *That big guy is going to hang us all and it will be over.*"

"I had no intention of hanging anyone. I knew by then some of their parents had money and they'd have it all over the news that we'd lynched their innocent boys. I intended to prosecute them in court to stop those raids on the stage stops."

"I cleaned up what I could after that and knew I'd die out there if you refused my request when you said you were taking them back as prisoners."

He nodded and hugged her. "Jesus found you a better horse and saddle the second morning. He never told me why."

With a shake of her head she said, "You know him. He is as tough as any man on earth, but inside he has a big, considerate heart. I'd worked hard that day before and woke early to help the cooks — you weren't going to complain about my services."

"I had lots on my mind about getting those prisoners back and I knew I'd face a high-priced bunch of lawyers that their parents would hire, and did. I sure wasn't thinking about that girl I brought back helping my crew make camp and cooking meals."

"You told me in Flagstaff that I could get off there or if I had no place you'd take me to Preskitt and find me work."

He nodded. "I knew by then you worked damn hard and that people listened to you. Can't say I really knew much about you but I knew you were showing signs of becoming a leader."

"Your wife and I talked for two hours that first day I got there. She told me about her plans to teach the ranch children English and to enroll them in school. Then she asked me to make that plan work. She wanted them dressed better — we sewed them clothes. Miguel treated me like I was some real important person not some woman of the night to use and toss aside. I saw he was a man of dreams, too. He loved so much to ride with you and when you told him he'd become the next foreman he about busted with pride."

"About then Monica had the heart attack and died. My wife asked you to be her replacement?"

"What a fix for me. I was planning my wedding and all that happened. But by then I also knew what I had to do — take that job and marry him. I talked to Elizabeth about my problems. She said, 'I'll talk to Chet. But you know he has chosen Miguel to be the next foreman and I am sure you two can live in this big house with us until then.' "

"I never hesitated saying yes when she asked me about you. I had seen your transformation, teaching the children English in a crash course, the dress-the-workers-better plan, then you stepping in and handling Monica's position."

"I sure worried about what you'd tell Elizabeth when she asked you about me. I still recalled that morning in the sagebrush — 'You either work hard or I'll leave you out here.' I knew you didn't need to be nice to me. I came there with those outlaws. You had no obligation to do a thing for me. But you did."

He kissed her. "You may be right. God planned it all."

# CHAPTER 15

Chet rose early in the morning. He didn't beat the house girls Oleta or Julie getting up — they were already fixing breakfast. Nor did he beat Salty, who already had a cup of coffee and was seated there at the table waiting for him.

"Morning."

"Morning, sir. You see all you wanted to out there on your trip?"

"I saw three of the ranches and all is well. What do you know?"

"I found those three suspects I think shot at her and you."

"Oh? They close by?"

"Close enough. We are watching them now." Salty moved forward on his chair and shook his head. "They are not smart enough to do this without some backing. I figure they were paid to do that and we are watching for them to make contact with those parties who hired them."

Chet looked hard at his man. "It wasn't robbery, then?"

"Takes some effort to rob folks. I think they thought they'd kill you or scare you into moving and were going to be or were paid for doing that."

"Who wants rid of me around here?"

"We are waiting for them to show up or these guys to meet up with them."

"Who are they?"

"You ever know of the Cassidy brothers, Roy and Elmer?"

"No. I never even heard of them."

"They have a place up on Twiller Mountain. Rough hillbillies, I'd call them. They have a son-in-law named Earl Gum. I didn't have his last name but we have it now. They've cut some timber, firewood, and posts for a living but they don't do a helluva lot more. Bo's got me an arrest record on the Cassidys. Drunk, fighting, but no arrest for stealing. That is why I don't think robbery was their purpose. They simply received some money for going after you."

Chet felt near to being amused by the idea. "Who would pay them money to get me run out of here?"

"That, I am not sure about. But I have those two helpers of mine watching them like a hawk to try and find that out."

"It's a shame we don't get along better with the law here and have them do that."

Salty agreed. "You were gone and Bo's advice to me on that matter was forget about going to the law."

Chet laughed. "He obviously knows about how it would work."

"I sure like the man the better I know him. He knows real estate and lots that goes on in town."

"It isn't costing much to keep an eye on them. Maybe we can learn something."

Salty agreed. "Like you said, the one horse is a dirty-colored roan, light marking, and their other horses are bays. We tracked them the next day from where they left the main road and over that little mountain, down the narrow twisty road to their junky place. That's what I have. You have a good trip?"

"Yes. We saw Toby and Talley. They have lots of hay put up. Those homesteads Bo has bought for near nothing, fenced in they make great hay farms. Toby has lots of hardworking Mexican boys handle things for him. They cut brush on that home place first, then learn how to cowboy, fix machinery, and work. He may not do it like you and I would but he gets lots accomplished. Then we went over to the Wagon Wheel Ranch. Spencer and Fred are doing great over there but they had some rustling going on and couldn't pin it down. We found out who it was and there are over fifteen men in jail in New Mexico."

"Spencer? He the telegraph builder they talk about?"

"He used lots of Navajo boys building that and several cowboys worked for him, too."

"Then we came back by Windmill and saw my sister and her husband, Sarge. They do the Navajo beef contract from there. Toby is handling his hay needs, too."

"Tom's son-in-law, Cody Day, takes that herd up to Gallup every other month for Sarge."

"Right."

Salty smiled. "I met him at the Verde."

"Has Hampt been by here while I was gone?"

"Yes, and his arm is lots better. Those three horse rustlers got seven years apiece. Bet they don't steal any more horses."

"Good riddance."

"Yes. I understand, sir, it is tradition for ranch folks getting married to honeymoon up at the Oak Creek orchards?"

"It is. Yes, quiet wonderful place."

"I am not some broke cowboy. I can pay for that stay."

"Salty, you have earned that stay. I know

the North Rim deal made us all money. But you have sure earned a week's stay up there. When's the wedding?"

"Two weeks on Saturday. And thanks. I know I'd made the decision of my life when Tom hired me on. I'd heard about the Texan-turned-Arizona-resident story but it was the best day in my life joining this outfit. I love the opportunity to stay on working for Vance and you. Married or not, if your two can't ride with you, I am ready to anytime or place you need me."

"I appreciate your support and we will have a place for you, rich or poor."

Salty laughed. "I damn sure am not poor any longer."

Salty left and Lisa joined Chet. "I overheard most of that. Not snooping. I saw him in action on the North Rim. He is another great soldier for the cause, isn't he?"

Chet agreed. "Tom told me that I needed him. I did. He is watching the three who shot at us. He thinks someone hired them to do that so I'd leave here."

"Maybe scare me — maybe — but I know they wouldn't scare you. Don't you have any idea who is behind it?"

"No, but we may find out."

"Tomorrow I am going to town with Oleta to get the dress started."

"I want a bodyguard to go with you."

"I thought we'd plan to leave about eight-thirty in the morning. It will take a long time to get the measurements and all that."

"I'll speak to Vance and he'll have a good man to ride shotgun."

"Kind of strange to need a bodyguard after all the adventures that I've survived."

"Different deal. Now you are my wife and I want you in one piece."

She came by, bent over, and kissed his cheek. "Thanks, Chet Byrnes. I love you. Maybe even more so here than anywhere else."

It was great to be back, though that theory of someone wanting to run him off hung in his mind.

They damn sure didn't know him and what he stood for if they believed that would happen.

# CHAPTER 16

The next day Chet was reading the back issues of the *Miner* newspaper in the living room. Lisa and Oleta were getting ready to go to town when he heard someone shouting for him in the yard. He ran through the house, and on the back porch he saw it was his foreman Vance hollering.

"What's happened?"

"Salty and those boys have finally found the man behind the shooting. He sent Ray to get you. Ray says he can take you up there. I am going after saddle horses for both of us."

"I'll get my hat and gun. Good."

"Where are Cole and Jesus?" Lisa asked him, trailing him from the back door.

"I'll have help enough. Those Mexican boys helping Salty have hit the jackpot. Vance is going, too. We will be all right. They aren't Jesse James."

"Yes. Don't get yourself all shot up."

"Honey. I need to go." He finished buckling on his holster and setting his hat on his head. "I'll be back. You be careful today. The buckboard and your guard are ready and waiting." He kissed her good-bye.

"I know. Oleta is coming down. We are going. You be damn careful."

"I will."

Hurrying down the long flight of stairs to the ground at the base he turned to wave at her. He smiled and swung into the saddle. Ray, Vance, and Chet left the ranch's yard in a flash.

"How far away are they?" Chet asked as they headed in the direction of town.

"Down in the Bradshaw Mountains," the boy shouted over his shoulder.

Hell. That could be forty miles away. But he rode stirrup to stirrup with the foreman and the youth.

On top of a rise they let their horses catch some breath. Elevation there was over a mile high. They'd have to put some restraint on their rush or they'd kill their mounts getting there. Again on the move, they were heading onto those untitled ruts that led into the mining district south of Preskitt. Soon in the pine forest, moving ahead at a trot, they crossed over some steep mountains. Chet sure didn't even want to ride his horse on the outside edge of the road.

Two hours later the boy pointed toward the end of a long, narrow meadow with steep sides of timber-size pine. "I left them down there."

Chet smelled their campfire smoke and nodded. They must still be there. Next, he saw some horses grazing and the light-colored one that had pursued them that day. He told his men to rein in their hot, hard-breathing horses.

They agreed and did so.

When they came in sight, he didn't know the seedily dressed three men but the hat-less wavy-haired man with them, somehow, looked familiar.

"Hello, Chet Byrnes. Remember me?" he asked, swaggering around.

Chet shook his head. The four of them were unarmed. Salty had a Winchester, and his teenage horse wrangler had another one like it.

"Aw damn, Chet, I can't believe I came more than a thousand miles to see you and you don't remember my name."

"You're a Ralston."

"Ha, you got half of it. Try for the rest, huh?"

"I don't need your name. Why are you here?"

"Now, is that a way to talk to a former neighbor of yours? Why, the years we lived right next to each other under the Lone Star flag of Texas."

"You know this guy?" Salty asked, a little on edge about the guy's sarcasm.

Chet nodded. "His family stole my remuda two weeks before I was to leave Texas for Kansas, then his family killed my brother when he was in Kansas."

"Yeah, and he hung my little brother and two of my cousins up in northern Texas — for no reason at all."

"Liar. They stole my horses."

Ralston made a face indicating that that was nothing. "Just a joke to make you squirm more."

"Don't tell me they were joking. To get rich, they drove them horses clear to the Red River and aimed to sell them to drovers who needed horses on the trail."

"Well, my name's Burl Ralston and I came here to kill you, you son of a bitch."

Salty struck him over the head with his gun barrel. Ralston went to his knees and Salty's second blow flattened him facedown on the ground. "You aren't calling my boss that."

Chet almost laughed at the savagery written on Salty's face as he stood over the

188

unconscious form on the ground. Minutes before, he was ready to kill this dark black spot from his past by himself. At the moment, though, he felt a little sympathy for the results of the man's poor manner. Yes. He needed to be shut up.

"What did he pay you to shoot at us?" Chet asked the closest Cassidy brother.

"Huh?"

"You want to be laid out like that?" Chet pointed at Ralston.

"No, sir. He paid us fifty dollars."

"What did he say to do?"

"Aw, he first wanted us to kill you."

"And?"

"We said we needed more money to do that."

"How much more?"

Cassidy shrugged. "Like two hundred dollars."

"So, he settled for you running us off."

"More or less. He said two was too much. He'd do that himself for that much money."

"Well, get ready. You're not going to see daylight for several years."

Rubbing the back of his head, Ralston sat up and asked, "What did he say?"

Salty hustled him to his feet, pulling him up by his arm. "That you four'd be in prison long enough to forget his name."

"I won't."

Chet stepped in, wagging his index finger in the man's face. "Then you come back to die after you get out of prison. I ever see your ugly face again I'll shoot you on sight. Salty, take them to the Yavapai County Jail. Have them charged with attempted murder and anything else the prosecutor can think up about what happened here."

"That won't be hard."

"Both of you two men who worked for Salty and have been trailing them will get a hundred-dollar reward apiece for a job well done. Good job. Salty, thanks. I wondered about the conspiracy theory but you sure read it right. Nice going. You and the boys have done a great job."

"Someday I want to hear that Texas feud story," Salty said.

"It's a long one." He wanted to tell Salty this might not be the end of it yet. Having Burl in an Arizona prison might draw more revenge-filled family members out there. But if he wouldn't spend two hundred bucks on having him killed, they might not have the travel fare. Time would tell about that.

# CHAPTER 17

Over the next few days, Chet spent some time with his ranch books. When they brought Chet the *Miner* newspaper, mid-week, the headlines read, GRAND JURY INDICTS FOUR MEN FOR ATTEMPTED MURDER OF A LOCAL RANCHER AND HIS WIFE.

Area rancher Chet Byrnes and his wife, Lisa, were chased by three men on the east highway a week ago under a barrage of bullets by the arrested three men. They were to stop Chet and his wife, but the two of them drove on to the Black Canyon Stage Coach offices. The company's employees saw and heard the pursuit and rushed outside armed to scare the shooters away. Their movements and threats soon ran them off.

Later a citizen brought the four men involved in the incident in under a citizen's arrest and swore to the deputy sheriff on duty they needed to be indicted for their involvement in the attack on the rancher and his wife. The two Cassidy brothers, Roy and Elmer, and their son-in-law Earl Gum were charged along with the fourth man also in custody charged for this crime, named in the indictment as Burl Ralston of (town unknown) Texas. Ralston was wanted in the Lone Star state by several communities for armed robbery, three counts of rape, and two pending murder charges. After his trial and sentencing here, Texas authorities will return him back there for multiple trials.

Poor Burl. It looked to Chet that if he was found guilty, he'd be serving those sentences somewhere else besides Arizona. Good. He had less to worry about his getting out. He hoped Ralston rotted in prison for that and when they tried him for those other crimes in Texas.

He took the newspaper in the kitchen and showed Lisa.

She shook her head. "I hope that is the last of the Texas invasions."

He wanted to say he hoped so, too, but he knew it would never be completely over until all involved in it were buried. "When

Salty and Oleta are married, let's go see Shawn and Lucy. Winter isn't many months away and travel up there later could be cold and icy. We can go south and see about the Diablo Ranch in midwinter and sweat."

"Fine with me," she said.

"I'll tell my bodyguards my plan and see who wants to go."

"Who will you take if one of them wants out for a trip?"

"Salty — no, I better let him honeymoon. I think Vic would be good."

Lisa nodded. "I'll be packed."

"Good. You know the story. Lucy showed Marge, my first wife, and I the ranching country up on top of the world. She later married my nephew Reg and they had one daughter. He had stayed behind in Texas and married a young woman who had worked in our house. They were running a ranch for an older couple in an exchange for when the people passed on and the ranch would be theirs for taking care of them. But he got a divorce from her and no one knew where he went. I know nothing about the reason for the divorce. One day he showed up here in Arizona. He never was the same person that I left in Texas, but he showed lots of aspects that he might return to being his old self.

"When Reg and Lucy met and were married, I hoped for the best. Then I think a bruja stepped into his life and threw a switch in his brain. He drank too much, turned inside himself, and I am sure his wife was treated the worst. Then he must have had enough so he rode off one night and shot himself."

"Bruja?"

"Yes. He wasn't her first victim. He didn't have the money she thought he had. The ranch was mine, not his. But she'd ruined another man's life who in the end lost all he had, too. He was not a particular friend of mine — but she ruined him and he lost it all.

"Lucy is married to Shawn now and they have a child. Shawn McElroy joined me and went to the border where I was a U.S. Marshal up on the U.S. side. He met Lucy at a family gathering here, as I recall, and began to write her. You know what happened next. They got married and have done wonderful with the ranch up there. His right-hand man is a short guy named Spud Carnes who has a wife, Shirley. Shawn and Spud make a great pair and the four do a helluva job. That country had lots of maverick cattle running lose, and we nearly stocked that whole ranch with those maver-icks."

"I met Robert and Betty at the sawmill. That business is a real moneymaker, isn't it?"

"Yes, it certainly is. Robert was coming down to the dances at Camp Verde and his wife, Betty, was tall enough he didn't need to bend over to dance with her. But her friends said he wasn't Mormon and she should stay clear of him. Think it kind of made Robert mad. He was making way lots more money than four boys his age could. Those two worked out a compromise. She kept her church and he takes her every Sunday. Today she has a big new ranch house like Tom, Sis, and Lucy have, and her husband makes a big living by the standards in Arizona today."

"They have a sweet daughter, too, I hear. What about the Oak Creek couple?"

"Betty and Leroy Sipes could not make a living farming vegetables on their small ranch. That orchard in Oak Creek came up for sale. I went and hauled them up there. They loved it and promised me they could make it pay. Now, he was a real gardener and you know he sends berries, fruit, and fresh vegetables to all the company ranches close by. I have never regretted a day on buying that place. It more than breaks even on his sales and we all benefit from all the fruits and vegetables he hauls us."

"I won't forget my honeymoon there, either. It is a heavenly place."

He chuckled. "It was nice. Salty said he could afford to pay me for using it. I told him no. It was for all of us and he did his part already."

"Heavens, yes. Sis told me part of her life."

"That was a tough one. She married a nice young man who worked for me. He had a horse wreck, broke his neck, and died. I had to go down and tell my pregnant sister he'd got killed."

"You two were very close, weren't you?"

"Yes. But we did what we could. Sarge, who you met, had asked me if he could date her before she married her first husband. He was too late, but when she became a widow, he didn't let any moss grow on his boots. She was concerned more about the baby in her but that did not bother Sarge. They finally got married and she had the son, who he raises like his own. He has the wife he always wanted."

"JD?"

"JD had a rough time finding himself. My brother's second son took up with the woman Kay, who is married now to our banker Tanner. She had been recently widowed. Her first husband had been older and his place was run-down. JD came to me to get some money for some things he needed to ranch with. She found out and had a fit. They broke up and he went wild drinking and not caring. We lost track until he managed to get a letter out of a New Mexico jail that he had been framed and in prison for having stolen a horse. Me and my men went over and they wouldn't let a U.S. Marshal talk to him. I telegraphed DC and then the locals couldn't do enough for me. We got him out and back home. He'd learned a lot. Tough education."

"After that he married Jenn's daughter Bonnie?"

"When I came here on my first trip looking for a place to light I ate at Jenn's Café. She's a great gal and when I needed help to take the Verde Ranch away from a crooked foreman she found all these men who'd once worked there but were boycotted by their ex-boss. Most other ranchers would not hire them because of him. I learned her daughter was working in a brothel in Tombstone. She asked me in tears one day could I get her out of there. I said I'd try.

"Myself, Jesus, and, I guess, Cole went down there. Valerie had gone down there with Bonnie but working in one of those places was not for her. So, Valerie worked as a waitress and wanted out of Tombstone. I could not convince Bonnie to quit. We gave Val a one-way ticket to Preskitt and shipped her to Jenn, plus promised her a place to live and a job helping in Jenn's restaurant.

"I can recall the day, sitting out there on the stage line porch, waiting for her stage, telling her we'd all help her."

"But Bonnie didn't come back?"

"No. Some white slaver kidnapped her and we had to go get her back. I think Cole had already married Val. Maybe JD was along. We found where she was, deep in Mexico, being held by a very rich man. I traded a Barbarossa colt out of my famous horses for her safe return.

"He wanted the horse and delivered her to us. We never knew if he paid for her or took her by force from the slaver. I knew I didn't have the force or the money to ransom her. When JD married her, I wouldn't have given ten cents for their marriage, but they made it and she's having child number three and loving it."

"And Elizabeth found you south of Tucson?"

"She told you that story?"

"Yes. How she shot the man who had

198

killed her husband. How later she learned that a rich man who owned Barbarossa horses was at a fancy hacienda just off the King's Highway and she went to see him to buy one. How she knew it was you striding from an old brown tent and you stole her heart.

"She told me about wading in the shallow river and you drying her feet afterward. That impressed her more than anything else. She said, 'He never said one impatient word to me.'

"You bathed her and she led you to a hay pile so you would not forget the experience of having her. Chet Byrnes, you lived a storybook life that day, didn't you?"

"Yes, I had one with her and now with you."

"I asked her if she had not been a widow would she have seduced you on that first day she met you."

"What did she say?" He shook his head amused. "I would never have asked her that."

"She replied, 'Even today I think so. I was riding a powerful horse in the clouds and I was in the arms of the man I loved from the first minute I saw him. To share my body with him was what I had to do. How else would he know me enough to make the effort to reunite us?' "

"It worked," he agreed. "I have never forked hay that I didn't recall those great moments we'd had."

"That is a storybook romance."

"No more than yours and mine. God gave her and me some lovely years together. But when we found each other it freed our souls. Life goes on and hand in hand we will continue. Our experience opened my eyes, I had found someone who loved me, and I loved her, and together we made good love. Let's pray?"

"Yes."

"Our Father, who art in heaven . . ."

# CHAPTER 18

Wedding day for Oleta and Salty. The big circus tent was up in case it rained. Cool air had slipped south and touched them. This setup, like all the ranch parties, had required lots of work and they expected many people. Everyone was dressed for the occasion. Ranch men wore starched white shirts and black pants, polished boots, and sombreros. Everyone was in a party mood and laughter rang across the yard.

The hardwood smoke that cooked the meat — beef, pork, and venison — shifted direction.

Ice cooled the tanks of draft beer and the lemonade in gallon glass jars. Sun tea waited in pitchers. Plus there was lots of spring water in buckets with dippers. Glass mugs were stacked on the side tables — the Preskitt Valley ranch waited with open arms for the big crowd coming for the wedding.

From Chet's seat on the porch swing he

saw the guests arrive and went to greet them. Sis and her two young boys were there. Sarge was on his way to Gallup with six hundred head of cattle.

Lucy and her three plus Shawn were there. May, Hampt, and their toddlers to babies were there. Tom and Millie attended the wedding, too. Chet's farm implement and mercantile folks attended. He knew the list was an arm long.

The ranch employees parked rigs, hitched horses on the picket lines, and fetched what the women had forgotten. The wedding came first and then the cutting of the creamy cake. The band struck up and the site turned into a square dance party. Daylight shut down early but the Chinese lanterns made it light enough to see by.

"How many of these have you sponsored?" Bo asked Chet, standing on the sidelines.

"I have no idea. We simply do them."

"Great parties. My wife and I always enjoy them. We meet people we didn't know and maybe never see again. The social event of the season, I call them."

"My ranch crew enjoys it as much as the town folks do."

"Oh, you should patent how to do it and sell it."

"Hey, what's happened? You haven't

bought a homestead for me in five months."

"More fools are outbidding me. We had a few liberal rain years. We have a dry one or two and there will be more ranches for sale."

"No ranches that I'd like to own are for sale?"

"I know of a lemon ranch in the valley."

"No. Things are sour enough now."

"With the railroad coming the land on top is selling. I understand you stole that place that Spencer runs over east?"

"We did okay. It is way too fancy for a working cow ranch. We call it Wagon Wheel Ranch."

"Will it work?"

"Oh yes, this year we will recover the cost of it."

"You are filling lots of those beef cattle shipments with your own now?"

"That crowds the market and there is not another that great to match it here yet."

"The train will be here?"

"Four years."

"Too late?"

"Yes. Too late."

The next morning a boy rode out from town with a letter and said he had to give it to Mr. Chet Byrnes. Through the messy party remains and trash that buried the yard the boy rode his skinny horse up to the house's back steps, and when the new house girl, Natalie, went down to get his letter, he coldly said, "You ain't Mr. Chet Byrnes. The man said to give it to no one but him."

Chet heard the boy's words and told him he'd be right down.

He thanked Natalie for trying to save him the climb and took the envelope. He sat on the step considering the barefoot boy and using his jackknife to slit the envelope open.

"You do this work regularly or is it a special-duty job?" he asked the youth.

"Mister, I do lots of things besides this."

"Thanks for the letter." Chet began to read it.

To Chet Byrnes:
The felon Burl Ralston has made several threats regarding you personally. He was found guilty last week of terroristic threatening and attempted murder by a jury. The state of Texas is sending officials here next week to transport him back to San Antonio for more trials. While he may be in jail for many years or even executed, his threats against you are very intense. His request for others to come kill you in his letters have been blacked out from his mail. We simply wanted to warn you about what you

might expect in the future.

The Yavapai County Sheriff
Department

Chet spoke to the boy. "Thank you very much. Thank who sent you. I am going to pay you a dollar for your services."

"They paid me."

"I am also going to pay you a dollar."

"You don't have a reply?"

"Tell them I said thanks for their information."

Chet put out his hand with the four quarters in it and dropped them into the boy's palm.

The messenger, without another word, reined his horse around and trotted off for town.

"Good news or bad?" Vance asked, joining him.

"Here, you can read it." He handed him the letter. Damn strange no one signed it. Simply *the Yavapai County Sheriff Office.*

"I have kept the night patrol on the headquarters that Raphael had."

"I know, but they don't know that and it was damn nice of someone there to warn me. But I'd bet the sheriff never authorized it. Through my years here those vaqueros have protected me and my family. Just tell them there might be intruders."

Vance nodded. "Some folks can't leave a dead deal alone, can they?"

"You are right. I am going to show Lisa the letter. Big mess to clean up here this morning."

"I was amused earlier. I said that to the men working and they said it was much better than the old days. They told me then the pews before were borrowed from area churches and had to be back there before the Sunday-morning services. It was much better now the ranch has their own."

Chet, amused, agreed.

"What did the letter say?" Lisa asked when he got upstairs.

He gave the note to her.

"Strange. The sheriff didn't sign it?"

"He didn't know they sent it. Some conscientious deputies wanted me to know that Ralston was still planning my demise."

"I believe that. I guess that gap can't be healed."

"No, it can't. But I am grateful at least some in the courthouse appreciate our efforts for law and order."

"When do we go to Hackberry?" Lisa asked.

"Tuesday. That'll give us a day to secure what we need."

"Both of your men are going?"

"Yes. We may be gone two weeks."

"That's fine. I saw Tad Newman is cooking and Billy Bob, who went with us to the North Rim, are also on your list."

"Things are slow enough at Tom's he can spare them. They know how we like things. Then later this fall we will slip off by stagecoach and go see JD and Bonnie."

"I enjoy traveling. You said there were no bargain land deals since the train is coming?"

"Bo thinks people have too much faith in the railroad's coming changing the economic culture of northern Arizona. I think it will take four years to reach here. You won't be able to go to California on it for several more years and people will realize this is a dry land with a small population and there are not many markets for the sand lizards and rattlesnakes we grow."

"Oh, that is funny. I know you, and I'll bet you'll find another perfect bargain like Wagon Wheel in the next six months."

"We may do that. I am looking."

She smiled and went to dress.

He did notice that morning between Julie and the new girl, Natalie, there was not the humor or fun that Oleta spread around every morning. Oh, they'd loosen up in time. Salty chose the right one to marry. Chet thought he'd better get moving. Jesus was down there, checking on things already.

He told his man about the letter, and Jesus laughed. "No 'dear Chet' or personal sign-off?"

"No."

"Well, it's good that we have friends. It's just, they can't tell us who they are."

Chet agreed and they went off to see how much was packed and what needed to be added.

"Great party last night."

"I thought so, too. Plenty of folks came. The wedding went well and they were off from an undisclosed hideout this morning for Oak Creek Canyon."

"My wife really enjoyed that place."

"Everyone has that I know about."

"You hear about the lion attack yesterday?"

"No. Where was it at?" Chet frowned at the notion.

"He was over at the west end of town. Snatched a young boy and started to carry him off. Two workers with shovels beat him off the boy and he is expected to live."

"He must be near toothless and couldn't catch a deer."

"Folks in town are upset."

"Good job for the sheriff to settle."
Jesus agreed.

They rolled north on Tuesday. One wagon
this trip, and Jesus drove it to the Verde
Ranch to pick up Tad, who drove it north
from there. Billy Bob appeared excited
about joining them. They pushed and
stopped on top of the rim on the north side
of the Verde. After supper, they all went to
sleep. Chet figured they wouldn't need a
night guard that isolated, and everyone
woke sleepy eyed.

"We ain't used to work yet," Cole complained.

While Tad and Lisa cooked breakfast they
loaded all they could and saddled the horses
for everyone. It went smoothly. No sign of
rain the night before so they never raised a
tent. In no time, they hit the road and
passed Robert and the sawmill without
stopping. By evening they were set up on
the ranch property past the stage stop facilities.

It was cool enough there to wear a denim
jumper or a blanket. A man in a business
suit came down and spoke to Chet.

His name was John Cosby. He was an of-
ficial, he said, with the Atchison Topeka
Santa Fe Railroad.

"Saved me a trip to Prescott. Is Mr. Emerson still your employee?"

"Yes, he's with me today."

"Good. I need to speak to both of you. But first let us talk — you and I."

"Fine. What do you need?"

"Well, my predecessor on this job obviously knew very little about running a stage line or telegraph wire and his idea to cut Mr. Emerson's wages was shortsighted. I saw right off why Emerson quit. But the man who cut his wages is no longer on our staff. What would it take, do you think, to get him to come back and run it again? We can see the rail laying taking many years more than we first anticipated or the men who were in charge then thought that it would. But they lived in castles and have no idea what is out here."

"Cole and I talked about that at the time."

"Well, we are being threatened by the federal government to lose our permit unless both the stage and the telegraph businesses are improved. See, the money for them came from Congress and they have an iron hand on it."

"So you need it fixed — now."

"I am not standing here because I like the thin air. Yes, now."

"I can't speak for Cole. But if I was Cole

I'd tell you to shove it."

"You don't know how serious I am. Could I hire you to convince him?"

"No. Cole is too good an employee for me to convince him to retake the job."

"May I talk to him?"

"Sure, it is a free country. He's past twenty-one. I can go find him."

"Can we go have supper someplace here?"

"We can eat at my chuck line. Come on."

"I wish to pay you —"

"No, I am not some broke cowboy. I can afford to feed you."

"I am sorry. I know you are a very successful rancher and connected to the U.S. Marshal's office in DC, but —"

"Just eat with us. I will introduce Cole Emerson to you as well."

"All right."

"Fine. Let's go back and I'll introduce you to everyone."

"I don't mean to be a burden —"

"Mr. Cosby, you are in Arizona now. I feed who I want."

"Come to DC and I will treat you."

"I doubt I'll ever go back there. I was certain I had my last kerchief out of my hotel room when I left."

"Many times, I wondered why I even took this job."

"Oh, how is that?"

"I was not born rich but like to live the style. You know what I mean?"

"Exactly. John Cosby, meet Cole Emerson."

The two shook hands and Cole tossed his head south. "You with them?"

"I am and I came here specially to talk to you, sir."

"I quit those cheap bastards a year and a half ago."

"Well, the stupid man who fired you is no longer with the railroad."

"He never fired me. He came, like some swaggering king, into my office and said, 'We're cutting your pay in half and if you don't improve this operation I will cut it that much again.' I told him where he could put it, took my things, and left."

"He no longer works for us. But you don't have to be a genius to drive by that facility and see how much it has gone downhill since the king ran you off."

"I have a job."

"I have a better one to offer you."

"I made over sixty thousand dollars doing it this year."

"You are lying. They don't pay big corporation leaders that much." He turned to Chet. "You paid him that much?"

"It was a windfall. We found a Spanish treasure and I split it with the men who were with us."

Cosby laughed. "Who else in this tent made that much money?"

Tad put the heaping platter of cooked steaks on the table and shoved his felt hat back on his head. "I did."

"What about you?" Cosby asked Billy Bob, standing there with a plate and silverware service for the man.

"I made that much. It's all in the Preskitt Bank, save for the twenty-nine dollars I give for a guitar."

Cosby, shaking his head, sat down in the camp chair. "What in the hell was in that Spanish treasure?"

"A bucket of rubies, a half bucket of emeralds, and, oh, forty gold bars and that much in free gold."

"Chet, you need any help?"

"No, not today."

"Cole, I can pay you forty thousand dollars a year on an ironclad ten-year contract to run the two businesses. We will have tracks to California from the coast by then and will have the railroad completed. That job hinges on those two companies breaking even or making money when you run them."

"I want two years to get it running again. Then time to make it better each year, with a fifty-thousand-dollar salary a year for the entire term of the contract."

Cosby stood up and stuck out his hand and they shook.

"Can Rocky come back up here with us?" Cole asked Chet.

Chet nodded. "Rocky wouldn't quit Val. I know that. Let's say grace, eat supper, and then we can talk business."

"Is that how you get those kinds of jobs, Jesus?" Lisa asked him.

He shook his head. "You see that mess down there we came by?"

She nodded.

"He may have a good-paying job but he's going to have to find some more damn good help."

Chet said, "Everyone bow their head. Our heavenly Father, we are gathered here in the pines. Forgive our sins, take care of all our people, and bless this food. Amen."

Cosby took a bite of his steak. "You need a job cooking under a roof, sir."

Tad grinned big. "Mister, I don't even need to work anymore. I wouldn't trade this outfit for the whole damn railroad."

They laughed.

"Great food."

"Thanks."

"You are his wife?" Cosby asked.

"I am Chet's wife."

"How did you get with him, if I may ask?"

"Oh, like a silly girl I ran off with some outlaws and Chet caught them in Colorado. He offered me a job as camp helper and a packhorse to ride back on. I took it and I have been working for him ever since."

They all laughed.

"She's telling you the truth," Chet said.

"I'm sorry. I have been laughing so hard I am crying. Now I can see how Cole ran a stage line and a telegraph wire so well that we bought it."

"How is that?" Chet asked him.

"He's just like you and her. He doesn't take too much seriously and still gets it done, right?"

"Lisa is not lying. We arrested those rich playboys who had raided one of Cole's stage stop stations and with two posses we had chased them down into the Four Corners country. They are in prison for ten years."

"Their parents have begged us to have them released," Cosby said.

Lisa put down her fork. "Don't let those sorry bastards out until the very last day. They hurt lots of people, including me, and didn't care about anyone they ran over or killed."

"I will see they serve their full sentence," he promised.

"John, I bet you never took an evening stroll and met such an outfit along the way, have you?"

"Chet, you have a neat outfit. Food is excellent and I have what I came for. Your ex–vice president."

Chet shook his head. "We just call them ranch foremen out here."

"No, I can see, from your wife on, that you have a helluva outfit even if the air is thin."

"You get better at breathing it the longer you stay."

"What is needed next, Cole?" Cosby asked him.

"Well, sir. I need to ride back down to the Quarter Circle Z and tell a short woman, she and that boy are moving back to Flagstaff. Is the telegraph working?"

"Fair."

"Damn, that ain't good enough." Cole chewed on his lower lip. "Can I borrow Spencer for six weeks, Chet?"

"Now we've got the rustlers in jail, I believe Fred can run the place for that long. If he will go along with it."

"He'll go along for a fee. Cosby. Spencer is the man strung it in such record time and he knows it. I believe with support he can get it running a lot quicker than anyone else."

"Sounds great. I will pay."

"Now I need to ask for one more person, Chet."

"He won't be back from his honeymoon until next Sunday." Under the lantern light Chet shook his head as if he was real disappointed about Cole's request.

"Salty Meeker is who can get the horses and coaches in line. What's wrong?"

"Who will take your place at that ranch?"

Cole shrugged. "Sarge may kill me. Cody Day, Tom's son-in-law."

"My sister might be madder at me than him if they lose him. He is the first guy Sarge ever trusted to move a herd to Gallup by himself."

"Who else do you have?"

"I guess Spud and his wife, Shirley. But then Lucy and Shawn will need help. I will find them someone. Cosby?"

"Yes, sir."

"I bet you right now, in two months those headquarters down the way won't look like a junkyard."

Cosby laughed. "I have never been around

cowboys before, but I know you aren't the ordinary ones. I can't believe all we've gotten done in a tent here tonight."

"Have you relieved your current management?" Cole asked.

"No, I wasn't sure I could hire you to come back with us."

"Save it for a few days. I am coming but I want to be right behind them going out the front door," Cole said.

"Probably the best thing. Will all of you keep it a secret?"

Everyone around the table nodded.

"Fine. They don't know who I am. They think I am an auditor. Those people have been sent here by the dozens trying to stop the losses but this operation has been a sieve. I saw the books they gave us when we bought the operation and you were in charge. It didn't take a genius to see the difference by comparison."

When Cosby rose to leave, Chet said, "Jesus, you and Billy Bob walk him back to his facilities. It's a dark night and Cole doesn't want anything to happen to him."

"I will be fine."

"No, you are in our land. A little precaution won't hurt. It is long ways out here between places, and further to police protection."

"Thanks. What will you do next?"

"Send Billy Bob out to tell my ranchers out west we will come another time. Turn around and head for home and resettle some things. I may go ask the man that strung the line if he'd join Cole on the telegraph business until it got going right."

"What will he charge?" Cosby asked.

"I am sure he would be expensive but getting it back on right is important, too."

"If he is that good, try five thousand a month for three months' work. Time is crucial."

Chet agreed that was a fair sum. "I am certain he would take it."

"Good. My dear, thanks for your hospitality. I want to see your home place someday."

"I'll be there. You would be most welcome."

"I am serious. And thanks, Cole. I'll be glad to have you in charge and know things will be getting straightened out."

Jesus and Billy Bob walked him back to the living quarters. Lisa and Chet told them good night. Plans were to be decided in the morning to lay out the future.

"He came out here to hire Cole." Lisa chuckled. "I about choked when Cole told him what he would take the job for."

"He may be losing that much or more

under this bunch he has in charge now. The federal government's involvement makes it important to a railroad. They count on them so much to get it built."

"I love Cole as a person. I hate to see him go back but he can make a fortune in those years. And do whatever he pleases in no time."

"Wild, isn't it?"

"Chet Byrnes, I love you so much and life is so exciting being your wife."

He smiled.

# CHAPTER 19

The first decision was for Billy Bob to take a letter to Lucy and Shawn. That letter explained what had happened, said it was all done in secret, and asked, if they could spare Spud and Shirley, then to send them to headquarters. Chet had a ranch for them to run. He went over things with the young man taking the message. It was two and half days' hard riding for him to get out to Hackberry. Chet told him to be careful of strangers and keep going. To buy meals instead of cooking them but to be aware that eating places were miles apart out there. To rest up after he got there and then come back to the Preskitt Valley ranch.

Billy Bob rode out. Later Cosby came by. Cole was ready to go south and shook his hand. They decided to meet back there in ten days, ready to take over the stage line and telegraph operation. They would use one of the empty houses that Chet owned for Cole to move into up in Flagstaff, before he took over. He would get Salty and Oleta over there and get him into the stagecoach business.

Jesus, Chet, and Lisa were going to see about Spencer taking the three-month job working on the wire to straighten that system out. They took bedrolls and food like raisins and peanuts to eat on the trail.

"Fred's wife, Josey, is having a baby in the middle of that," Lisa said when they finally got on horseback and rode east.

"We can move her to our house a month early. Those boys will work for him. We'll do whatever we can to work that out," Chet said.

Tad was taking the buckboard back to the Verde Ranch and shook his hand when they parted.

Two days' hard pushing to get to the Wagon Wheel and a slow, chilly, light rain was falling when they reached it. Jesus told them to dismount at the front door and he'd put the horses in the barn stalls.

Fred opened the door and looked for more people.

"Jesus is putting the horses in the barn. There are only three of us."

"Okay. Come in. The rest are in the kitchen."

"What did we do wrong now?" Spencer said, hugging Lisa. A completely different guy from the man they'd found several weeks earlier, a man who'd been plagued by rustlers.

"Did you get the house girl married?" Lucinda asked.

"Last Saturday, but we have more plans. Everyone, sit down. Jesus will be here shortly."

They sat around the long dining table, and the large fireplace had a warm fire going.

"The railroad hired Cole to run the stage line and telegraph company again. There are some problems in the wire. Cole said you knew more about it than anyone. I know you are happy here. But Cole needs you to cover them and get it all straight. The railroad is willing to pay you five thousand dollars a month for you to find the weak spots from New Mexico to California and you have three months to do it. I told them I could spare you for that long and Fred could run the ranch."

"Wow, that is lots of money but it will be winter soon."

"It will give you some money for emergencies with your ranch wages. I'll keep paying you and all. It isn't finding gold but it isn't bad."

"When do they need to know?"

"Within a week."

"Honey, that would give us a healthy bank account. Tell him yes."

"Fred, if you need help when he's gone telegraph Flagstaff. You can reach Cole and he will have men up and down the line who could come help. The last month we will move Josey closer in, perhaps to Flagstaff, and have her stay with Val and be near a doctor. Just in case."

Fred thought that should be safe enough. Josey agreed.

"What kind of problems are they having in the line?" Spencer asked.

"I think connections. Loose wire in places."

"I will need some pole-climbing rigs and some Navajo boys to help."

"Find them and have them ready to be on the payroll ahead of your going to work. Make a list of equipment you will need. In two weeks, Cole will be in Flagstaff and in charge."

"Pretty damn nice of you to find us a job while we work for you."

"Listen, you guys are making these ranches work. You know Cole quit them when they walked in and cut his pay in half. Well, that dumb guy is gone now. They made Cole a helluva deal for ten years to run it, which fits what I thought. They'd be that long getting to California. The last years of that term they will be building tracks east from California. The government told them to fix the stage and the telegraph service. They can't afford the government to be mad at them."

Spencer chuckled. "Hope it's an easy winter. But I get it done and I get my money?"

"You will get three payments and all your expenses."

"Damn. Having that much money means anything ever happens to me, she will have a nest egg. I never worried about it, being single. But with her and the kids I have to worry about that now. Damn good deal. You three staying a day or so?"

"No. We're going to Sis's tomorrow and then home. I have to find a man to run the ranch Cole runs."

"Who's that?"

"I am going to try Spud and Shirley. He's a hard worker. Shawn taught him a lot about handling cows and calves."

Spencer smiled. "I thought it might be Tom's son-in-law, Cody."

"He is the first guy ever pleased Sarge enough to let him be the boss of the cattle drives. It gives Sarge every other month off. I'll raise his wages. Give him a few years to get used to the role, and I'll need another foreman."

"Hey, we love it. Getting those damn rustlers out of our hair made Fred and me a lot easier to live around."

"Amen," Lucinda said. Josey agreed, too.

Next morning, they rode for the Windmill. It was cloudy and the trip took a long day's ride. It was after sundown when they rode into the yard. Dogs barked and lights came on.

A cowboy saw who it was and met them, then took their horses to put them up.

"Back again?" Sis asked.

She fixed the three of them some food and Chet told her about Cole going back to work running the stage and telegraph deal for ten years. Sarge was off to Gallup with the Navajo cattle.

In the morning, Cody came up and was surprised at who was there. Chet and Cody had a short, private talk — Chet promised him a hundred-dollar-a-month raise starting in January and thanked him for the job he did.

Cody about choked thanking him. Chet knew he'd made that boy's day. Good enough.

Next day they rode on to the big house on the Verde Ranch and after dark woke Victor, Reba, and Chet's son Adam. They'd been at Salty's wedding and also knew about Cole's secret plans. Lisa was too tired to talk and she went upstairs to bed.

Jesus said he'd leave early in the morning and for Chet to get a ranch hand to ride with them up the mountain. He was anxious to be in his own bed.

So a cowboy named Earl rode up the mountain with Chet and Lisa, and they were home.

They ate a meal Julie fixed, took a hot bath, and went to bed before sundown.

Damn glad to be home.

# CHAPTER 20

Chet was up before the sun and grateful to be there. He dressed, went downstairs, and the girls jumped up from the table.

He laughed. "I spooked you. Been alone so long I scared you?"

"It has been very quiet while you were gone. What do you want to eat?" Julie asked him.

"Mexican omelet, some German fried potatoes, and thin rings of fried onions with them. Plus, some coffee and hot biscuits."

"Yeah, Natalie, our breakfast customer is back."

"Glad you missed me." He chuckled as they carried on like it was parade day.

His first day back he talked to Vance and found out everything was going good on the ranch and on Cole's as well. Billy Bob would be getting up to the Hackberry Ranch and in less than a week Spud and his wife would be down there looking over the ranch next door and deciding if he wanted to run it.

Chet took Lisa to town to shop with a ranch hand riding along in the buckboard. A precaution he had promised to keep. His replacement of Cole as his other guard would not be easy to fill. His mind was searching and weighing the people he knew who might take the job. Someone that he could really trust, but none stood out as a real candidate for the position.

While in town, he spoke to Bo and told him about the deal that was about to open for his ex-employee Cole. He needed a real sharp man who understood lots about other things. Perhaps wasn't married so he could leave on a minute's notice.

Bo had no individual person for him to pick.

Tanner at the bank was in the same boat as Bo about him finding a man to take Cole's place. The possible candidates both had little children, and one of them might not like the travel. The end result was no name came to be seriously thought about that day. Chet drove the guard and Lisa home in the last light of sundown.

At the ranch, a boy took the horses to put them up and told Chet there was a man over by the house waiting to talk to him.

Chalk, his guard for the day, stopped Lisa and asked her to stand there until they knew who this stranger was.

"Señora, we don't know his name. One minute please."

She agreed to stand there. Chalk caught up with Chet. The man rose in the last shadowy light of day and removed his hat.

"Chet Byrnes?"

"Yes."

"I am Johnny Forge. We've never met but I was told you hired cowboys."

"Where you from, Johnny?"

"Denton, north Texas, sir. I'm not riding the chuck line looking for work. I have some good reference letters and I want a permanent job. They tell me you are one of the best ranch operators in this Territory."

"Lisa, come on. It is all right. He's looking for work. Thanks, Chalk."

"*Sí. Muchas gracias, señor.*" And he was gone in the night.

"Forge, we've had some problems and that is why we are being careful."

"I completely understand. I can come back —"

"No need. The lights are on up these stairs. The girls will soon have food cooking and no doubt you have not eaten. We can talk up there."

"I'm grateful for your hospitality. Thank you, sir."

"No *sir* here. I am Chet and the lady ahead is my wife, Lisa. We simply live here with our people. You have come a long way?"

"Yes — I came from north Texas. Took my time but never realized it was such a long, dry ways out here."

Chet laughed and held the door for both Lisa and Forge to enter. "On a map, it doesn't look that far."

"Not on the map. Right."

"Have a seat. Ladies, this is Johnny Forge."

The busy girls bowed toward him and went back to their preparations.

"This is some place you have here."

"Lisa and I enjoy it. I guess you know I left Texas several years ago to avoid a family war and bought a place north of here in the Verde Valley. I moved my family here and it was a long way. How did you hear about me?"

"A friend of mine, Sam Oliver, mentioned you one time. He knew you from the trail drives to Kansas. I was curious. He said you came out here and built an empire in the jumping cactus."

"I remember Sam and those trips to Abilene, Kansas. That was not all peaches

231

and cream, either."

"None of them were. I took some to Dodge City later than that."

"Never made it to Dodge. I was out here before they moved those railheads. What did Sam say about me?"

"He said I should go out there and meet you. Maybe you had room for a jingle bob boss."

"You have no family?"

"More or less why I came. While I was on my last cattle drive to Dodge my wife and children were — murdered on my small ranch."

"Oh," Lisa said. "That is horrible. Did you get the killers?"

"The law did, and they were hung. One of them got away. Conroy Miller. No one knows where he went. I put out all kinds of rewards. Looked all over. He left no easy trails. And living and sleeping in that ranch house brought back too many memories. The ride out here was enough of a challenge to occupy my mind."

Breakfast was served despite the time of day. Scrambled eggs, fried potatoes and onions, crisp thick-cut bacon, biscuits, and flour gravy with fresh-perked hot coffee.

"Johnny, I can't even imagine the deep shock to come home to that. Any reason why they did it?" Lisa asked him.

"They were simply that mean is all I could figure out of it, ma'am. They were drunk. I think they knew I was out in Kansas with a herd. My wife was pr—" His eyes were wet, and he shook his head and pursed his lips.

Lisa reached over and clasped his arm. "We don't need to hear the rest. We understand — I am so sorry."

He blew his nose in an old kerchief. And he nodded in agreement. "So am I."

"Excuse me," Chet said, putting down his napkin. He went to the back door and whistled loud.

An armed guard with a rifle came to the bottom of the stairs. "Have someone put that man's two horses up for the night. Water and feed them. He's staying with us."

"*Sí, señor.* No problem."

"*Gracias.*" Chet went back in the kitchen to sit down and eat.

"You didn't have to do that," Johnny said.

Chet smiled. "Ask my wife. I do lots of things I don't have to do."

Lisa agreed, smiled, and then shrugged like it was normal.

Both men laughed with her.

"When we get through," she told him, "the girls will have ready a hot bath upstairs. There will be soap, towels, and clean clothes for you to wear. Leave the rest of your clothes there. I am sorry. I do have good help but none to scrub your back. There are some long-handle brushes in there."

Amused by her comments, he smiled. "Most generous of you."

"The bedroom across the hall will be your room tonight. Be sure you are wide-awake in the morning. It is a long way from the top to the bottom of those stairs. A few guests have tumbled down them. It is not a nice trip."

"I will be wide-awake when I descend them."

"Good."

"We can talk more about the job deal in the morning. The girls will have coffee ready shortly after six a.m."

"Why, this meal, a bath, and a bed is worth the whole trip."

"I know it isn't bad, but it is not worth you coming this far." She chuckled.

"It is, Lisa, when you didn't expect to even be considered two hours ago."

"I guess it would be."

Chet smiled and began to tell Johnny about his wife. "I found her in a patch of sagebrush in Colorado. Told me she was broke, had no horse or way to get home."

"You did?"

"He told me under no uncertain terms that for an extra packhorse he had for me to ride, I had to help the camp crew set up, take down, repack, and make meals. If I didn't work hard he'd ride off and leave me at the very next stop."

"You must have done it. You're here."

"She made a hand, but back then my second wife was alive. Elizabeth meant nothing to me."

"I hadn't had a bath in weeks. My clothes were rags and my mind was barely working."

"We are going to bed and will continue the story line tomorrow."

"Thanks. I have to finish this coffee. It is so good."

"Arbuckle's."

"Señor, there is no rush. We have more coffee," Julie said.

"Thank both of you. Good night." Johnny rose to tell them that.

Then he sat back down and the two of them left him with the house girls.

At the foot of the stairs, Lisa stopped and looked back to the lighted kitchen door. "Hmm. He might get his back scrubbed, after all."

"You never can tell." Chet laughed quietly. Forge was a nice-looking guy.

235

# CHAPTER 21

Morning came early. Chet dressed and went downstairs. He found his guest in the kitchen conversing with the two girls and sipping fresh coffee. Its aroma filled the room, but he noticed that both girls looked polished for this early in the day. He sat down and Natalie brought him a steaming cup and took his breakfast order.

"Sleep good?" Johnny asked.

"No one had to rock me to sleep."

"The girls were telling me about your foreman Cole. Can you tell me about him and this giant job?"

"Cole was one of my right arms. A few years ago, a rich man came to my sister's ranch house to meet with us about me becoming a partner in building a stage line from Gallup to California over the Marcy Road. I was busy enough but that man knew we could do that better than anyone he could hire. So I put Cole in charge. It was not easy but we got the stage stops set up. They raided and burned them down to discourage us. That was why I chased down Lisa's bunch way up there. They were some of the ones that did it.

"We arrested them and brought them back and, despite their rich parents' fancy lawyers and money, they are serving long prison terms. She had soon discovered that boy she went with on that journey was not going to marry her. Lisa came back here, worked for my second wife, Elizabeth, taught the Spanish children enough English so they were able to enroll in the public school nearby, and took over running this house when the lady who did that died. Lisa married one of my foremen and later he was shot by outlaws in a raid on the east ranch. Next thing, my wife died of cancer very suddenly and Lisa and I got married."

"Arizona, despite your successes, has not been easy on you."

"No, Johnny, I have had some tough patches to get over."

"Back to Cole. He is taking that job back over?"

"Yes. My business partner and I knew we had some time before the rails came. But when it finally arrived up there the stage operation would be dumped. The telegraph would prosper but we owned both so when they started bugging us to sell the wire to them, I explained to my partner to sell them both. That way we would not have a dead horse. The railroad knew the telegraph would really cost them much more when it was on a train track, so the big corporation bought both companies. It was making good money when they bought it. Their man in charge at the time told Cole his pay was cut in half — Cole said, 'Shove it in your ass' and left."

Johnny laughed and agreed.

"At one time after he left, they had six men trying to do what Cole did and they were losing money every day. They still may have that many. Don't say a word — the chief officer for the railroad jumped us going through Flagstaff and he made a wonderful deal with Cole to take it back over on a ten-year contract."

"It sounds exciting."

"It has been but I lost Cole again as my sidekick and guard."

"Chet, I am looking for work."

"Obviously. I may send you out to the Hackberry Ranch to help Shawn McElroy and be his number two man and learn our ideas about ranching."

"That's what I need — a chance."

"Or we may start you down at the Verde. Tom has two things you need to see. One is a blacksmith shop that makes barbwire and windmills for our ranches. He also has a great herd of purebred Herefords we are mighty proud of."

"I bet you are."

"He was my first foreman when we had to take the ranch back from a crooked foreman who wouldn't let us have it."

"Man, you have had problems."

"A big share of them, but we rose from the ashes."

"Where can I start, then?"

"You never asked what I'd pay you."

Johnny smiled and shrugged. "I figure you'd know what you paid folks right off."

"I do. Thirty bucks a month and I'll feed your two horses."

"I'll accept that. And, Chet Byrnes, if I don't make the grade, fire me."

"Tell the boys to saddle two ranch horses. We'll go to Tom's first. You have lots to look at."

"Girls, my wife is sleeping in this morning. She needs the rest so tell her Johnny and I went to see Tom. We will be back."

Going down the stairs he'd noted that Johnny still wore a black-powder-and-ball .45 on his hip. "I have something else I need to do. I see my foreman Vance coming."

"Morning," Vance said to them. "See you met him. He and I talked some yesterday. I encouraged him to wait for you."

"We finally made it back. Vance, he needs a cartridge model .45 from our armory to wear and a box of shells."

"I'll get him one. And two saddle horses?"

"Yes. We're going to meet Tom. The boys put up his horses so there is a saddle that's his."

"They can find it. I'll tell them and get the gun for him."

"You like those model Colts?" he asked Chet.

"When Cole, Jesus, and I got my nephew out of jail and some crooked deputies tried to take us, we had a real gunfight and we won with those Colts. They are not breathing today."

"I heard it was too expensive."

"The cost is nothing if, when it's over, you are still breathing."

Johnny laughed. "Thanks, then."

He carefully loaded five fresh bullets from the small cardboard box of cartridges into the new pistol, made sure the empty chamber was under the hammer, and closed the side gate. "Nice gun."

When the boys brought the horses, he put

his extra bullets in the saddlebags.

"They won't fly out. I'd leave mine un-buckled so I can get to them in case I need some."

"That makes sense."

They swung into their saddles and headed for the gate.

"Does this horse buck?" Johnny asked.

"Cold morning, he might. Old man down in Texas told me, as a boy, any horse he ever owned who didn't buck a little wasn't worth his salt."

"He probably was right, too. Tell me, how did you got this neat setup you have here?"

"My first wife was married to an army officer when her father bought this place. Her husband got shot and killed — I never remember the details. Marge came out to Arizona and was living here when I met her. She paid all my bills. Guess she thought, after we met, that I was broke. I had to make her stop that and take my money. At the time, I was committed to a woman in Texas. I told her so, but we kept going places and being friends. My nephew was with me — he was about fourteen. He'd been a problem to his mother, my brother's widow, so I took him along.

"We were headed back to Texas. Stage robbers stopped us fifteen miles south of here that night. They took him as hostage. I took a stage horse out of harness to ride bareback and borrowed a rifle and went after them.

"I caught them in camp the next dawn. I shot all but one of them and asked him where the boy was at."

"He acted tough and said, 'At that first canyon on the right we cut his throat and threw him in it.' Well, I filled him with the rest of the bullets in that gun. Took one of their best saddle horses and rode back there — it was getting to be daylight and I found him deep in that canyon — dead.

"Out of my mind, I carried him up to the road. A posse met me at the road and offered to take him. I said no. I guess Marge heard about it and arrived to help. We put him in the back of her buckboard and left. That woman saved my life, handled his funeral. All my family was still in Texas. I had no idea how they were getting along — but she knew I had promised a woman in Texas I'd come back for her. She was okay with that. I went back to Texas and that woman couldn't move her mother and father, they were so bad off health-wise. So she stayed there.

"I brought all of my family out on the Fort Worth–Denver Railroad to the end of the tracks by railcar. Horses, wagons, and all we brought along, and we drove across New Mexico and Arizona on the Marcy Road. Took the cutoff to Preskitt and settled on the lower ranch, where we are going today. Marge was there waiting.

"She liked jumpers. She'd rode them all her life in competition. And she was good at it. I wanted to see the high country, and she offered to go see it with me. My sister said that I would ruin her reputation, so we got married. Her dad gave us that ranch for a wedding present."

"Wow. Neat gift. I love this place."

"I did, too. We had a son and she went back to jumping. She always wanted to jump higher. I warned her. Did no good. She had a wreck, broke her neck — died — and I had to destroy the horse. Victor and his wife are raising Adam down there on the Verde. Victor runs the farm operation down there. Another time I will tell you about wife number two."

"No one handed you much of this on a plate, then, did they?"

"I have made most of what I have from cattle sales to the four Navajo subagencies at Gallup, who I ship six hundred large steers or cows to every month. They bring forty-eight hundred dollars a month. Snow, drought, or heat we deliver them on time and send them good beef."

"That's quite a sale. I mean, I have been to Dodge and even Wichita with big herds but not that many head every month."

"Cattle we can't supply we buy locally at a fair price."

"How many ranches do you have?"

"Nine."

"Some deeded?"

"Most of them are deeded. My land man has bought several homesteads. We fence them then cut and stack the hay."

"Thanks. I am getting in on the whole history of this."

He introduced Johnny to Tom and then they met Victor. His wife served them lunch and then they went by the blacksmith shop. Johnny shook his head at them making barbwire. He'd never seen that much speed in a barbwire plant before in his life.

A steam engine powered the operation.

Victor said, "I am getting a steam-driven tractor this winter and a thrashing machine for our barley crop."

Before they left Chet told Tom that he was sending Johnny down there to learn all about his part of the ranch.

Tom agreed and they shook hands.

His foreman turned to Chet. "Is Cole

really going to take that job?"

"He never told me anything different. He wants Salty when he gets back from the honeymoon. Spencer is going to fix the telegraph line on a contract. Fred said he'd make it all right over there while he was gone. I sent for Spud and Shirley to take Cole's place. I think Shawn and Lucy can get help over there. Or I will find them some."

"He's shorter than Toby but he's a worker, too."

Chet laughed. "Johnny will be your shadow for three months."

Johnny nodded. "Tom, I came clear out here to forget some things that happened. My wife and children were murdered while I was taking cattle to Dodge City last year. I appreciate the chance you and Chet have given me to start over."

"Fine. I am glad to have you."

They rode back to the top ranch and Chet answered questions.

"I bet Victor gets busy with a steam tractor and a thrashing machine. There is lots of farm acreage up and down that valley back there. I see why he wanted one."

"But the closest place they can deliver it is off a train in Tucson and they will come up here like a slug crossing your yard."

"I'll bet on Victor. He's a go-getter, isn't he?"

"All my men are."

"All right, tell me about Julie in the kitchen."

"She was raised on this place. Her father is a vaquero and she can read, write, and cook."

"I knew she was not stupid." He laughed.

"Several in that family came up from Mexico to work for my old foreman Raphael. They are great ranch hands. Some tough outlaws came up here one night to kill me. The vaqueros turned out, shot some, chased down the rest, and hung them all. They buried all the ones they shot at the ranch and no one knew who hung the rest."

"How many were there in the gang?"

"I bet a dozen. None got away."

"I may be lucky to be alive."

"That vaquero who was riding guard with us last night didn't know you and he stopped Lisa before she got too close."

"I heard him."

"I had told Vance there might be some trying to get us. But he obviously checked you out."

The lights were on in the kitchen when they gave the boys their horses down in the yard. After they washed up and climbed the stairs, Natalie showed up in the lighted doorway — hands on her hips.

"Don't show that new man he can come in this late and still get a meal."

Both men put their hats on their heads and turned. She caught Chet's arm. "Get back in here, both of you. Lisa told me to say that."

"I imagine she did," Chet said. Then Lisa ran over, welcomed Johnny, and kissed Chet.

"Johnny, did he wear you out today?"

"No, ma'am. It damn sure was interesting."

# CHAPTER 22

At breakfast Cole came by and the girls fed him and their other two regular customers. Chet introduced the two men.

"Nice to meet you, Johnny. How did you do?" Cole asked Chet.

"I hired Spencer for five thousand a month, like you offered. He is getting some of the Navajos who helped him build it the first time, and he will have a list of needs to start out."

"I am sure he can fix those problems. I need to get two good men for him to train at that."

"Yes."

"Your wife told me to expect Salty and Oleta, who get back here Sunday."

"He will be here. He's dependable."

"I know that. I want to get up there and try to find some good help. They cut back on those boys' wages so much they lost all the good ones I had working for me. They may be cheaper but I never saw so many wrecked coaches as they have piled up there in their yard at Flagstaff."

"We all knew they bit their own hand when they ran you off."

"They never ran me off. I quit."

Johnny laughed.

"I'd say Cole is high enough today about the pending job to bite nailheads off."

Johnny agreed.

"My wife told me I was crazy to go back."

"You are, but their pay will overcome that."

"I can only imagine, from all the wrecked coaches they hauled in there stacked up, how many they've crashed, huh?"

"It will be interesting."

"I am wound up. Wish I knew more about the books. They may not be right."

"Trying to hide losses, huh?"

"It must be pretty bad. Cosby wasn't down here looking for me for his health. All the problems he must be having getting track laid back in New Mexico and him hanging around Flagstaff."

"He may be doing one thing at a time?"

"I think that's his plan," Cole said.

"I understand part of this," Johnny said. "You two and a rich man set it up and then sold it to the railroad?"

"My partner and I started with the stage-coach business. He knew nothing about it but folks were making money hauling gold, mail, and money shipments as well as passengers. He came to us to set up those stage stops on the Marcy Road. We bought some used coaches and buckboards to make the four-hundred-mile run from Gallup to the Colorado River crossing.

"We had lots of opposition. One of his own men was working for the competition to stop us."

"Four hundred miles?"

"Yes. That's how long it is across there. He knew I was getting along with the Navajo, and their land has to be crossed."

"Had you ever run a company that big before?" Johnny asked Cole.

"No. But the boss man here wasn't worried. I was, but Chet told me not to worry, that I can always come back to him and ride guard. When I left the company, it was making several hundred thousand dollars a year and we had the telegraph wire humming. They were afraid not to buy it. If they didn't then it would've cost a lot more later."

Chet said, "I told Hannagan to make them buy the stage line, too. Railroads were closing down stage lines all over and a close-out auction would have made it tough to get bids on that stuff."

Cole laughed. "This big, fat vice president came in my office smoking a big cigar and said, 'Boy, I'm cutting your pay in half. You make too damn much money.'

"I stood and told him I was no damn boy. That I would not take a cut in pay and he could have the whole thing lock, stock, and the barrel."

"What did he say then?"

"I don't think he thought I'd quit. I didn't care. I took my things and left.

"The man who secured horses for me quit that day, too. So did the telegraph man. The man in charge hired more folks — people I'd never have hired, but he didn't know the difference. I heard all the complaints and I expected management to do something sooner. But big companies, they say, have that problem — not acting quick enough to see what is wrong clear out in Arizona."

"What will you do for help?" Johnny asked.

"Pay them a better wage. Worry about them on and off the job. Make them family, like we do on the ranches Chet owns."

"I can see that. What outfit ever paid for a worker's wedding and honeymoon?"

"The Quarter Circle Z." He paused. "I wasn't his first cowboy, but close to it. We set out to deliver that first herd to Gallup. I wanted to work for him. He wasn't some lazy guy who slept in and didn't do anything to improve his herd. Chet was a man on the move. He sold the Navajo agency six hundred head a month. The last bunch handling this deal never got the cattle to the agencies on the day designated and those people had to come a long ways to camp out and wait. One person told Chet the cattle that were delivered were so thin they could read a newspaper through them."

Amused, Johnny shook his head. "And the two businesses, stage and telegraph, were making money?"

Chet nodded. "We made half a million dollars the second year."

"Then they bought it?"

"You bet, and the good help quit. They cut corners and wages until all the good workers were gone. Lost business. It got so bad the government told them to fix it or else."

"Good luck. And thanks a lot for taking me on."

"Glad to have you, Johnny. We always need a good man."

Having finished talking to Chet and Cole, Johnny, leading his packhorse, rode off to go to work at the Verde Ranch.

"He'll make a hand," Cole said.

Chet agreed and they went into the living room to talk. "Are you going to have some time to ride the line with me and make sure we are doing all we can?"

"You need me?"

"I can damn sure use you if you can spare me the time. I'll pay my two guards seventy dollars a month. You pay them a little extra, but only for the days we work on the stage line."

"Fair enough. I can hire you."

"No. Pay the men trailing me around. Then no one can complain about me."

"As soon as Salty gets back I want to move up there."

"How many wagons will you need?"

"Eight. Val has added to her stuff since she's been down here."

"Vance can handle that. Things are slow here for now."

"Where can I find a good accountant? One thing worries me. Figures don't lie, but liars don't figure."

"There won't be many out here to pick from. I'd bet Cosby could find you one back East that would like to fish and hunt who'd move out here and do that job."

"Damn good idea. Thanks. What are you doing next?"

"Kind of waiting to talk to Billy Bob when he gets back from Hackberry."

"Oh yeah. You had him take word to Spud and see if he wanted to run my ranch."

"Vance told me he'd handle that one, too, until I got someone. It being so close."

"Good idea. Hey, hay sales. I don't know where they buy theirs, but Toby has lots of hay to sell, doesn't he?"

"He's three hundred miles from the last station in Arizona. Unless they're robbing you, we couldn't compete."

"That's right. I am thinking about everything. Hal Bowers was my horse buyer. You haven't seen him since he quit them, have you?"

"No. But I bet we can find him. I'll send out some letters. He may be back in Fort Worth."

"Who is that auctioneer who holds those stage line closeout sales?"

"He still mails me bills. The last one is in on my desk."

"I'll go get it. He might be a cheap way to buy used coaches."

"It isn't the cost to buy them. It's the freight to get them here."

"Right, I recall that. I've been looking in every corner for new ideas to save money. Didn't I hear you bought a steam tractor and thrashing machine?"

"It is ordered. Victor takes delivery of it in Tucson sometime this spring. Then he has to drive it up here."

"How fast will it go?"

"Smooth road, about fifteen miles an hour but they turn over easy so unless it is smooth, only five or so."

"Does it have brakes coming over the steep mountains?"

"It says they do and we can use a belt on it and saw lumber. We can use it, can't we?"

"Sure. And pump water?"

"That, too."

"Be handy as a pocket on a shirt. I'll go back up there and help Val."

"Thanks for coming by. I won't see much of you unless I go to Flagstaff, will I?"

"Damn quit talking like that. Money ain't everything."

"It helps a lot, though." Cole left him for his own place.

After he'd gone, Chet read the *Miner* back issues.

Lisa came in and told him they had lunch ready. He thanked her.

Later in the day Billy Bob made it back. Chet went out to welcome him and the couple he brought back.

His messenger waved his old felt hat. "I

brought them, Chet."

He hugged Shirley and shook Spud's hand. "You did good."

Spud looked around. "Where is our place at?"

"South a few miles. A big two-story brick house. You two will like it."

Shirley's eyes almost bugged out. "Two-story brick?"

"And Cole is going back in and run that stage-telegraph deal again?"

"Oh, he is going to run it, but it is a mess."

"Billy Bob had never seen the place where Cole lived?" she asked.

"No, we bought it a while back. Leveled some land and have some artesian wells to irrigate alfalfa. Those girls will have food fixed. Wash up and come up in the kitchen."

"Chet, we are so dirty. We have been riding for days."

"Shirley, eat some lunch. You can go upstairs and take a bath after that."

"You are the boss. Come on, guys. I am starved."

Everything went great. Shirley and Lisa hit it off. Spud made them laugh about his version of the trip down there. Things were going smoothly at Hackberry. Shawn had several guys capable enough to handle his job. And Lucy was going to have another baby.

After they ate, had baths, changed into clean clothes taken out of the bundles on the packhorses, which the ranch boys had unloaded for them, they hopped in two buckboards and ran for the other place.

When Shirley saw the two-story house, she began crying. "I can't live in that house."

"You damn sure can, sister. You are as good as any woman in this world. Quit crying."

They met Cole's wife, Valerie, Chet's son Rocky, and Cole. Neither Spud nor his wife were very tall, and standing inside the doors on the polished floors at the foot of two winding stairs, they looked like lost kids to Chet.

But he knew in time they'd love it.

He found a chair while they took the tour, led by Valerie. Still lots for him to get done but they had the time. In no time, the short man would finish straightening out the entire ranch. Cole had it all going and Spud would finish it.

They were back for supper, and Lisa gave them bedrooms, including Billy Bob, who was going to sleep in the barn but she stopped him.

Things were going well. Salty came back

with Oleta, and Chet told him he needed him to help Cole. Salty agreed it would be a good opportunity for him, and Oleta wouldn't care. The housing up there was much better than the casa they'd had to live in on the ranch.

The overloaded wagons wagged their way north. Lisa found lots for Valerie and Oleta to take with them to their new residences. Chet kissed his wife good-bye and took off after the wagons that had left a couple hours earlier. He knew he would catch up, knowing going down the hill would slow them down. He planned to get some of Victor's big draft horse teams to help them up the steep road on the north side of the valley the next day.

It all worked out fine. Three days later they made Flagstaff and were on the ranch-owned property. In the sunset, wearing his businessman suit, the railroad president strolled in their midst. Cole introduced him as Mr. Cosby.

He even lent them a hand unloading.

Chet, Cole, and Cosby were talking during a break they took.

Cosby said, "The wire was down three hours today. How it got repaired, I don't know."

"It may take a month to get it all checked

out but Spencer can fix it so it will not do that. We ran for days with no problems when I had it before."

"I understand, but what a waste to have equipment and you have to repair it all the time."

"Come back in a month. It will work or I'll know why."

"Cole, that is why I hired you."

"I want the sharpest accountant I can find. Chet said you might have a person, somewhere, that works for you and likes to hunt deer, elk, and antelopes. He can fish down in Oak Creek Canyon. This isn't New York or Chicago but it is a hunter's paradise. He can do that and work on the books."

"Brilliant idea. I will find him and send him to you."

"Tomorrow we sweep the place clean?"

"Eight a.m. You must be ready?"

"Exactly."

To start with, Ivy McKinney, the manager, didn't show until ten a.m., but they were ready for him and sent him packing. Cole told the current employees, after McKinney was gone, they had jobs as long as they worked hard, were on time, and did things correctly.

"You must be at your places when the

clock strikes eight. People waited this morning for you. I won't stand for it. People who schedule coaches, meet in my office in ten minutes. Thank you. This man, here, is my right arm, Salty Meeker. If I am not here he knows what to do. And thank you, Mr. Cosby, for all you have done for me and the railroad."

Chet and Cosby kind of faded. Cole knew what he had to do. Billy Bob and the women were getting things settled in the first house, and Tad had come along to cook.

To the evening meal Cosby brought two bottles of champagne and some bottles of sarsaparilla. Tad had found some really good beef he'd cooked in the oven at Cole's house, along with some yeast rolls. The gals found an assortment of glasses to use and they toasted his first day.

Chet sat drinking his sarsaparilla, agreeing they had set Cole up well to run it and that he had had a wonderful day. He and Lisa were riding home with Billy Bob to the Verde Ranch, then on home the third day.

# Chapter 23

Someone had gone after the mail and had it stacked on the dining table with the back issues of the *Miner* newspaper. Lisa found them and told Chet there was a letter postmarked from Kanab, Utah, for him. He took the envelope and slit it open with his sharp pocketknife.

She leaned over. "Who sent it?"

"Rory Lincoln at Joseph Lake."

"What's it say?"

"I am reading it."

"Fine, tell me later. I am going to talk to the girls."

"No, stay here. This is a very tough letter and you need to hear it."

"What happened?"

" 'Dear Chet, I am sorry I have to write you this very bad news. Someone murdered the entire Meadows family. They shot him six or more times. They had her tied on the bed and must have raped her — it was a horrible sight. They cut the two children's throats ear to ear. It had happened a few days before anyone found them, and they rushed to get me. There was no way to get the law to look at the crime scene. I wrote the Yavapai County sheriff about the crime and I know he won't send anyone up here at this late date. They needed to be buried.

" 'I wrote Michael's brother, too. The killers had tried to burn the cabin to hide the crime but the fire went out. I have few clues but if you had time —' "

By then Chet had to hold up his sobbing wife and pulled out a chair for her to collapse on.

"Why kill those lovely people and those dear children —"

"Darling, I have no idea. I can't imagine anyone that bad to do such a thing."

"What will the law do?"

"Nothing. They have no evidence and the bodies are buried. It will be another unsolved crime maybe two hundred fifty miles away from us."

"But someone has to try to do something about it." Lisa threw her arms on the table, hid her face in them, and cried more. "I can't even get pregnant and they killed two children I loved."

"We can go up there and see what we can

find, but finding help will be a problem — you understand?"

"Yes, I know everyone is busy. You have solved greater crimes than this one. At least we can say we tried."

"I understand. I'll go talk to Jesus this evening. See what his plans are."

"Vance, maybe you could spare Vic and another vaquero?"

"Yes, and Tom might have someone. Johnny, he can go. He's been in a similar situation, but he's tough."

"Fred can't. Spencer is gone to help Cole. Cole needs Salty. Would Sarge let Cody go with you?"

"I can ask. We can't be long about getting ready. It is a damn long way up there and winter isn't far away."

Lisa dried her eyes on a handkerchief from her pocket. "I'm going, too."

"You certain?"

"Damn certain. I am not with child."

"It's some hard, long ways up there. It's a rough land."

"I think we need packhorses. No wagons."

He agreed. "We can move faster."

"In the morning, I'll send Billy Bob to Windmill and ask if they can spare Cody."

"Make a note to Tom that you need Tad, that horse wrangler, and Johnny as well."

"Hey, is anyone home?" Spud came through the kitchen. "There you are. What's wrong?"

Chet explained about the murders on the North Rim.

"You are planning to go after the murderers, aren't you?" Spud asked.

"I want to try."

"Vance and the men here can take care of my place. I want to go and Shirley will, too. I haven't had anything exciting to go after in years."

"That can be arranged. Lisa is going, too."

"Good. I'll be ready."

"Billy Bob is going to Tom's early tomorrow and get some of our crew from there and a new man. Then he's going to ride to Sarge's place and see about another young man to help us. Everyone else is working with Cole on the stage-telegraph redoing."

Chet wrote his letter and told Tom what happened and what he needed. They would pick up those men and Billy Bob on the way. Plus Cody, if he could get away. They needed things packed and loaded on packhorses. No wagons this trip. They were going to move across country fast, this time.

He added he'd like for Tom and Millie to stay up at Preskitt Valley if they could.

Then he wrote his sister and Sarge why

he needed Cody and asked if they could spare him. If not, it was fine either way. He sent Billy Bob the next day.

Every man would have a sound rifle, cartridges for it, and their Colts. Raincoats and jackets in case it got cold, Jesus promised the nine men and two women. Chet would have enough force to stop most any outlaws.

His ranch crew got busy making sure every horse they took was well shod. The coal smoke was boiling out of the blacksmith shop chimney. Hammers were tacking away on the shaped plates to hooves. Others were rapping on top of anvils to make them fit. Everyone making the effort to send them off properly outfitted.

Like on all occasions on the ranch, there was lots of teasing going on but Chet made sure they were doing a good job. They had a real long way to go to get there.

Late in the afternoon, Billy Bob came up from the Verde Ranch to get some personal things. He found Chet and announced they'd let Cody Day go with them.

"That's good news."

"He's at his in-laws tonight. Tom and Millie will be up here to look after things while you're gone."

"That's a job done good."

"I've been trying."

"I know and thanks."

Lying in bed that night, he'd run so much all day he couldn't calm down enough to fall asleep. He knew that at daylight they needed to ride out under the overhead gate bar and push to be on the north side of the Verde Valley and on top of that rim by sundown. Finally, he fell asleep.

Breakfast was served under lamps, and the riders were loaded up and went out the gate before the sun peeked out. The sun wasn't up on the sheer journey down the canyon to Verde. In the shadowy gorge, steel-protected hooves clacked on the rocks going downhill. The riders from the other ranch were out at the main road waiting and they put their packhorses into the string and started jogging their mounts northward.

Tad and Cody Day both shook Chet's hand, and he saw the horse wrangler was back there keeping the packhorses moving. It was quite a procession but they'd be well north of that rim before dark. They were making good time. They took a break on top to rest the horses and check their tack. One rider put on a new cinch Billy Bob found for him and they soon were back on the march.

Before they left, Chet told Vance they'd push for sundown to quit. When they finally stopped, they watered the horses and things moved fast. Horses unloaded and fed grain in nose bags. Cooking fires lit. Bedrolls set out.

He saw his wife in the last red light of sundown, stirring a large pot with a wooden spoon. She stopped, took both hands, and pushed on her hips. Obviously she was stiff after all day in the saddle. She was still as tough as she was coming down from Colorado. Someday the two of them would connect and she'd have a baby.

When they sat down on the ground to eat their supper, he asked her if she was stiff.

Her reply was, "Not too bad."

"Good."

"But you could help it some by rubbing it out."

"I will." He laughed at her not complaining. She was tough.

Cody came by and dropped on his haunches. "Billy Bob said they buried the victims."

"Had to. They were dead several days before anyone found them. Warm weather and they were a hundred miles from an undertaker."

"The sheriff never investigated it?"

"No. That's why I am making this trip to try and learn what I can. Lisa and I met them on our trip up here. Not many folks live up there."

"They have any money?"

"I don't think much. He couldn't afford a ranch so he brought his cows up there and homesteaded some ground, built a cabin."

"Not many people saw anything, then?"

"I didn't say it would be easy."

"Yeah, Billy Bob said — he said the killers were bastards and needed to be stopped. He met the family, too. Said they were real western ranch folks."

"Cody, I know it is a hopeless case but someone has to try to find and stop them killers."

"Amen. Glad you asked me along. I needed a break."

They reached the Little Colorado Crossing the third evening. Things were holding up well. Chet shared his thoughts about there being too many horse thieves at that location. He set up a lookout schedule and they managed it. No horses were missing. Two hard days later they talked to Mrs. Lee and never explained a thing to her about their purpose. He paid the crossing fee and they rode west toward the Kaibab Plateau.

When they got to Jacob Lake, Lincoln

came out of the store and recognized him. "Well, bless the Lord, Chet Byrnes, you did come after all. I am ashamed of my doubting about you not coming. People said you are a man of your word. Thank God you came, sir."

"Rory, several of us met that family and we share your loss. What we can do right now is look. No one found and secured any evidence from that scene that we could use as proof of who was there."

"I was there the first time when we felt we must bury them. Many of us walked about looking, but no one said they found any evidence left by the murderers."

"Do you think they had any money worth killing them over?"

"They were sincere young people but I doubt they had any large amount."

"Did anyone say who they thought was responsible for the crime?"

"No, sir."

Chet rose in the saddle and asked if anyone had any more questions to ask him.

No one did. "Thanks, Rory. We will look around and see if we can find anything that points that way. She didn't have any jewelry?"

"Not that I knew about. She had a single gold band wedding ring that his great-grandmother Betsy Cates wore. She was proud of it. Come to think of it, she didn't have it on when we buried her. Funny. I never looked for it. Her hands were stained with her own dry blood —" He shook her head. "From all I saw they really mutilated her, aside from the rest they did to her."

He turned away to overcome his sorrow. Gathering his strength, he turned back. "If I caught them I'd choke them to death with my bare hands. God forgive me."

"We do, sir. So you say her ring was gone?"

He managed to bob his head. "God be with you and these fine people who work for you. I am going to have to go somewhere and find myself. That funeral haunted me for days. Just talking about it has me beside myself. And now you point out those mad men took her ring."

"Was it marked?"

He swallowed hard. "*Betsy Cates* was written inside by the jeweler. How he did that I never knew but she showed me and I read it on the inside of the ring. It was Michael's great-grandmother's name."

"Thanks, Rory. We will try to find out what we can."

They all rode south in silence.

"You all right, Chet?" Jesus asked.

270

"Sure. That was hard back there to be in the prosecutor role. But I want these mad people."

"So do I. We need more evidence."

"The only people that saw a bunch of outlaws that close were Salty and Cole. Think we can find out where they lived?"

Chet nodded. And maybe at the cabin they'd find something that the burial party didn't.

By late afternoon they were at the cabin. He asked everyone to stay away until a few had looked at the scene. Six people slowly walked over the grounds outside the cabin. He slipped inside the door. The smell of death filled his nose and also the aroma from when the murderers tried to burn it down.

In the fading light, Chet saw where her hands had been tied with rags to the head of the bed. A sourness rose in his throat and he rushed to the open door to vomit outside. It even poured out of his nose and burned his nostrils like fire.

"You all right?" His wife had run over to check on him.

"I will be, I promise. Don't go in there. It is sickening."

"Obviously. Learn anything?"

"Nothing to learn. They tied her hands

271

with rags to the metal headboard rails so she couldn't fight them off."

"Nothing in the yard out front. I want to check the house."

"I'll go with you."

"You still look sick."

"I am feeling better."

"Liar."

"Go ahead."

She went to the bed and slow-like pulled the bloodstained sheet loose. "There is something in it."

He removed a common, open pocketknife. Dried blood on the long, open blade. It was what they stabbed her with — one of them, anyway. No initials scratched in it for ownership. He almost wished he had not come back in this cabin. He snapped the blade shut and pocketed it.

"It took more than one to hold her down."

His wife nodded. "Not much here. But that woman lived through several hours of pain and punishment."

He agreed. Then he went to stand in the doorway and spoke to Jesus. "Find anything?"

"No."

"At daylight, we'll widen the circle."

They all marched on back to the camp, set off from the area that the owners used.

"Where to tomorrow?" Jesus asked.

"Widen our circle." Chet swept his arms out.

Then Spud and Shirley came out of the brush, waving a pair of old army field glasses.

Shirley said, "Chet, we think one of the killers had been spying on them."

"Go ahead, Lisa. I want to go look where they found this old pair of glasses."

She smiled. "Your Spanish sword is worth more."

There was now no doubt that someone using those old glasses had spied on the Meadowses from that pine tree.

"I bet they did it from about six feet up this easy-climbed tree. He must have thought he had those glasses tied on good enough and went out through that dense cedar cover, lost them, and didn't come back to find them," Spud said.

"What next?" asked his wife, who sounded worn-out.

"Go eat supper, Shirley."

"Good. I am tired as all get-out, Chet."

He hugged the shorter woman's shoulder. "So am I."

# CHAPTER 24

They discovered nothing more at the murder scene or around it, except that Cody found a few very small pieces of ruby. The reflection off them struck his eyes. In an instant, he dropped to his knees and gently freed them from the dirt with the blade of his jackknife.

"What is it?"

"Didn't you find rubies in that cave?" He held the small pieces in his palm.

Chet nodded. "Michael asked me where they got them — the Spanish. I said, probably in another cave around here."

"Think he found it?" Billy Bob asked.

"No telling, but it would give those outlaws a reason to kill them. I never saw any of that in the ground samples we took around here. Nor are there any other tiny pieces in the ground here in the yard — so maybe these fell out of his pocket or hand, handling the rubies."

"Where do we look?" one of the other boys asked.

"Keep looking. We find some, we will all share."

"We're looking," Shirley said.

They began to make wider circles around the homestead but the few grains of red were all they found.

It was obvious to Chet that the gang had abandoned the previous camp that Cole and Salty had scouted out. No one had used that site west of their first camp in a long time. Chet and his crew searched, but the outlaws weren't anywhere near that area, and when they talked to a few prospectors on the move, Chet learned that no one had seen the Meadowses' murderers.

Chet's posse was camped nearby Joseph Lake that cold morning and Chet told them that unless they found out more, they'd head home in the morning. He hated to give up but no new evidence about the murders showed up nor did any leads to the possible killers appear. To admit his investigation had come to a dead end was not easy, but he told Lisa the night before he had to face the truth — they'd done nothing to solve the deaths of that family.

The storekeeper thanked him for his efforts. "Everyone up here appreciates you

and your people coming up here and looking into this matter. No one else did it. And
I knew it would be hard to solve the matter,
but I knew if anyone could — you had the
experience to do it."

"Rory, there is nothing I can find to point
a finger at who did it. A horrible crime, but
without more evidence it goes unsolved."

"Yes. But thanks anyhow."

"I have some ranches to run. Good luck
to you." They shook hands and he went
back to their camp setup.

Lisa met him coming in. He dismounted
and walked to where he planned to unsaddle.

"I know this never happened to you before
— but some things can't be solved."

"Exactly. Well, we're five days away from
Flagstaff and everyone needs to go back to
work. You all can go from there."

The gathered crew stood around, nodding
at his words.

"I'll be back in time to head another herd
to Gallup," Cody said. "But thanks for
thinking of me. Nice break for me to get off
the Windmill and meet all of you."

"When you come to Preskitt Valley gather-
ings bring your wife," Shirley said. "I'd love
to meet her."

He agreed to do that.

Tad told everyone thanks for helping him get the food out.

And Lisa said, "If you come to the ranch for any reason, plan to sleep in my house. I have lots of beds."

The horse wrangler thanked them for letting him come along.

Chet repeated his appreciation and told them they all tried hard. But deep inside he knew the failure to solve the crime would bother him for years.

The overcast sky the next morning wouldn't produce any rain. They'd not accomplished one damn thing to solve the murders. The second day at the ferry he had to listen to Mrs. Lee's complaints about there being no law in that region. That wasn't his fault.

Across the Colorado River he looked back at the empty ferry barge being dragged back to the west shore — and thanked the Lord he was, at last, beyond Mrs. Lee's sharp tongue.

They put in the third night at the Little Colorado Crossing and guarded their horses in shifts. No loss of ponies and two days more of pushing hard and they made it to the ranch's holdings in Flagstaff.

Valerie and Chet's son Rocky greeted them.

"Cole's gone to check on some things east. He should be back tonight," Valerie said. "Learn anything?"

"Not one damn thing. Those outlaws that had been camped close took a powder and we never found a sign of them nor any evidence to point a finger at anyone."

"That is a real shame."

"We agree, but nothing is nothing. How is his business going?"

"Cole had a fistfight with a driver he fired and maybe won it but he has a black eye. He needs two telegraph operators and an accountant." She laughed and threw her arm over Lisa's shoulder to hug her. "You and Shirley keep those men straight?"

"Ask her. I don't think you can do that."

Shirley dismounted. "We damn sure tried."

The girls laughed. Rocky took their horses' reins to put them up.

Chet's son received some thanks and walked with his dad to the pens. "See anything unusual this trip?"

"No. Things were pretty plain. Didn't see much of anything."

"That was a long way for you to go, wasn't it?"

"Yes, and then come home empty-handed. But I felt someone needed to go look at the situation."

"Cole is really busy. I decided he likes doing all that and it told me I needed more education than he's got so I could handle more business when I was grown."

"You planning to work in business when you get old enough?"

"Mom says I can't be a saddle bum so I better get educated, huh?"

They both laughed. Busy unsaddling the horses, Chet heard Cole call out, and he swung the saddle on its horn to stand it up.

"We're over here, Dad," Rocky shouted. "That's okay, isn't it? He tries hard."

"Good. He works at it, huh?"

"Oh yeah."

"What did you learn?"

"We didn't find another cave. That bunch had drifted away from that part of the North Rim and we didn't learn much more even about the murders or who did it."

"Whew, long ride for nothing, huh?"

"I felt the same way. But since nothing opened up, I decided to come back home. How is your deal going?"

"By tomorrow we will be on schedule again."

"That's quick."

"No, it isn't. When we were brand-new we made the schedule work. These people have never done it since. I think all these wrecks they had, the drivers had been drinking — so they take a sobriety test now and the station agent can decide if they're sober enough. So far, we have fired four drivers. I am not too popular. But off work for six weeks, they can come back sober. And they will need the money by then."

"It takes an iron hand to get on track."

"I know it does. Wells Fargo put us back on their list to use. That in itself will make us solvent. I have the postal inspector satisfied and Cosby sent me a wire telling me I've done good work in such a short time."

"I bet he's pretty smug over his new management."

"Some of those people in the office can't believe he really was the president of the board and came out here in-go-neeto. Now they know."

"Everything taking shape?"

"If I had two more Saltys to run down things I'd be fine. Whew, he gets lots done. He's culled some horses, found me some more at a fair price, run down folks who've been overcharging us for hay and grain. He and Toby have the hay business settled east of here. You may make more off your hay than the cattle. He'll find some contractors west of here."

"We can use it. Tad says he has supper ready. Come eat with us."

"I guess so, huh, Rocky?"

"Yes, sir."

They were soon seated under the big tent. And they brought on the food — beefsteaks, corn on the cob, beans, fresh sliced bread, and coffee.

"You headed home next?" Cole asked.

"You don't need us? Then, yes."

"I have things running pretty smooth. Spencer has lots of the problems on the east end straight. He'll be up here in a short time and working west. Tells me they were not splicing it back right in most cases."

"Then I'll go back home."

"It really is going easier than I first thought. But thanks."

In bed in the guesthouse later Lisa asked Chet, "You disappointed he didn't need you?"

"Not really. I think he's even doing better than he did last time."

"Good. I'll have you around more. Who is going to ride with you besides Jesus?"

"Billy Bob."

"He's not Cole, but he is sharp enough."

"He's single and fits in well. I thought when Jesus got that money from the cave he might retire."

"No, he has really stepped up. This job is an achievement for him and he is proud of it. Anita realized that was his job when he married her."

"Shirley and Spud did well on our trip. They were anxious to get back."

"Both of them are hard workers. I'll spend some time with them and they'll get along fine up there. Cole had most of the projects completed."

"I am like you. I wish we could have learned more up there. But with no one to talk to up there, there wasn't anything left to do."

"Someday we will learn the facts, if we live that long."

"I don't doubt that."

He reached over and kissed her. What a neat partner he had found in her.

# CHAPTER 25

The morning after Chet got back, he was opening mail that came while they were gone.

Dear Mr. Burns,

My name is Jennifer Greystone. My husband, Earshal Greystone, is several years older than I am and not in good health. He learned about the Spanish rubies you found on the North Rim of the canyon from a story in the Tucson newspaper. He told me that thirty years ago he was at that place where the Spaniards earlier mined those gems. But at the time he was very short on food and water. He only took a few gems and hurried to get back to civilization up in Utah.

No one believed he had found rubies in the Arizona Strip. He was never able to go back because of a wreck that made him a cripple. He is willing to draw you a map for a small sum of money. If you are interested, let us know.

Sincerely yours,<br>Jennifer Greystone

"What came?"

"A lady says her husband was at the mine the Spanish mined up there on the strip. She offered me a map for a fee."

"Where is she at?"

"Oh, Lisa, I bet it's a phony way to get money out of me."

"What if it is real? Where does he live? Why not find out more?"

"You are as bad as Jesus was about finding the Spanish horses." Amused, he turned over the envelope. "Mesa, Arizona."

"You could take a guard and run down there and know if he is lying or not."

"All right. I will write her back and get directions to her house. But I bet it is a fraud."

"Billy Bob is in the kitchen."

"I'll go see what he needs." Chet left his office and went back to the kitchen.

"Can I help you, Billy Bob?"

"I needed to go see about a fellow I know who lives down near Phoenix. They said he had a bad horse wreck and I figure it's a four-day trip down and back. But if you needed me I won't go."

"I have a deal over by Mesa I need checked out. You take the stage, I'll pay the fare coming and going. See your buddy, then look up this man who heard we were in the ruby business. He wants to sell me a map to the mine."

"Wow, you reckon he's honest?"

"I'm leaving that up to you."

"But — but it ain't my money."

"We were all over that country. If you don't recognize the place he's talking about don't buy it."

"I'll go. Thanks. Herman Boyles must be in bad shape. He's a helluva good man — sorry about cussing, ma'am."

"No need to be sorry. Go find us the direction to the ruby mine, Billy Bob."

"Yes, ma'am, that would be a great trip, huh?"

"I'd sure go along."

Chet laughed. "I bet you both'd get to go. Here's the money for your trip. Two hundred is enough for his map. Tell him if we find it we will pay him more — if you decide to buy it."

"The Mesa postmaster should know where he lives."

"I bet you can find him."

"I'll catch the midnight stage tonight."

"Stay in a hotel. Eat meals in a real restaurant. Rent a horse. You are part of the Quarter Circle Z ranch management now."

Chet would have sworn the cowboy blushed. "Yeah, I'll do it."

After Billy Bob left the house, Lisa chuckled. "Poor guy can't get over being so rich, but when you said he was ranch management you liked to have blown him over."

"Billy Bob did his part on those trips we made with him along. Money has not changed his disposition or sincere efforts."

"Hey, I am a fan of his. I'll be anxious to see what he comes up with."

"We will see. That worked out well."

"Yes, it saved you a trip. What are you going to do today?"

"Go over and visit with Spud and Shirley. They really never got to know much about their place before I drug them off to lower Utah."

"Those two have grown up, too. I never knew much about him. She was another hand-me-down from here?"

"I haven't done bad myself — I got you out of it."

"Yes, you did and I am glad. But I'll let you go up there alone. I have some household chores to accomplish today."

He buckled on his gun belt, took his blanket-lined jumper and put it on, kissed her good-bye, and put his hat on as he left.

The stable boy saddled him one of his horses. In a few minutes, he rode off in the cool mountain air for the new place. The roan horse had a long, swinging gait, and Chet wasn't over an hour getting down there. He knew it would warm up as the day grew longer, but it was giving him a forward page of the weather ahead. The cottonwoods were golden in the low-hanging sun.

As he reined up in their yard, Shirley appeared in the front door. "He's down at the corrals."

"Thanks." He rode on down there.

He found Spud and three of his men replacing posts in the corral. Spud shed his gloves and came out to meet Chet and shake hands.

"Morning." The men nodded and Spud stepped away from them. "We had a few posts had some rot around the base. Figured they might break off when we worked cattle in here."

"Good idea. Finding lots to do?"

"Oh, just jobs like this. Cole had some work similar, and we've already fixed most of them. I've been riding through the cows when I had time. When we get ready, I want to cull some. Shawn and I had that herd up there about straightened out. I learned all about checking if they were bred. That was what Miguel taught us. Shame about him getting shot."

"Yes. He'd have made a helluva good foreman for the ranch. Vance is a fine man but Miguel was a special person."

They were beyond earshot of his workers and headed for something Spud wanted him to see when he asked, "I hope you are satisfied with what I get done. I know I am not the smartest guy on your payroll and, seriously, I never expected to have a place of my own to run. I count on Shirley pretty strong since she has more education than I do. I really didn't believe you'd choose me for this job or any other, running things."

"Spud, don't think small. You have lots of common sense, lots of cow sense. I had no fears about your ability to be the foreman. I know it is wearing different shoes, but I felt I needed you here. I think you probably do too much physical work. Your job is to get them to do that work and you supervise them doing it."

"Kinda hard, Chet. I've been a worker. Now Shawn treats me more like I was his right arm, but you gave me more credit than

I feel I deserve."

"No one gave you anything you didn't deserve. Don't worry. You will make a great foreman."

"You say so, I'll believe you."

"Let's go talk to your wife. These guys have enough work to do."

"I'll tell them I'll be back."

He did and they went to the house.

"Shirley, he wants to talk to us."

"Anything wrong?"

"No. Let's sit at the kitchen table."

"We sure never expected to live in a mansion." She shook her head and pushed a lock of hair back from her face.

"Lisa and I have talked about one thing we wanted to advise you two about. Spud becoming a ranch foreman, and you his wife, need to dress up a little more. A foreman makes more money than a ranch hand and you need to dress a little better. I told Vance that when he took the job. He doesn't wear a suit but he looks a little sharper. His wife does, too. It isn't to show off as much to be a little prouder-looking."

Shirley nodded. "And I guess that's my job. Since I handle the clothes. You see what he's saying? Chet wants you to look like a boss."

Spud laughed. "I guess we can make that grade."

She nodded. "I can see that now, looking at the others. We dang sure want to keep this job. I believe you don't have a happier foreman than him on your payroll. Now, if we had some kids —"

"Lisa and I are the same way."

"I guess it is up to God." She became caught up laughing. "We try hard enough."

All three laughed. That was good. They got the word. He'd done his part. He didn't stay for lunch and wondered how Billy Bob would get along on his trip down to Mesa. Somehow, he hoped they had a solid lead on the mine. It might bring him more leads to the murderers. The whole thing was left undone and he hated that, but he had no more leads to the crime.

Back at home the girls fixed him some lunch and he told Lisa about his words to Spud and Shirley on dressing up.

"Good. You will have things straight one day. You have a man for Shawn and Lucy?"

"I bet he has one. He has several hands that would be good prospects."

# CHAPTER 26

Chet and Lisa attended a meeting to raise money for the Thomas family, who had lost their house in a fire. Chet had sent an order for three wagonloads of lumber from the mill to use to frame a new house. Lisa presented the order to the Thomases after the auction, and they both cried, up there on the stage.

Chet was standing below the stage and told them he'd bring a hammer and help frame the house when they got ready. To just send him word. Henry Thomas came to the edge of the stage and shook his hand. More neighbors made offers of labor. It was a good gathering and a successful fund-raiser.

The liveryman and his wife and kids were there, and Luther Frye, the liveryman, spoke to Chet.

"I have a man who would like a Barbarossa horse," Luther said. "Your nephew selling some?"

"He says he will."

"I'll go see him, then. Can I say you sent me?"

"Sure. But he isn't liable to give you a discount."

They both laughed.

When Chet got back to Lisa she quietly asked him, "Didn't that liveryman get his wife out of a house of ill repute?"

Chet nodded, and when they were outside the hall, he explained, "She was a widow with three children. Her husband was killed in a buggy wreck. She had no skills, so she took a job there to provide for them. Frye heard about it, went down there, and brought her out with him right then that night. Married her, and they've done well ever since."

Later that week, Chet received a request from the U.S. Marshals to arrest a man, if he had the time, who was reported in the area. The man's name was Rupert Cosgrove and he was wanted for embezzling money from a bank in Coal Hill, Arkansas. He had stolen about four thousand dollars. He supposedly had relatives in the Preskitt mining area.

Chet sent the U.S. Marshal, John Stone, a

wire that he would look for him. When Jesus came by the house he had him look over the description of the man. *Age 36. Stands 5 feet 8 inches tall. Partial bald. Brown hair with blue eyes.*

"I figure we can ride down to Crown King and start back-checking for him."

Jesus agreed. "Who else is going with us?"

"Vic. Billy Bob had a friend down, I guess, at Hayden's Ferry, who was laid up from a horse wreck. He wanted to go down there and see about him. Then a man's wife at Mesa said her husband could draw me a map to the ruby mine up on the North Rim for a price so I sent him down on the stage. I think he planned to see his injured friend and then ride from Hayden's Ferry to Mesa and test out the man with the map. He knows enough about the strip to know if the man is lying."

"Oh yeah, we rode over part of it enough. What will it cost?"

"Not over a couple hundred and a share, if we get some."

"Sounds fair enough. We going down to Crown King in the morning?"

"Yes. Set up two packhorses for the trip. We can cover it all, I figure, in three days if he's around. Vic and I will bring them by in the morning on our way down. No need for you to ride out here and have to ride back."

"Thanks. I'll get some more sleep, too."

"How is your operation going?"

"Good. Anita and the baby are fine. I have thirty head to calf in the spring. Things are going great."

"One day we will wake up and there will be snow on the ground."

Jesus laughed and agreed. "It sure isn't far away."

"Tell Anita hi," Lisa said when he prepared to leave.

He agreed and thanked her.

Chet walked him down to his horse, and Vance must have seen them coming and met them.

"We need two packhorses tomorrow, and Vic to go with us to Crown King and look for an embezzler. Billy Bob went down to Hayden's Ferry."

"You know what the three of us need on those packhorses?" Jesus asked him.

Vance nodded. "They will be loaded by the morning."

"We are on a U.S. Marshal request."

"I figured that. Vic will be glad to go along with you. They are working on cleaning out the horse stalls the rest of this week. He won't miss that."

Everyone laughed.

■ ■ ■ ■

Up early, Vic, the vaquero in his mid-twenties, was at the breakfast table flirting with the house girls and sipping coffee when Chet reached the kitchen.

"Good morning. They say you are missing all the fun?"

"They are cleaning out the horse stalls this week," he told the girls. "I won't miss that job."

They laughed.

"They may save the pigpens for your return," Julie said, and then poured Chet's coffee.

Vic shook his head at the notion. "They'd like to, I bet."

"Scrambled eggs, fried bacon, and pancakes suits me," Chet told her.

"I will have the same."

"I have your orders. Is Lisa coming down?"

"Yes. She will be here shortly."

"Good, we don't need to leave her out."

"She coming along?" Vic asked.

"Not this time. These run-off crooks we're after can be dangerous."

Everyone agreed.

Breakfast went smoothly. The two finished

eating and stood up to leave, washing down the last cup of coffee when Chet's wife arrived.

He kissed her good-bye and the two men were ready to leave for Jesus's place.

Vance handed Vic the lead ropes for the three packhorses and said, "It would all not fit on two."

"Thanks," Chet said, and waved to all the pitchfork cowhands about to start on the horse barn cleaning. "Save some for Vic to clean when he gets back."

They all laughed and promised him they would do that.

When the pair went out under the gate bar they were in a trot and the horses were breathing steam in the cold mountain air. It had frosted over the night before and the grass along the road wore a silver cast.

Out from under some pines going down the road, Chet studied the big cloud bank to the north over his shoulder. "I bet that's our first snow coming."

Vic looked back, made a sour face, and nodded. "It is coming."

They picked up Jesus, who was already mounted, and moved on west to take the little-used trail that went up into the Bradshaw Mountains to join the main road that swung in from town. This cut off several miles and they were in the pine forest, climbing into the Bradshaws and the mining district that straddled the range, headed south.

Noontime they took a break and ate some burritos wrapped in flour tortillas for lunch. By midafternoon they reached the town of Crown King. They hitched the horses and climbed the long steps to the Miner's Glory Saloon. Once in the smoke and rotgut smelling air of the room, they went to the bar.

Chet ordered two drafts and a sarsaparilla for himself. Then before he paid him he asked the bartender if he knew Rupert Cosgrove. He shook his head.

"For ten bucks, have you seen him?"

The bartender held out his hand.

"Start talking and it better be good."

"He's with the Harmon brothers. They've got a mine called Ozark Queen. About five miles north of here."

"I saw that sign," Jesus said.

Chet threw the ten down. "It better be the right place."

They went out the front doors and, going down the stairs two at a time, he told Vic to bring the packhorses, that the two of them were going on at a faster pace.

Vic agreed and those two both made a

quick bound into their saddles and headed
north. Racing around lumbering ore wagons
they headed up the rutted highway and scat-
tered some vehicle-chasing dogs. The dust
wasn't bad but it grew thicker and there
was more wagon traffic to duck and dodge
through.

They reached the sign for the Ozark
Queen mine and reined up. The deep ruts
led to some log buildings up a steep slope
through some slashed timber. Chet took the
lead and reined up at the office. He searched
around. There were kids playing in the dirt
and they grew quiet when they saw Jesus
and Chet.

Their horses hitched, Chet used the lever
opener on the door. From his seat at a desk,
a man in a white shirt looked up, surprised.

"I am a U.S. Marshal. I am here to arrest
Rupert Cosgrove."

"There — ain't anyone here — by that
—"

A near-bald man came in the back door
and demanded to know who those guys out
front were.

"Cosgrove? You are under arrest. I am a
U.S. Marshal." Chet's pistol was pointed
right at the flush-faced man. "One move
and you are dead."

"How in the hell did you find me out here?"

"Believe it or not, we looked for you."

"Who are you?"

"U.S. Marshal Chet Byrnes, that's my deputy Jesus Martinez putting cuffs on you. Where is the bank's money?"

"I don't have any money."

"What did you spend it on?"

"You have the wrong man."

"I doubt it. You fit the description. Prove who you are, then."

"John Green."

"Try harder. You, behind the desk. Yes, you. What is his name? You lie to me, you will do two years in the federal pen. Name him."

"Cosgrove." The man was white-faced and shaking all over.

"Listen, there are children outside. I don't want anyone hurt. Is there anyone here might try to free him?"

"No. I — I don't think so."

"Jesus. Real careful, you check and see if anyone out there knows we're here."

His man shoved their prisoner to the door, opened it, and he peered past him. "Looks clear."

Chet spoke to the seated man. "Don't you try anything. Get away from the desk."

"I am going." He turned his chair over backward getting out of it.

Jesus used the prisoner as a shield. Guiding him outside with one hand. His other hand had his pistol ready.

Chet followed him, realizing it was darker outside than when they went inside. Then, when he stepped off the porch, something cold struck his cheek. It was snowing. The kids were shouting plus jumping up and down as the heavy snow began to really fall.

Chet could hardly see anything for the snow. They needed another horse for their prisoner. Oh well, when Vic got there they'd use a packhorse even if they had to discard the load.

Drivers on the main road were cussing their teams as the snow became a problem for their horses' footing. The white stuff never let up falling. Where was their partner? Then he appeared like a white ghost.

"You got him?" Vic asked as if shocked it was him.

Chet was off his horse and stripping off the hitch. "We need a horse to get him back to town."

Vic joined him and they soon had everything but the cross-buck pack saddle unloaded. The two tossed the grumbling prisoner on that horse.

"We going to leave it?" Vic asked.

"Yes. We need to find some shelter next."

Vic threw up his hands.

"Jesus, can we find the road off this one and go on to Preskitt?"

"I think so."

"You lead the way. If we can use that side road we came in on we don't need to go back to town. We can go back to the ranch and hold him there."

"You guys are crazy," the prisoner said, and added some swear words to his complaint. "We'll all freeze to death."

"Just shut up. You have no say. You could be walking on foot and I could still make you do that."

Jesus took the lead. Vic led the prisoner and his horse. Chet brought up the other two packhorses. The footing under the horses, in places, caused some slippage of hooves. But the situation was not real serious. Still, it made Chet very observant of his own horse and the ones he led. The steepest part of the road he could recall was where they turned north off the main wagon road.

They passed several wagons and rigs in the ditch or turned over, along with ones that were stuck in the middle of the road — their teams unable to track them. With their prisoner, there was little they could do to help them. The snow let up only a little then more fell in the next deluge of flakes.

Chet could see the pine tree branches bowed under the weight of the wet white stuff. He'd been in snowstorms before but never with a prisoner to guard. After perhaps an hour of descending the grade they reached the lower level and Jesus nodded. "Better footing here."

"Amen. We may make it, guys."

"You doubted that, too?" Vic asked over his shoulder.

"Coming off that steep grade, I did."

"Good. Then I won't worry about me fretting over it."

The three laughed.

"Did anyone shoot at you two when you arrested him?"

"No. Why?" Chet asked.

"Fellers, this is the first arrest I ever was in on and I damn sure didn't know what to expect."

"You did damn good finding us in that snow."

"I admit I worried some about finding you."

"We worried, too," Jesus shouted back.

After dark, they reached the main ranch. The snowfall had leveled off to small flakes falling but there was over a foot accumulated on the ground. They dropped out of their saddles and Vance met them.

"You got him?"

"Yes. We will need a guard and someone to feed him something for tonight."

"We can handle that."

"Jesus, give him the handcuff keys in case he needs to take them off."

"I'll put the horses up," Vic said.

"No, we will do that. You look like a snowman," Vance teased the vaquero.

"Come on up to the house and thaw out," Chet said, handing his reins to a boy.

"But I've got snow all over me."

"Vic, they won't care. Get up the stairs."

"Yes, sir. And don't laugh, Jesus. I came home like this one time when I lived in Mexico and my mother beat me with a broom for coming in her house like that, with mud from a sudden rainstorm."

"My wife won't do that. Get up those stairs."

"Yes, sir."

Both of the house girls and Lisa were there to help them get off their outer clothes. And they used brooms to get some of the snow off their britches. Laughing and teasing one another, they soon were seated at the table.

"Your trip must have been successful?" Lisa asked.

"Yes, we were. Vance has the prisoner. Aside from a long, slick ride we had few other problems. We never got to interrogate the prisoner but we listened to his complaints all the way back here."

Lisa said, "I am glad you are back in one piece. This snow started here not long after you left and I worried you would be snowbound."

"No. Jesus, with his snow experience in Mexico, led us back to the ranch."

The house girls laughed.

"The only snow I ever saw in Mexico was way off on a mountain in the Sierra Madres."

Chet thanked Vic after they finished eating, and he headed for the bunkhouse.

After the meal, they showed Jesus a bedroom and said good night. Chet and Lisa were in their own bed, and she said, "I can't believe you rode out and got back in one snowy day."

"I had enough of being away from you, I guess."

"Chet Byrnes, sometimes I could beat you with my fists."

"It's the truth."

# CHAPTER 27

The next day Chet sent a ranch hand to ride into town to wire the U.S. Marshal that he had the prisoner Rupert Cosgrove and, due to snow, was holding him at his ranch, but he would transfer him shortly for holding to the Yavapai County Jail in Prescott, Arizona Territory.

After breakfast, Jesus rode home. Chet had not made any plans about what they'd do next. There was no word from Billy Bob. With the snow that deep, Chet knew his man would be a few more days getting back from the valley.

They got a telegram from him that he'd be there on the midnight stagecoach. Lots of the snow was gone and the temperature was high enough that it was not freezing at night.

That evening he and Vic, riding a buckboard and with a robe on their laps, went to meet the stage. Plus, they'd brought a blanket for Billy Bob to wear back, because he left without much winter gear on his body and sure didn't need that much down there.

They got him and his war bag off the stage and started for home.

"Hey, guys, I am damn grateful for this blanket to get under. Man, it was eighty degrees down there today. I had no idea you got that much snow here. But my buddy Earl, who had the wreck, is doing good. Better than anyone expected. And I bought the map to the mine. That old man seriously broke his leg after he found the mine. It healed stiff and he doubted he could get around to ever go back. Said he'd thought about doing it many times but never saw a way or anyone he trusted enough to go find it for him."

"What did you pay him?"

"Two hundred, and he gets ten percent of what we get, less our expenses."

"What made you think about that?"

"I knew we couldn't go up there for nothing."

"Good thinking. We will have expenses. Think you can find it from his map?"

"I do, Chet. You know those three buttes?"

"We called them the Sisters?"

"Yeah. Those are the ones and it is north

of them."

"Well, if you think you can find the mine, great. But I am not going to rush up there in the wintertime. It has been there that long and it can wait until springtime. Coldest days I can recall in my life was coming back from Utah with prisoners on that road."

"Jesus wouldn't go up there, either, in the winter."

Vic was driving and laughing. "Jesus told me one time that every cold day on that trip he watched out for polar bears. Figured they'd eat him."

The snow soon melted and things leveled out. The U.S. Marshal sent two men to take Cosgrove back for trial. Between snows, Chet and his two men slipped into Flagstaff to check on Cole and see how things were going for him.

They met in his office.

"How are things going?"

"Not bad. I have some new ticket agents. Some were stealing, others were going to work drunk, and one told an important man he didn't care if the individual got to Gallup or not. Someone, unknown, chopped down two telegraph poles way west of here. We guessed he needed firewood. It took several days to replace them but Salty can splice them now, too. Spencer keeps fixing the small things that pop up and he's training two people what to do."

Chet looked around before he said, "Billy Bob bought us a map supposed to lead us to the ruby mine."

"Is it good?"

"The man found it says so."

"I hope you all do good going after it."

"That won't be until next spring," Jesus said.

They all laughed.

# CHAPTER 28

Billy Bob, Julie from the house crew, and Vic took a buckboard and a saddle horse along to the Wagon Wheel and brought the very pregnant Josey Taylor back to the Preskitt ranch to have her firstborn. Lucky for them, it didn't snow or turn hard cold. She bragged on how good a job the three did, and it was all smiles when they helped her down.

Lisa welcomed her to their house.

Chet noticed that Julie and Billy Bob talked to each other for a long time after the others went inside the house. Business as usual for the ranch. A herd of cattle each month delivered to the Navajo at four delivery points and then the wait for government money to be paid. Tanner handled that part at the bank — he watched very closely for notices of availability of federal warrants to be paid. And he told Chet when each one came to his account.

Chet settled with Ben Ivor when the last piece of farm machinery finally made it to Preskitt. Then he and Ben shook hands and the dealer thanked him for his business.

"You said you may go back up on the strip again?"

"When it warms up we probably will. There was a serious murder case growing cold up there. But I doubt anyone can ever solve it."

"The family they killed?"

"Right. So little to go on but they didn't deserve to die."

"Chet, I knew it bothered you but there are things you simply can't solve in this world."

"I know, but I damn sure hate it when it happens to me."

"I moved here because I saw an opportunity to become a successful merchant. Not to give up on my marriage. I guess I put too much of my time in on the business, getting it started. My first wife took our kids and left me. I was lost. I thought I'd been a good husband. No matter, she thought she was being punished to live in this outpost. I know Preskitt had much more going on than many places back East. But she left me.

"You brought Kathrin down from Utah.

After her bad experience, she was very afraid of any man but you. You saved her from the fate of ending her life in a brothel, and you never asked her for anything. That affected her because she felt she owed you her life. She was a very good business-woman — a meticulous bookkeeper, and she guided me in recovering bad accounts, too. I asked her to marry me. She refused. I knew her obligation was pinned on her desire to repay you for saving her."

"I didn't need to be repaid."

"No, I knew that and I finally got her convinced I was serious. I didn't blame her, as bad off as she was up there, and you would not take a penny for doing that. We married and have two wonderful children. Next week my two teenage children are coming to live with us. Their mother is go-ing to prison for selling property she did not own.

"My boy asked me in a letter, do you have any customers who are cowboys? I told him yes and I knew you have two sons close to his age."

"Rocky moved with his parents back to Flagstaff. But if he likes horses and animals he and Adam may make friends. He lives at Camp Verde."

"Well, thanks. We will see how things go.

Kathrin is excited. I am, too, but wish they were coming under better circumstances. A good friend wrote me what was happening and I hired a lawyer back there to get custody of them. But I want you to know I appreciate the things you have done for the Territory and the county. As well as for your business."

"Ben, thanks. You have helped me since the start. Hug Kathrin for me and thank her. When you do something like that you never know if you did the right thing. Obviously, I did that right."

"Very right."

He left the busy mercantile and joined Vic, who had the team and buckboard waiting at Doc Jones's office. He spoke to him and decided his wife was still inside. He entered the empty waiting room and could hear someone crying.

"Now, Lisa, stop crying. If it had been a fit baby you could have carried it. Not every seed makes a tree in life. Some, not ready for life, pass on."

"Oh, I am just so upset —"

Chet opened the door and said, "I am not. I still have you."

"Doc says I lost one."

"You may lose more. But, my dear, you won't lose me."

"I'm sorry for crying. I just wanted one so bad for both of us."

"She will be fine, Chet. Losing a fetus is always hard. But she's young and healthy and she will have more."

"Let's go home." He hugged and kissed her until she smiled, and they thanked the doc and left for home.

It snowed again before November was out. Great wet snows that made ranchers smile and melted off in a week. Hay requests began to come in and Chet wasn't sure how many tons of hay Toby sold but plenty went by the ranch house, and then his haulers would spend a night at the ranch before driving home, saying their job would never be done with all the orders Toby had to fill.

Chet, Lisa, and Billy Bob took the buckboard and went to the Verde on one of those sunny, warm days. Most of the ice and snow were gone off the north slope and wagon tracks had cut through any snow on the rocky surface. They emerged out of the shadowy canyon in the brilliant sunshine and drove on down to Tom's house.

Lisa wanted a list of all the helpers, family members, and children for her Christmas list, and Lisa and Millie went to work on it in the kitchen while Chet and Tom talked in the living room.

"Rumor is, a guy sold you a map to the ruby mine?"

Chet, seated on the leather couch across from him, nodded. "I have a map to somewhere. Man swears it will take us right there. I don't know. Next spring, we'll go back."

"I hope it is as big as the last one."

"I doubt that. Everything quiet down here?"

"I don't have a problem to speak about. My blacksmith people want to make more barbwire. They say we can make a profit off it. They found a used boiler that is for sale and they say they can build two more machines for next to nothing."

"How much to set it all up?"

"Twenty-five hundred."

"Do it."

"They will be excited. Thanks."

"Tell them not to slight building more windmills. The ranch foremen say the extra water tanks really spread out range cattle to graze the whole range."

"I can handle that."

"What else?"

"Nothing here, Chet. I went to Flagstaff one day to see the roadbed they built to make folks think the train will be there in no time and talked to Cole. He has that stage line running slick as a gut. Spencer has the telegraph wire singing. They want a second wire strung and want him to do it."

"I guess he will ask me for more time off."

"He likes being a ranch foreman but he can make a damn sight more money building telegraph lines."

"I'll cross that bridge when I get to it. But thanks for the tip."

"Anything else?"

"No. Toby is the hay king of northern Arizona."

"That is no kidding. Hay comes through here all the time. But Robert has hay and I have plenty. I guess he may make record sales if we keep having snow. Has that girl had her baby yet?"

"No. But she's close."

"They stopped here and stayed at the big house for the night. Billy Bob is making you a hand, isn't he?"

"You didn't think he would?"

"That boy was country dumb when he first came here. This isn't that same boy. He was so efficient about Josey's needs when he brought her by here. What she needed, he handled, and that he was doing it shocked me. You made something out of him, that is for sure."

"I like him. He's going to make a good hand."

"Cole has all that junk gone and the area around their headquarters looks like a park. You know, cleaning that up assures people he is running a first-class company. His fares sales are up thirty percent. He got a letter from the post office in DC saying how much they appreciate the job he did straightening that mess up. And Wells Fargo has doubled their shipments already.

"Plus Salty has shut down the highway robbers overnight."

"Good man for the job. Cole knew that when he talked about the job. Tom, he was your discovery and we both lost him."

"Oh. He is a super smart guy."

Chet, Lisa, and Billy Bob went on back home after lunch. She was talking about the Christmas party and Chet was thinking about the long trip back to the strip and what he'd find up there in the spring. Really, he wanted those young people's murder case solved but nothing pointed him to it being solved.

A week later, on a cloudy, cold December day that threatened to perhaps snow some more, two riders drew up in the yard. They had a packhorse and their bedding tied on the back of their saddles. Chet noticed them coming under the gate bar and he went back through the kitchen to see if they wanted to talk to him.

One of the men pointed toward the stairs and Chet went to the back hall to meet them.

He opened the door and greeted them.

"Mr. Byrnes, I understand you met my late brother, Michael Meadows." The cowboy was in his early twenties and had long, blond hair and sparkling blue eyes. "My name is Jamie Meadows. My pard is his wife's brother, Hines Ball."

"Hang up your coats, come inside, and we can talk. I had no way to contact you. They told us you helped them, but we never heard your names. Julie, please make us some fresh coffee. This is Jamie and Hines. Have a seat. I am anxious to talk to you two. We went back up there."

"Mr. Lincoln wrote me a letter that you really tried to find the killers. We both appreciate your efforts and we are lost on what we can do next about it."

"That's why you came here?"

"Yes, sir."

"Jamie told you we have tried to solve the hideous crime of their deaths — I'm sorry, I get choked up. My sis and I were close. We came over here to ask if you knew anything at all about who did it." Hines blew his nose hard and mopped his tears in his kerchief.

"It will be a tough crime to solve. No bodies. No close detective work looking for evidence. We found a common pocketknife in the sheet on the bed, and the bloodstains on it told me they'd tortured her. I am sorry but there was no denying that. But who held the knife, we have no idea."

"Did you interview any of that gang everyone says is behind the crimes up there?"

"No. We never found them on our second trip back there."

"You reckon they split up after they did that?" Jamie asked.

"I have no idea. But that might be the case." Lisa came in the room.

"Lisa, this is Michael Meadows's brother, Jamie, and Jeanie's brother, Hines Ball."

"Oh, it is good to meet you. Neither Chet nor I knew your names, or we would have contacted you two."

"They came to see if we knew anything to help them. Lisa went up there with us and she's as disappointed as I am that we couldn't link anything to some suspects."

Both men stood and shook her hand across the table.

"Nice to meet you. We ranch over east," Jamie said. "We're not as large as you are.

We met your foreman Fred Taylor on your big Wagon Wheel ranch and he told us that you'd talk to us."

"Fred is a hard-worked young man. His boss is working on the telegraph line to get it working again."

"Yes, he amazed us, telling us you found him two years ago."

"Fred was living in the alleys then. He's a smart young man and he is tough."

"Oh yes, sir. But he told us you would help us. We decided we'd ride over. These long trips sure take time."

"I bet you two have calluses." Chet chuckled.

"Let me show you a letter the undersheriff wrote me about them investigating the crime."

Lisa shook her head in disgust. "The sheriff must be illiterate. His staff wrote us a letter and signed it 'Yavapai Sheriff Department.' "

They laughed.

Chet read it.

Dear Mr. Meadows:
In regards to your letter inquiring about a supposed multiple murder on the North Rim of the Grand Canyon. I find I cannot find any use in sending a deputy

over to the strip to investigate the deaths since I have no death certificates or recorded record of their death. So I am sorry but I cannot justify the expenses of such a useless, unsolvable situation. If you have evidence or witnesses of this crime, bring them to our office in Prescott and we will interview them, weigh the evidence, and decide whether it is sufficient to face a grand jury.

*John D. Boyd*
Undersheriff of Yavapai County,
Arizona Territory

"This letter shows how well run our law is in the Territory."

"Collecting property taxes is more important to the sheriff than enforcing the law." Hines shook his head.

Chet agreed. "They will obviously be of no help in solving this crime."

"What should we do next?"

"Did Michael ever find the ruby mine?" Chet asked.

"That was what he was looking for," said Hines. "He told us in the last letter, he thought he'd tracked down an old Spanish mine."

"My expedition last year found a cave and recovered a lot of rubies that the Spaniards

320

had gathered and stored in this cave. But we never found the mine. We told Michael we'd not come back to look for it and wished him good luck. You two have any idea where it is?"

Both men shook their heads.

"We were at the ranch after you were there the first time. Michael said he had a deal that would put us all into ranching."

"He never showed you any rubies?"

"No. But he said he was onto something and figured he'd have more to say in his next letter."

"You never got another letter?"

"No, not from him. We got a letter from Mr. Lincoln informing us they had been murdered and were buried."

"Nothing else he could do — just bury them."

"Right. We appreciate all he did. Hines and I wondered if you were going back."

"I plan to really look harder in the late spring. You can freeze to death up there in winter."

"Would Hines and I bother you, going along with you?"

"No. Safety in numbers, isn't there?"

"Well, Hines and I would sure be pleased to ride with a man who has arrested more men than I can count."

"That's right, Mr. Byrnes."

"Chet will do. I will let you two know when we get closer. You may ride along with us."

"Whew. Thanks."

"Either of you have a first name for this Logan?"

"I think Claude, but I am not certain. What are your plans?"

"I have a U.S. Marshal badge and I will request what they have on him."

"That might help."

"Yes, any clue will help."

"Chet? I think the girls about have lunch ready."

"Oh, we didn't come here to mooch a meal."

"This is not mooching. You are welcome to spend the night and don't worry, we do have enough to cover the cost," Lisa said with a big smile.

"That sure is generous. Thanks."

"Hey, you two are very welcome here."

"There is hot water to wash up on the back porch," Natalie said.

After washing up, Jamie shook his head at the table set for lunch, filled with the hot dishes the girls had set out for them.

"This is pretty impressive, ma'am," Jamie said to Lisa.

"Grass does not grow under their feet."

"I see that."

They took their places and Chet said grace.

The bowls were circled and the visitors looked amazed at what there was to eat.

"If you have time I'd love to see the maps of your ranch. I have heard so much about them."

"Fine. We have one for each ranch."

Hines laughed as he passed the meat tray of cooked beef. "I can draw mine on a postage stamp."

Chet nodded. "You have to have a place to start."

"Have you considered that North Rim?"

"To ranch? No. It is so poorly watered, for one thing. Where would you drive them to market?"

"Maybe grow camels there?" Jamie asked.

Chet laughed. "I might could grow them there. Today I have all the ranches I need."

"You ever hear of the Bar Ten Ranch?"

"No." Chet passed the butter for the homemade sliced bread to Hines.

"It is maybe twenty sections and goes clear down to the Apache reservation."

"Is it for sale?"

"Yes."

"What do they want for it?"

"I was afraid to ask." Hines's words made the others laugh.

"Any idea?"

"Is it stocked with longhorns?"

"No, it has had English breed bulls for a long time."

"Any idea how many mother cows?"

"Fifteen hundred, they say."

"That count real?"

Hines nodded. "Jamie and I usually get to work roundup for them and they have lots of cows and calves."

"Where does he sell them?"

"He paid the tribe for letting him drive them across the Apache reservation, sold them down in the mining district, and shipped the rest on the train to Texas, I guess."

"Is it as good a ranch as Wagon Wheel?"

"Range-wise it might be better. But no one has a headquarters like that Wagon Wheel place. Well, this isn't bad, either. But from the back of a horse I'd say it was really good."

"Why is he selling it?"

"A year ago, he married a Texas woman who owns a fancy place south of Fort Worth. I think she wants to go home."

Lisa smiled.

"So neither of you heard his price?"

Jamie shrugged. "I heard he'd take two hundred fifty thousand."

Chet sat back in the chair and shook his head. "You serious?"

Hines nodded. Now that Jamie had mentioned the price, he remembered that that was what he had heard also.

"Lisa, please send word to Vance. I need to talk to him."

She told Julie to have his foreman come to the house.

"Would you two take on the job of being foremen?"

"I have a better idea. Make my dad, Thurman Meadows, the foreman. He's fifty years old and healthy. Let us be the jingle bob foremen."

Hines moved to the edge of his chair. "We'd like to have Thurman to help us and teach us all we need to know."

Jamie nodded.

"Would he take the job?"

"Chet, he'll make you a great foreman."

By this time, Vance had come into the room and listened quietly.

"Keep it all under your hat. I am going over there to Holbrook and try to buy it. Vance, send someone to town and tell Bo to bring his suitcase out here; we need to look at a ranch in the eastern part of the Territory."

"Yes, sir."

"That word needs to be left quiet. Oh, and meet Jamie and Hines. They ranch out of Holbrook."

They rose and shook his hand with a friendly smile and nod.

"Nice to meet you both."

"You run a neat ship here, sir," Jamie said.

"I have lots of good help."

Jamie shook his head in wonder.

"I'll get someone on a fast horse to go get Bo," Vance said.

"Thanks. Have him stop on the way and tell Jesus that we need to go in the morning."

Vance agreed and was gone.

"Well, this has certainly been an interesting day. Hines and I came to ask for help and got jobs instead. Thanks."

Lisa stood looking out the west-side window. "You can't leave. They set your personal things on the ground at the foot of the stairs and put your horses up. I have hot water upstairs. Take a bath, rest awhile, and this evening these girls will serve a great supper. Tomorrow you can ride home and Chet can go with you."

"Amazing. I have never slept in a house

this nice."

"Welcome to the ranch team. You will find you like it. There will be clothes for you to wear after your bath while we wash your clothes. Later they will be dry and ironed and ready for you to put back on in time for supper."

"Thank you."

# CHAPTER 29

For the second time since Bo had arrived, Chet asked him if he could ride that far.

"Hell, yes."

"Good. We will ride horses over there. We leave at sunup."

A boy took his reins to put him up. Bo took a war bag off the saddle horn. Chet took it away from him.

"You bring your long-handle underwear?"

"I sure did."

"Good."

"I haven't ridden much lately, but I'll make it over there."

"Fine. We are not taking a wagon to haul your carcass back in."

"Tell me about this deal you're working on."

"Bar Ten Ranch. A brother and brother-in-law to the couple I told you about that were murdered on the North Rim came by asking for my help in the investigation. And in our talk, they told me about a large ranch on the east border of the Territory that is for sale. The man married a Texas woman and she wants to move back there. It goes by the Bar Ten brand."

"Twenty sections. He wants half a million for it. I saw the listing."

"Cut that in half. Maybe two hundred thousand cash."

"I don't think he would take that little."

"We are going to go see. These two young men suggested one of their fathers for my foreman. They know ranching and were willing to be the jingle bob foremen under him. They also know the ranch."

"You going back up on the strip again?"

"After branding in the spring. You want to go along?"

"Hell, last time you paid the ones who went along a fortune to each of them."

"Bo, the chances of doing that are one out of a hundred."

"I'd still like to see it and the opportunities I might find. And I doubt very strongly this guy will take your offer for his ranch, but we can ask."

"We have not asked him."

"Right."

At the top of the stairs, Lisa had the door open and smiled to welcome him. "You ready for this long ride?"

"You going, too?"

"No, Fred Taylor's wife is here and expecting any day to deliver her firstborn. I better stay and help her."

"I understand, now that I have two of them."

"Wash up. Billy Bob is up here already. Vic's coming for supper. He is a vaquero here, and our cook, Tad, we will pick up at the Verde Ranch tomorrow. Jesus will join us here in the morning. Six of us are going over there with packhorses. It will take three or so days to get to Holbrook. If we can make Windmill tomorrow night, Wagon Wheel the next, then Holbrook, and we can sleep indoors all the way."

Everyone around the table laughed.

Chet shook his head. "What is so funny?"

"Chet, you always push those places as if they are closer," Lisa said.

"We can do it. So that is the plan."

"How are the real estate sales going?" Billy Bob asked Bo.

"I sell some houses in Preskitt. But no one wants to sell their ranch. What I mean by that is they want such a high price they don't have to make any moving plans."

He drew some laughs.

"There is a place west of Jesus's that has a

'For Sale' sign out front?" Vic asked him.

"Charlie Overton. Eighty acres. He wants twelve thousand dollars for it. It is worth maybe two thousand on a very hot day."

"What are some of those homesteads we bought worth?" Chet asked.

"Those near the Marcy Road? Probably would sell at three times what you paid for them."

"None are for sale," Chet said, and sipped on his hot coffee.

"I'd say so, too. Toby has fenced them, has windmills on them, and you can mow fence to fence on most of them." Bo shook his head, studying the apple cobbler one of the girls put on his plate. "I should have bought the Oak Creek orchards. But I didn't know you could hire that couple who runs it."

"They are wizards at growing things," Lisa said.

"Didn't you save him from some kidnappers in Utah?"

"Yes. And Jesus and the crew nearly froze to death coming home."

"I've heard his story about it being so damn cold, too."

"It may be that cold this trip."

"No excuses. You get back here for the Christmas celebration," Lisa said.

"Yes, ma'am."

She came around and hugged him. "I know this may be a very good deal. But I want you back here for Christmas."

"You guys heard her. We have to be back for the ranch party."

They all nodded.

His crew rode out with him on a mild winter morning. Jesus had joined them earlier and they pushed off the mountain, then gained Tad and three more packhorses. They pushed hard for the Windmill. They trotted their horses a lot that day but it was still past dark on the short winter day when they reached the Windmill and Sis's hospitality.

Billy Bob saw that the horses were grained and watered, for they had another long day to Wagon Wheel next. When Billy Bob slid into his seat at Sis's dining table he told them, "The horses are all fed and watered, and they will be rested for tomorrow. Lucy, you tell your men thanks for helping me."

"What are you going after?"

"Look at a ranch."

"That figures. It must be a bargain?"

"It ain't, we won't buy it. It is, we will."

The men thanked Sis for the food and got ready to sleep in one of her many beds in the warm house.

"Breakfast at five. I know you have a long day tomorrow. Chet, how is Josey doing?"

"Lisa says very well. She is healthy and ready, she says, to have it."

"I know how that goes." She smiled and shook her head. "She is in good hands with Lisa."

Chet agreed.

The weather was cooler, in the predawn, than the day before. Chet, seated in the saddle, turned the collar up on his wool coat. He was a little amused at seeing Bo, stiff-like, getting on his horse.

They rode off at a trot. Tad was driving the packhorses that Vic led that day. Billy Bob had that chore the day before. He was riding stirrup to stirrup with Chet.

Midmorning, they were on the Marcy Road. Chet felt they'd be, at their current pace, at the Wagon Wheel by evening. It was one of those sharp days where the wind cut a person in half with its sharpness. Even wearing long-handle underwear, a wool shirt, vest, and his coat, the wind still let Chet know it came from the North Pole, and the message it sent was cold.

The lights on at the ranch house were a beacon in the night for them to bear down on crossing the basin. Chet felt relieved they were making it at last. But even so he felt worn out riding across the wide-open country under the star-sparkling sky.

Fred met them, and three of his men came, dressed warmly, to put up their horse stock.

"Kind of shocked us, you all riding in this late in the day."

"Fred, we are damn glad to see you. Been a cold day getting here."

"No baby before you left?"

"Josey is doing fine. Lisa says she is very healthy and strong. She's in good spirits. No baby before we left."

Fred nodded that he heard him. "I appreciate all you and your wife have done. I'd like to be closer but we both understood it took a lot of work to get her over there so nicely. She really thanked Billy Bob. He's a pretty nice guy for doing the job he did to make her trip over there so easy."

"He's a good guy. Did two guys from over by Holbrook drop by here?"

"Yeah. They came by and said they planned to go with you to the strip."

"Did they tell you it was their relatives that were murdered?" Chet had the latigos undone on his girth and swung his saddle and blanket off his horse.

"Here, I'll put it on a rack. Yes, they told us it was his sister and the other guy's brother they murdered."

"Fred, it was a horrific crime and there's no evidence to point a finger at anyone."

Fred lowered his voice. "You must be over here on business?"

"Those two want me to buy the Bar Ten. They say the man who owns it is ready to sell."

"Wow. I heard he has a new wife. The guy who owns it."

"Yes. He met her on a trip to Fort Worth. Pretty woman, but she comes from a rich Texas family and she's spoiled, from what I hear. Holbrook damn sure ain't Dallas."

Tad and the two Mexican women who worked the kitchen soon had a hot meal on the table.

In the warm house, most of his men had recovered from the cold and were glad to be there taking their places at the long table.

Bo asked Jesus if it had been that cold on the strip.

"Almost."

The answer was still funny in the face of the relief and warmth they'd found inside the fine house. Chet even decided Bo was a damn sight tougher than he had imagined, to have made the two days' hard riding

335

under the cold weather. But there was no other way to get over there.

"Is there anything I can do for you while you are here?"

"No. We'll go look, talk, and if it is a bargain we will try to buy it."

"It is a big outfit."

"Do you know a man called Thurman Meadows?"

"Yes. We worked with him at roundup. He has a small herd of cattle, but, yes, he is really respected among all large and small ranchers."

"He's Jamie's father."

"Yes. I had not connected that. But it makes sense."

"I am going to talk to him about running it if we can buy it."

"You know where he lives?"

"Maybe you could show me."

"Yes, I could. I have some men who can handle the ranch for a time. Just say when."

"You know the railroad wants more telegraph lines?"

"No. I have not had anything but some short letters from Spencer. I am doing all that."

"Fred, you may be running this ranch before spring."

"Chet, I'm not up to being Cole or Spencer but I believe I can run it. The men work well for me. I know what I need to do. Toby is going to put up the hay. I am not afraid."

Chet slapped his shoulder. "It will be better here for you when Josey and the baby are back here."

"Amen. That is right."

"After I make this deal I'll leave Jesus and Billy Bob to run the ranch and you can go join Josey at my house."

"I don't —"

"They understand such things. So do I."

"Good. What else can we do for you?"

"I want to meet Thurman Meadows tomorrow."

"As I said, I can take you there. He's a few hours from here."

"Thanks."

Chet found Jesus before he went to bed. "You will be the foreman tomorrow along with Billy Bob. Vic can ride with Fred and me. Bo can rest. I am going to talk to Thurman Meadows about the Bar Ten superintendent's job."

"We can handle it," Jesus said.

Chet nodded. When he went down the hall to his assigned bedroom he felt his plans were going well so far. Was owning the Bar Ten simply a dream? In a short while he'd know.

# CHAPTER 30

The weak sun was near twelve o'clock when the three of them swung into the orderly yard of the Three T Ranch. A man he suspected was Thurman Meadows put down an ax he'd been using to split stove wood and removed his leather gloves.

"Thurman Meadows, I am Chet Byrnes. How are you, sir?" He stepped off his horse.

"They said you were tall. Nice to meet you, sir."

"No, sir. I am simply Chet." They shook hands.

"Maggie has some coffee. Hitch your horses, man. She has some sweet raisin bread. Be a good excuse for me having you for my guests to eat it."

"Thanks. Nice place you have here."

"I guess I am a coward about borrowing money. I could have done that, to build bigger, but I have built this small ranch with money I had in my hand."

"My dad did that. I guess I was too anxious and I borrowed money since I took over our original ranch back in Texas. Kansas cattle deliveries crossed those debts out."

Meadows nodded he'd heard him. "The boys said you made them an offer if you bought the Bar Ten?"

"You interested in the job of foreman?"

"Helluva big job for a man my age to be offered."

"Those boys said they wanted you to run it."

"And they'll be the jingle bob foremen?"

"Exactly. You'd earn three-fifty a month, ranch house, and expenses."

"The boys?"

"Two hundred a month."

"I didn't take the job I guess they'd hate me."

"No, I bet they'd respect your judgment."

"You can introduce your men to my wife. Maggie, we have company."

"I'm Chet Byrnes. That is Vic and this is Fred, my foreman over at the Wagon Wheel Ranch. He said you know him from round-ups."

"Come into my kitchen, gentlemen. Our son said you'd come and ask Thurman to work for you."

"Has he decided?"

"Well, Thurman?"

"How foolish do you think I am? Yes, Mr. Byrnes, I would appreciate being your superintendent." Gesturing, Thurman said, "Sit down, gentlemen," then continued. "I consider this is the greatest day in my life. Thank you, sir — I mean, Chet."

"Good. I must warn you I have not bought the ranch yet but I had to be sure I had some real leaders if I do."

"Those boys already consider you the next owner of the ranch."

"Are there fifteen hundred mother cows on that ranch?"

Thurman smiled and shrugged. "I'd have to count them. There are lots of them."

Things settled, they rode back to Wagon Wheel.

Jesus met them on the front porch. "Well?"

"We have a superintendent and two foremen."

He nodded in approval.

The Bar Ten was a good distance south of Holbrook and farther yet from the Wagon Wheel. Chet and his outfit, including Bo, left the next morning and found it mid-afternoon. When they reined up before the rambling house, a man put on his cord coat and hat to come out to greet them.

"I'm John Arnold, may I help you?"

Chet dropped out of the saddle and stuck out his hand. "Chet Byrnes, Quarter Circle Z, Preskitt, Arizona. These men work for me. I heard you'd like to sell this ranch. We rode over to talk to you about it."

"Nice to meet you. I want half a million dollars for lock, stock, and barrel of this place."

Chet nodded. "I'm thinking two hundred thousand, cash."

Arnold smiled, shook his head as if amused at Chet's offer, and started to turn away.

"Arnold, it'll soon be snowing here. How much hay have you got?" Chet had not seen a stack in sight.

"You talking cash for this place?"

"I am talking cash."

"Where is the money at?"

"Preskitt."

"That your best offer?"

"Yes." Chet gathered his reins as if ready to leave.

"How long will it take to get it here?"

"Oh, it's already at the bank."

"I would have to see a clear deed," Bo said.

The man blinked at him. "It's clear."

"That's Bo. He's my real estate man."

"The First State Bank have all the papers on it in Holbrook."

"This is Tuesday. We can have your money there Friday. We will meet you there at ten a.m. Friday, but I will meet you at the bank at nine a.m. tomorrow to see the papers on it. I must see that there are no liens or judgments against it — you understand?" Bo said.

Arnold stood there nodding his head. "You understand I only had this week to sell it?"

"No. Why is that?" Chet asked.

"My wife was moving back to Texas without me if I didn't. Gentlemen, I will meet you at the bank tomorrow."

Chet reached out and shook his hand. "Tomorrow at the bank."

"Yes. I'll be there." Chet watched him head for the front door like he was under a spell until he disappeared inside and closed the door behind him.

"Now, what was his problem?" Bo asked.

Chet took off his hat and shook his head. "I reckon she planned to leave him here."

"How serious is his hay situation?" Billy Bob asked.

"I have no idea. Mount up and we will look at it while we are here."

Chet noted the nice spring-fed creek that divided the wide, grassy swale the ranch headquarters sat in. This would be some outfit and might be the best ranch he'd bought so far. There were several haystacks and no immediate forage problem. The corrals looked extra stout and well designed. A few ranch hands waved at them passing by.

Chet reined up and spoke to one, a man in his thirties. "Who's the foreman here?"

"We don't have one right now. His wife fired him three weeks ago. He's the boss. I mean Arnold. And I think he's at the house."

Chet checked his horse. "I plan to buy the ranch this week. Tell the men to sit tight. I'll be back here and I have a good man hired for that job."

"That is damn good news, mister."

"Chet, Chet Byrnes."

"I've heard of you. Boy, that will be good news to this outfit."

"See you Friday."

"You damn sure will."

They turned their horses and headed back to tell Thurman Meadows his job was about to begin. Riding back to town they passed several sets of cattle — in Chet's opinion lots of calves needed to be weaned. But he had a man coming who could handle all that.

Maggie made a fresh pot of coffee for them and they gathered at her kitchen table.

"So, you bought the Bar Ten?" Thurman laughed. "I knew he wanted to sell it badly. Might I ask the final price?"

"Sure. Two hundred thousand cash on the barrelhead."

"You bought a real bargain. I have no idea about conditions over there, but Sam Barkley quit three weeks ago. He must have had a big fuss with her. Several folks tried to get him down but he wanted a million bucks for it."

"Until, I guess, she told him she was leaving after this week if he didn't have it sold," Chet said.

"Oh heavens, yes. I bet that spurred him into selling it to you for any price."

Chet chuckled. "We never met her. A ranch hand said she fired the last foreman a few weeks ago."

"That woman came here from hell," Maggie said in a low voice. "He married her two years ago. His first wife died a few years before that. Arnold always was such a nice guy. Helped his neighbors. Did things that were needed in our community. But she stopped all that. She's about thirty and bossy. She may be fifteen years younger than him. But, boy, he found a loser."

"Now, Maggie —"

"Thurman Meadows, I have not said one word was not the truth."

They all laughed.

"Devil or not. I want you two to live in the big house when she's gone. I will even buy some furniture. I want you to hire some house help. Now, wait, Maggie," Chet told her. "My friends and businesspeople will come by and spend time there. I don't expect you to have to wait on them, but you will need some household help."

"Why, that house is as big as a hotel."

"I just said, hire some help. You are going to think you are a hotel owner before this is over."

She laughed as she refilled the coffee cups. "I won't ever embarrass you, I swear on a Bible."

"That's great. You and my wife, Lisa, will get along fine."

"I am anxious to meet her, too."

"Many times, she rides with us. You will meet her shortly. Thurman, Wells Fargo is shipping the money over here. All is going like directed and we close on Friday unless Bo finds a problem with the title."

"I'll get my foremen ready to meet the

crew at the ranch that day. I guess he still has a cook for the ranch crew?"

"I bet she fired him, too," Maggie said.

"I can loan you Tad until you get one. It's important having a good cook. We made a quick appraisal. He has hay. We have a hay specialist and he has more if you need it but don't wait till the last minute because it is west of here a good way."

"I'll keep that in mind. It doesn't usually snow here like at Flagstaff."

"I know that. See you Friday at the ranch."


They rode back to the Wagon Wheel Ranch.

Lucinda greeted them with a "Did you find it?"

Hanging his gun belt, coat, and hat on top in the front hall, Chet smiled. "We bought it."

"Wow. Is it a big place?"

"Twenty sections. We will see when Bo gets through."

"He didn't come back with you?"

"No. He's staying in town to examine the title."

"Does it have a big house?"

"Yes. We did not get invited to look inside."

"You should have taken me along. I would have gotten you inside to see it."

"I wasn't too worried about it."

She went off, shaking her head like she couldn't believe he didn't want to see the inside of the house before he bought it. "Supper will be ready shortly."

"What was wrong?" Billy Bob quietly asked him.

"She wondered what the house looked like inside and couldn't believe I bought it sight unseen."

"Cheap as you bought that place it could have been a tent."

Chet agreed and went to find Jesus.

"Everything go all right?" Jesus asked him.

"Yes. But Arnold is a strange man. He asked his price of half a million. My offer was two hundred thousand, cash. Something about the cash offer stopped him and he agreed to accept it. I didn't expect him to do that, but he did and it was, I think, her threat to leave him."

"Did you meet her?"

"No. She never came outside. It wasn't that cold. It is a nice-enough-looking ranch. Thurman had no idea, either, why he accepted that little. He and those other two are ready to take it over by the weekend. It is a grassy outfit. Not a place like my home ranch but a working one."

"Did Bo doubt anything about it?"

"No. He is being careful and tomorrow making certain there are no liens or lawsuits against it."

"I guess we may miss meeting Arnold's wife." Jesus shook his head. Then he dropped his voice. "Spencer's wife is a little too bossy for me."

Chet nodded he understood.

They were called to supper and more questions were asked during the evening meal about the Bar Ten. Chet told them the sale would soon be completed and then they could see it for themselves.

Wells Fargo delivered the money on time. The bank president in Holbrook was Jeremy Priene, and he tried to be helpful. Arnold's wife did not attend the exchange. Bo was satisfied with the paperwork.

Chet tried to talk to Arnold but the man had little to say.

The ranch sale completed, they rode out to the ranch, met up with Thurman Meadows, and were introduced to Riley Day, the man left in charge for the time being, and he agreed to show Chet's crew everything about the ranch they might need to know. He told them there were six ranch hands, two yard workers, and four domestics. They all told him they would like to continue working there.

Thurman asked him for their salaries, and he produced a paper. Ranch hands were paid from twenty to twenty-five a month, room and board. The rest were paid eighteen dollars a month.

Arnold and Day promised to move their things out in the next few days. Chet and his bunch left and met the other two young men, Jamie and Hines, at a local café for lunch.

"Boy, we never expected him to sell out that cheap," Jamie said.

His partner agreed.

Chet sat back with a coffee cup in his hand. "Neither did I, but who knows? When you are satisfied with the hay situation needs, count the cattle. I think we have plenty of hay but distance may hurt, so if local sources can't supplement your needs economically we will ship it over to you.

"Also, we need a report on the ranch's haying equipment condition and needs. No matter how small the problem, we want this operation to work so let us know any problem you three have."

"Are you going back on the strip?"

"Yes, after roundup next spring."

"Okay."

Back to the ranch. Chet and his crew

joined Thurman and his men in lining things up — checking the remuda, the farm equipment, range condition, hay on hand, where they mowed it, and cattle count — until he was satisfied they had things in pretty good shape.

Before they went back west, Chet saw he had purchased a great ranch with low needs to boost it. It could use some windmills for better range distribution, needed some perimeter fencing, but like he told Jesus, it all would come together in time.

They would have over half his investment back by the following fall in cattle sales and perhaps even more than that.

Jesus and Tad stayed to run the Wagon Wheel for a month, so Fred could go back and see his wife and newborn child. The decision was an easy one to make. Fred promised the pair he'd bring her and his son back short of that time.

Sis, that first night out en route back home, asked them lots of questions about his latest acquisition. She shook her head at his reply: "Just another working ranch we needed."

They made a hard push and reached the Verde Ranch house long after sundown, waking Reba, Victor, and Adam. Tom came down for breakfast and Millie joined him.

Chet and the others explained about new ranch and then they left and rode on for the top place, reaching it after lunch. Lisa and the house girls fed them. Fred, his wife, and son had a big reunion.

Chet and Lisa drove over to Jesus's ranch and explained to Anita that her husband would be back in a month or less. He was watching Fred's place until they got back. She thanked them and said she and the men working for them had everything under control. It was after dark when Chet and Lisa and the man riding guard got back. Chet felt very tired after all their running around but the big house welcomed both of them and he and Lisa sat up talking to each other about the events that had happened.

"You know your railroad man wants Spencer to build a four-line telegraph system across the Territory and run a good one down here?"

Squatted down on his boot heels to put another log on the fire in the fireplace, he nodded. "I don't blame Spencer for taking on the job."

"I am stingy, I guess. He took both Cole and Salty, who I adore. And now Spencer?"

"They have great opportunities to advance their lives."

"But who will fix all our places?"

"Fred and Billy Bob are making real good leaders. Tad is no slouch."

"You know, I have worked a lot helping him cook, and in the past half year I think he's really taken a hold. Was it the money from the cave?"

"Probably. But he is doing some powerful thinking for the ranch's benefits, too."

"Good to have you back home. Let's go to bed."

"I thought you'd never ask."

"Chet Byrnes, I have almost been crying for your return."

He kissed her and laughed. "So have I, girl. So have I."

Things settled down into winter. They had a big Christmas party for the ranch workers and one for everyone else who could come. Valerie and Rocky came down for the event from Flagstaff. Cole bowed out of attending, as he was busy solving problems with his stage lines and the telegraph operation.

Chet spoke to Valerie about Cole's involvement in his job.

"Of course, they want him to fail, Chet. And he is fighting almost one-handed against the people stacked in those jobs by the past bosses, people who want the old, easygoing system to replace his on-time orders. He knows who they are, but it is hard to throw them out without any more infractions than what they've tried to pull on him. In time, he will win but they fight him underhandedly.

"He's even caught them sawing axles to cause wrecks."

"You reckon I could help him?"

"You know, outside of Salty there is no one else."

"I'll get involved."

"Don't tell him we talked. He wants to beat them by himself."

"So do I, Val. So do I."

Chet and Lisa discussed the problem that night after the party. He planned to move up there, stay in one of his own cabins, and start seeing what was going wrong with Cole's employees.

Joel Hart had been one of the first drivers that Cole hired earlier. The past administration, after Cole left, had fired Hart for complaining the harnesses needed repairs. He was back to driving for them because Cole sent for him.

"There is a lady here knows more than I do about the undercover crap they are pulling on Cole," Hart told him. "She can really tell you all about them bastards."

"What's her name?" Chet poured some more whiskey into Joel's cup. He'd just come in off his run from New Mexico and had two days off.

"Amanda Dodge. She's a shady lady but some of the ones that got hurt in their so-called *accidents* were her best customers. She and some of the others made a list of the underhanded men, but there are no sheriff deputies up here to turn it over to. They didn't trust anyone — figured they'd get their own throats cut for doing it."

"How do I get secretly in touch with her?"

"Leave your door unlocked at night."

"What will she charge me?"

"Oh yeah. Well, I never bought any evidence from her."

Chet laughed. "I'll ask her, then."

Two nights later, she arrived. Chet was sitting up in a chair as she carefully slipped inside the dark room and closed the door. She gave a start when he whispered, "Hello."

"I'm not here to hurt you, Amanda. My name is —"

"You're Chet Byrnes. I know who you are."

"Take a chair. I am prepared to pay you for your help."

"Anyone ever knows it was me, they may

kill me."

"No one will ever know. I guarantee you that."

"I want these bastards to rot in jail. They killed some of my best friends."

"All I need is a list."

"Here. You can't read it in the dark, but I can tell you the names on my list."

"Go ahead."

"Carl Stokes, Norman Hadley, Hop Franklin, and Butch Horns."

"What do I owe you?"

"He said you won't want my services." He could see by her silhouette that she tossed her shoulder-length hair back like she would do, propositioning a man in the daylight.

"I have a wife."

"Don't stop many men. Oh, how does twenty dollars sound?"

"How does forty sound?"

"Robbery."

With her loud perfume in his nose, he grasped her hand and pressed two twenty-dollar gold coins in her palm and closed her fingers on them. "Learn more and come tell me."

"Hell, mister, I'd fly to the moon to tell you for this much money."

"You be careful."

She slipped away in the night with the

slick swish of her silk dress and high heels on the porch.

Chet latched the door and lit the lamp to read the names on the list. She had a very flowery penmanship. He didn't know one man on her list, however, starting tomorrow he'd start getting acquainted with them.

In the smoky confines of the Texas Darling Saloon, playing two-bit poker the next afternoon, he met Hop Franklin. Dried tobacco juice crusted his lower lip and his flannel shirt sleeve cuffs were worn to shreds. He cussed all the time about everything wrong in his life and bet wild as all get-out. His height was about five-eight and he weighed more than two hundred pounds. Needed a haircut, a shave, and a bath. He stunk.

Chet won all his money, and Franklin left, grumbling about the cowboy bastard who got it all. Drunk two nights later, two men he didn't know beat the fire out of Hop with batlike sticks and told him Flagstaff was not the place for him to live and if he wanted to continue to breathe to leave the village at once. Hop must have accepted their words of encouragement and was never seen again in the Flagstaff city limits.

Norman Hadley's cinch broke riding

down to the Indian village where he kept a squaw. Before losing his saddle, he may have been warned that his company was no longer wanted around there.

Carl Stokes found a live rattlesnake in his oven. He left his cabin screaming that they were after him. Butch Horns woke up drunk in the alley behind Lord's Livery to find the crack of his ass had been highlighted. He left town, yelling and trying to stop the pain by fanning his bare posterior with his hat.

Amanda Dodge received a crisp twenty-dollar bill in an envelope at her general delivery box at the Flagstaff post office a week later. And Joel Hart looked good underneath his new Boss of the Plains Stetson hat, driving the afternoon stage off toward Gallup.

There being no more business for Chet Byrnes to do in Flagstaff, he rode that cold day for home. It snowed lightly the second day coming up the mountain but on his arrival his wife rushed to him in their house and assured him she'd given the house girls the day off.

He really loved that woman.

# CHAPTER 31

The following week, midday on a Tuesday, a small rancher named Rolla Kincaid came by and asked for his help. Someone had broken into his ranch house while he and his wife were gone and stole all his wife's jewelry, and while it was not worth a large sum, her grandmother had owned it.

Rolla stood there with his hands jammed down in his jeans pockets and looked to be on his last legs. "Gawd damn, Chet, that was all she had worth ten cents in her life besides our five kids. Anyone could find it, I figured maybe you could."

"Better come inside and I'll make me a list."

At the kitchen table with pencil and paper, Chet listed the gold chain necklace, two brooches, and two gold bracelets. He wrote *Irma Kincaid's Jewelry* on the top of the page.

He told Rolla he'd see what he could do.

If Fred had still been living around there Chet bet he could've given him the list and recovered the jewelry that afternoon. But he didn't know anyone living on the fringe like that who might know where to find the robbers. "Tell her I hope we can find them."

"I told her you were the guy to ask. Thanks again." He left.

Lisa asked what he wanted. He told her.

She shook her head. "People think you have a telegraph wire to God."

"Maybe because I use to own such a company."

She hugged him, laughing. "You simply can't say no."

"Well, that's probably the truth. Weather's holding off. I may ride up toward Deer Valley and see if I can find out anything."

"Take two guys with you," she said, going down the hall.

Vance sent Vic and a younger hand named Alfred along with him. Dressed warm enough for the temperature they rode across country to save some time and, by going up into the timber on a steep trail, they were forced to ride single file through the tall pine growth.

Chet heard a shot then another coming from above them. He waved on Vic, who had the lead. His own cow pony scrambled to match Vic's horse's cat-hopping. Rocks were rolled back by their horses' hard-pressed effort to climb the mountain as fast as they could. Alfred was bringing up the rear.

Vic gained the edge of open meadow and he reined his horse onto the level bench. There was an empty saddle on a hipshot horse standing about a hundred yards to the east.

"Someone is on the ground," Chet shouted, and spurred his pony down the narrow field.

The body facedown on the ground was not moving. With his six-gun in his hand, he reined in his horse to a skidding stop, slid off the saddle, and, seeing no one, dropped to his knee to examine the person's condition.

He was still breathing.

Vic had his own horse stopped and looked down at Chet for an answer.

"Check it out." Chet turned back to the wounded man. Really a boy. He couldn't be older than twenty.

Vic charged off eastward.

"Lay still," Chet told the wounded victim.

"What can I do?" Alfred, the second rider who came with him asked, and hurriedly dismounted, looking around like he expected the shooter to be right there by them.

"The shooter is gone," Chet said. "Get my raincoat off my saddle."

Alfred nodded and got Chet's raincoat. "What else?"

"We need to transport him to a doctor."

"Where's one of them?"

"I am not certain —" He watched the wounded one draw away from them. "Keep fighting. We —"

His body gave a last shudder and everything went quiet.

"He died —"

Vic came riding back with the pistol in his hand. "Who is he?"

"He's dead, Vic. I never saw him before in my life. Does that horse over there have a brand?" Chet gave a head toss toward the grazing one the dead boy must have been riding when he was shot.

"We better load him. Nothing we can do for him now."

"It's a double seven."

Chet had never heard of anyone who had that brand. "No help. Bring him over."

He rose to his feet. "Either of you see the shooter?"

"No, sir."

"So, this young man is shot. We heard the gun crack but never saw the shooter. He's dead and no gunman is in sight."

"What do we do next?"

Chet warily shook his head. "Take his body to the sheriff in town. Tell him what we know, which is nothing. And we go home."

"Is that against the law?" Alfred asked.

"It is not supposed to be." Chet guessed this youth from Mexico had concerns they might be blamed for the dead man's demise.

The corpse tied over his saddle seat, they headed toward town with him. At the courthouse Chet went inside and spoke to the desk officer.

"My name is Chet Byrnes. A few hours ago, we heard some shots and rode up on Kilmer Flats to find a man freshly shot. Very shortly after, he died on us. We brought his body in. It's outside, across his horse. He never told us anything before he died and we saw no sight of anyone nor another horse besides the one standing over him. We did not search him."

"He shoot himself?"

"He didn't wear a gun. Nor was there one on the ground around him."

"Take his body down to Harold at the funeral home. Someone may show up who knows him. Is his horse worth a damn?"

"No."

"Take him to the livery and you can pay the feed bill and claim him or donate him to the livery."

"We can do that."

"You live at Preskitt Valley, right?"

"Yes."

"Sign here that you brought him in, just in case we need to do something more about him."

"Okay."

Chet left the sheriff's office. They delivered the body to the undertaker, dropped the horse at the livery, and the three rode back to the ranch. Chet wondered all the way who the dead young man was, who shot him, and why. Alfred, riding with him, could not understand the meaning or the reason for the poor man's death and must have worried some that he'd be implicated in his murder.

When they returned to the ranch Chet met with his foreman Vance and talked to him about the matter. Vance saw no reason for it, either, but was glad they were all right.

At the house, he told Lisa all about it and she thought it was strange, too. A man was murdered and the sheriff's office acted like a dog had died and weren't interested in who it was or anything else. Even in bed later Chet couldn't sleep. In the morning, he'd send word to Jesus and maybe they'd go in to talk to Bo about it. The more he pondered on the matter the more he wished he had someone like Fred or Cole there.

The murdered man was a gringo. But nearly all his people around Preskitt were Hispanic. Maybe Billy Bob could learn more. He was down on the Verde helping Tom. Or even Tad the cook — damn, he couldn't sleep. So he got up, put on a robe, and went downstairs to sit in the dark living room.

In a short while Lisa came down in her robe and found him. "Are you sick?"

"No, that damn murder today has me wondering like a madman who was involved."

She sat on his lap. "What can you do about it sitting down here in the dark?"

"If I knew that I wouldn't be so upset about the whole thing."

She laughed softly. "I knew the matter bugged you."

"I don't have the gringo side up here to go look into it. I think it would take someone like Salty or Fred to get to the bottom of it."

"Fred's off running the Wagon Wheel. And he could solve it, I bet, if he was here. He knew every rumor that went on in Preskitt.

Salty has been kidnapped by Cole, and Cole knew how to find things out, didn't he?"

"I would bet either one of them would know in a few hours."

He kissed her and they smooched awhile. Finally, he gave up and they went back to their warm bed.

A little groggy from not sleeping well, he found Vance in the kitchen, talking to the two house girls, when he got down there the next morning.

"Anything wrong?" Chet asked.

"I talked to Vic and the boy awhile last night after you came up here. I knew you were upset not knowing the dead man's name and the way the sheriff's deputy acted. I sent three men to town with a little silver money last night. When they came back about midnight, they told me the dead man's name was Andrew Styles. He was wanted in Colorado. There is a reward for him, dead or alive. It sounded like someone was going to collect a reward for him — but they won't try to grab his body until the last day they can to collect the reward."

"How much is the reward?"

"They thought two-fifty."

"Did they know who would pay the reward?"

"Wells Fargo."

"Good. They will tell me who claims the reward."

"Does that answer your concerns?"

"Yes." Turning to the girls, he added, "Scramble me some eggs, fry some potatoes. Do you girls have biscuits?"

"We sure do."

"Make some gravy, then, too. Vance and I are starving."

"I just came to tell you what I learned."

"Let's celebrate. You did a helluva job figuring this one out. It isn't a sin to eat up here."

"My wife might think it is."

"Bring her next time. I know you don't flirt with Lisa's girls."

The girls laughed in the background.

Amused, Vance nodded his head. "That might prove I don't."

"I'll write the Wells Fargo rewards man this morning and flat out ask him for the guy's name that collects the reward and tell him why." He lowered his voice. "I am sorry I doubted you could learn those facts. Cole and Fred spoiled me with news about what white folks were doing."

"Tell us what they wanted him in Colorado for," Natalie asked, refilling coffee cups. "Julie and I are curious."

"I bet I can do that." Chet lifted his hot coffee mug up to sip it. Things would work out. "That Alfred, who went along with us yesterday, I think was afraid they'd arrest us for killing him."

Vance chuckled. "I'll send a tougher guy with you and Vic next time."

"No. He has to learn how to live up here."

"You're right. But he would have sold his soul if he thought he would be arrested."

Things settled down. Everyone in ranching was getting ready for spring roundup. Chet and Lisa were in town to handle some business. Judge Roger Hannaby stopped them in the bank lobby and Chet knew he had something on his mind.

"I had been wondering if I could speak to the two of you in private."

Chet smiled. "We under investigation?"

"No. This is more personal. About an individual minor."

"They serve soft drinks in the pharmacy and have private booths. We could be pretty private in there."

"Excellent. Let's stroll down there. I guess you are busy ranching?"

"It never quits."

"I understand the railroad came and stole your man Cole away from you again."

"Yes, they did. It is a great opportunity for him, no doubt."

"Generous of you to let him go back."

"They needed him. They are paying him well and when he comes out of that job he will be able to do anything he wants to do."

"How can an ordinary cowboy run a stage line and a telegraph company and make them money?"

"Your Honor, Cole Emerson is no ordinary cowboy."

Hannaby chuckled. "He must not be, Mrs. Byrnes."

"Trust me, he isn't."

"He got that stage back on the timetable in ten days. His telegraph business is doing four times the business they had when he took it back over."

"Wonderful." They took seats in the booth. "Do you know the Lindsey girl, Mrs. Byrnes?"

"I am Lisa, and no, not well. I heard she lost her mother."

"Yes. She lives with her maternal grandparents. She is twelve years old."

Chet nodded. "A little older than my oldest boy."

"Her grandparents asked me to find her a home. They live in town and she is, well, a tomboy cowgirl. Well, I wondered if you two would consider her as a visitor out at your place."

"My oldest son lives with Cole and his wife up at Flagstaff. The other, Adam, lives with Victor and his wife at the Verde Ranch."

"They are both planning to live with us for a time this summer," Lisa said.

"Well —"

"I guess she and those boys could ride horses?"

"I understand she rides very good."

"I'd damn sure be sad to know I couldn't ride horses all summer as much as I like to ride." Lisa shook her head. "Would she become ours if it worked out?"

"I believe so. Her grandparents are really too old to be parents. But they would want to know her foster parents wanted her."

"When could we meet her?" Lisa asked.

"Tomorrow?"

Chet bobbed his head yes. "Didn't her father die two years ago?"

"Yes. I heard he was a good businessman."

They drank their sarsaparilla and set up a ten a.m. meeting at the grandparents' home, then drove home. Lisa was excited.

"What was her first name?" she asked him as they were going downhill.

"I didn't catch it. He'll tell us again."

"Will the boys approve?"

"If she's not stuck up and doesn't mind riding horses she will get along with those two."

"It might be a great summer for the three of them."

"It will be a great summer anyway."

"I plan for it to be that."

"What about the trip to the strip?"

"We can just play the whole thing by ear."

Lisa hugged his arm. "I think that having her will be a dream come true for me or the worst thing I ever agreed to."

Chet laughed the rest of the way home.

The next morning came quickly, and they were on their way to town.

"What were you like at twelve?"

"Horsey. I went to roundup when I was twelve. I learned boys peed standing up and kept their back to you doing it. I never had a brother. That may be why I ended up in Colorado with that pretty boy. Here I was, in a world no one explained. I had no mother to tell me a damn thing. She died when I was eight. I've been pondering on how to talk to a twelve-year-old girl ever since yesterday."

"You told me you hoped you had a girl so you could point out your mistakes."

"Yeah, but not twelve. I wanted some

practice time on her at two and three years old."

"No such deal. Today is the deal."

"I know and I am shaking inside."

"I think you will get along great with her."

She punched his arm. "Silly, I don't even know her."

"You will, Lisa."

"Will the boys share you with her?"

"I guess so. Never thought about it."

The girl's grandparents' house was one of those large, rambling mansions with a butler. They didn't have one of them at Preskitt Valley. The butler took Chet's good hat and placed it on a hatstand in the hall closet, closed the door, and led them into the living room.

On a raised voice he announced, "Mr. and Mrs. Byrnes."

A redheaded, freckle-faced girl rose and came over to shake their hands. "I am so pleased that you came today."

"So are we," Chet said. "Your grand-parents here?"

"No. They feared that they would cry. I told them I'd be fine on a ranch with two guys."

"The boys aren't there yet. But they are coming, and Lisa wrote them that you would be coming as well."

"That was very nice of you. My suitcases are in the hall."

"Then it's off to the races."

"Do you go to the horse races, Mr. Byrnes?"

He stopped her. "My name's Chet. No *mister*. I go sometimes but never thought about having a girl to go with me."

"Your wife doesn't attend them?" She looked down at her polished shoes, a little crestfallen.

Lisa hugged her. "He's been busy all spring but this summer he's taking both of us to every one of them."

"Wow. I'd love that."

"So would I." Lisa winked privately at him while he was loading the buckboard. "My name is Lisa."

"My proper name is Ringold, but I like to be called Renny."

"You are christened Renny for all summer. Have you ever driven a team?"

"Oh yes."

"Why don't you drive us home?"

"I have never been there."

"Here, hold the reins. I'll get in back."

"Cluck to them," Lisa said.

The team began to move out and their new ward did a professional job of turning them around and they were off to the ranch.

Lisa coached her through the town traffic and then onto the open road eastward at a trot. Chet enjoyed watching Renny, filled with excitement as she handily handled the horses. His wife was busting her buttons. He felt it was neat to get off to such a good start with the girl. If this was any sign of the summer's future, they'd have fun with the boys and her.

On Saturday, Cole and Valerie brought Rocky down. Chet and Cole had lots of time to visit and talk about the stage and wire services. The telegraph was running well and Spencer was busy making up a list of needs for a four-line setup for it across Arizona. His plans were to be at Wagon Wheel Ranch for roundup before he seriously tackled that job.

Cole told Chet that the railroad was going to repay the ranch the salary that Chet paid him while on the repair job and did not expect for Chet to pay him for the construction of this larger line.

"They think with the hookups on each end they can really make it pay for itself before the train arrives."

Then Cole lowered his voice. "Whose girl is she again?"

"Renny's mother died first, and then her

dad was killed two years ago. She's been with her old grandparents. She is with us for the summer. Judge Hannaby thought she'd be happier riding horses out here than living in a mansion in town. She's a cowgirl and she gets along with Lisa well."

"I bet she can beat those boys at anything."

Chet agreed. "They have their work cut out for them."

"How is the new ranch doing?"

"Thurman's son says well. He writes his father's letters. They have recorded over eighteen hundred mother cows. That is a bigger outfit than they promised me, which is usually the opposite. Roundup may show more. I may move some cattle from there over to Toby's Rustler's Ranch. He has the hay and feed and I don't want to eat the range to the roots over there. We have lots of open range that Toby opened with water sources at the homesteads and windmills to spread them out."

"Are those alfalfa fields we set up working?"

"Yes. They will mow them in a few weeks. They look great. Cutting them in two parts worked."

"I knew a shorter run was the way. We are getting more jobs from Wells Fargo on the stages, too. In fact, I met a man named Dodge who knows you from the marshal days in southern Arizona. He's one of their top men now and he laughed when he met me. Said why in the hell did they fire me in the first place? Why anyone who knew anything would have kept a Chet Byrnes-trained guy in charge. I told him they cut my pay and I quit. He laughed and said they were lucky to get me back and to tell you hi."

"Your boss figured that out, too."

Cole agreed. "In a few months, I will have all that junk cleaned up on our locations from New Mexico to the Colorado River. All sound top horses, sober drivers, and on schedule."

"Will Val be all right without her son over the summer?"

"She understands. He's growing up fast."

"Yes, both him and Adam are."

"You going back to the strip?"

"After roundup. One of the brothers is going. Can you spare Salty for a month to six weeks?"

"Things go this smooth, yes."

"Sarge is lending me his man Cody again."

"Billy Bob?"

"He's really grown up. Made a great hand."

"Tad handling the cooking?"

"Him, and the boss lady. Same crew except you almost."

"I know and you know this job is a great deal for me. You know, too, that lots of guys have been crowded out and never got a chance to go back and kick it back into shape again. I am glad I did have that chance."

"Nor do many men, like Cosby, come back and look at things that were going wrong, bust up the wrongdoers, and hire right again."

"You ever hear about the guy who dropped that ranch on you? Him or his wife?"

"No. I never saw him after I closed that deal."

"He must've gone back to Texas with her."

"I guess so."

"I need to get back to Flagstaff tomorrow. I have a stage line to run. Have fun this summer."

"Thanks. I hope the boys and Renny will have fun. I'll be fine."

"Lisa's worked great for you, didn't she?"

"Oh yes. She is a very thoughtful lady. No big storms. She also thinks deep and she's really good for me."

"Hope you find a trunk full of rubies."

"I bet we found them all."

Chet saw the two of them off the next morning. Val was a little sad parting with her stepson as she kissed him good-bye on the cheek. He and Lisa stood on the porch until Val and Cole's dust was gone.

"What is on for today, now that both Rocky and Adam are here, too?"

"Horse racing at the fairgrounds this afternoon. Remember, we promised her. Billy Bob is set up to go along. The kids want to ride horses over there. I'll take you in the buckboard."

They left midmorning with food packed in two wicker baskets and Natalie along to help. Billy Bob rode horses with the kids while Chet drove Lisa in the buckboard.

Their drive into town gave them ample time to get to the grounds. It was all new for his kids, but one of the grand social events of the spring for the town.

There were hundreds already there at the grandstands and track. A warm day for that early in the spring and there was lots of talking about the horses running.

"Now, guys, Renny is your ward. You be sure she is with you and not in harm's way, understand me?"

"We'll watch her," Rocky promised.

Billy Bob nodded that he'd keep an eye on them, too. Then they were off and gone that quickly. The ranch had a reserved covered picnic spot with four tables under it. Lisa and her helper began to set out the lunch and lemonade. She sent Chet off to be social.

The church crowd wouldn't be there for at least another hour. Chet had crossed off their attending it for the day.

By twelve-thirty the grounds would be busting at the seams with families and horse racing activity.

Chet spoke to some other ranchers. Several asked if he would go back treasure hunting on the strip. To answer them, he said they planned to do some more but had no schedule yet, that their discoveries and subsequent finding were probably a once-in-a-lifetime find. Folks always suspected such finds abounded in a land not too heavily explored.

Tom and Millie joined them.

"Heckuva crowd here already," Tom said.

"People getting ready to break out," Chet said.

His threesome soon joined him and took him aside.

"Dad?" Rocky began. "Renny wants to

ride in the novice girl's race on a horse belonging to the Bar K Ranch."

"Is he rideable? Sometimes they bring colts here green as grass."

"No problem. She's already ridden him in the pen. He's not a plow horse and she can handle him. But you have to tell the stewards it is okay for her to ride."

"They wouldn't take your word?"

"Dad. You have to be an adult to do that."

Adam shook his head. "Hell, no, we tried that."

"Better drop the cuss words. I better speak to Lisa and I'll be right back. Renny, I guess you'd like to do this?"

"Oh yes."

"Wait here. I'll go ask her."

He strode back to the shade and excused Lisa from the crowd there.

"What is it?"

"They are having an all-girl horse race. Your buddy wants to ride and her grooms want her to."

"Wow. One to ten, how dangerous is it?"

"Two to three if she falls off."

"Those boys haven't planned her demise?"

"No. They were annoyed the judges didn't accept their approval of her riding in the event."

"You decide. She's a pretty smart girl and

she can ride."

"I say yes. I think a win or close win would bind those three together."

"I never thought about that. Go ahead."

"Thanks." He strode back to the waiting threesome.

"Well, Lisa said, all right. Keep Billy Bob informed. You two look out for her. We will be down at the winner's circle waiting for the roses."

Rocky made a face. "Dad, we aren't sure this colt can even run."

"If I get in a horse race, I plan to win from the get-go," was Chet's reply to his son.

"Thanks, Chet. I plan to win." Renny looked pleased and behind those freckles there was a determined set to her smile and in her brown eyes. If she didn't win this time, watch out for the next time was how he saw it.

Billy Bob saw it, too, and chuckled. "Maybe we better ride him in that pen some."

"Listen to him, kids. He's a hand with horses."

"The girl's race is the third one," Adam informed him, and they left to sign up for it.

Chet figured that was their goal. He overheard Adam ask Billy Bob if he'd ever won a race.

The answer was not loud enough for him to hear.

Carl Evans, who ranched south of the new place, asked how Cole was doing up at Flagstaff.

"He has the stagecoaches back on a real-time schedule and they are close to quadrupling the number of telegraph lines."

"I hated when I learned he was going back to work for them. He and Val made real neighbors. The new man you have up there is very polite and friendly but that Cole is a real manager. He had that stage deal working well and the folks they hired to replace him didn't know a damn thing about running it. Be real honest with me. Is that train running across through there really going to help us prosper?"

"I believe it will but how long will it take to get here is the question. On that I have no idea. It may take ten years."

"Oh Lord. That is way too long. Thanks."

They shook hands and Chet went on back to the shade.

"She entered?"

"Billy Bob's handling that. It is the third one on the card. They said the colt was gentle and she is ready to race."

She swung on his arm. "I never thought

about the bonding part. You can snack on the food or we can go be at the finish line."

"I'll get a bite now and when the race is over we can come back and eat."

He took a plate of cherry cobbler and a spoon from Natalie then motioned for Lisa to start for the finish line. They stopped and spoke to Bo on the way.

"Where you going?" his land man asked.

"Lisa's new ward is in the girl's-only race."

"Where did she come from?"

"She is a trial deal. The judge asked us to see if we could help her."

"She a jockey?"

"Both my horse experts think so."

"Who's that?"

"Adam and Rocky." Chet was laughing by then.

Bo was rocking his oldest in his arms, laughing. "You hear that, Shelly?"

"Yes. I am anxious to see this race."

"Here, Lisa, hold my plate. We can go up to the finish line."

"This must be kids' day at the track," Bo said, switching the baby to his other side.

They soon were in place. Race number one was between three spotted Indian ponies, and the riders were all young Indians riding them. Howling like coyotes, they gave it all they had, and the fattest brown boy in a loincloth, feathers in his hair, and riding the fattest spotted pony, won the race.

Next the track announcer called for race number two. This was for young horses and teenage boys only riding them. The starter gun went off and at least four of them left the starting gates bucking like double-jointed critters. The crowd laughed and applauded. A swift black horse won the race, and the boy was riding low with only the finish line in his eyes the entire quarter mile.

His name was Huey Craft, and they presented him the bronze trophy.

Race number three was for previously unraced colts ridden by girls only. Anyone entering a previously run animal would be barred from racing for two years and fined two hundred fifty dollars. Pretty strict rules, but they obviously meant business. Two horses entered were withdrawn at the last minute, leaving a field of five entries. Obviously they feared being exposed.

The starting pistol had a similar effect on the entries. Two of the entries ducked their heads and had no ambition to run but rather bucked while the other three swept away like haints.

Renny on a sorrel was on the outside, bent low in the saddle, and she must have been challenging her mount to run. She was nose to nose with a black and a bay, and the race looked to Chet like it would end in a dead heat, but Renny used a bat on her red horse and it shot ahead, crossing the line first.

"We will have the results for you in a minute, ladies and gentlemen."

A silence smothered the crowd. Billy Bob and the boys on horseback rode up and shouted, "She won fair and square. Why isn't she being announced the winner?"

Dressed in a business suit, big Tom Drake for F Bar Ranch came running over to Chet. "She is your daughter, isn't she?"

"She's my ward."

"What in the hell are they stalling for? She won by a full neck."

She and the two boys leading the dancing colt came up to the finish line.

"The winner is Calvin Arnold's colt Horacio."

The crowd shouted, "No!"

Tom Drake waved his arms in the air to quiet them. "What ruling made you make that call?"

"The girl on the Bar K colt used a false name on her entry."

"What name did she use?" Chet shouted.

"Ringold Byrnes."

Tom looked at Chet.

Chet nodded and then shouted, "Today

that is who she is. My adopted daughter. Ask the judge."

Renny and those two boys were dancing hand in hand in a circle, celebrating, and the crowd was on their feet, roaring.

Lisa ran out and kissed both Tom and Chet. "She won the race. Flat outran both of them."

Soon his entire crew was on the track, waiting for the retraction.

"After due consideration, the Bar K Ranch entry ridden by Ringold Byrnes is today's winner in the third race."

The crowd really roared.

Tom shook his hand. "You have yourself a winner, Chet."

"I had one before that."

"I guess you did. Young lady, anytime you want a horse to race, come holler."

She swallowed and, a little red-faced, thanked him.

"Well, the horse racing committee for the Quarter Circle Z ranch better get down there and eat with Natalie. Before it is all gone."

Lisa had Renny under her arm ahead of them. Chet and the two boys followed them.

"Dad?"

"Yes, Rocky."

"Any of those clay bank horses we own —

can they run?" Rocky asked.

"I bet they can."

"Renny, we need to go see May's son. The family owns those horses that Dad brought from Mexico."

She flashed a smile at him and called them what they were named. "You mean the Barbarossa horses."

Lisa looked to the sky for help.

Chet laughed. "They can run."

They drew a crowd. Not expecting this many, they soon ran out of food, and Lisa spoke to Chet. "I brought enough for twice more than I expected and we still ran out."

"You didn't know you'd win a race, either."

About then Tom Drake's man arrived with the cooked leg of a steer on his shoulder and his men carrying two more and lots of French bread loaves. The party continued. Lisa shook her head at the sight. But they'd have enough to eat for everyone.

Tom said, "I seen they was all down here. More power to you. You and that girl made my day. This is the best day I have ever had on this track. Thanks."

Tom's three men sharpened their knives and they went to work on the beef and the bread.

"Mine, too," Chet agreed. He was prouder

of the kids than anything else. Besides, he saw the bond they'd made with her over the win. It was going to be a helluva summer. He knew it right off.

No one had to rock them to sleep when they made it back to the ranch that evening after dark. He dropped into bed and Lisa mumbled, "Next time — we camp — over there . . ."

# CHAPTER 32

There was a cold-water creek east of Camp
Verde, so his winning horse racing party all
went trout fishing over there. Camping for a
few days under the deep canyon sheer walls,
they caught trout and had a great time. Billy
Bob gave guitar-playing lessons and they
discovered Natalie could really play the
mouth harp. After a week of camping and
some rain they rode back to the ranch, tired.

The threesome, Rocky, Adam, and Renny,
were assigned to help Vance and the crew at
the roundup branding process. Keeping the
branding iron fire red-hot was their job and
they did good at that, according to Vance.
Things moved right along. Chet, Jesus, and
Billy Bob made a run out to check on the
Rustler's Ranch roundup. They were impressed with the crew and all they accomplished. Several of Toby's hands could
heel a calf in a loop, slide them to the fire
on their back as careful as they could be,

and go right back for another.

With three packhorses to pack their camping needs they left to see how Spencer and Fred were doing. Same story. Branding was going smoothly. An hour on the job, Chet saw Spencer was letting Fred lead, which was super — he'd be the man, next year, who would organize it again.

They learned the new baby and mother were doing fine. They spent the night in the cow camp satisfied all was going right. Very early they saddled, ate some jerky, and rode west for the Windmill to pick up Cody. Jamie from the east ranch was to meet them in Flagstaff in four days at the ranch property there. Those guys didn't need any looking after.

They were headed west under a blanket of stars. Midmorning his sister greeted them as they rode into her place.

"You guys look tired."

"We are," Chet said. "How are you?"

"Fine. Breakfast is about cooked. I want to hear about your horse racing team."

Chet's crew laughed.

"Those men will put up your horses. Wash up and come inside. I want to hear it all."

"We are coming."

Seated at the long dining table, drinking some good coffee, he began the story of how

Renny came to Lisa and him. How they were attending the Sunday races with his two boys and Renny and how Fred had offered to let her ride his untried colt in the novice race.

How Chet told Lisa that Renny could safe enough ride him, and so she entered. And how she outran the others and the judges decided he had no daughter so they disqualified her. But the so-called judges quickly learned she was his ward by the court orders and they called her the winner.

"Neither of your sons rode?"

Chet shook his head. "When they get home, they are going to look at the Barbarossa stock for possible entries in the next races."

Sis was laughing. "And you have three teens this summer?"

"Adam's a little short on years but the three of them are fun to watch. They are going up on the strip with us."

"Isn't that dangerous?"

"No. I've got to settle some things while we are there."

"Chet Byrnes, you have not changed one lick. It all has to be straightened out, doesn't it?"

"I like it that way."

"It is the only way you will have it."

"All right. But things in life need straightening and there is lots unsettled up there."

"And I want our foreman back in one piece. Cody has grown into the best man we've ever had, and I get some time to take off and go see a few things — time I never had before. So you remember, I need him back here before the summer is over. Is the railroad coming at all any faster?"

"No, but they are adding three more lines to the telegraph system."

"Why?"

"Cole has that much business."

"I heard he was blowing them away. They need him in charge of the track laying."

"He might be someday. The railroad president knows where he's at."

"That wouldn't surprise you, would it?"

"No. But don't say anything — I don't want to have to run that iron path. Cole can if he wants to and if they will pay him enough."

"Does anyone think it strange that ranch foremen like Cole and Spencer can get things done that no one else can?"

"There is nothing stupid about being a ranch foreman. They all are not that smart but the ones that are make good supervisors anywhere."

"I never would have believed it when we

lived in Texas. But just look at what you have done."

"We better eat and run. Tom can help you if you need anything when Sarge is gone."

"I know. You be careful. I love your wife. I thought Miguel was robbing the cradle but you didn't."

"She's having lots of fun with a daughter."

"How did that happen?"

"Her father was killed in a wagon wreck two years ago. Before that her mother died and so she went to live with her grand-parents, who are old folks. The judge picked for her to stay with us. She's happy. A tomboy like you, and those three together are a big kick."

"I understood the boys were looking forward to this summer with you."

"It had been planned. Roundup is over and we're headed north in a few days."

"You better eat. Those men will be anxious to get on the road."

"Yes, ma'am. Thanks."

They left thirty minutes later, headed west. They stopped for only a short while at the Verde Ranch. Tom was pleased that roundup, across the board, went so well. He'd bought some high-priced Hereford herd sires in Kansas for the purebred herd and had a new hauler. He hoped this guy didn't eat one moving them out to him like the last guy did. He'd been a damn expensive meal, as far as Tom was concerned.

When they reached the top place, Jesus set out for home, in a long lope, on a fresh horse Vance loaned. Lisa and the house girls were all excited to hear how the other ranches were doing with their roundups.

"Fine. We didn't go clear over to see Thurman and the brothers but we saw everyone else east."

"You have been in the saddle a lot," Lisa said, and kissed him. "Boy, are we glad you're back."

"What did I do wrong now?"

"Nothing. Just making a fuss about you being home in time to leave for the strip."

Chet held up two fingers. "I have that long to get ready. Is Salty here or is he going to join us going by Flagstaff?"

"He's up there. But he is going along with us."

"Where are the kids?" He cranked his head around to look for them.

"They're running late. They'll be here any minute."

"It is about dark, isn't it?"

"They have a surprise."

"They just rode in," one of the house girls reported.

Under her breath, Lisa said, "Act surprised."

"Oh — sure."

"He made it back in one piece," Adam said, then they laughed.

"Come down here, Dad. We have your late birthday present, or it might be an early one." Rocky stepped off a saddle in a sweep of his chaps. Pointing to it, he said, "I was just breaking it in a little."

"You mean they finally got it made? They must be out of work."

"No, they fit this one in," Renny said. "Looks great, doesn't it?"

"Yes. Hey, let me give you all a hug. This is certainly nice. I'll enjoy it."

After his hug, they scrambled up the stairs, washed up, and took places at the large circular table. Chet said the blessing and then they ate supper. It was good to get real home cooking after their whirlwind trip. Everything looked fine out there with the spring flush of grass getting up. The conversation at the table ranged from the threesome's hoeing the frijole rows to irrigation of alfalfa.

His young farmers were ready to ride out and be cowhands or at least horseback adventurers for a while. Hampt and May came by on the final night before they left to visit with them and wish them good luck. Chet knew his ranch foreman would have liked to have gone along — but he felt he needed someone steady at home in his absence.

Up before dawn, Jesus had gone over the supply list, checking what was loaded, and agreed they had all they needed. Leading a string of packhorses, they rode out from under the crossbar for the Verde Ranch in the predawn. Not one horse bucked or even acted up — too damn good to be true, Chet decided.

Midmorning, they reached the lower place. Tad Newman, the head cook, his helper Eddie Maine, and the head wrangler, Eldon Grimes, were all ready to ride.

Before he rode out, Chet shook Tom's hand, and his foreman wished him good luck. Victor's wife, who was Adam's step-mother, was introduced to Renny and she wished them a good time.

"Next time you win a big race I want to be there," she told her. The word was out clear down there. Chet laughed.

A little red-faced, Renny nodded and promised her she would invite her if she had time.

Lisa spoke to Millie, who promised her

she'd be up looking after her house in a few hours.

They rode north across the valley and red rock mountains that clustered in the valley.

Late afternoon they camped in the pines on the north rim of the Verde. They even had spooked up four elk. Renny's first time to see one of them. She was impressed by their size.

By the time they had the supper dishes done, it was bedtime, and no one complained about that. Next evening they rode past the stage line offices, and Cole's wife made them stop.

She went past Rocky and slapped him on his chap-covered leg. "Things all right, brother?"

"Yes, ma'am. This is Renny. She won the race Sunday."

"Way to go. Nice to meet you. I need to catch Chet. You all don't have to fix supper tonight or breakfast, either. My crew is feeding you."

A cheer for her went up. She caught up with Chet. "My people will stable your horses and unsaddle them. They will be under lock and key and I have tents in case it rains."

"You are spoiling my crew," Chet said. "Thanks. You meet Renny?"

"Yes. My son introduced me."

"You must've raised him right."

Everyone laughed but Rocky.

Salty and Oleta joined them for the meal. He asked if she could go along. Chet told her she was very welcome.

"See, I told you so," he said to her, and received the side of her hand on his arm.

Before the meal was over, Cole joined them, lamenting he could not go along, that he was jealous of them going up there. "Find me a nice ruby I can have cut and set into a ring."

"Why didn't you take one out that first time?" Chet asked.

"I never thought about it."

"You hear about our new member?" Chet asked him.

"No."

"Renny, this is Cole Emerson. He runs the stage line east and west and the telegraph wire."

"Nice to meet you. Rocky told me all you do."

"She won the open amateur horse race Sunday at the fairgrounds."

"That is wonderful. Teach these two boys how to ride while you are up there, will you?"

She was laughing and shaking her head

too hard to answer him.

"I knew he would say something like that," Rocky told her in disgust.

Jamie Meadows joined them that afternoon. He reported they got along fine at roundup and he had close to nineteen hundred head of cows. Said they were amazed at the number of cows they found and yearling stock.

"Do you imagine that was to keep his taxes down? Most counties charge a dollar a head in taxes," Chet asked him.

"By damn, that's probably what he was doing."

"Thurman wouldn't ever have done that. He was too straitlaced."

"Honesty is not a bad way," Chet told him.

"No, I agree. It is hard to believe a man would cheat that much for that little."

Chet thanked Jamie for coming on this trip and helping him buy the ranch. They discussed moving some of those cows to other outfits in the fall. He thought it would help that range a lot.

The meal was done well and Chet thanked Valerie. So was breakfast, and after it, they headed east to go around the mountains and then head north. Chet reminded them about the thieves and rustlers at that last jumping-off place on the Little Colorado River ferry, their next stopover. They promised not to let them have a thing.

This time he allowed for three days to reach Lee's Ferry and the Englishwoman who ran it. He used the entire short stopover to make sure all the pack saddles were properly on their horses. But the whole time she clucked at his heels, like a scolding hen, about what must be done about the numerous outlaws and gangs roaming the strip.

Away from hearing her at last and on the road, Lisa rode in and told him he had his lecture for the day.

"Well, thank God it is over."

The second day they reached Joseph Lake and the store. Chet and most of the men spoke with the store owner, Rory Lincoln. He had no new reports on criminal activity over the winter and no new clues on the murder of the family. He knew the Logan gang were somewhere in the strip but he had no idea where they might be.

"I guess we will go down to that cabin and search some more. No telling what we might find. You learn anything, I will pay for any information on anything we need to know."

"If you can't find some more treasure, I

hope, at least, you can settle this once and for all."

"That is why we are here."

The next day they rode south and two days later were perched on the North Rim. The cabin was still standing and the cow herd had calved. Plans were made to brand them with Michael Meadows's MM iron. But they'd do that before they'd leave.

"I dread having to drive them out of here someday," Jamie said, shaking his head. "We busted our butts getting that handful up here. Nothing would do but get them up here. Now the family is dead. Damn it. Excuse me. I'm not over it even now." He went off to pull himself together.

That hurt Chet, too. The kids had ridden off on a short horseback ride to see more country. He warned them to be watchful. The rest sat on some leftover logs and discussed what they should do next.

Salty started in, "Fixing that stage line I met a man who prospected all over for those rubies and he found them. He told me that at the beginning of time, when volcanoes were losing their caps a long time back, they blew molten rubies out of a pipelike structure and spewed them all over a small area. If you ever found one you might find a wagonload or only a single one that some caveman dropped.

"He said, if you find a field of them you'd be lucky. Most were small deposits shifted around by eruptions and blowouts. He said he found emeralds in veins. Like they were once in a layer of mud and set there until they were made into stones. He doubted the rubies and emeralds were all together, but were in separate deposits. The man had some rubies and emeralds to show me. But I think he found them west of Preskitt in the Williams River area. I never mentioned our find over here. He said someone found a lot of them somewhere in Arizona that the Spanish had hoarded."

Chet smiled. "That must be us. Thanks. Now we can go look for some more, huh?"

"You want a few of us to go look for this guy everyone blames for everything? Last year they had moved from where Cole and Salty originally found them, right?" Cody added.

"They'd moved from there and there was no trace, we could find, where they went. I don't even know if they came back. If they murdered the family, probably not. But why don't you and Salty take a couple pack-horses and start crossing the country? You two are our best scouts. See if you can find them. But whatever you do, be careful."

"Can we take Oleta in case we find them, and she can come get you while we watch them?"

"That might be dangerous. But you three decide."

Cody nodded. "Then we wouldn't lose them if they pick up and move."

Jesus agreed with him. "She can outride most men."

"I simply don't want one more person hurt."

So those three rode out to find the gang. Chet was sick that they had no more leads. The rest rode down to the cave site and discovered there were other ropes used to reach the cavern since they'd been there last.

Rocky looked over the side and shook his head. "Dad said it was a long ways to the bottom if you fell or the rope broke. I'm not going down there."

Renny agreed.

Adam shrugged. "I'd go if there was any treasure left."

Chet tried not to laugh at the three comments. He enjoyed them — they were funny and neat.

The next two days passed slowly. Adam was teaching his horse to crawl on his front knees, and the horse was learning it, to the rest of the party's amazement. Chet saw the animal trainer in him immediately.

"You train dogs?" he asked him.

Adam wrinkled his nose. "They're too easy."

"No, honestly. You train dogs, you can sell them for money."

"How much?"

"How many tricks can they do?"

"Oh, say, a dozen."

"If he's real good, fifty bucks."

"Hmm, I might try that."

Adam made the horse get up and rear on his hind feet and circle like he was dancing. "What would he sell for?"

"Two-fifty."

"He cost me seven-fifty. An Indian boy sold him to me. But I will look into trained dogs, too."

Lisa came out and stood, arms folded. "I made some bear tracks. Get the crew and I'll put them out. Adam?"

"Yes, ma'am?"

"What would you like to train next?"

He smiled. "A mountain lion."

"You better wait a few years to do that."

"No, Miss Lisa. You need to start when they are born. Bottle-feed them."

She threw her head back to stare at the azure sky. "What does your mother think

403

about that?"

"Oh, she worries but said she didn't doubt I could do that."

Lisa paused, bit her upper lip, and then shook her head. "Get the bear track experts in here."

Chet was laughing and shouting. "Miss Lisa has bear tracks ready. You don't come, I get to eat them all."

"I bet that boy has more dare than you had as a kid growing up, Chet Byrnes."

"You're right. I'd never thought about a mountain lion to break for a pet."

They both laughed.

Jesus offered to take the crew fishing for trout the next day, in the side stream canyon.

Lisa planned to go with him and the kids. The others, when they went last time, caught so many they wasted them. Chet and Billy Bob wanted to try the map to the ruby mine since there was no sign of his scouts that day. Tad, his helper, and the horse wrangler were going to keep camp.

Chet told Jesus to keep a sharp eye out, and they left before dawn. Billy Bob had tried to recall the Three Sister rock formation they'd gone by last time. Then it did not mean much to them, but this time it had become the main deal on the hand-drawn map. Lisa packed them a lunch and they made good time searching the country northwest of the Meadowses' ranch.

By noon they located the Three Sister Buttes. It was obvious to Chet that they got more rain down near the canyon than they did farther north. They were out in the desert sagebrush and not much more. They ate their lunch and washed it down with canteen spring water.

Lunch consumed, they studied the formation and there was no doubt there had been a cave at one time in the face of that butte. Chet traced the outline, but the roof had fallen in and closed the rest under a hundred tons of rocks and huge slabs.

They crawled all over the formation. Billy Bob crawled into one small space and said he could feel air escaping from it. But it was too narrow for him to get in past that point.

"We might drill some holes, set a blast off to open it more?"

"I am game."

They rode back to camp to find Jesus and his party were back. Tad was frying fish and there was still no sign of his scouts. Those three might ride their horses into the ground to find that Logan gang.

"You do any good?" Jesus asked.

"We are going back to do some blasting. You see any fresh tracks?"

"None. We may go with you tomorrow," Jesus said.

Behind his white apron Tad said, "I want to watch your blasting. Eddie, you are the cook tomorrow."

"If you die of the ptomaine, don't blame me."

They all laughed.

The next day they left the horse wrangler, Eldon, and Eddie, the camp cook's helper, and went to Three Sister Buttes with blasting powder, caps, lanterns, rock drills, and shovels. And lunch, of course.

The rock they drilled was medium hard according to Tad, who had worked mining jobs. They all agreed they might blast away in the bowels of those buttes. By noontime they had the blasting bores in the rock, loaded the blasting powder, and exploded them, all lying facedown at a safe distance.

The explosion rocked the ground they lay on and it was a while until the dust settled. Anxious to see what they had done, they had to wait until more was blown away by the soft, hot wind.

"It's bigger," Billy Bob shouted. "But I won't fit."

"Tie this rope around me and lower me in that hole," Adam said to his father.

"Let's light it first with a lantern and see how deep it goes."

"That's not a bad idea."

The lantern illuminated the cavern and, top to bottom, it was large. Chet moved back as some bats flew out the new opening and flew away.

"It won't be peaches and cream in there," he told his son.

Adam wrinkled his nose. "I can see if it is worth making the hole bigger."

The rope tied on his waist, he backed inside trying to find a foothold in the wall. "Hand me that lantern so I can see something."

Renny did that. "Now what?"

"It is six feet more to the floor. I'm fine, Dad."

Chet lowered him more, and Tad joined to help him. At last he was on the floor and the rope slacked.

"Untie it from you. I am coming," Renny said.

"Bring your own light."

"I will." Hand over hand, she hauled up the heavy rope. Then she stuck her head in the hole. "What's down there?"

"Oh my God —"

Renny shook her head, frowning. "What's he got to do with it?"

"There are steamer trunks of gold coins down here. Hurry up. Red jewels. Turquoise. Silver."

She turned to shake her head at the others trying to see past her. "He's either gone crazy on mine fumes or there are some treasure ships sunk down there."

Chet closed his eyes. "He found the *Pinta* and the *Santa Maria,* men."

"How are we going to get it out through that porthole?" Jesus asked, laughing.

"We can make that door larger. But we will need a fleet to get it out of here."

"Lower me down there," Renny said with the rope tied around her waist. "He's too spellbound to tell you a thing. It's just money."

Jesus and Tad lowered her into the great cavern.

"Guys, you better go find several wagons," she said up to them while holding her lantern head high. "No wonder they didn't go back for the others in that cave. There's a lot more here."

"Oh!" Adam said as if taken aback. "They died in here, too. Stay over there, Renny. Piles of skeletons."

"Put me in there," Rocky said.

"Two is enough for now. We need to chisel out a door around here someplace," Chet said.

"What did you find?" Lisa asked, out of breath, catching up to them.

"More Spanish treasure."

"Really? Where are the kids?"

"Don't fall in there. They are on the room floor where the trunks are at."

She jerked back. "Are they safe?"

"It hasn't bit them so far. Everyone, get back up here. We need a usable entry cut into this mountain."

Both kids were pulled up dusty, and came out shaking their heads.

"Whew. It was hard to breathe down there," Adam complained.

"Did you see a crown for a king or queen?" Renny asked. "I didn't."

Adam shook his head.

Anxious to get the cavern opened up, they worked into the night until Lisa finally made them quit. Earlier, Jesus had ridden back to camp and he, Eddie, and the wrangler loaded everything to bring it all up to the buttes.

Since there was no road, they had to go around dry washes and tall rocks. It was slow, but when they learned why they were hauling so much, the two helpers could not believe that more treasure than the last time had been found.

Chet and the boys met them with lanterns. "You didn't have to kill yourselves getting here. No one has the wagon power to haul this away."

Later in their bedroll, Lisa snuggled to him. "What will we do with all this?"

Amused at her words, he chuckled. "Ranch until the cows come home."

"I guess so. Did you ever expect to find so much?"

"No. That doesn't happen in dreams, even. Twice is unheard of."

"Can you get it out of here?"

"I will, or my name is not Chet Byrnes."

It was predawn before he knew it. In the soft darkness, he pulled on his pants under the covers, then he put on his boots, seated on top of the bedroll. Out of nowhere he heard an iron shoe strike a rock.

"Don't shoot," a familiar voice shouted.

"Salty?"

"It's the three of us plus two. Why in hell are you clear up here?"

"We found Columbus's ships."

"What ships?"

"The ones he sailed to the U.S. to find us."

"You found even more treasure?" Salty shouted with his horse reined up.

"Yes, a real serious amount, too," Lisa said.

"Holy cow, girl, you awake?"

"I am now. You won't believe it."

"Oh hell, I can't believe you did that," Cody said. "We brought you two guys, too. They've got plenty to tell you."

The whole camp was awake by then and that must have spooked the neighboring coyotes. They were howling from all over. Lisa, in her bathrobe, scurried to the kitchen area. Renny, already dressed, helped her. Tad joined them. Both the boys and Eddie were washing dishes left undone from the night before.

Salty and Cody set their two prisoners on the ground, on their butts, back to back, and chained them that way. Salty said, "More about them later. I want to see the treasure of the other world."

"Grab a lamp," Chet said, shaking their hands. "This mountain was tied somehow to a ruby find some guy made years ago. Billy Bob made a deal with him for a map. He's a cripple and could never come back up here. Billy Bob found a small opening. It looks like, a long time ago, the front of the cave collapsed. That's why we searched for

411

a way in from the back. Some drilling and blasting got a hole the kids could slip through and we found the main portion of the cave."

Salty held the lamp in the widened opening. Chet caught his sleeve. "There is a good ten-foot drop."

"Yeah, I can see it. Is it all full of loot?"

"Adam and Renny say it is. They were the first to see it."

Cody looked in next. "My heavens, Chet, there is a fortune in here."

"Easily. Now, getting it out of there and back to Preskitt and staying alive is what will count."

A smile swept Salty's face as the sun began to rise behind their backs. "I bet you have a plan."

"Twenty wagons. A couple water wagons. There is not enough water around if we get that many horses and men up here. There must have been more water when the Spaniards were in operation here."

Cody nodded. "I wondered about that myself. Pretty dry country."

"Sounds like they have breakfast ready. We can talk more after that."

Salty caught his sleeve. "Those two guys were all we found. They say they found the Meadows family's bodies and told us what

412

they did about it. You are going to be shocked if it is the truth."

"I want to hear it, but let's eat first."

With a stern warning that any wrong move and they'd be dead, Salty unchained the prisoners. They quickly agreed. One looked to be forty, with gray hair and whiskers, Salty called him Frank Mayes. The other one was red-faced, younger, plus had a nasty look to his bloodshot eyes.

He went by Lucifer Krye.

After breakfast, Lisa and the kids took off riding and exploring.

Salty told the two to tell their story.

Mayes began, explaining his part. "We went over to see the Meadowses about something and found them all dead. Right off, talking among ourselves, we decided if we buried them then everyone would think we killed them. It was a sickening sight. I never saw the like in my life."

"Who do you think killed them?"

"Why, Injuns, of course. They scalped them."

"No one told us that." Chet couldn't believe the man's words.

Mayes shook his head. "You know why?"

"No. You making that up?"

"No, I am not. You ever hear about the slaughter of the Fancher wagon train?"

"Yeah. What's that got to do with this?"

"Well, if it was Indians kilt the Meadows family, they'd be liable to send the army down here and they might have some of those warrants left from the Fancher train massacre."

"That happened a real long time ago."

"They don't throw murder warrants away."

"And you think the LDS people hid the fact they were scalped from the authorities?"

"They never mentioned it, did they?"

"You're right," Chet said, and looked across the table at Jamie Meadows, silent all this time and probably in agony hearing all of this.

"Where is the tough guy that used to lead all of you?"

"Fallen?"

"I never caught his real name."

"Floyd Fallen was what I heard was his real name. Vigilantes hung him and two more over in Nevada last winter. They were riding the wrong horses."

"You both wanted?" Chet asked.

"Yeah."

"Me, too," Krye finally spoke.

"What are the crimes?"

Mayes nodded. "Killing a guy who raped

my wife back East. They said I couldn't prove he did it. Hellfire, she told me he did it to her before she died. I warrant them damn Injuns raped Mrs. Meadows, too."

"The bastard I kilt raped my teenage sister. They said, when I chopped him to small pieces with an ax, that it was murder."

"That's all that is left of the gang?"

Cody gave a head toss toward them. "There's four women in their camp. Three kids."

"They have food?"

"Cody and I shot them a deer before we left."

"All right. You two men are on my payroll. It is all secret. But you do it right I'll pay you for your work and beyond. That all right?"

"Damn right!" Mayes said. "Neither of us kilt them. Injuns did."

"Remember, I can kill you in the blink of an eye."

"Yes, sir."

"Eat."

Chet stood up and he walked away from the table with his men. "Now, how do we get the treasure out of that hole?"

"We need some track and ties — wait, there is a mine cart up at the Joseph Lake store. I saw it lying on its side," Jesus said.

"Where would we find track?" Cody asked.

"We can make wooden tracks. Fifty trips won't wear out wood that fast."

"There has to be a sawmill somewhere up here."

Everyone agreed.

"Now, we send a wire to Tom at Camp Verde to send us forty wagons, two water wagons, armed men, and plenty of supplies."

"We can meet them at Joseph Lake as soon as they can get there."

"Where do we wire him from?"

"I'd say Kanab up in Utah. We need to bring some wagons here while we wait. A water wagon would be nice, if we can find one. Put on your trading hats. Salty, were you with Cole last time?"

"No. I was on my honeymoon, but I do recall that they didn't have a water wagon at the store. We bought it in Kanab, Utah."

"If they don't have a working telegraph in Kanab, you will need to go down to the Little Colorado Crossing and maybe even Flagstaff."

"Can you hold this place down with the both of us gone?" Salty asked.

"Jesus, Billy Bob, Tad, and I can. Few know we have this much treasure, but word will get out fast."

"What about that mine cart?"

"A couple of us may ride out with you two and trade for it. Haul it back here. On something. What a damn mess." Chet had dropped his head laughing.

They soon were all laughing at how unhandy it all would be.

When Lisa and the kids came back, he told her the plan. She told them good luck and the four rode to Joseph Lake.

It was farther than Chet thought, to Joseph Lake. Rory gave them the mine cart. They loaded it onto a hauler's wagon. Billy Bob and the kids led him westward. The store man said the telegraph in Kanab, Utah, was working. Chet sent Cody and Salty up there to make arrangements and to stay there until Tom wired back he knew what they wanted. Then they were to look for a water wagon or a wagon filled with watertight barrels and a supply wagon.

Rory knew a man who needed work and would haul the water out to them. Plus, the guy who left with the cart would haul whatever they needed from the store to their site.

Things were going too good. They didn't get back to the site before sundown. Chet guessed the kids spent the day ahead of him, getting the wagon hauling the heavy cart unstuck from the loose, sandy dry washes they had to cross a hundred times on the route.

The driver Jasper Andrews could not believe they were Chet's children. "Why, them scudders bailed in every time like beavers building a dam to get me going."

He smiled and thanked them. Rocky shook his head like it was nothing. "We got him moving every time. No big deal."

"Do you think those other two got a wire off?" Renny asked.

"If that line worked I bet Tom already knows."

"Good. I thought Preskitt was a bad place to have to live." She looked around the desert camp. "This one beats all of them."

"Why, Renny, you don't like this place?"

"Chet, I have so much sand behind my molars I may never get it all out."

They laughed.

Before they turned in, Chet spoke to Jasper Andrews about going after a wagonload of lumber next.

"Mr. Byrnes, they'll charge you a fortune for it."

"No matter. Tomorrow, I will give you the list of what we need. But I will need those boards."

"Anyone look at that cart?"

"What fur?" Adam asked.

"Not *fur* but *for*. Those heavy iron boxes weigh a ton. We need a flatcar to haul them out on."

"You getting boards to make a box?"

"Are you enough of a carpenter to do that?"

"Me and Rocky, with a hammer and cold chisel, can get it off."

Rocky, seated beside him, nodded.

"Good. One less thing for me to worry about."

"You planning a railroad to get them out of that hole?"

"Tad, I don't want to blast too much more. The roof may fall in."

"I saw that front and you were right. It collapsed."

"We can pack those trunks and containers onto a flatcar, then pull it up and out that back door and into the wagons for removal to our ranch."

"Those boys going to strip the body off the mine cart?"

"They may need some help but we have time before the wagons get here, even if they hurry."

Billy Bob smiled and agreed. "I'll help if they need it."

"Thanks. I want them to do all they can. It builds confidence in them."

"Right. My dad would say, 'Try it, son.' That's how I learned."

"That's sure the right way to learn." He saw Lisa was coming over with Renny.

"Can we get in the mountain and see some of the treasures?"

"We have a ladder, and you will need some lights. Be watchful of snakes. We have not seen any so far but they may crawl in there in the heat of the day."

"We can avoid snakes."

Renny nodded. "I'll go get us two lamps."

"That will be great." Lisa turned to him. "With this heat, Renny says she can appreciate Preskitt's climate much better."

He wiped his sweaty face on his kerchief. "I agree."

"The wagon man Jasper Andrews has gone back for lumber?"

"That's the plan."

The three started, via the ladder, into the cavern. When Lisa got down he lowered her a lit lamp, then one for Renny. He came down in a hurry. A little polish on a coin he picked up from the top of the bin and the features popped out on the face like it'd been freshly minted.

"This is amazing. They have been here for

two hundred years and polish up easier than a new one." His teen companion shook her head and raised the lamp to inspect another.

"Renny, any gold or silver is amazing."

"But this is mostly coins. How did they make so many coins this far from a mint?"

"Good question, Renny. I never thought about that. Why, we couldn't melt gold alone out here, much less make coins."

Lisa laughed. "Or even have a place to spend it. Lots of this is spending money. Not near as much of the first batch you found in the canyon was money. Why so?"

"Lisa, these folks have been dead for over two hundred years. They can't tell us, and unless we find their account books we may never know."

"Nice of them to leave it for us."

He hugged and kissed her. "I agree."

"May I ask you a question?" Renny asked.

"Sure. What is it?"

"I am sorry to have to ask, but I never lived in a house before, where the two people who were married kiss as often as you two do. I don't mind. In fact, I think it is sweet, but I wondered why and maybe how it would happen."

"You have a good answer for her?"

"Well — I am not sure. We both had happy lives and lost someone we loved. So,

I guess we consider ourselves lucky to have someone again and we show our affection to this pairing."

"That sums it up," he said.

"If I ever find a mate I hope it works out this well. You two don't argue. You are thoughtful and good to each other, and to me, too."

"Oh, I bet you'll find someone grateful for you being yourself."

"I don't consider myself wild, but I appreciate the opportunity to be myself. I would never have been allowed to ride that horse at the fairgrounds in my past life. After it happened I knew I made a step up in my life and you two gave me that boost because you trusted me. I am very grateful for the chance. And those boys could have said *No she is a girl, she doesn't need to ride.* I never had any brothers or sisters. I was concerned they'd be mad about me sharing their time. But instead they were my boosters and never put me down."

"Renny, I'd say that you were as big a treat to both of us as finding this king's ransom."

"And I feel the same way," Renny said. "You are making me cry. This money is nice, but being a part of your family has lifted me up so high into the clouds we have at home. And to think I felt locked in a prison having to live in Preskitt, before you two came and got me."

"Lisa and I are proud of the boys and how they treat you. Both of them have lived with foster parents as only children because of my busy life."

"They are enjoying this trip so much. You can hear them banging on that miner's car. You will have a flatcar by dark. Both of them think they are you, Chet."

Renny hugged him and then pulled him down and pecked on his cheek. "I am going to do that, too."

No one needed to tell Lisa — Renny had found one of Lisa's traits to follow. She gave Chet the lamp and used her kerchief to dry her eyes before going up the ladder.

# CHAPTER 33

Andrews brought the first load of lumber and showed him how much they'd over-charged him for the load.

Price wouldn't matter if they could get all the loads out. "They cutting the rest?"

"Damn right. I'll have the second load here day after tomorrow. They'll have it to load at daylight."

"Don't you figure that is worth some-thing?"

"Whatcha mean?"

"I mean, they are cutting it fast."

"Yeah, but the price they're charging you is too high."

"Eat supper with us. You'll have time to get back."

"Aw, you don't have time to feed me."

Lisa took his arm by the elbow. "I do. Now, if you could find me a tall post, a large sheet of canvas, and a fat yearling steer, my boys would butcher it and I could keep meat fresh for four days. So when my other men get here, I'd have food on hand."

"I can get two posts and a crossbeam on the next load and the canvas at the store. I'd have to bring the steer on the next day."

"Andrews, you are a genius."

"I been called lots of things, missus, but never that." He snatched off his weather-beaten, old felt hat. "I am proud to be a part of this operation."

"We're proud to have you."

Chet had become concerned. They were going on day four and there was no sign of his two men coming back. He'd hired the water man, Casey Boyd, to fill the barrels, so there was water for their horses and people. They were doing fine.

Chet ordered four more posts. The men set them to make a platform for a two-barrel sheepherder shower he bought at the store. It was set up, plumbed, and ready to use after the sun warmed it for two days.

Meanwhile, he and all the hands were carefully building a stout trestle inside the cave to run the flatbed cart on wooden tracks over the hump to the outside dock. Then they'd load them into wagons.

After supper the next evening, the two women had the privacy of the shower. They thought it was kind of chilly, at first, being behind blankets hung on the south and east sides, but their last word was that the shower was great.

The boys were next. Then they refilled the barrels and the men took their turns. All enjoyed it so much they thought they'd been to some great fancy city.

At noon the next day, the lost scouts came in one nice farm wagon.

Chet walked out to meet them and frowned at the brand-spanking-new Studebaker wagon and two big Belgian mares. "Only one?"

"No, siree. We need to unhitch," Salty said. "The mules and the loaded water wagon are stuck in a sandy wash and we need these gals to pull them out."

"Was Tom excited when you got his message back?"

"He couldn't hardly believe it."

The mares unhooked, the two boys came racing in on horses, wanting to hear about the mules.

"Ma'am," Cody said, "have the men set up your new dining hall tent. There's tables and chairs and a new cook stove for Tad. Some outfit ordered it and when they couldn't pay for it, we got it for half price."

"Well, you boys help them get unstuck.

We'll set up the tent," Chet said, laughing.

"Did he say Tom didn't believe him?" Lisa asked Chet.

"He did say that."

"I'm shocked. As long as Tom has worked for you, and he can't believe you struck it rich twice."

"Heaven, girl, not many people do that in one lifetime."

They were raising the tent when the mules began honking, pulling the water wagon into camp. The boys each led a harnessed mare back with them.

"Dad," Adam said as he swung around by him on his horse. "These mules could pull hell up on the topside. The mares are great, but, man, those mules are something to see pulling."

"We better leave hell down there for now."

"You'll be impressed. I sure was." Adam rode off, shaking his head.

What next? The new tent shone in the last sunlight as they secured it. Now they had it up and it would soon be time to leave it all. It made no difference. He needed to spoil all of them. He had not put a price tag on the loot inside the mountain, not even a wild guess.

No matter. He'd go on ranching as long as he lived.

Where were the rubies? He hadn't even looked, he'd been so busy making the trestle that he'd forgotten all about them. They celebrated completion of it òver two Dutch ovens full of peach cobbler that Tad and Lisa had rustled up.

"Well, what's next, boss man? In a week or so we'll pack all this home?" Jesus asked him.

"Probably. I found no books in the top of all those chests. Did you?"

"What I looked at — no. But there's got to be a reason for all this treasure being stored in that bluff."

"Maybe the books are under that caved-in roof in the front."

"Maybe. Strange. That cripple man in Mesa was only after rubies. It was why he wrote me. He had no idea all this was hidden inside the cavern."

"What do you suggest we try?"

"We dig a trench around these buttes knee-deep and look for rubies."

"That'll work. It will be many days before they get the wagons we need up here."

"We have a tent. Water supply and shower. Trenching starts tomorrow."

At breakfast, he told them about his wild idea and why he wanted to do it.

Everyone agreed it would be interesting. Work was work, so the trenching started at the southeast corner and continued northerly. The first thing they found was a single silver Spanish spur. One of the two men they brought in handed it to Adam. It didn't look like anything of much value but twenty minutes later it was shining in the sun.

"Where did you find it?" Chet asked.

"Over there."

The two walked back and they plowed up a large circle. The second spur showed up. Adam was shouting and ran off to wash it. Renny helped him. They brought the pair to Chet.

"Who dug them up?" Chet asked.

"I guess they belong to Lucifer Krye?"

"Yes, I'd say so. If he's the one that found them."

Adam and Renny took them to the man. "Dad says these are yours."

"No."

"Mister, those spurs are made of silver and the rowels are on them. I bet they were made in Spain. You could hock them for a hundred dollars anywhere. And they have been engraved. Renny and I didn't find them. You found them."

"Oh, okay, I will take them."

"Good."

Nothing else of any consequence showed up that day. Adam asked his dad why the man didn't want to accept them at first.

"I guess he thought we still suspected him of killing the Meadows family. He has lived all his life being insecure."

"What is that?"

"He never had any place he could stay at."

"Oh, that would be bad, wouldn't it?"

Chet nodded. He walked over to where Mayes and Krye sat on the ground. "I think tomorrow you should get Cody to take you two in the wagon and go get your families."

They both scurried to their feet.

*"O gracias, señor."* Both shook his hands. So grateful.

Cody said, "I can handle it."

Later Adam stopped his father. "I saw what you meant. They are both insecure, huh?"

"Yes."

# CHAPTER 34

Cody left early with the two on horseback. Jesus went with him, driving the buckboard.

Everyone else dug on the trench. It was past lunch when Eldon, the wrangler, shouted, "I found rubies. Oh my God, I found them."

Renny set down the water pail she used to serve the workers liquid out of a dipper and ran over to him. The stones were in the dirt and Chet saw his shovel of dry dirt was full of them. Despite the dirt clinging to them, they gleamed scarlet in the too-bright sunlight.

"Eldon. You have really done it now!"

Eldon began screaming. He put down his shovel, then he and Renny began dancing to celebrate. Pretty soon they were polkaing all around in the dry grass. "Found it! We found it!"

Chet was laughing so hard but not without some concern. "Easy on my daughter."

431

"It's all right, Dad, I'm as excited as he is."

Chet, Renny, and Eldon dropped on their knees and began picking out the larger stones.

Lisa brought a towel to put them on. "Oh, Eldon. You have found the mother lode."

They had done it again. How lucky could they get?

By the time the crew quit for supper, it was obvious they were in the ring where an explosion had burped up a rain of rubies. No telling what else they'd find.

In their bedroll that night, Lisa said, "I saw the father side of you today. It was sweet. That boy was innocently wild over his good fortune and he had a girl in his arms but it was sweet for her father to say, 'Go easy on my daughter.'"

He was chuckling. "I felt that way, too."

In the morning the quest was on for more rubies, and by noontime they had a large ring of dirt turned up and were down three or four feet deep. The first wagons that Tom sent from the Verde Ranch arrived that day. A tall cowboy in the lead dismounted his horse, took his high-crown hat off, and wiped his sweaty face on his sleeve. "Ma'am, you must be the missus. I'm Earl Butler, and Tom told me you were very pretty. I'm sure glad to meet up with you at last. It is a long ways up here."

"Thank you, Earl. That's my husband, Chet, coming there."

"Whew, this is about the last jumping-off place, isn't it?" He searched around on the flat, glad to be there.

"We're glad to have you."

They shook hands.

"Tom said for me to get up here. You had some valuable things needed gathering. It wasn't hard to find your tracks after I made Joseph Lake. All tracks lead out here."

"Lisa, I am going to show him what we're doing. Tell those men to unhitch and relax — they made it to where they were supposed to land.

"Come with me. Those boys of mine and others are finding rubies on the other side of these three bluffs. That's what we came out here for. Earlier I found some Spanish treasure that had rubies in them. A cripple man down in Mesa told me there was supposed to be more around these buttes. He offered me a map. I paid him a small sum and promised him a share. So we came out here and found the treasure train in a cavern under these buttes. Yesterday we found the rubies on the west side of them. Watch yourself and duck your head. This bridge is low."

"You've made this ramp very recently I can smell the pine."

"Yes, we've been busy. We didn't want the mountain to collapse. This back entrance is low. We use a ladder here to go down inside."

"Big cave. It really echoes, doesn't it?"

"Yes. These trunks were the first thing we saw." Chet opened one lid.

"Oh my God, are they all full like this?"

"Yes. We load that flatbed mine cart, built that ramp, and push it out so we can load the wagons."

"How in the hell did a cowman ever figure that out?"

"We would've faced a lot of pickup and carry, so we figured it out."

Earl was laughing. "I've been talking to Tom about finding me work. He got me up one morning before daylight and said he had a job for me. I never expected this. He said, 'My boss must have a real find up there. He needs forty wagons to bring it home.'"

"We have hay coming today for all the horse stock. We import water, too."

"I saw the water wagon when I drove up. And you simply found all this and now rubies on the outside?"

"Yes. Well, I have laid out some cash to assemble it all."

"I'm sorry to be so damn nosy. You put a value on all this?"

"No. I really have not tried to. I have been so busy building that trestle and getting what I needed set up."

"You have done one helluva job. I reckon we should load those wagons and haul it down to Preskitt. That will be slow going."

"Dangerous, too. If the word gets out about what you are hauling."

"Yes. But I have some damn tough men with me. We will deliver it. Mr. Tanner will be set up to handle it there at the bank. Tom has more wagons coming after me."

Chet dropped his butt on a trunk. "Earl, it has been a trying deal, but I figure we will make it with all of us trying so hard."

"Hell yes." They shook hands.

They went down to camp. Four suntanned young men were waiting to see Chet.

"Mr. Byrnes, sir. I brought four racks of hay. My dad, Greenville Houston, said to see when you'd need some more."

"Four-day turnaround?"

The youth looked concerned. "I can make it in six, sir."

"Make it six wagons. Then I will have to

see again how much I will need."

"Oh, that will be fine."

"I owe you eighty dollars a load?"

"Yes, sir. It is fresh-cut alfalfa."

Chet nodded that he heard him and counted out four hundred to hand to him.

"That's too much, sir. It was eighty dollars a wagonload."

"I saw the hay you brought me today. I am paying you a bonus."

"Well, thank you, sir. Six days we will have six loads here, sir."

"Stay for supper. My wife has plenty of food and you can get an early start."

"We will, sir, and thanks so much."

"I invited them to supper," he said when Lisa joined him.

"Good. See you shortly," she said to the boys.

"Earl wants to get several loads back to Preskitt."

"Good idea. I don't know who'd steal them out here but, yes, I am ready for Preskitt's cool breezes."

"You can go back with him."

She cut her eyes around sharply at him. "You aren't getting away from me that easy."

He hugged her and kissed her cheek. "I wasn't trying. How did the ruby picking go?"

"Nearly double of what you brought back from the other place."

"Who'd ever believe that?"

"I do. I carried one pail with two hands to our bank. Oh, Jamie Meadows needs to talk to you."

"Fine. But I have no answers for him."

"I don't know what he wants."

"I can handle it."

They parted and he found Jamie finishing washing up.

The two sauntered off to talk beyond the others, cleaning up for supper.

"Chet, I am maybe a little sturdier now than I was earlier. I helped them load and I want to thank you for all you've done for us. And the families appreciate all you did, too. I appreciate all you've tried to do solving the murders, but it's kinda closed for my part. There were no Indians going to tell us who was there that day. I even don't care we never knew they'd been scalped. But, even more so, I don't really feel like coming back here and driving those cows back home. Take me six months and I'd hate even looking at them by then. I'd like to give them to the two men and their four women."

"The drifters, Mayes and Krye?"

"Yeah. They have kids and nowhere else

to go. They done their part. They aren't my kind of people but they ain't afraid of work. I know the family would do that."

"You can't tell who is married to who now anyway."

Jamie chuckled. "And I have been dreading that drive back home."

"Let's see after supper what they want to do."

"Thanks."

Later, Chet and Jamie went down to where the *family* was camped. They all jumped up from eating when they saw who it was.

"Ease back down. We want to talk. You know Jamie Meadows. It was his brother and sister-in-law and their children that were murdered. He has some good news for you and I also have something to say."

Everyone got settled back on the ground. One of the darker women bared a breast to hush a hungry baby.

"We came to find the killers and we feel none of you had a hand in their murders. That place down there reminds him too much of them for him to stay and ranch there. But he thinks you, and I mean all of you, deserve that ranch. It is a homestead claim to three hundred sixty acres. You must improve it and live on it, and one day he will sign it over to you so you will have a deed. You know the cabin will need to be added on so all of you can squeeze inside."

They laughed.

"He has a registered brand he can give you and twenty some cows and calves to start a herd."

They sucked in their breath.

"Why give us all that?" Krye asked.

" 'Cause I can't take it home with me."

"Oh, Jamie, we are so sorry." They all rushed over to hug and pat on him as he cried.

"Then you will accept his gift?" Chet asked.

"Yes. And we appreciate all you have done for us," a part-Indian woman said.

"I will pay you for your time, too."

In bed later with his wife, he explained what Jamie did.

"I see why he cried. He came to find some peace, didn't he?"

"And in the end, they showed him they cared."

Yes.


Four trunks per wagon was enough for each team to haul back to Preskitt. Chet and Earl reached that agreement after loading the first one. The trestle worked well and Adam

439

showed Earl all the bolt holes in their flatcar's topside rim that he and Rocky left after unbolting the box from it. Twenty-two wagons were loaded and they hardly looked like they'd made a dent in the numbers of trunks still resting on the cavern floor.

They'd leave in the morning to go back.

Barrels of water and sacks of grain were in one wagon, and in another, camping gear and food. There was one spare wagon, just in case. Earl didn't want that much loot simply waiting, alongside those desolate stretches of road, for another wagon to get there to pick it up.

Jamie had all the papers that he'd need to switch the ranch over to the settlers. They'd get them back in the mail sent to Joseph Lake. They all hugged him, one at a time, before he rode off. Chet promised him his share when it was settled.

"You don't owe me anything, Chet Byrnes."

"Listen, I owe you. It will come to you."

"I wish my brother had lived to really know you. You two came from the same past world. He'd have made it big up here, too."

Chet agreed and they parted.

A week later wagon train number two arrived at Three Sister Buttes. A rancher Chet knew climbed down along with a woman he recognized. Curt Baker and his wife, Adeline. They ranched south of Preskitt.

"Howdy, Chet. Tom says you have worlds of stuff to haul back. I visited with Earl, who was going south on the Navajo Trail a few days ago. This Spanish treasure business is sure treating you all right."

"Keeping me busy, anyway."

"Tom said your sons and daughter are even up here this summer with you."

"I have two sons, Adam and Rocky, and the judge asked us to consider adopting a girl who lost her parents. Renny is a very nice young lady. You may have heard that she won the novice race at the fairgrounds recently."

"We missed that one, though I recall someone saying you didn't have a daughter?"

"I do. And she and the boys are around here somewhere. Earl showed you the treasure we're hauling back?"

"Yes. There's a lot more of it, he said."

"Yes, there is. My concern is someone will learn all about it and try to rob the train."

"I definitely have some tough men with me, but, like you said, it would be a concern. There is only one route in and out. I'd been to Utah a time or two. It hasn't gotten any better. How in the hell did you find this one?"

"We first discovered a cavern on the north wall of the Grand Canyon. The men took ropes and went off there to investigate it. It was about thirty feet down and thousands more feet of air under that. The Spanish had hidden three men in that cave and all the treasures they must have had. No one ever came back for them. The Indians may have gotten the outside force. Those men left notes. We recovered a pail of rubies in that cave and there was some interest in them. A man in Mesa offered to sell me a map to this spot here because he had become injured after finding some rubies on this site and could not get back up here. Instead, we found these trunks inside the caved-in cavern. We have not found any letters in these trunks, and only later did we find the rubies."

"Wow, you have been digging it up. But why was it hidden out here?"

"Another question with no answer. Lots of this loot comes in minted coins. Our first find was raw gold and gold bars."

He introduced Curt and Adeline to Lisa and they went to have coffee and bear tracks in the tent.

"Nice tent."

"I sent men to wire Tom for help. They brought it back along with that water wagon and a new Studebaker wagon. Spent my money like water. But we needed it."

"We have had some hard rains so it was nice to have this over us," Lisa said.

After coffee Chet and Curt went up and looked at the cavern and the trestle.

"You built this?"

"Yes."

"My lands, had it been up to me, all that would still be down there."

"Invention sometimes is necessary. I could improve on it now but it worked smoothly the first time. I figured the face of this cave was once open to the south and they had all this stored in here. Maybe an earthquake shook the front portion down and the men who brought it in there were buried. We found an air leak back here, widened it all we dared, drilling and blasting. We don't spend a lot of time in here since we finished the delivery system."

"I don't blame you."

"You and your men rest a day or two and then we can load you up for the trip down."

"You earned this treasure, Chet Byrnes. There will be two more trips coming, won't there?"

"Earl thought five in total."

"I know he brought an empty wagon out in case he had a breakdown."

"I won't object to you doing that."

"Odds go up the more trips you make, don't they?"

"More outlaws to know about them, too."

"Most outlaws hate robberies like this. They have to have a way to pack it off. Money is light."

"Yes, paper money and notes are easy to handle. But one of these trunks could be worth a lot more than some small-town bank's total deposits."

"Damned if you do or don't. I bet you and Lisa are ready to head home."

"The ranches are in good hands. We are surviving."

"I met Jamie Meadows. That was a shame."

"We met the family he lost and really liked them. He gifted those other folks because he didn't have it in him to drive those cattle back home."

"Tough enough dragging this loot back. That isn't cow country going south. He said his brother was a larger adventurer than he was."

"He must have been."

"What do you think this strip of country is ever going to be good for?"

"Raising lizards and rattlesnakes, I told my wife."

They laughed.

In two days, Curt, his wife, and his bunch left for Preskitt with one empty wagon, two others for supplies and water, and the others filled with trunks. Things went smoothly. Chet had offered for Jesus to go back home with that last wagon train. His man shook his head and sent his wife a long letter via the train.

Chet ordered more hay and they hauled in more water. Rocky got to drive the mules to town empty and they filled the water wagon from an artesian well. Salty drove it back full or near that. Chet and the others rode on horseback. The trip took all day. Renny stayed with Lisa and they mended clothes.

Coming home that day with the water wagon, the riders ran for the tent when they got close because a monsoon shower turned up. They barely beat it to the site and, from the dry tent, laughed at a water-soaked Salty and his umbrella.

Ten days later Earl, his men, and the wagons were back.

"Mr. Tanner at the bank is not sure where he will park all this. We are fast filling his

vaults. But he says not to stop bringing it."
Then he laughed. "Oh yeah. Those coins
were minted in Mexico before 1800. Some
ruler — perhaps a governor — may have
stolen them."

"Finders keepers, losers weepers."

"No one has claimed them and they can't
believe anyone found them."

"Hey, you hear Rocky shot an albino mule
deer? Nice rack. I never saw one of those in
my life."

"Me, neither. Bet he's proud."

"Busting buttons. We rode up to a small
lake and caught lots of large trout."

"How far away is it?" Earl asked.

"One day up there and one day back. I
didn't see a sign of anyone ever being there
but the storekeeper at Joseph Lake told us
where it was at."

"You ever fish up in the Apache country?"

Chet smiled. "Good fishing. They don't
eat them."

"Man, yes, wonderful fishing. Well, two
days and we go back. No trouble on my part
and Curt got along good, too. He was near
to Flagstaff when we met them."

"Everything's holding together down
there?"

"As far as I know, yes. Tom said it was the
smoothest summer he could ever recall. Oh

yeah, Millie said to tell you Bonnie had another boy down on the Diablo Ranch. That makes four kids now."

"She didn't plan to have that many when she married my nephew JD."

"Time changes things."

"It really does."

Later Chet reported to his wife about the number four baby at Rancho Diablo.

She shook her head. "I'm really losing that race."

"I don't feel we have missed that much. We travel and enjoy and at this rate, we will be back home by September."

"Well, I am sure not pregnant." She looked around to be certain they were alone. "Our girl found out about Eve's curse."

"This early?"

"She will be thirteen soon. Many girls start earlier."

"I didn't want her to grow up."

"I can tell you one thing. She is not stupid, badly spoiled, or as crazy as I was at that age."

"Good."

"I agree and she talks to me. Which I appreciate."

"I hope that this business continues as smoothly as it has, but I will be glad to be back on our mountain."

"Me, too, but you have done a super job managing things. The showers, the tent, horse feed, and the meals Tad serves. And the lack of problems."

"Good people who have worked hard."

"You know who I think are the largest winners?"

"Who?"

"The girl and your two boys. They have learned how to work and play. I really think this summer will pay off in making them better adults."

"They will be better adults."

She looped her arm in his elbow. "Let's go to bed."

"Amen."

# CHAPTER 35

Earl and his crew left for Preskitt and the cavern had begun to look half-empty. In three more weeks, maybe four, Chet felt they'd complete the job. The last train would be headed for Preskitt and Chet's summer work would be done. Salty had been scouting with Billy Bob in new places every time he found a chance to go look. Chet and Jesus made shorter circles but nothing showed up to interest them nor were there rumors to run down.

Curt and his wife arrived back with their wagon train for another load, rested a day, thanked Chet, and then took twenty-two more wagonloads of loot and were southbound.

Things were fairly quiet among the original crew. Some men from the Dixie branch of the LDS church came one afternoon and visited with Chet.

Oliver Pettigrew was the highest-ranking

man in their group. He asked Chet if he wanted to consider investing in ranching there. His expenditures had certainly been welcome in the area.

Chet thanked him and said he had no plans to do that. Pettigrew then asked, if not, would he get them connected to a telegraph line from Flagstaff up to Kanab, in Utah.

"I am much better at herding cattle. But you could go south yourselves and speak to Cole Emerson, who is heading that business across the northern Arizona line."

"We understand he was, formerly, one of your foremen?"

"Yes, he was. But he works for the stage line, the railroad line, and telegraph now."

"Will he talk to us?"

"If it would make the railroad money, yes."

"Fair enough. How much Spanish treasure did you recover here, if I might ask?"

"I will be flat honest with you gentlemen. I have no idea. We loaded it up and sent it down to Preskitt."

"Compared to the Grand Canyon cave site we heard about?"

"Maybe twice as much. We had more large gold bars in that recovery."

Pettigrew nodded. "I must say, few outsiders come in, hire our people, buy from us at reasonable prices, and get along as well as you and your men, sir."

"You come by my home place on top of the Mingus Mountain side of the Verde, I will sure feed and host you at my house."

"Very generous of you to offer."

They parted. Getting a telegraph wire connected to the one at Flagstaff might make a good connection for Cole to add. But that was Cole's business, not Chet's.

In another week, the last wagon train arrived at Ruby Buttes, his men's new name for the structure. They loaded nineteen wagons. Chet considered dismantling the showers, since they had room in the empty wagons. They did that. No one wanted the water wagon and mules. Salty was to drive it back down to Arizona. The cooking stoves, tables, chairs, silverware, and Lisa's huge tent were all loaded.

Chet thanked everyone, then gave a short prayer, thanking God and asking for protection going home. He, Lisa, and his kids, as he called them, saddled and left the region at daylight.

It took a day and a half to get to Lee's Ferry and a half day to get every rig across the wide Colorado. Day five they crossed on the Little Colorado ferry and he had

everyone ready for some trouble in camp —
none happened.

Three more days on the Navajo Trail, and
Valerie, with three railroad policemen on
horseback, met them a half day east of
Flagstaff. Her son, Rocky, rode out to greet
her and the other two kids went with him.
Lisa and Chet joined them.

Chet waved the wagon train on and said
they'd camp at the ranch property ahead.
He didn't see a dry eye when his son
dropped out of the saddle and hugged Val.

"He's grown a foot this summer," she
sobbed.

"Maybe more than that. He drove those
mules with the water wagon and made a
great hand. We had lots of fun. I want you
and him at the fairground first Sunday in
September."

"What for?"

"Rocky, Adam, and Renny are all going to
be in one race to see who the best is."

"What horses will we use?" Rocky asked
as he and Renny got down from their horses
to stand with Rocky.

"That's up to the riders."

The kids, in their excitement, hugged one
another and jumped up and down.

No sweat. They'd be damn tough on one
another.

Back in the saddle, Chet shook Rocky's hand. "You take care of Val. I'll see you in camp tonight."

Rocky stopped him. "It has been the best damn summer in my entire life."

He stepped back and saluted Chet.

# CHAPTER 36

The cool afternoon air swept Chet's face as he was coming up the new hacked-out road to the ranch's yard and houses above Flagstaff. Survey stakes with ribbons tied on were where the roads would someday sprout off. The air reeked of pine sap, and he felt at home.

A monsoonal pile of clouds swept in overhead and they raced to the property to get set up, but to their shock a large tent setup awaited them and a note: *Glad you made it back. Cole and Val.*

"Cole and Val did it," he shouted to Lisa and the kids.

"Just like him," Rocky said, and laughed.

They unsaddled and one of the hands took their horses as the rain began. Thunder rolled across the mountain peaks secured in the billowing storm clouds. For Chet, it was good to be there. The others would come in under slickers, but the drop in temperatures felt great.

He didn't miss the strip's hot temps one little bit. He'd be home in two days and could pick up the pieces from there. How much did he have that they brought back? No telling. It would all help the ranches he was building on.

They'd been up there for the bulk of the summer, but he wouldn't trade the time he got to spend with Lisa, his boys, and Renny for another king's ransom.

Some spy must have told Cole they'd arrived. He swept off his wet hat and hugged Lisa, shook hands with the boys, and hugged Renny. "I see those boys didn't kill you, missy."

"No way I'd let them do that," she told him with a grin. He agreed.

"Tanner showed me some of it. My lands, there is a lot of it. Anyone bother you?"

"Not to speak of."

"Well, you people are the talk of the Territory. And no one knows how much money you got from up there."

"I can't help them. They had a cave-in at some time, and I guess that answer is under tons of rock and dirt."

"You mean you left some up there?"

"Lisa, give him those rocks we picked out for him."

"You remembered me?"

"Who could forget you?" Rocky teased him.

"Heck, they are big ones. Thank you."

"How is business?"

"Terrific. Read this letter he sent me." He fished it out of his pocket.

Dear Cole, I just saw accountings report for the third month. It is larger than any month you had before they ran you off. Great work, my friend. It goes to show what happens when you mean business, even way out there. Our land sales are brisk in your Territory. I am certainly proud. You need anything, wire me.

"Be careful. He will have you in New Mexico laying track."

"Whew. He plans to have three more wires strung before the snow flies. I told him he had to have it up before then."

"I am going back up to my mountain shortly. I appreciate you loaning me the boy. He's a mule skinner now."

"He wrote me several letters and told me how much rope you gave him. They had a great summer."

"So did we," Lisa said, joining them. "And thanks, we really got to know the three of them. I'm helping Tad fix supper. Oh, Salty said he'd be back in the morning. He's gone to see his wife. And Jesus is napping."

Cole frowned. "I told his wife when I thought you'd be down here."

Lisa shrugged. "He's fine. I just wanted both of you to know."

"Well, Chet, what next?"

"Check on my ranches, I guess —"

"I think you may lose Spencer permanent. They will have more line expansion for him to string up."

"Utah wants to connect. I told them to come see you."

"Wonderful. Then I'll get the credit for the line."

"I will find Fred an older man to help him run the Wagon Wheel. Have they gone back to more track laying?"

"Slow. Shortage of everything." At that, Cole excused himself to go back to work.

Chet went and lay down on a cot and napped. Lisa woke him at suppertime. The wagon train had made it in. No trouble. Good.

They took another day's rest at Flagstaff. A combination of worn-out and at ease about being in a safe place. Robert heard about them being up there and came to see Chet.

"Things going all right at the mill?"

"Usual things. Lost a horse last week when a log pile rolled over on him. It wasn't a mistake, just an unfortunate accident." Robert shook his head. "We are making our quota. No one is complaining that I hear."

"Last statement I saw was fine."

"We have really hauled a lot of logs to the mill. They have three shifts running now. That's the Flagstaff expansion. I figure that will back off. But I have still not heard a train whistle."

"It will be years getting here. Everyone is building tracks and can't get something they need."

"I'd like to have some jewelry made for my wife, if you have any I could get set."

Chet took a tobacco sack out and held it over Robert's palm, spilling some rubies into it. "Try these."

"Wow. Those are big. What do I owe you?"

"Just keep things running. That's your Christmas bonus."

Robert laughed. "I can damn sure do that."

He bound his gems up in a kerchief. "I can't believe all you have found."

"To be very frank with you, neither can I. But our treasure searches are over for now."

"Those boys of yours are really growing. But who is that girl with them?"

"Renny. Her parents died so the judge asked Lisa and me to take her and see if she liked us and we liked her. The feelings are mutual. She's had a ball with those boys and can beat them at many things."

"This the first summer you ran off with them, isn't it?"

"Yes, and we'll probably do it again."

"I better get back to the mill. I never expected rubies that big. Thanks."

"I never expected a superintendent as good as you are, either." Chet clapped him on the shoulder. Robert was blushing and shaking his head over his praise. Good. He deserved it.

"Nice of him to come by," Lisa said. "He could have stayed for lunch."

"No. He's pretty fussy about his job."

"Someday you will be famous and others will come and steal all of your super men."

"Took a railroad president to steal Cole."

She hugged his waist and laughed. "That's what I mean."

He said grace — that was what they waited on — and he announced they'd go south in the morning. When lunch was over, Lisa rushed off to get something.

Renny slid in beside him. "I want to ask

459

you a question."

"Sure. What did I do wrong?"

"Nothing. But the boys said I should ask you. They weren't that brave."

"What is it?"

"When can we get together again? I mean, the three of us."

"I don't have a calendar with me."

"They mentioned the county fair meeting for the race."

"Yes. I told them we will do it then."

"Chet? Two more things I want to clear with you. You know I don't have a father but I'd like to call you my dad if it won't make you mad."

He hugged her to him. "I would be proud to be your dad."

"Those two said that you would say that. I appreciate it more than I can even say. When Lisa said the boys were coming along on this trip — well, I about panicked. I never had to share anything in my life. But it was the greatest summer of my lifetime. I'll be ready to go in the morning and ride at the head of the parade going south. Dad."

"See you then."

Lisa, when they were in bed that evening, said, "She picked a good one, to be her dad, of course."

"Thanks." He reached over to kiss and

hug her. Life sure turned out great for him, night or day.

Two days later they were at the Verde and ready to leave, and Chet saw Renny and Adam to the side, talking. He booted his horse over there.

"Hey, it is time we went home, girl."

"Coming, Dad."

"Adam. See you, pard."

"Hey, both Rocky and I think she's great."

"I agree. Now, get in the saddle and let's go."

When he joined Lisa at the head of the train she was laughing. "I thought she might want to stay down here."

He sighed. "Not yet."

Under her breath, she asked him, "Who's going to win her?"

"Damned if I know." They both rode on, laughing, and Chet waving for the train to follow him.

Someone rang the yard bell when they got in sight of their house. *Company coming.* When he came under the bar his horse was single-footing to the bell ringing. Folks were running in to join the rest, welcoming the boss and his wife, returning triumphantly with a wagon train of loot they found in the strip.

Chet saw the young reporter from the *Miner* newspaper in the crowd. His head would explode before the afternoon was over.

# CHAPTER 37

Chet Byrnes knew they'd swarm him first time he went to town. Everyone who saw him would want to shake his hand and borrow money. But with Vic riding shotgun and Lisa beside him they drove to town. They left her at the dress shop and went to Bo's. He locked the door and twisted the CLOSED FOR BUSINESS sign around toward the outside. The onlookers' noses were pressed to the glass.

"From all the rumors and Tanner having guards twenty-four/seven at the bank, you must have done well." Bo sat back in his swivel chair.

"Over forty steamer trunks full of money. Most was money that was made before 1800."

"How in the hell did it get up there?"

Seated in a straight-backed living room–like chair facing Bo's desk, Chet said, "I have no damn idea."

"It is not at some crossroads?"

"No, nor any water hole, nor rich farm-land, or in a grove of timber-size logs."

"When I heard you'd found another treasure trove, I screamed, 'That SOB knew where it was at all the time.' "

"No way. I showed you the ruby mine map I bought from the man over in Mesa when we bought the east ranch, but I had no idea that under that mountain they'd left a fortune in treasure."

"Of course, if a poor man had found it he'd not had the money to guard it and get it hauled down here."

"Oh, that much, someone smart could have worked it out secret-like."

"I doubt it." Bo shook his head. "Well, what comes next?"

"I want to check on all my ranches and get ready for fall and winter."

"Not such a tough job with the help like you have. If I owned a ranch and didn't know a damn thing about it, I'd sure want your help."

The noise outside grew greater. Bo shook his head. "I'm going to tell them you aren't loaning money today. To go see Tanner at the bank if that is their business."

Stepping to the door, Bo cracked it open. "Whoa. Whoa. He isn't loaning money today. Leave my doorstep. Go on, now. He is not going to loan you any money. Period."

"How do you know that? I ain't asked him yet."

"I know him pretty well. Now, go before I have the city police arrest you. Get!"

Bo shut the door. "You are really in for it now."

"They'll get tired of it after a while."

"Tanner got a handle on it?"

"Not yet."

"You can go out the back way."

"I'll start out that way and Vic will drive the buckboard up."

"I miss having a nice, quiet meeting with you."

"No deals today?"

"No, but I get a real one I'll drive out there and tell you all about it."

"Thanks, Bo. See you."

Vic drove up. Chet nodded to him, jumped on the spring seat, and they were off.

His man cut up the alley, stopping at the back door of the bank. Chet got off, checked his pocket watch, and told him to be back in thirty minutes. Then he beat three times on the metal door. It swung open, Chet went inside, and they closed the door.

Tanner came back to get him. Trunks were

stacked higher than their heads. They scooted sideways down the hall crowded with trunks and went into his office. With a sigh of relief Tanner stood with his back to the door. "Banking can be hell on days like this."

"Problems?"

"I am not used to having this many trunks stacked in my bank. We are emptying them. I don't want you to think I am complaining, but how did they get to where you found them and why?"

"Other than a robbery, I have no idea, and I think all a mule could pack was one," Chet said.

"I bet we never find out anything more than we know now. One of the haulers said the cavern had many body bones on the floor, skulls?"

"Yes. They all didn't ride away from there. I looked at the front of that mountain and decided it had caved in. Buried under tons of rock and dirt. We went around and found a place with an opening in back and blasted open a hole. My two boys and adopted daughter climbed through and then we had to let them down about twelve feet to the floor inside."

"Were they scared?"

"Those three would have taken on anything. Told me it was a bunch of dusty old trunks.

"We bored holes in the rock wall and blasted our way in. We worried if we did much more it might collapse the roof into the cavern. I built a trestle to roll an old mine cart in to get the trunks from the floor to the hole in the wall and out to be loaded into wagons. Each trunk required five to six men to load it."

Tanner shook his head. "I heard about that structure you built to get them up and out to the wagons."

"My friend Lincoln at the store up there gave us an old, rusty mine cart. We took off the barrel and made it a flatcar and used the wood for the tracks. We were careful. It was all we had."

Tanner could hardly handle all the wealth he had stacked up in the bank. "There may be half to three quarters of a million dollars here."

"I knew we had lots," Chet told his banker. "I have to go to Mesa and pay that man for the rubies we found. He is a cripple and in bad shape, according to my man. Billy Bob, who struck the deal, thought forty thousand would be plenty."

"Bet he would be pleased."

Chet agreed. He might get Jesus and Billy

467

Bob and go find this Earshal Greystone. His wife's name was Jennifer, and Billy Bob knew where they lived at Mesa.

Chet drew out forty thousand dollars and had one of the tellers wrap it in newspaper and tie it with string. The clerk used several big bills in five-hundred and thousand denominations so the package didn't look so big. Chet shook Tanner's hand and prepared to go back to the ranch.

Out in the alley Chet put the package of cash in the box with the groceries under the seat and nodded to his guard that he was ready to go pick up his wife. Several people tried to wave him down when they recognized who it was in the buckboard going to the dress shop.

Chet didn't talk much about anything concerning the treasure in public. Lisa loaded her things and they went to the ranch with no problem.

He told Vic to send word to Billy Bob down at the Verde that in two days he needed to make a trip with him and Jesus to Mesa. He'd know what that was about. Lisa heard him and nodded. At the house and alone he told her what he planned to do about the Greystone deal. She agreed.

They caught the midnight stage on Thursday, and Friday midday they were in Mesa in a buckboard rented over in Hayden's Ferry. Billy Bob told Chet that Greystone lived in the barrio north of the square.

Billy Bob drove up to the casa. A woman in her thirties came out of the house. "Oh, Señor Kimes, how are you?"

"Just fine, señora. This is my boss, Chet Byrnes, and his man Jesus Martinez."

"Oh, have you been to the mine?"

"Yes, and we came to settle with you, if we may?"

"That would be a miracle. My husband is not doing so well."

They went into the adobe casa and she seated them in chairs at the wooden table. She went into the bedroom, woke her husband, and rolled him in his wheelchair into the room.

"Billy Bob, you found it?" Greystone's face lit up at the sight of him.

"It was not exactly a mine that we found. But we did find some rubies."

"It was so long ago I was there. Things go this and that way in my mind. There were three columns of tall red stone maybe a day's ride west of the road fork."

"That is where we found the stones, all right. But it was only part of the find."

"I was out of water that day. Delirious,

maybe? I had to go find food and water. I only found a handful of rubies."

"We won't do any more mining up there, but I told Chet you were a man who needed money and that you had been honest with me. He wants to pay you."

"Sure. How much was my part worth?"

"Forty thousand dollars in cash." Chet used his jackknife to cut the strings on the package he was holding.

The man's wife sucked in her breath and peered over to see Billy Bob as he unpeeled the paper from the money.

"Jennifer, there is forty thousand dollars in this package. There are some one-thousand-dollar bills in here so the contents didn't draw any looks like a suitcase would have."

"None is counterfeit?" the man's shocked wife asked aloud.

"No. It came from my bank in Preskitt. The money is good," Chet said.

She crossed herself twice and, white-faced in shock, looked closer in.

"I never saw a bill this big before. But it feels like money."

"It truly is good."

"What do I need to sign?"

"I have the paper. Would you like me to read it?"

Tears streamed down Greystone's wrinkled face. "No. God bless all of you. Jennifer and I live on the generosity of her church and food our neighbors grow for us."

"We can take you or her to the bank and deposit it. I don't want you robbed."

"Thank you. I can't read or write but I can sign and she can witness it, and then take her to the bank. We owe them a small sum but we will pay it. Right?" he asked her.

"I worried I would die before we got it paid."

"How large is the bill you owe?"

"Sixty dollars."

"When you get her to the bank, Billy Bob, pay them that amount. Be sure she has a correct deposit and a receipt for the loan payoff. She won't need to take the money out of this. And break a twenty-dollar bill. That will be her grocery money." Chet handed him four twenties.

"You are too generous," she said.

"No. When you come back, I have a purse with rubies in it for you."

"A purse, too?" her husband asked.

Chet nodded. "You men take her to the bank. I will visit with him."

Jennifer wiped the tears from her eyes. Greystone waited until they were gone.

"What do I owe Billy Bob?"

"He doesn't need anything. He is richer than most ranchers I know. I share my findings with my men."

"Have you ever been to the Goldfield mines?" Greystone asked Chet.

Chet shook his head. "They around Superstition Mountain east of Mesa?"

"Yes. I have a claim there that is good, but I never gave it to anyone because I figured they'd just steal the gold. I thought that drawling Texas boy Billy Bob was honest when he came the first time, and I never met anyone that honest before in my life. I know I am talking in circles. She didn't think so. Some days I know who I am; some days I don't have any idea who I am. I am glad you came. We don't need a paper wrote up. That mine is still there and I will sign it over to you today."

"I won't take your mine. If it is workable I will pay you for it."

"My wife will get the papers. I can sign them."

Billy Bob, Jesus, and Greystone's wife came back in the door, laughing. "Chet, I wish you'd been there. Seeing me deposit my money, the banker was shocked."

"He asked if the man who found the

Spanish gold in the Grand Canyon was you."

"Yes, that, too."

Earshal asked his wife to get out the Goldfield gold mine claim.

"What are you going to do?"

"Form a partnership with Chet, here. He will get the gold out."

"Well, I hope he can." She went for the claim.

Jesus was shaking his head in disbelief. "That will be another rich mine."

She came back. "I won't tell you all my story, but the man I was married to — maybe living with — he said we were married, but the Territory had no record of it. That man beat me up all the time. He didn't need an excuse. We were up in the mountains. No one was around."

"How long had you been married to him?" Chet asked.

"I think two years."

"How old was this man?"

"Maybe forty — I didn't know. But Earshal came, and I left that camp with him and married him. He had this mine and it was paying us but he had a wreck with a wagon and we had to close it down. We had no one to run it and he was not well. But his claim is good."

"We may go out there tomorrow. I will see what it looks like and let you know what I will do."

"I am very grateful. I read that story to Earshal, that was in the Tucson paper, and he told me he knew where that ruby mine was at."

"You think there will be a claim jumper on your claim in Goldfield?" Chet asked her.

"No telling."

"That is what I thought."

Chet handed her a tobacco sack of rubies. Her eyes bulged out when she peered down into it. "Are they real?"

"Would I bring you glass?"

"I don't believe so, but you never know."

"They are real. See you after we look at the mine."

"God be with you three."

They got a hotel in Mesa that night. After breakfast, they rode out to east of Mesa. Chet had a map they had studied the afternoon before. Since Goldfield was a town, and they brought no camping gear, he told them if they stayed out there, they'd get a hotel for the evening.

Their horses were livery stock but they kept them going. They reached the town at the base of the huge Superstition Mountain in midafternoon. The other two had cold draft beer, and Chet had sarsaparilla.

He bribed the bartender for information about the Calico Mine.

"Been shut down for several years. I think he ran out of vein. Wasn't worth a hill of beans for years. That's why no one's done anything with it."

Chet thanked him.

"What do you think now?" Jesus said.

"We found a fortune hanging off a bluff in the Grand Canyon. Went to the end of the trail and found a Spanish fortune and some rubies in no-man's-land. I want to invest some money in this Calico Mine. Bring out some rocks and bust them. I don't know how to make a tunnel. We have some investment money so we aren't using money we need to eat on. There was gold in there once. We might get lucky and find some more and we won't starve if we don't.

"Let's get some supper. Find us some clothes, get these washed, take a bath, get rooms, and meet some contractors."

"With all I know about mining you could fit it into this empty mug," Billy Bob teased.

Chet sent his wife a wire.

STAYING IN GOLDFIELD ON A MINE
PROJECT. TELL ANITA MORE COMING
IN A LETTER.
CHET, JESUS, AND BILLY BOB

They took a hotel room and by nine a.m.
the next day had interviewed several possible contractors in the Gold Dust Saloon
at an empty card table. Jesus took notes and
names on a Big Chief tablet. Several men
wanting work went out and looked at the
mine setup with Billy Bob then came back
and talked some more.

Chet felt he was getting informed on mining. He was convinced some of the men
were fairly straight, others braggarts, and
some worthless.

By four o'clock that afternoon they had
settled on a young man in his twenties to
mine a hundred and fifty feet. Jed Carlisle,
age twenty-four, had graduated from Colorado Mining School and wanted to make
good. So timbers were ordered. Jed had
men. They rented an air hammer run off
steam and had an option to buy it if they
wanted it.

In three days, two pickaxes were pounding and dust and rocks were being hauled
off to be busted and smelted. Jed showed
them some rich pockets of gold they'd

476

found that raised their hopes.

Billy Bob took the livery horses back to Hayden's Ferry to save the rent and livery charges. He took a stage back that afternoon. By Saturday, they were more excited about the rich ore coming out and they were handpicking through the tailings.

Jed was smiling. "I think we are going in the right direction. There is some side-tunneling we can do later."

Jesus began to talk about going home for a few days and checking on his wife. Friday, Chet sent him home and told him to bring Lisa back. He sent her a wire to come back Sunday with Jesus.

Chet and Jed looked at other mines for sale. But Chet wanted their current project to become more profitable and use that money to run a second one. They really had a good week. Jesus came back with Lisa, and midmorning they had a big breakfast at the Gold Dust Saloon.

In three days she had a two-story house rented and they moved in. It was the fall and the desert temperature made the area livable. Things were really doing great at the mine. Chet had full confidence in Billy Bob and Jed running the Calico Mine.

In the mine office, with the doors shut, he warned his two superintendents the things to watch for. High-graders leaving after a shift with their pants pockets full of gold nuggets, teamsters hauling rocks to the crusher putting aside high-grade ore and coming back after shifts to get it. They'd caught some employees doing that and fired them.

That all in place, Lisa, Chet, and Jesus took the stage back to Preskitt.

Chet found everyone in good health and, with things going so smoothly, he wondered why he came home. With Lisa, Jesus, Vic, and Tad to cook, and Eldon for their horse wrangler, Chet set out to check on things at the other ranches. They went by the Rustler's Ranch first. Toby and Talley were doing fine. They had four of their hands married and living in the casas they built for them. They had a lovely time and were ready to move three hundred cows over from the east ranch. Chet and Thurman had plans to use the crew coming back from the Navajo drive to bring them over to Rustler's Ranch.

Chet got a kick out of the thinking and planning that went into the move.

Thurman and his foremen wanted their cow count down to fourteen hundred, so Toby was going to be up to capacity at his house. Of course, that suited Chet. His range was really being utilized with all Toby's water development on the home-steads watering the range cattle. More of his places needed that.

In bed at night, Lisa told Chet that Talley was expecting number two, and she herself didn't have number one. But she also said how proud she was of Renny helping teach at the Cherry School.

They rode clear over to the east ranch and stayed with Thurman and his wife. They were ready over there for the drive of cows to Toby and had hands borrowed from Fred.

Lisa teased him, "You are getting to be one of the largest cattlemen in the Terri-tory."

Fred, Josey, and their new baby were next. Fred had settled into running the vast Wagon Wheel Ranch. He and Chet dis-cussed upping his numbers of cows and the future. He didn't need an older man to help him — maybe a younger guy to break in.

Next was Flagstaff to see Rocky, Cole, and Val, who were making it fine. Cole had to hear about everything, and Chet told them about the gold mining operation.

"Man, you did good on the strip this last time, too. You know, I think the railroad is going to pick up and go when they get out of that Rio Grande gorge down there."

"They might."

"We are hard-pressed to get the three new telegraph lines up before it snows. That Spencer is a whiz, isn't he?"

"Yes, he sure is."

"Stay for a day. You and I can put our boots up and visit."

"I've been gone so much that I better get home. I wanted to go see Lucy and Sarge, but I better haul my butt back home."

"Good luck mining."

"I may need a lot of that. One day you have gold — the next day you have sand."

"I want to tell you that Rocky is still talking about his time with you and Renny. He has never looked at a girl before she came along."

"You coming to the horse races?"

"I will have to. I have three racehorses in training now. If Rocky doesn't win he may never be the same again."

"He'll be fine. He and the other two really worked well together on that trip."

"He drove that big water wagon and mules and told me all about it."

"It was one great adventure."

"Something he won't ever forget."

"None of them ever will."

Chet and his crew made it down to the Verde. Adam joined them and they had some laughs. He had plans to be at the races. He had two horses in training.

"Is Renny teaching school?"

"Oh. Yes. She helps the teacher at the Cherry School."

"Bet those kids are learning lots."

"I bet so, too."

They were back home before lunch. Chet learned that Renny had stayed home that day to greet them. It was a nice reunion. The house girls fixed a frosted cake. He swore that Lisa and Renny both bawled.

About bedtime, a youth rode in with a telegram. Chet heard the commotion while readying to go to bed. He went out on the back steps.

"Telegram for Mr. Byrnes."

"What is it?" Lisa asked.

"I have a telegram."

He took it from the youth and read it in the lighted back room.

"It is from Goldfield. From the sheriff deputy in charge."

DEAR MR. BURNS
BOTH YOUR MAN BILLY BOB AND YOUR MINE SUPERINTENDENT JED CARLISLE WERE SHOT IN AN ATTEMPT TO ROB YOUR BUSINESS OFFICE. I HAVE AN ALL-

POINTS BULLETIN OUT FOR THREE SUSPECTS AND THINK OUR LOCAL LAW MAY FIND THEM. BOTH MEN ARE IN SERIOUS CONDITION AND IN THE HOSPITAL AT DR. REDDING'S HOUSE. HAROLD FREDRICK, DEPUTY SHERIFF IN CHARGE, GOLDFIELD, ARIZONA TERRITORY

"Oh my God," Lisa said, reading the telegram. "How will you answer it?"

"I'll get a paper and pen. I am going to offer a thousand-dollar reward for information and help finding the men responsible."

"Yes, do that."

"What is wrong?" asked Renny, coming into the room.

"They have shot both Billy Bob and his mine superintendent, Jed Carlisle, over at the mine."

"Why shoot Billy Bob? Oh, that is terrible. He is such a nice man."

"We think they had a robbery at the mine office."

"What will you do, Dad?"

"Get Jesus and go after them tonight."

Lisa took charge. "Renny, please tell Vance to get Vic and tell him it's going to be for days. Chet is going to need him and Jesus.

Tell him and Jesus that they are going to Goldfield. That Billy Bob and the mine superintendent were shot in a robbery. Then have Vance send someone to the stage office to hold the stage so they can get on it. Tell them it is very important they wait for them."

Turning to Chet, she continued, "You better come inside and change clothes."

He nodded. "Pay that boy for the outgoing telegram and give him a tip, too."

He headed upstairs, on the run, to change clothes. It was still August but he'd need fresh ones. His heart was pounding in his throat. He dressed quickly, strapped on his gun and hat.

"Chet, you have to be careful. I know you are mad. And upset. But be cautious, because Renny and I need you. We don't need you dead. We need you to help us run this vast empire. Do you hear me?"

"Yes, I hear you fine. I won't be careless. I love both of you. I will be fine." He kissed them, and his boot heels rumbled down the stairs. What had he forgotten? He could not even imagine what it was.

Vic was mounted, and a boy handed Chet the reins to his horse.

"We sent a boy ahead to tell Jesus you were going to Goldfield."

"Vance, thanks. Watch the women and tell everyone to be careful. I will be coming back when this is over."

His foreman nodded. "God be with you, hombres."

The two tore out in the long twilight.

"I am so sorry I had to call on you so suddenly. Let's ride — hard."

"There is a boy coming to get our horses at the stage line and take them back home."

"Wonderful. We will make the stage fine."

At Jesus's house, Jesus kissed his wife and baby, then tore off the porch, mounted his horse, and joined Chet and Vic.

"God bless all of you," Anita shouted after them.

"You, too," Chet shouted as they rode out.

When they reached the stage station, they stripped their saddles off their horses while Chet ran and bought tickets. He thanked the ranch boy standing there.

"Mr. Byrnes, we aimed to wait for you. You didn't have to ride that hard."

"I have two men down there that were shot. I had to catch this stage."

"I understand. But we'd have waited."

"Thanks."

There wasn't much sleeping on the rocking stage. How the driver ever held it on the gravel road going south under the stars,

Chet never knew. But they rolled on, changed horses at various places, and drained their own systems at the stopovers.

Chet had explained to Jesus all he knew about the robbery and shoot-out. Of course, he knew nothing about the men's wounds or even if they were alive. Past dawn they arrived at Hayden's Ferry. They ate breakfast in a diner, then hired a buckboard, loaded their saddles and gear, and charged off into the rising sun toward Goldfield and the purple Superstition Mountain range.

They went through miles of flat desert and irrigated farmland that spread out in orange groves, cotton fields, and milo, beginning to end. They passed many farm vehicles and Indian wagons going to town or home, through the Mormon town of Mesa with its wide streets, and trotted on through the city limits. Out again, they were in the saguaro cactus–staked desert, and by evening, with the livery horses sweaty and worn down, they made Goldfield. They drove to the mine. Two men with rifles guarded the office in the golden light of sundown.

"Señor Byrnes, Ramon and I have guarded the mine since they shot both Billy Bob and Jed. We are so glad to see you."

"Are they alive?"

"*Sí.*"

"Where are they at?"

"The doctor's house, behind the Longhorn Saloon."

"Thanks. You two be here a little longer. We must eat and put these worn-out horses up and we will be back."

"Fine. Fine."

He turned the team around and went to the doc's house. Chet and Jesus ran up the stairs while Vic tended to the horses. A male nurse met them and Chet explained who he was.

"They are both sleeping."

"Chet — you made it —" His head wrapped in bandages and looking wobbly, Billy Bob stood in the doorway, shaking his head.

"Good to see you." Chet and Jesus ran over and took him back to bed. The entire time, the Texan was trying to explain and apologize about what happened.

"We will get them," Chet promised him. "Now, get into bed and get your rest."

In the unlit room, in the other bed, asleep and looking more bandaged, was Jed.

"We had some — pure gold that day. Those three busted in and shot us. I swear, they aimed to kill us."

"Billy Bob, you did all you could."

"No. Damn it. We didn't do anything

about it."

"We can talk about it later. I know you did the best you could —"

Billy Bob didn't answer. He'd slipped back into sleep.

The nurse said he was heavily dosed with a sedative to keep him down.

Chet thanked the doctor and the nurse for all they had done for the pair. Then he explained they needed to stable the horses, get hotel rooms, and a meal.

"Sir, there is nothing you can do for them tonight. Get some sleep. They will be all right for now."

Chet introduced Jesus, who shook the doctor's and nurse's hands, and they went to get set up.

With the horses stabled, they left their things at the hotel and walked over to the lit café. Close to shutting down, the six-foot-tall waitress saw how worn-out they were and promised she wouldn't close until they finished their meal. She even made them fresh coffee. Chet tipped her ten dollars, and they went back to the hotel and stumbled into bed. Chet slept on top of the covers, still dressed.

Past sunrise, Chet awoke to a knock on the door and answered it. It was Jesus.

"A deputy sheriff is downstairs in the lobby. Vic is down there."

"I'll be right down. Thanks."

The deputy's name was Frisco Holden. The four went into the hotel restaurant for breakfast and a waitress took their order, poured them coffee, and welcomed them to Goldfield.

"There were three men robbed them. Jack Newman, Rodney Harte, and Jewels Roberts. You'd hired them ten days earlier. They had not caused any trouble. I have found out Newman and Harte were in trouble over at Silver City, New Mexico. Roberts, they had never heard about."

"I recall one of them," Chet said. "Harte, he had run a jackhammer."

Holden laughed. "More than likely a sledgehammer. He was an ex-con from Texas."

"Any idea where they went?"

Holden nodded. "I understood they took the Salt River Road, which goes east."

"You can go to the copper mines at Globe or turn left and take Tonto Creek to Strawberry or go out east. Jesus and I took it once to recover a pig farmer's wife kidnapped in Hayden's Ferry."

Jesus agreed. "Cold damn trip in winter."

"I figured a posse wouldn't overcome them."

"Well, we have a trail, anyhow. I will offer a thousand-dollar reward for them dead or alive. Can I pay you to make wanted posters and mail them out all over?"

"Cost you fifty bucks."

Chet rose and dug out the money. "Handle it. I need a mine superintendent."

"What does it pay?" Holden asked about the time that the waitress brought breakfast.

"Hundred a month for a good one."

"Make it two, and I know the man," Holden said.

"Send for him."

Holden scraped his chair on the floor. "He will be here in an hour."

The deputy put down his napkin and, straddling his chair, he excused himself.

Chet nodded. "When we get up from breakfast, Jesus, buy us some horses and one packhorse with gear. Get us what supplies we need. You can meet us at the mine office. Maybe the mine men know more than he does. No telling. They have almost a week head start on us but I bet they don't expect pursuit."

"I have money. I'll bill you later."

"This is the best meal we've had so far," Vic said.

"Yes, it is."

Holden came back. "The mine man's name is August Malloy. He is to meet us at the mine. The job he had, the gold petered out. He knows mining real well."

"I can use him if he's good."

"Yes. I wouldn't have given ten cents for that mine of yours, but it really is producing the gold. We can go by the banker. He was impressed, too. He said you have deep pockets already."

"You knew he found the Grand Canyon treasure?" Jesus asked Holden.

"I heard about that."

"The second story isn't out yet. He discovered a larger treasure hoard the Spanish left up in the bluffs."

"Then you guys came down here to Goldfield and reopened a dead mine and have it going full steam ahead. I'm impressed."

"Tell us more of what you've learned about the robbery," Chet said.

"I am told that a large amount of gold was found at the end of the week, and they were storing it in the mine office. I heard it was a surprising amount, and I guess your men thought the employees were too busy to notice it or be tempted by the gold. But obviously those three saw it and figured they could steal it.

"The shift was about over. Those three had a wagon ready. They broke into the office and began shooting up everyone and everything. That's when your men were shot. Then they flung all the gold they could into the wagon bed and charged out of town. I admit we had no idea there was that much gold in boxes on the office floor.

"Jed was able to tell me he thought there was over ten thousand dollars' worth for them to steal. We found where they transferred most of it to packhorses about a mile east of town and rode off. I wired the sheriff in Globe and asked if they could head them off up at the junction of Tonto Creek and the Salt River. I told them the value of what they'd stolen and that they were mad-dog killers. But the robbers must have detoured. His men never caught them."

"Well, you obviously did all you could."

Just then, August Malloy walked in. He was a man of medium build. He shook hands with them. "I guess you are the mine owners here?"

"Yes," Chet said. "Do you know this operation? We are running it for a man who lives in Mesa. He is crippled and in bad health. He ran out of funds and boarded it up."

"I have never been in this mine, sir, but I

have managed several mines in New Mexico, Colorado, and the Huckleberry until it ran out of gold. That can happen in any gold mine."

"I understand. Let's go look at it."

When they got to the mine, the steam engines were shut down to do some timbering, and Malloy approved.

"You have a safe crew," Malloy said, going through the operations. "And good equipment. You also bought it at a bargain."

When they came out of the mine, Malloy said, "Your mine super hired some good men. Holden said you'd pay two hundred a month?"

"Yes. And a bonus if you exceed the past month."

"Fair enough."

"We can cut a contract over at the bank."

Malloy nodded.

"Good, let's go. Jesus come back yet?" he asked Vic.

"No. I haven't seen him."

"Come on. We can get the paperwork done."

All that complete, the banker aimed to wire the amount of any large expense checks for Chet's approval.

After that was settled, Jesus was there with loaded packhorses, so they went by the hospital and talked to the doctor.

The physician shook his head while talking about Chet's mine superintendent. "It will be a miracle if that young man survives. But he is very strong and maybe he will. The cowboy, Billy Bob, if he doesn't have any infections, will recover. But it is a long, twisted path even for him."

"Were any of the robbers wounded, did they say?"

"Billy Bob said with certainty that he thought he had hit two of the three men. But he was hurt and in a turmoil from their attack. He said he had trusted two of those men and they were the last ones he'd ever suspected of doing that."

Even as they stood outside at the hitch rack, the glaring sun reflecting off the sandy ground, Chet could still smell the ether's and antiseptic's strong fumes. Both victims were weak and their conditions stabbed his heart. If he'd known there was such a threat he'd never have left the pair by themselves. He felt knifed by the results of the attack on them.

Greed like that stole men's hearts and minds. But the fact was, these were his men lying under sheets as white as their faces, and he took the blame for their injuries. He wanted those bastards who did this behind bars or hung by the neck until dead.

They rode out of Goldfield on the dusty road that followed the Salt River into the mountains, on a crooked, steep, winding path eastward. He and Jesus could recall using it another time but he'd liked to have a guide or someone more familiar with the way.

Miles ahead at the forks of the Salt River and Tonto Creek he could hope that the thieves left a sign or someone saw the direction they took.

The descriptions of the individuals in the party were vague enough they might pass them on the way and not even know them. Several times along the way Chet removed his felt hat and wiped the sweat from his face onto his sleeve. The sparse desert vegetation left great, open spaces on the huge rock formations.

Soon juniper brush began to replace the mesquite and fingerlike saguaros. A band of javelinas burst off into the brambles, snorting, disturbed from their siesta. Jesus's spooked horse tried to buck. Jesus held him in check and they laughed about it.

At the junction of the streams, they spoke to a young, pregnant Hispanic woman camped under a canvas sheet.

Chet asked her to sell them some supper if he'd furnish the food. She agreed and told them her husband was supposed to be back. He had gone, several days earlier, to Globe to see about work in the mines. All she had to eat was the fish she caught, so they shared some of their food and ate some of her fish. Of course, she knew nothing about the pack train the robbers had taken through there earlier.

After the meal, Chet sent Jesus to the small store close by to buy her some staples and to ask about the pack train. He returned with lots of food for her and word that the pack train answering his description went north from there.

The girl was very grateful and cried. Chet dismissed her wanting to somehow repay them, but was suspicious as to why her husband left her there alone with not enough food. His men agreed with his concern. The next morning, they rode north.

They talked to a whiskered old prospector coming south, riding a mule and leading a few more with packs. His name was Harris.

"We are looking for three men with a pack train. They stole some gold from my mine and shot up my superintendent and guard."

The old man was packing his pipe. And

went over the names, nodding his head. "Newman and Harte, huh?"

Chet said, "That's two of them."

"I ain't found much color lately, but, by Jesus, I know where they are. What's it worth to you?"

"Name your price."

"Thirty dollars would get me a long ways."

Chet peeled off fifty. "Where are they?"

"Two days ago, they were on Cotter Creek. Gambling with guys and showing lots of color."

"How far is that from here?"

"Thirty miles."

"We are going to load up right now. You draw Jesus here a map in the dirt."

"I can sure do that."

Vic and Chet began loading the horses.

"Can you believe that?" Chet asked Vic as he was cinching up his girth

"I damn sure think that is a miracle."

"Big a miracle as finding that Spanish treasure."

"I agree."

They had the animals loaded, and Chet couldn't stop thinking about the girl. "Harris, there is a pregnant girl camped by herself down there at the fork in the streams. I want you to take her twenty dollars and be sure she's all right. I have a deep concern her husband dumped her."

"What if she's gone?"

"The twenty is yours."

"Hellfire. What is her name?"

"She's a teen and pregnant. You can't miss her."

"If she's there, I'll pay her."

"Good. I want those crooks." Chet swung in the saddle and they pushed hard.

The Cotter Creek handmade sign nailed to a post was barely visible in the sundown.

They decided that close they'd make a dry camp and hustle in there in the morning. Horses hobbled, they ate jerky and slept some.

Before dawn peached the eastern horizon, they were in the saddle and headed up the deep draw headed for the camp. Over two mountain ranges, midmorning, they smelled the woodsmoke and soon saw the camp of tents and some shacks made of lumber taken from old buildings.

Chet considered it a typical prospectors' camp. The residents all needed baths, and many were sucking on crock jars of mountain dew as they staggered around. An assortment of Indian squaws and Hispanic women tended fires, made food, and dodged drunks anxious to kiss or fondle them.

497

One of the females stopped Chet. "You need a woman, hombre?"

He dismounted. In a low voice, he said, "I need Jack Newman. You know him?"

She stepped right up to him. "What is he worth to you?"

"Twenty dollars."

"For that I show you him and my body."

"Show him to me."

Both Jesus and Vic had their rifles out and scouted the crowd for any movement toward them. Chet gave them a *follow us* head toss and they parted the crowd, moving forward with their horses and pack animals.

The crowd gave them dirty looks. A few of the women shouted offers of sex to them but the woman he'd hired kept walking, leading the way through the camp and woodsmoke. She gestured with her hand out. "Here is his house."

Chet dismounted and handed her a gold twenty-dollar piece and checked the rifle's chamber. The crowd began to back away, realizing his purpose was not going to be a friendly reunion between him and Newman.

Someone flung the canvas flap back, cussing about who the hell was out there while buttoning his fly.

The muzzle of Chet's Winchester stuck in his face. He gasped.

"Jack Newman?"

"Nooo. I'm Jewels Roberts."

Chet slashed him in the face with the rifle butt and he went down screaming. Jesus had spurred his horse around the wall tent and Chet heard him shout, "Stop!"

Then the .44 caliber blast from back there made many hit the ground. Vic was there and had the screaming Roberts, spitting bloody teeth, by the collar as his other hand waved Chet aside.

His gun barrel at his waist and cocked, Chet stepped into the tent. He saw the man on the cot reach for the holstered pistol on the floor as the naked woman, screaming, fell off the cot on the other side.

The black-powder gun smoke boiled up in the room. The woman was gone and the man lying on his back clutched his bloody wrist where Chet had shot him.

Chet's ears were ringing from the shot. The fumes burned his nostrils and smoke made his eyes water. He grasped the screaming Newman by the collar with his left hand and dragged him outside, next to the moaning Roberts.

Jesus came around the tent on the side, walking his spooked horse, and dragging Rodney Harte by his belt.

"Any more?" he asked Chet.

He shook his head. "I think we've got them all."

"Where is the gold you stole?" Vic asked Roberts.

"We ain't got any gold."

"You want more loose teeth?"

"Hell no. It's in the tent."

"Get your ass up and get it."

"I can't. Hurt too much," Roberts cried.

"You are going to hurt worse than that." Vic gave him a swift kick to his side, and the man, on his hands and knees, scurried inside the tent. Vic followed.

In a minute, Vic stuck his head out. "Part of it is here."

"Good. Thanks," Chet said to the woman, his guide, who was wrapping up Newman's bloody arm. When she had his arm wrapped, she rose and held out her palm. "Twenty more."

He paid her. "Now, get us some food. A couple of you boys, here, round up our horses and packhorses."

Then he shoved his rifle in the boot.

"Come back up to my tent." She kissed his cheek. "I like working for you, mister." With that complete, she sashayed off to the other side of the camp.

There was quite a lot of the gold left. His men filled the panniers on the packhorse with it and stuck the rest of the stuff into bags on their horses. The job completed, Chet spoke. "These three men robbed my mine office and shot up my men. I aim to take them back to Goldfield for trial."

"Hang their asses."

"Men, I did that one time. Not that they didn't deserve it. Not that they weren't as bad an outfit as these outlaws, but prosecution and prison sentencing shows Arizona has the right to be a state. I want that to happen. My name's Chet Byrnes, I live and ranch at Preskitt Valley. You need a meal or a cot to sleep on we never turn anyone, with manners, away."

"Didn't you find some Spanish treasure in the Grand Canyon?"

"Yes, my men and I found it."

"Ha. All I found up there in those caves was bat shit."

They laughed.

"That's all I found, too, except in one was gold and jewels."

The old man threw down his hat and stomped on it. "By damn, I forgot to look in that one."

They all laughed.

After they ate, they loaded the three handcuffed outlaws on their horses and rode back to the main road and south. They took the left fork in the road to check on their friend down where the streams forked. Chet wanted to be sure she was all right.

She met them about sundown.

"No husband?"

"No. I guess he left me." She dropped her chin. "I thought he loved me."

"What is your name?"

"Maria Conswaylia."

"Maria, these men work for me on my ranch. Come to us. I will send a wagon for you. I have many single men who need wives. Don't worry. They will love your baby, too."

"I have had enough fish."

Back in Goldfield, he hired a man with a wagon to get her and bring her into the town. When she arrived, Chet had the doctor check her. The doctor told Chet she was doing well. That night, Jed died. On crutches, Billy Bob stood in the cemetery and with wet eyes said, "I wish it had been me instead. Jed was such a smart man."

"No, he wished for you to become one of my grand ranch foremen."

Chet liked his new mine superintendent. The mine was really putting out the gold.

He thanked the man, told him he'd be in touch, and to send a wire if he had an emergency. With that fixed they took a buggy back to Hayden's Ferry.

Chet wired his wife they'd be up there at midnight and bring two buckboards.

They made it to the ferry. The night was cool compared to the desert temperatures they were getting used to.

When he introduced the new girl, Lisa kissed her and hugged her. Renny was along and told him, aside, she had the fastest horse in Arizona and the race was Sunday.

Sunday at the fairgrounds they all had lunch at their pavilion. Several of the ranch family members were there for the noon meal. Bo, his wife, and kids. Tanner, wife, and babies. Cole and Val came with Rocky, and Adam came with Victor and Reba. Plus, half a thousand other folks. Toby and Talley even came down. Tom and Millie, too. Jesus and Anita were there, and Vic brought Maria.

Chet teased the three teens that he dare not cheer for any of them.

At the end of the second race, the announcer said the next race coming up was a simple, friendly, family affair. Everyone laughed.

The starting pistol set them off. All three horses came out of the gates like professional steeds. Rocky had it by the nose at the halfway post. Then, as Chet watched, Renny leaned over and whispered in her horse's ear. Next, Chet saw her mount speed away and she won by a length.

Afterward, when it was all quiet and the horses had been cooled down, as Chet was fixing to let the ranch boy lead her winning horse back home, he turned to Renny and asked her what she said to her pony to make him run so fast.

"You won't get mad?"

"I won't get mad."

She wet her lips. " 'Get the hell out of here. We're losing.' "

He nodded. "You said the right thing."

# ABOUT THE AUTHOR

Author of over 85 novels, **Dusty Richards** won two Spur awards in one year (2007), one for his novel *The Horse Creek Incident* and another for his short story "Comanche Moon." He is a member of the Professional Rodeo Cowboys Association and the International Professional Rodeo Association, and serves on the local PRCA rodeo board. Dusty is also an inductee in the Arkansas Writers Hall of Fame. He currently resides in northwest Arkansas. He was the winner of the 2010 Will Rogers Medallion Award for Western Fiction for his novel *Texas Blood Feud* and honored by the National Cowboy Hall of Fame in 2009.